PRAISE FOR MICHAEL BOTUR

"Michael Botur's writing is a breath of fresh air in a country gone stale on its own literary midgets' bad breath. Just read him. You'll see what I mean. This dude can write."
—Alan Duff MBE, author of *Once Were Warriors*

"Michael Botur's work grabs you by the throat and won't let you go. His stories throb with what feel like real people, real conversations, real moments of pain and hope, misunderstanding and reconciliation, remorse and surprise. And that's the magic of this collection."
—Maggie Trapp, *New Zealand Listener*

"Crimechurch is a wild wild wild ride, and this reader found it utterly fascinating despite the confrontation, brutality, and dysfunction."
—Karen Chisholm, Australasian Crime Fiction

"In four previous volumes of stories Botur has claimed for himself a piece of literary territory occupied by the desperate, downtrodden and damned. He tells his tales in what would have been called an "amphetamine-fuelled" prose style until all suggestion of acquaintance with amphetamines became socially unacceptable. Let's go for 'breakneck' and 'febrile' to describe the prose."
—Paul Little, on *Crimechurch*

"Michael Botur's talent shows a skill broad, diverse and still very focused. He has mastered the art of the short story. The authenticity is so scary, you wonder where this man has been and what demons followed him home."
—Paul Brooks, *Wanganui Midweek*

"Written in unvarnished street language about the rougher side of life - drugs, jail and death, the book shows rare bravery and honesty [...] The thing about Michael Botur is his voice is very much a street voice. His language is street language: it's raw, it's coarse, it's obscene. It's tough and it's confronting [...] There are gems – some of them are absolutely great."

—*Ian Telfer, Radio New Zealand*

"It's as if Mr. Botur hung out at CBD fast-food outlets after midnight – swilling bad coffee on a hard-plastic seat, listening to conversations, and jotting observational notes under the garish yellow lighting. There is a ring of authenticity about these stories – both in the language used by the characters and in the physical descriptions of their environments. Botur is not so much a moralist, as an informer – without ever becoming a show-off."

—Jeremy Roberts, *Takahē*

"Botur wields demotic vocabulary, and agitated rhythms, combined in collages of invective and obscenity, with much skill. It's a neat trick that's easy to stuff up, but he consistently gets it right."

— *Paul Little, North & South*

"As a former journalist he has perfected the skill of telling a story and evoking emotion. Botur is a clever writer. He has mastered the art of leaving things unsaid."

—*Rebekah Fraser, New Zealand Book Lovers*

"These stories are energetic, often breathless, containing concrete detail, close observation, originality and power. Most of them use street language in a playful, or serious manner. The collection is peppered with expletives, topics about sex, drugs, viciousness and breaking the law."

—Patricia Prime, *Takahē*

BOOKS BY MICHAEL BOTUR

My Animal Family

Hell of a Thing

Crimechurch

True?

LowLife

Spitshine

Mean

Loudmouth: Page and Pub poems

Moneyland

Hot Bible!

MORE BOOKS FROM THE SAGER GROUP

The Swamp: Deceit and Corruption in the CIA
An Elizabeth Petrov Thriller (Book 1)
by Jeff Grant

Chains of Nobility: Brotherhood of the Mamluks (Book 1-3)
by Brad Graft

Meeting Mozart: A Novel Drawn from the Secret Diaries of
Lorenzo Da Ponte
by Howard Jay Smith

Death Came Swiftly: Novel About the Tay Bridge Disaster
of 1879 by Bill Abrams

A Boy and His Dog in Hell: And Other Stories
by Mike Sager

Miss Havilland: A Novel
by Gay Daly

The Orphan's Daughter: A Novel
by Jan Cherubin

Lifeboat No. 8: Surviving the Titanic
by Elizabeth Kaye

Hunting Marlon Brando: A True Story by Mike Sager

See our entire library at TheSagerGroup.net

THE DEVIL TOOK HER

TALES OF HORROR

MICHAEL BOTUR

THE DEVIL TOOK HER

TALES OF HORROR

MICHAEL BOTUR

THE SAGER GROUP

Artifex Te Adiuva

CONTENTS

The Writing on the Rat 1
Urban exploration is about scoring successful sneaks and never getting busted. There's double the risk when you're a woman of color on her own, so it's important to tell my best friend if I'm going somewhere dark and dangerous.

Somewhere like a coal cellar.

A coal cellar where I lose my cellphone, and the lid slams shut, and I'm trapped, with only vermin for company.

That vermin may be my only way out—if one of us doesn't devour the other first, bit by agonizing bit...

The Day I Skipped School 27
Susan and Tsuru, two lonely introverted high school girls, find themselves unexpectedly bonding as an ordinary morning of skipping school descends into something horrifyingly awful—something they'll bury under mountains of memory across the next decade, desperate to forget.

Club Hundred 55
Before me and my best friend raced to see who could be the first to have sex with one hundred women on Tinder, we had integrity and family and hope.

Before our lives became a nightmare, we had an opportunity to commit to our wives, to be happy with a single lover, not to consume women as if they were disposable, violating morals and rules and cultural codes to get to that significant number and one-up each other.

Before we displeased the gods, we had 99 chances to turn back and abandon our selfish quest.

Now all we have is a curse we'll give anything to undo.

Everyone Rachel looks up to is in a hip band, and Rachel demands those in her orbit be famous – or friends with someone famous, at least.

When Rachel's colleague, a rapidly-rising musician, walks out of their office to enter a never-ending Auckland party scene, Rachel follows, abandoning everything. All-night social events become all-week, then all-month.

Even though it's probably going to kill her, Rachel knows there is an exclusive club deep underground where there's a hell of a party, and she's dying to get in.

My wife Melanie is missing, so I hire a San Fernando Valley private investigator to find out what happened.

The only way to truly know, he ultimately reports, is to read her personal journal.

See, Melanie was a journalist—or *is* a journalist, if she's still alive—and it turns out Melanie disappeared while investigating the Golden State Dementor, a killer who seems to paralyze people with a wasp-like stinger. She's written strange things in her journal about the killer collecting a choir of children and taking them to his dimension, not unlike the Pied Piper.

Melanie's increasingly disturbing journal entries have to be the delusions of a woman losing her mind, because if they're not, there's something terrible out there, snatching runaways from the soulless California night and taking them somewhere unspeakable.

On a rainy Friday afternoon, I meet school badass Matt McAnulty in the deserted area behind Science block. I'm sick of exams and boredom and my abusive parents. I buy Matt's fake ID and proceed to purchase a box of beer. My life is about to get instantly exciting.

The problem is when Matt's parents –formerly renowned brain surgeons banished for conducting ugly experiments– offer me a ride home, I find myself in the biggest test ever. A test of how far I can take this fake identity–perhaps so far that I never see my original self again.

The Strange Paper 145
Aged 15, I'm grounded by my father for two weeks.

If I'm not at school or saxophone practice, I'm supposed to be in my bedroom. Lying on my bed, depressed, I begin to read *The Strange Paper*, a mysterious monthly magazine exploring unexplained events.

I'm hooked, enraptured, entranced–and when I turn 20 and stumble into an opportunity to write for the mag, I come under the spell of a captivating, commanding editor.

The only problem is the editor is going from confident to overbearing to obsessive. He's becoming convinced he needs to rise up against monsters disguised as men be believes are infiltrating his office, his city, and taking over the globe with each vaccination.

Suddenly my dream job has become a nightmare which could kill the people I care about.

You Dream of Jail 177
Sad sack office grunt Henry feels trapped. If he says No to the corporate bullies pressuring the company he works for, he'll lose his livelihood and be buried under a mountain of debt– although Henry can't bring himself to give the bullies what they want just yet.

As stoic meditation sessions help Henry to picture what life will be like if he loses everything, he becomes unable to tell which upsetting events are fantasies and what is reality.

It appears the episodes Henry believes are nightmares could turn out to be real, and what seems real to Henry may be something else entirely....

Being a popular cool kid at school gives me everything–everything, that is, except deep love. I can only find that by entering a secret, impossible-to-admit relationship with Kristina, a nerdy, shy exchange student from Germany.

I string her along for a while and show Kristina my sensitive geeky side, though when I want to ascend in social status, I decide to dump her swiftly and painfully.

Years later, I've forgotten most of the hurt, and it seems okay to reconnect with Kristina in her remote Black Forest village while I'm a tourist in Europe. We even start a little romance, and I prepare to make the most of an upcoming weekend with Kristina's parents.

Unfortunately Kristina hasn't forgotten. She wants me to make up for the hurt. Her powerful parents will do anything to help her–and in the castle where they keep me confined, I learn exactly how much power they possess.

After a violent outburst at his university, young Kevin is assigned by the court to teach English literacy to refugees as a form of community service.

Our hero, however, is paired with two refugee brothers who have come from a country where violence means a lot more than simply smashing things. Where these boys come from, violence means life or death, and after it emerges there has been a murderous curse transmitted from a dictator to his minions, Kevin begins to suspect one of the brothers is much more keen on death than the other.

As Kevin is exposed to more and more of the boys' dark history each Saturday, the badder of the brothers reveals what it means to really hurt somebody—and how good it feels.

My best friend doesn't want to die, but his cancer is irreversible.

It seems all we can do is count down the days until death takes him—that is, until we learn about Tukdam, an eerie extension of Tibetan Buddhist meditation.

Pretty soon, my friend is breathing so slowly that the cancer can't grow on him and he seems to sleep through his own death.

Then my friend wakes up, and the terrifying end begins.

Jasmine Tauariki is a student in a computer coding course who endures bullying from her sadistic supervisor Warwick.

Desperate to hang onto her grades and graduate, Jasmine evens the score with a prank which seems harmless at first—just a little itching powder, which Jaz doesn't even expect to work. She shakes some into Warwick's hoodie, watches him writhe, and forgets her gripe.

When Warwick plays his own revenge prank, a tit-for-tat war breaks out. The pranks get more and more vicious—and the stakes become more and more disfiguring.

* Winner of the 2021 Australasian Horror Writers Association Short Story Award.

GLOSSARY OF KIWI SLANG

Bufty—UK derogatory slang word for a gay man.

Dox me or Doxx—To publicly identify or publish private information about a person for revenge or punishment purposes.

Furred up /Furry—Humans who dress up in furry animal costumes for pleasure.

Going flatting—Leaving the family home to live in a shared house or apartment.

Narthex—An antechamber or large porch in a modern Christian church.

Pashing—To passionately kiss.

Smoke a cone—Smoking marijuana with a pipe or bong.

Seinen comics—Japanese manga comics marketed toward young adult men.

Urbex—A contraction of urban and exploration: The exploration of manmade structures, usually abandoned ruins or hidden components of the manmade environment.

Vantablack—Polymer-based, super-black coatings considered the "blackest of blacks."

Whānau—New Zealand Māori term meaning an extended family.

Yonks ago—A long time ago, ages ago.

THE WRITING ON THE RAT

THEN

Istood in front of the fenced-off St. James' Church, waiting for my eyes to adjust and my heart to chill out.

The bus drove off, I squeezed through the security fence and sealed it behind me. I'd be out of here in an hour, and in that hour, I couldn't risk some pedo security creep fucking with my shit. Urban exploration is about scoring successful sneaks and never getting busted. Plus, there's double the danger when you're a woman of color on her own. There are monsters out there.

The mission: break into the abandoned church, score some souvenirs, snap some selfies to post on the urbex subreddit, and get the fuck out within an hour.

I went into the recess behind the church where a forgotten dumpster skulked in the darkness. Beyond the dumpster was a shed painted a pale, reflective color—white, probably—mostly likely a coal storage shed from the dinosaur days when it was cool to burn fossil fuels. I could see a flaking sign fixed with cable ties to the chain link fence around the rim of the school pool: NO SKATERS.

Pfft. Yeah, right. I knew people skated the pool whenever it was dry, and that was at least nine months a year. I'd walked past on weekdays and seen the caretaker dragging his cart and shaking his head at the graffiti. He'd waterblast just before summer and that was all. He had to cede control to the skaters for the other nine months.

Cede control to urbex, too. Badass bitches like me, with a Swiss army pocketknife and a sports bra and a pocketful of joints, sniffing for geocaches on weeknights, while the rest of the world is living their dumb, safe lives watching TV.

Edging through the narrow gap between the church and the neighbors' wooden fence, smelling their curry, spying their Burmese flag, I crawled up onto the dumpster and shattered a stained-glass window with a wet green chunk of firewood and stepped through.

Phone books on the floor. A pyramid of Bibles with the same tan cover and tiny red cotton placeholder. Dead flowers in a crystal vase.

In a wardrobe I discovered a bottle of dusty merlot from 1989. I chugged it and listened to my stomach wince. I put one hand in my hoodie, danced with the other, and laughed, drunk.

"XANDERRRR?"

Nothing but the drumbeat of pigeon wings.

"YOU REALLY OUGHT TO BE HERE, FURRYBOY."

Xander was my friend from Reddit—well, frenemy, I guess. We had like a competitive buddy thing going. We'd explored a lava cave together, all wet walls and pools of clear water. We'd rummaged in an abandoned meat works where chains swung, brushed by ghosts. We'd sat in puddles of paper beside tipped-over rusty file cabinets in the psych ward out at Kingseat. Tonight I—Joyce Koh, urbex pro—was going to be the first person to sneak in and complete the St. James mission. Steal Xander's glory. Rub it in his face. Bitches one; Dicks, zero.

I kicked in the door of the church library. Books about the Soviets. Pamphlets on abortion. I stroked the pages and walls and codices, reading with only moonlight.

I drew chalk pictures on the narthex, smoked a cone in the kitchen, watched my smoke bob along the ceiling. Cans, tags, shriveled condoms, and one huge motherfucking rat.

"Jesus, you scared me," I told the little twitching dab of darkness. A big rat, curious, snuffling, like a little scurrying piece of shadow. Sniffing everywhere my shoes kicked up leaves and plaster dust. "Yo: I'm not feeding you. I don't like you bastards."

The rat scampered a few inches, stared at me.

"You speak English? Aw'right mate. Jog on, guv'nor. Eh? Fuck off then if you're not gonna be my faithful companion."

I walked three lengths of the dark dusty complex, stroking the balustrade, the columns, the portraits of St. George and Jesus Christ and cherubs and harps. Most exquisite in the building were the pews, lit up in stripes of blue and cream where the moon fell. They had *fleur de lis* carved into them, intertwined with crucifixes. Nice native hardwood rails and steps. I tugged on a pew to see where it would go. A black bat-shape flapped diagonally, rising as it approached the exit, then vanished. Behind the pew were mountains of pigeon shit.

I felt breath on my neck. I whirled. *Jesus—Xander? That you?*

It was the rat, wavering like a praying mantis.

"You want a show, then, Rat? Watch this."

I strode onto the altar, walked through the vestibule, and put my fingers on the t-shaped wood cross, positioned with maroon curtains behind it. The focus of the church. A meter of dark wood with nice grains, thick as my arm and polished. I hacked out one of the screws with my knife. Immediately the top swung down, scraped my shoulder, swung right, then left, then slowed.

Heavy oak.

"Jesus Christ!"

Nobody replied.

"You wanna fuck with me?" I asked the cross. "You wanna fuck with the JoyceCo, huh? Eat THIS."

The cross was pinned to the wall with a single remaining screw. I revolved it so it was positioned upside down. Suck on that, you bible-bashing, guilt-tripping losers.

I took my phone out and snapped a selfie with my middle finger in front of the camera lens. Then I re-did it with a joint in my teeth and my forefinger and little fingers up on both hands. Devil horns. Throwing the goat. Hailing Satan.

Xander would be so fucking jealous.

I clicked the button, snapped a second selfie. The photo was perfect—except my phone couldn't find a signal to send it.

"Let's go check out that coal shed. I need a smoke, anyway. You coming, Rat?"

I shunted a pew against the window, got up on the ledge, vaulted out into the wet black air, sprinted across the tarmac like an alley cat from shadow to shadow.

When I reached the coal shed, I hefted the roller door. It rose ten inches and stopped with a shudder. Spiderwebbed leaves rained on me. Steel chain. Another padlock. And I didn't have my crowbar.

Fuck.

I crawled around, hoping for a miracle. A forgotten piece of paper with the code on it, perhaps. A welding torch. Even a tire jack would do.

I lay on my belly and peeked under the door. Cold, dusty concrete floor. A drift of crispy leaves, and a sheen of—what was that—something oily and stinky—coal bricks? Motor oil?

Before I knew it, my arm was under the door, cellphone out, thin light licking the walls. Last time a caretaker worked in here had to have been ten years ago, maybe more. Rakes, shovels, a chair with foam bursting out of the seat. A Commodore 64 computer with dried moss on the screen. A 2001 calendar with an ancient porn actress on it. My shoulder wanted a closer look, and so did my shoulder blades. To let them get a peep I had to wiggle my bum under, then my right leg, then the left.

Within ten seconds, the outside was reduced to a thin wide letterbox slot of moonglow under the roller door, and I found myself inside the coal shed.

I hissed Yesss. Snapped a selfie. Mostly black. D'oh.

Scanning my cellphone light around, I could tell the place was mostly empty, a cinderblock bunker with relics on the walls and a pair of doors in the floor.

Massive doors with steel handles. It had to be a coal cellar.

I managed to haul one of the coal doors up a centimeter, doubled down on my effort, got it up an inch, stuck the toe of my sneaker inside, then my ankle and knee, then slid under the heavy steel panel, propping it up with my back. I shone my light into the underworld, wincing as the hundred-kilo rectangle of steel squeezed me.

At the bottom of the sunken cellar my cellphone light revealed an iron furnace, its face grilled like a knight's visor, a few square meters of empty floor, a few black rocks, bare walls, and nothing else.

Empty. Forgotten.

I tilted my phone, let it scan the cellar walls one last time.

In a second, my hand became three hundred grams lighter.

I watched my Samsung smack onto the concrete floor of the cellar below.

I listened for Xander's sneering voice making fun of me for diving after my cellphone. "You suuuuck, JoyceCo. Lost your phone, bitch. Epic fail."

Yeah right. I wasn't gonna pussy out and forget my

phone.

Attagirl, I told myself. In you go.

After it.

What, you scared of creepy crawlies?

I took a breath, sucked my stomach in, wriggled under the cellar door, and dropped.

THEN

Pebbles under my palms. Tiny rocks glinting. A flat, freezing floor. Concrete polished smooth.

My phone's screen was streaked with cracks. I squeezed the On button hard enough to crush it. The phone remained black.

I stood, reached for the ceiling—and reached—and reached.

"Helloooo?"

A strip of milky light a millimeter wide hovered above my stinky, methane-y cellar. The bunker stank like car exhaust.

I jumped toward my bar of light.

My fingers scraped air.

"ARE PEOPLE EVEN HERE? HELLOOOO? THIS IS SERIOUSLY NOT COOL."

I took four paces before a pale rectangle emerged. My nose hit the wall. I cursed, shuffled along the wall. Three paces before I was walloped by another featureless rectangle of cinderblocks. My fingers caressed the surface, hoping for gaps. Nothing. God damn it. Not even a pile of coal to stand on.

It was six paces back to the far wall. I returned the way I'd come. Above me, where the cellar doors met, there wasn't even a hairline crack.

Swallow your pride, girl. Walk through the blackness,

emerge into the light with one motherfucking epic thrill of a tale for Xander.

DONK.

Phone working again, sorta, briefly, kinda-not-really. I shone the last dribbles of piss-thin cellphone light on whatever it was I'd hit. Black eyes in a face of metal. I shrieked, fell on my butt, wriggled away—

The furnace. Cast iron. Like a black iron fridge with a handle on a little door. I stared at it for ages. The last photon of light in the universe helped me discern its shape. Edges, yes. A charcoal-colored surface a fraction less black than the rest. An island-shaped patch of colorful rust.

I approached the furnace, begged it not to bite me. I opened the squeaking door, gently extended my head into the mouth. Little piles of coal and dust on my lips. Ash in my nose.

I pulled my head out, sneezed violently, snorted snot out, put my foot on the lip of the furnace, found a fragment of balance, begged my feet to behave and remain ankle-to-ankle.

This is it, Joyce. You've reached your lowest. The bottom of hell. This is your getting-the-fuck-out story. Get home at 2 a.m. Be grateful it's not later. Make a post on Reddit, with photos. Massive sleep. Check your social in the morning.

I reached for the lidded ceiling and leaped—

And hit the ground. Daggers in my cut knees. They'd need scabs to heal.

I leaped for the ceiling doors again.

Hit the hard floor.

A twitchy, snuffling beak.

"WHO'S THERE?"

I screamed. I covered my ears. The snuffling sound vanished.

Calm, Joyce Koh, calm. Get control. All of this—it doesn't matter. First world problems. A caretaker will be here in the morning, or security, yeah. Cops, paramedics, news media.

They had to come. I didn't believe in God, but that didn't give him the right to fuck me.

I lay hugging my head, trying to hold my bladder closed cause there was nowhere to piss.

I pulled the battery out of my phone, put it back in.

Pulled it out, put it in.

THEN

As soon as I woke, I sparked my lighter. My stomach bubbled and whinged. Might as well smoke up, I thought. Hotbox the place. Enjoy life a little while I waited for rescue. The science protected me. Even though I hadn't parked a car or told anyone where I was going, every minute I endured in here had to be a minute closer to rescue. Simple mathematics.

I sucked my spliff for four minutes in my dark, sightless box, watching the tiny red eye of the joint. I counted every second. There was nothing else to do. Something squeezing my guts. A burbling bubble. Trapped gas. Eventually I noticed a tapping and scuttle. I counted to 32. The sound returned. Counted to 29. Another shuffling, snuffling whicker.

A rat. *The* rat.

My rat.

"Ben, the two of us need look no more. You like that song, you little shit? Eh?"

My words echoed half a note. Not enough echo to even have fun with. Almost zero light coming in, except a small glow inside the belly of the furnace, but I thought I saw the rat, its little caper berry eyes absorbing the pathetic sight, judging, or so my trickster brain told me.

When I kept the lighter off for a few minutes and let my eyes chill out, I realized there was a tiny spot of light inside the furnace and only one possible place it could've come from.

If I was actually seeing a circle of light within the coal furnace, and not going schizo, the light probably had to have come 80 meters through the pipe, and presumably the pipe was designed to heat the pool in the school next door. A super-old retro heating system—possibly my only way out of here.

I decided to suck my tummy in and flatten my tits and crawl into the furnace.

All I managed to fit in was a single hand and half a wrist and a mouthful of dust.

I stretched and craned and pushed. The heating pipe was only inches wide, smaller than my head. Sticking my pocketknife in got me only a couple of inches further out of here. If I wanted to get out via the pipe, I would have to chew off my limbs and post them out one by one. Cut my own head off with my damn pocketknife.

I could send Ratty out, though she couldn't speak English. She had no way of telling strangers that she knew where to find me. I needed some way to write on her. A pen. Liquid paper. Tattoo needle.

"C'mere. I'll feed ya," I told the darkness, unsure of where to point my voice. *I'll eat you*, more like. If Xander were here, he would undoubtedly bust out some Asian joke about my family eating household pets.

I watched for the rat all afternoon, or morning, or midnight, and didn't see it. There was a whisker of light in the ceiling that I tried to jump to. Every time I jumped, I got less and less air and hit the ground harder and harder, 'til finally the hairline of light was gone. And everything was coma-black.

Until I got rescued.

Unreal, I know.

Saint spraised over joyed privilegegratitude heav

enlydivine fuck in RESCUED!!!!!!

The light that flooded in when the cellar doors were pulled open purified my dirty skin. Xander was lowered down first. He wallpapered me with his arms, told me he was sorry for ever thinking he was smarter than me, that he'd treat me like a queen forever onwards now. We ascended a ladder, and Xander laid me in a pure white ambulance with cotton wool, while kind paramedics with white angel wings slid needles into the blue veins inside my wrists and gave me a drink of morphine. The tickle began in my clitoris, flowed up into my organs, my heart. My head radiated light. I drank papaya juice, so sweet that flowers bloomed in my throat, and my clitoris sparkled, and all the world was warm. I sat up in bed. Mum and Dad showed me a receipt. They'd paid off my student loan. They smiled so hard their faces cracked and split and melted and dribbled into oil, blackening the ceiling lights, popping and fizzing and stinking up my nose, the windows hardening, the bed concrete.

My—eyes—were they open? I couldn't tell. Did I even bring my eyes? Idiot, girl. Rule number one. Should'a brought 'em. I dug my fingers in and pulled on my eyeballs 'til my skull screamed.

My nose was running. Dinner! Yes! And a feast of hard flesh around the cuticles of my fingernails. I cried and snuffled and licked the salty goodness off my top lip. My stomach growled, and I needed to go toilet. There was nothing to piss and shit into but the bed of white dust in the furnace. I squirted my guts out, scraped ash over my scat, and looked at the ceiling.

Oh God, I told the heavens above from my place down in hell, I'm so so soooo epic-sorry for disrespecting you. Are you there, God?

God was there. God was my āyí, in Xiamen, my aunt, stirring a pot of soup and beaming down on me, patting my head, while little cunty too-good-for-her-family Joyce Koh played Nintendo Game Boy.

I had a lot of sorries to give God before I got out of there. Sorry for smoking weed, sorry for trolling people on 4Chan, sorry for busting through the security barrier and especially—oh man—especially sorry for turning that cross upside down in the church.

I said sorry all night.

THEN

When I pulled the scab off my knee and tossed it into the dark, the furry nose lunged, seized it, and retreated to a corner, nibbling.

"So, you got a taste for flesh, Ratgirl?"

It was a Thursday. Or Monday. I dunno. Five days, I think. A thousand and one nights.

I scraped my knife on the concrete, but it didn't spark. Pointless waste, anyway. Blunting it wouldn't help.

I had almost no sparks left in my lighter. I flicked it once, cast a little orange glow.

The rat paused, quivered, then resumed munching.

"I don't have anything else to feed you, so . . . what d'you wanna talk about?"

I watched Ratty, well, the shape of him, her, it, they. I imagined my rat friend. I pictured my life playing across the wall like a slideshow. I saw a future with Xander. Give it a few more days. He'll owe you so much for leaving you down here. Milk it, girl. Cash it in. He'll have to beg for forgiveness. You can sue him, yeah. Get millions out of his family. I watched myself investing in eradicating coal cellars. I watched myself winning the Nobel Prize for exploration. I watched the vice chancellor put a cloak and mortarboard around my shoulders. I watched my mum bless me, pulling my face into her boobs and rubbing my skull and pressing a plastic-wrapped moon cake into my chest. I saw the police and ambos scanning St. James with flashlights. People wearing rubber gloves. Questionnaires proffered at joggers. *Have you seen this girl?*

HEEEELLLLLLLP, I yelled, HELP MEEEE. My hoarse, cracking screams directed at every corner. Aimed through the furnace pipe, hoping cockroaches could send help. My stomach was a coiled python, flinching each time I emptied myself into the air. After a hundred screams, with ten seconds exact spacing between each, I could only form the vowels. ALLLLBBBB. ALLLLLLL. My throat was on fire, my body hollowed out.

EEEEEEEELLLLLLLLP.

HAAAAAAAAALLLLB.

I threw my knife at the ceiling. Tried to catch it. Failed, with jittery hands. Listened for the thunk as it fell.

Something shifted. The furnace was possessed. Should've realized ages ago. Those slits in its front were spider eyes. Vantablack patches in the milky cave. I unsheathed my knife and pointed it straight as a ruler. I was seeing things in the black, now. Or just seeing things.

"Fuck with me. Go on. I dare you."

I watched it for sixty straight seconds. I didn't need to blink. I went to a hundred seconds, then two hundred. Five minutes without blinking. Confronted. Overcame. Kicked its ass.

I spent the rest of the day—or night—or year—tickling the walls then reaching quickly behind me, trying to grab my rat friend. She was coming in and out of the cellar through the furnace pipe like a cuckoo clock, up and down, up and down. Telling me something, maybe. Trying to give me an idea.

I slept the night with my head on my hoodie, curled in a piss-free corner, knife out, furnace door open, hoping she'd come back.

THEN

When I woke, I treated myself to a breakfast joint. It made me so happy, I didn't mind licking the dew off the ceiling of the iron furnace. The droplets tasted tangy. The double-droplets with hardly any metal particulates tasted pure, flavorsome. My tongue mixed extra spit. So long as I licked the furnace lid twice a day, I'd be fine, I decided.

I had some reserves of strength, so I called for help for a few hours. Eventually there came faint voices. Something hauled the cellar doors open. Firemen, burning skylight, fluffy clouds, breathing apparatus, flashy yellow hi-vis. They pulled me out like a little bitty baby.

"Koh?"

"JoyceCo," added a sarcastic saint.

There had been a pole all this time. Xander spiraled down it and embraced me.

They asked how the hell I ended up in here. What I was doing in the church grounds in the first place. Why I pushed past sign after sign after sign saying STOP and YOU ARE TRESPASSING and HAZARD ASBESTOS DO NOT PROCEED.

It all began when I was a baby, lol. Then, in high school, I was the sarcastic, skeptical bitch with nerd-glasses to protect me from people's offence. I got into spelunking, exploring, a spirit quest, lol.

That's water under the bridge. God's given me a break, yeah, the Jehovah my parents worship at Asian Interdenominational Unitarian Church on the south end of Princes Street in Otahuhu.

"Oh, hello."

Ratty was snuffling between my legs. I stroked her spine. She flinched, went away. Came back a moment later. Getting braver.

"I've got a secret. Wanna know what it is? Yeah? Lean closer. Closer. A little closer. Thassit."

I snapped my thighs shut and pinched my fingers in a ring around its neck.

That was the day everything changed. The day a tiny seed of an idea in a dirty corner of my brain bloomed and took over and became my everything. My all-or-nothing.

As I kept Ratty clenched between my legs, wheezing and nipping, I peeled off my knee-scabs piece by piece like cornflakes. I mashed the scabs against her snout for ages, practically pulling her sharp little teeth apart before I felt Ratty's head lunging forward like a baby velociraptor, tugging fragments into her gullet.

That's it, baby. Eat a piece of Mama.

A whisper of air on my knee. Bleeding. I urged Ratty's little head towards it. Keep going, gorgeous girl. Drink my blood. Me, I needed the blood, too.

While my daughter drank, I drew four letters in her fur with the only ink I had. The red warm ink. I spelled H-E-L-P in beautiful strokes, then reached up inside the furnace, put Ratty in the pipe, and told her to go get me rescued.

THEN

Days. Nights. Weekends. Years. Months. Public holidays without Joyce. Rotations of the earth. My aunty strolling the house, turning photographs of me face-down. Pouring out rancid Tupperware pity-dishes my parents' friends had brought round. My dad clawing his ears, slapping himself.

I hadn't seen her in forever, and I had to get Ratty back. I began slicing off bits of skin, forcing myself to resist the temptation to eat them. I lay every little sliver of Joyce Koh on the lip of the furnace, nicely positioned to look tantalizing for my rat. Just the surplus bits of skin at first, of course. The bottoms of my palms. The crusty corns of my feet. My knees. A tiny sliver of my labia. Every cut electric-shocked me, knocked me against the wall, but I cried and licked my sweat and got the job done. Some slices took a thousand Mississippis, but I had forever to recover. The pain was entertaining, like a movie. My skin was all wasteful, decadent First World excess anyway. And it was just the outer layer I was slicing off.

Usually, Ratty joined me for daily activities—yodeling on Tuesdays; playing Random Number Generator on my fingers, masturbating, singing Cantonese opera, talking to Satan.

Worse than the pain of my bloody muscle sticking to the floor and peeling it off with a wet smack was the pain of drowning. That's what being on my own felt like—hot moist suffocation. Abandonment.

Except it worked. I wasn't abandoned.

My babygirl came back, snuffling up the pipe from God-knows-where. Emerging in the furnace to snaffle my skin. I held my breath, terrified of scaring her away. The only sound was an occasional hard drop of blood on concrete as I sawed my skin.

One of the best morsels was my heels. To get the difficult, thick chunks of skin off, I smoked an entire jay then cut the thick skin off my left heel in a curved slice like a Pringle. My tummy threw up a fistful of puke that burned my lips. When I set about cutting the right heel, my knife chinked against something hard, and a chill fizzed through my circuits. I'd scraped my ankle bone.

I couldn't walk for the rest of the week, and I had to do laps of the cellar on my knees. But we were doing this. Entrepreneurship. Excitement. New frontiers in exhilaration. Puking all the time. Dying. Feeling lighter and thinner each day, like a ghost.

Next thing to feed Ratty were the backs of my hands. I sliced behind the knuckles and peeled back. It was exactly like taking the fatty skin off a salmon steak. It parted nicely and stickily, and Ratty chugged it like a duck, gulp-gulp.

My bestest gal pal rolled on her back while I stroked her belly, peeing once, just a quick, single spurt. I wondered if Ratty had drunk much apart from my blood.

Are you getting drinks on the outside, girl? Rainwater? Sewer cocktails?

How many days, babe, realistically—fifteen? I think fifteen. I believe fifteen.

Long enough to fall off the front page of the paper and get forgotten.

By day sixteen—if it was day sixteen—I was playing sports all the time. Well, getting the thrill of sports, anyway. The chase, the agony, the success, the sting. The relief when my nerve endings dried up and I lost feeling in my cut-open hands as they turned to jerky. They didn't hurt so long as I lay on my back and kept them in the air, so the blood didn't come up them. I even took a drink myself, though the blood had gotten thick, and it smelled like fireworks. Hard to swallow, thick and pukey and sulfury. The best drinks were when Ratty came back soaked wet from the rain outside and I sucked the moisture out of her fur. The H-E-L-P letters I'd painted on her were gone, probably, washed out by wet grass and rain, but it was okay, so long as she came back.

Sometimes when I cut, I flicked my lighter for a glimpse at what I was doing. If my lighter gave a flame for a couple seconds, I'd light a joint and suck 'til I was numb, then slice off another fillet of me. My weed-induced joy was always gone within a three hundred count, and I was back to talking to Ratty when she visited me in the dark. We talked about Xander and politics and the weather and TV. Then I let her go and do her thing, hopping up inside the cold furnace, crawling out through the pipe. Her visits weren't free. I had to show Ratty I valued her time. It's essential to feed your guests. She rewarded me by showing me the inside of the cold iron furnace. If I skinnied down to the thinness of a snake, I could enter the pipe and flow through 80 meters.

Stretching that far would be no problem because my body had dissolved all its fat and bones. I was liquid. I'd crammed my head and shoulder inside the furnace and put my hand in the heat pipe, and I could feel my atoms trickle through and emerge in the school pool.

Twice, I'd even heard the noise of skaters, shouting, jabbering, shrieking, the trucks of their decks on concrete. One of them was screaming, desperate. Almost sounded like Koh, Koh, calling Koh, but I accepted that couldn't be. No one was rescuing me, silly, tee hee hee. Not my old deaf parents. Not Xander.

I hadn't sacrificed enough of myself, that was the problem. I was holding back. Aunt God was telling me I had to sacrifice a little more before she'd let me out. That's why I cut a deep rectangle into my thigh, passed out, woke up, then peeled off a postcard of skin. It curled up like a crepe. I slept the rest of the week, shivering, thinking about nothing.

THEN

Me and Ratty had our first fight. Looking back now, it was stupid. We couldn't even see each other. I was letting her sniff my private parts, it was a new level of trust in our friendship, important to broach. I'd cut off a lot of my skin down there; she was excited about the blood, though, and she nipped me, and I shrieked and tossed her across the room, then went roaming from corner to corner trying to find who was in here that'd shrieked like that. It wasn't me. I don't make a peep. I'm a good girl. Joyce Koh lay down low. Joyce Koh low zero. Joyce Koh don't bother God. Joycey sit in her bad girl room 'til it time to come out.

Our fight went for days. At first, I shut the door of the furnace to force Ratty to stay inside the cellar with

Mum-Mum. Then, I realized that was cruel and had a smoke and sawed off my left earlobe and offered it to her. I didn't need it because I'm right-handed. Right-eared, too, I think. It was from my right that I heard little clue sounds, like the scrape of a skateboard wheel reverberating through the pipe, a scrape which travelled sixty five meters, limped another ten, then dribbled its final few decibels into my vault. My only contact with the outside world.

There were people out there! I sprinted to the furnace, stuck my head inside and yelled HAAAALLLLLLP.

Nothin. No rescue. Just time out. My brain floating in black space. One teency star at the end of the heating pipe. I was in a coma, I decided. My family were just outside my sealed eyelids, yeah, that's why I couldn't see shit. Deep sleep. Wake up eventually.

I got stoned after that. Totally baked. All I had in this world was one last joint. I smoked it and practised holding my breath to thirty seconds, thirty-five, fifty on the eighth go, and finally held my breath for a minute ten. I didn't die, so instead I sawed the helix of my ear, then the lobule, then the antihelix, then the hard-to-grab twist of cartilage plugged into my head, watching the letters of words from Year 13 Advanced Biology swirling in the black air.

Ratty came. Bitch only wanted me for my ears, though. She nibbled while I stroked her spiky fur, sticky, thorny with clumps of something dry and hard. I listened to her tongue smack against her teeth. I heard her throat pull chewed-up meat into her tiny belly.

"I'm gonna treat you a whole lot better," I promised Ratty, "'Cept you gotta get me out of here."

She paused for a minute, digesting what I was saying.

And then it started. Accelerating the speed at which she devoured me. Racing through my plan.

To get Ratty to fully love me and trust me and lead me out through the furnace's heat pipe, I had to spoil her. REALLY spoil her. I cut my right ear off. It filled my gorgeous girl's tummy. She chewed for an hour. There was constant feedback in my ears, like a microphone squealing in front of a speaker. I tugged fistfuls of hair away from my scalp and hacked those off and stuffed the hair in my sore earholes. Then, I hacked out a rough fillet on the back of my right leg. It wasn't dinner time—it might've been midnight—but my little rattygirl had to have something to keep her strong.

The day after, I woke, peeled my sticky leg off the floor, accidentally dragged myself through a gooey floor puddle, found the juicy calf muscle steak I'd been selfishly hiding on the back of my left leg and fed my babygirl. I told Ratty about the world I come from. Where I come from, veal is calf meat. Call it veal!!!! Calf!!!! Get it?

I gave Ratty an affectionate rub on her head.

In the vomit that came gushing out of me, I felt a couple of hard curled-up chunks. I licked the puke off the concrete floor, chewed and swallowed. Spicy, but still warm, and very soft. The chunks had been tenderized in my tummy. It was nice, dining together.

Next day, I cut my toes off. They were difficult, thick, knobbly, slipping side-to-side, rolling out from under my blade. I tried to ration them over ten days, but I think Ratty really liked the texture, the hard bits of bone in the middle like prizes. I gave her two toes a day, sat against the wall and listened to Ratty's tiny nibbling. Then they were all gone.

There was some little artery in my toes nobody had ever mentioned to me. Helix, hexadecimal, hex on me, hee hee hee… . I felt light-headed after a few minutes of bleeding. Ratty licked up every last drop then groomed herself, licking the backs of her paws then wiping off with the backs of her wrists.

In the black, I could feel her looking at me.

Her face was like, What next?

BEFORE

We did the lava cave on a steamy day in late summer when the rain was baking on the warm basalt. We pulled off the motorway and onto the avenue, slowed to a crawl beside the diggers parked along the rim of the quarry. We both got out of our cars, battled through prickly bushes, and looked down at a small metal circle with a handle on it set in the rock, chained shut.

"Thought you'd be all furred-up today," I told Xander, kicking a rusty can his way.

Xander was called x@nomorph on Reddit. A respectable handle—an H. R. Giger reference. He'd shared his Deviant Art profile with me, and I knew he was a Furry, total internet weirdo like me, so it's not like he was waiting to ambush and dox me, reveal my dumb, dorky body and ugly face and shitty shoes. He broke down the icky introduction-y part by making fun of my last name, Joyce Koh. He wore Converse and denim and a *Stranger Things* t-shirt. I decided he was legit. Safe.

"Today's support mode."

"I don't need support. I know what I'm doing. We go into the cave, we get the shivers, we hit the end, revolve one-eighty, we get out."

Xander wiggled his eyebrows. He was uglier than his profile photo, but to be fair, so was I. I have rings of fat sitting on my hips. I was so skinny when I was 18, real nice cheekbones, skin hard and moist as crème brûlée. Then, all the pizza and beer we ate in the dorms at university added up and by 20, I had the Freshman Fifteen, fifteen pounds of fat on me I was hoping to get rid of with some private exercise, crawling round in the dark.

Exploring tunnels around the city was the ideal way to get fit undercover, with zero chance someone I knew would ever see me. Except Xander, of course.

First step in entering the lava cave was twisting the metal chain which was padlocked around the handle of the cave lid. I used my beautiful new crowbar. With enough torque twisting the chain, the padlock stretched, bent, then let go. It took two of us to haul the heavy steel lid open. Someone had told me on Reddit that the city council had originally found the cave when looking for new sewer routes before sealing it up and abandoning the door, assuming no hipsters would ever come crawling around a quarry on a Saturday.

They assumed wrong.

I had pretty good arms from moving all that fat around. I guided myself down the old, wooden ladder, taking most of the weight in my biceps. When the wood moaned and began bending, I gulped, said a prayer, and dropped into the ink.

"YOU OKAY?!"

I was standing, ankles clenched together, knees scraping, in an inch of cold, milky coffee. I pictured little slithery things probing up my vag. But I wouldn't give Xander the satisfaction of seeing me worry over eels and slugs. I'd done more spelunks than him. I intended to stay ahead.

I caught Xander as he dropped down after me. We used the torches on our phones. The light parted the blackness. We moved into the gaps behind the light. We stroked the rust-orange, dripping walls. The air tasted of moldy sandwiches. I dropped into a void, hit something beneath me. Winced. Cried out. When I put my torch back on Xander, he was reaching for me. I was close to saying something sarcastic, but that would've made his hand shrink away like a snail's eye.

"You don't have to," I said, "we're almost at the end."

Xander snorted. "You're about as experienced as me, JoyceCo. By the way, has that got one of those little trademark symbols after it?"

"What, you think your little puns are gonna make me come out of my shell and fall in love with you in the dark? Don't try to be some kind of leader, dude. We're both fucking incapable."

We sat there in the void. From inside my denim breast, I pulled a Glad bag and my pocketknife. Apart from my little log of weed, I had a decent joint in there, glazed with resin to hold the paper together, and with extra-fine, kinda dry, dusty weed that burned perfectly. Zero tobacco.

I sparked up, gave it a test-toke, and handed Xander the next hit. Me and Xander smoked in the darkness, feeling awkward.

"So," I said, sensing his nervousness, "you come here a lot?"

He looked at me like I was insane. Then he laughed so hard, I watched wet droplets dance in the beam of the torch. After the echoes of his laugh died, we listened to something drip for ages. We turned off the light, counted to 100, then 200, conditioning ourselves to the dark, watching the blue streak of glow worms crawling somewhere on the ceiling.

We watched our joint's orange eye twinkle and die.

"Nice down here, huh? No one judging you."

"Feels safe. Totally."

"So, listen, there's this, like, cellar," Xander said. "It's under this Christian church-school thingy, St. James', with the church all walled off 'cause they're gonna demolish it? By Mt. Eden."

"I know the place. Sounds awesome."

"Slow your roll. I never said you could do it without me."

"Fine. I promise I won't go near saint JAMEsizzizzizzz without you. Apostrophe after the ess, by the way. Your English sucks."

"This is coming from an Asian eh, *Koh?*"

I punched him on the shoulder. We laughed and enjoyed our darkness. The slime, the puddles. All bearable, as long as someone else was with me.

"Joyce."

"What?"

"Promise you'll tell me if you plan to go on your own."

"Maybe," I said.

THEN

"Here."

I took a big lick of the furnace walls, sucking up as many milliliters of condensation as I could. My tongue let go of my throat. I called Ratty to her meal.

"*HEEEERE.*"

I dangled a square of meat so succulent and fresh that it dripped on the floor. Ratty seized it like a piranha. Her tail, slick from the puddle of blood, sounded like a reeled-in fish slapping the deck of boat.

I watched my girl chew for a few seconds.

I seized her. She struggled and bit. I tightened my fingers.

"HOLE TIE, WOULDJA," I growled through gritted teeth, "jus givin'—jusgivinyou—lil—haircut."

Ratty didn't like me melting the hair on her left side. She didn't like me sawing and scraping with the knife either. I had to soften the follicles with the hot lighter then pinch the hairs out one by one with the bones of my fingertips.

First, I plucked a pattern in her shoulder, then on her ribs, then on my babygirl's big rear thigh.

I had one final flame in my lighter. I sparked my lighter once, twice. Five times. Ten.

When my lighter flamed for a few quick seconds on the twentieth try, I used the light to look at my handiwork.

I'd pulled out a patch of fur resembling a K. Next letter I'd burned and scraped and plucked out of my rat's fur was O. Then an H.

"Walkim billboar," I spewed, and giggled drunkenly. "Wall they thinga nex'?" I had no lips to form words. Only half a tongue. My neck was floppy. My head bounced on my chest. Before I fell over, I shoved Ratty into the heat pipe and pushed her little bum forward. Mama needed a rest while she waited for rescue.

I couldn't put my hoodie under my face—the blood would've stuck and dried and the cotton would be glued to my weeping wounds forever. I slept on my back, staring through space in a direction I used to think was up.

My thoughts sailed past Neptune, then Uranus, hit Pluto and the Oord Belt, and the edge of the galaxy and sailed beyond.

I thought about cave fish. They're happy without eyes.

NOW

Chased by smoke, the rat bursts out of the pipe and lands in a splat at the feet of a 10-year-old skinhead on a scooter.

"Hoooleeeee . . . *shiiiit*. You guys, check out the size of this fuckin' MONGOOSE, yo."

The de-furred rodent gets up, waddling and swaying, teeth pinching a ragged mask with a triangle of flesh-colored plastic in the middle.

It almost runs—before the scooter pins its spine.

The rat lets go of the fleshy, bleeding, dribbling rubber mask it has in its teeth.

"That ain't a mongoose, G. That's a rat."

As the scooter crushes it, the rat eyes its pipe, which is puking grey smoke that makes the boys clutch their shirts and hoods against their mouths. In the pipe which the rat has run from is a wad of hair. Soaked in sweaty oil, it burns stinking greasy, grey smoke.

Somebody calls the cops. Thirty kids gap it. Five are left behind, toeing a mask that looks exactly like a ripped-off face—with a human nose with a ring in it. The face-shaped flap of meat comes with lips, cheeks, chin, and eyebrows.

The critter itself is crimson, except for two white eyes where it looks like somebody has scratched the rat's pupils out to force it to become blind.

Scratched, too, are three letters on its side spelling K-O-H.

"Like Joyce Koh?" Carlos said. "The urbex chick? What do you think, Tim?"

"I gotta ring Xander, man," Tim says.

*

Xander Walsh is weeping into the arms of a Victim Support when the roller door is hacked open. When three strong firemen split the cellar doors. When the light leaps into the hole and the rescuers can see that, although she grins with thirty white, exposed teeth that go all the way up to her cheekbones like a Day of the Dead mask, there is something wrong with Joyce Koh.

Joyce appears to have rubbed dark red peanut butter all over her face which has hardened into gritty purplish-black chunks. Her eyes, wide dusky pools, don't blink. Don't reflect. Her face is brown where the muscle has dried and cracked and bled and dried again.

"'Ey guyz," says a throat without a tongue.

Unbothered by the light, she stands on bony, dripping legs and proffers a hand with two white balls in it. Ping pong balls or cue balls or hardboiled eggs. "I got a couple eyes left over. I don't need em. Wan' one?"

THE DAY I SKIPPED SCHOOL

1.

Tsuru, the Japanese goody-good girl, is sitting at the front of geography class and I totally want to throw darts at her back, or a knife, blades, needles. Just something to ruin her perfect posture. So uppity and show off-y, like she's a different species, her white polo shirt sitting perfectly on her statue body. Her hair is shinier than mine, her eyelashes thicker; her bra is newer and sturdier, her tits harder than everyone else's. This school is a write-off, and we all wish we could stay away, and it's frustrating that Tsuru seems oblivious to the shithole her parents have enrolled her in.

The mean girls from my class throw a Green Rocket towards the front of the class which crumples as it hits her back. It's a paper dart with boogers in it. Tsuru feels the snotty plane tap her spine, shivers once, adjusts her shoulder blades, continues to absorb the lesson, acting oblivious.

Bitch. Fuckwit. Dumbass moron. Girls' High sucks balls, Tsuru. The least you could do to, like, raise the level of dignity is give us some push-back by reacting when we hassle you, girl. Jesus. Things are different where she comes from, I suppose. Tsuru is from Japan. Her mum is a grumpy lawyer, and her dad is an accountant for the Japanese embassy downtown. I saw them once, and they looked frightened of the world, walking in front and behind her, protective of Tsuru like she was a little baby bird. The protectiveness just made it worse, at school. Kids still call her Slanty or say "Love you long time" or biff condoms at her and she doesn't say shit.

Our class right now is geography. It's boring as hell. Ms. Bowker is tapping the whiteboard where she has projected a map of the world, showing all these exotic locations, Polynesia and Easter Island and Tierra del Fuego and shit, talking about human migration and blah blah blah, Koreans have more Neanderthal DNA than the rest of us, and the land bridge from Asia to Canada, and how Japan's Crane Wife fairy tale was transported to the Aleut people of Alaska through continental drift or some shit, cultural memetics, and the Kamchatka people, and the Kodiaks and….

I've tuned out, honestly. I have two things to care about, hunched in my corner: I care about hiding my manga comic under my geo book, and I care about Connie and Francine and Hannah not fucking with me and stealing it. 'Uzumaki' is this super-violent *seinen* comic about a curse that's taken over a Japanese town in the form of a spiral. It pulls people's heads into vortexes or vortices or whatevver, curls people's spines into ropes and stuff, bends people like cinnamon rolls…. It'd be super-awesome if the Uzumaki curse hoovered up Connie and Francine and Hannah's three-headed bitch-dog trio and contorted their faces with agony, let them know what it's like to suffer. Sitting midway down the class, far enough away that Ms. Bowker can't hear them, the Cerberus bitches are planning a keg party, and they're discussing the invite list loud enough for Poppies and Losers to hear if we've made the cut. I know I'll be on the Pop list because I play my way through the ranks, I put in effort to not-be-a-loser so I can survive school, throwing out strategic compliments and lending the bitches money and giving them cans of Rockstar energy drink.

Honestly though, I barely keep my head above popular water. I'll go to their party if they invite me, but I literally hate crowds. My idea of a good time is sneaking out of school to throw rocks at the windows of an old factory or wandering by myself round an art gallery of naked drawings, something that'll really give my parents reasons to fret over me. Or breaking into the basement of Mr. English's big white house and looking for an old lamp with a genie in it. Yeah, that'd give me the thrills I need. Al English is the saggy-necked almost-60-year-old silk dressing gown-wearing Jaguar-driving creep who hits on me every time I accept one of his smokes when I'm dawdling in the alleyway to get to school slower. Mr. English stains my day every time his yellow alcoholic eyes touch me. I'll be kicking through drifts of leaves in the alleyway then find myself accepting a cigarette while he rests his fat frog throat on the fence, breakfast cocktail in his right hand, stroking the cord of his dressing gown, bragging about how his property management business has, like, a thousand clients, how he gets to spend all day in his slippers, how many kids he's put into this world, how dating is better than ever in his 50s, how his pescatarian diet gives him increased "virility," whatever the fuck that means. The gross old paedo just starts my day dirty, that's the point.

Ms. Bowker's voice cuts into my daydream.

Since we're talking about cultural traditions in Japan, she goes, "Caaan anyone tell me the tale of the Crane Wife?" No one puts her hand up, so Ms. Bowker claps her hands together and goes, "Alrighty then!" with her big dumb enthusiasm and begins explaining.

"There was once a gentleman who randomly stumbled into a relationship with a woman—it could've been any one of you girls! The woman in question was, in fact, a crane disguised as a human. The hero of the tale didn't know this at the time, bear in mind. Now, to help her man make money and keep him happy, the crane wife plucked her own feathers to weave a silk brocade, which the man sold. Their lives increased in affluence, girls, and d'you know what? Everything was going swimmingly... . Swimmingly, that was, until one fateful day."

"Scuse me, miss?" Hannah has her hand in the air. "Just wanted to say: Connie looks like a crane with her bony white ass."

"Oh, shut the ACTUAL fuck up," Connie responds, and the girls start laughing and fighting.

Tsuru swivels her head and half her body to study the Pop girls. Just a little swivel, as if her parents will be notified if she turns away from the teacher for half a second. It's not the first time I've seen Tsuru study us, looking down her curious beak like she's an eagle up in the canopy. As she turns, her skirt rides up her thigh. I can see etched lines, like a barcode of scar tissue. Places where she must've accidentally—holy shit, she's a cutter! Damn, I never thought Tsuru would be the type. My eyes are fixed on the notches in her thigh. I can picture the right-hand slicing into the pure, soft bulge of flesh. Two-inch slices at a time. Consistent, evenly-spread cuts. Yeah girl. I feel you. Space the cuts consistently so a girl knows she's got control over something in this shitty world.

Me? I'm a slicer, too. I make a notch recording every cold criticism from my mum. I'll show her someday, too. Look what all your rules and critiques and going on about getting a boyfriend made me do, Mum.

"LADIES." Ms. Bowker claps. "Seriously, now, girls, I haven't finished: let's see if we can't squeeze in the ending. Now, according to the legend—"

BLIIIIIIIIIIIING. The bell is ringing above Ms. Bowker's head, making her hair shake. We become a tsunami of green skirts and white shirts, crimson ties, swinging bags. Tsuru is nearly sucked into the hall as the class pours out until she comes too close to Francine, who pulls the bag off Tsuru's back and rifles through it, helping herself to exotic Japanese perfume, and to Tsuru's panda pencils, plus her calculator, which looks like it's worth money.

"Thank YOU!" boss bitch Hannah Kitchin pipes, as if it's been a fair exchange.

"Pleasure, anytime," Connie adds, lifting a bank note out of Tsuru's purse.

Francie blows a mocking kiss. "*Konnichiwa*, skank."

The bitches dissolve into the river of shirts and skirts flowing out to lunch. I want to catch Tsuru's eye and let her know that I don't approve, this isn't right, the girls in my seinen comics would fight back, surely?

Tsuru's eyes will probably ask me why I didn't stick up for her, though, and I don't have an answer, so I melt into the river myself, flow into another depressing day, wishing I'd had the guts not to come in the first place.

*

I'm skipping school today. The fog is heavy as a wet blanket and it's probably going to rain, my skin is dewy and my breath is white and I don't know where I'll go. I just know school is a miserable prison and it's safer to stop midway up my street and not take another step closer.

At the end of the grass berms, where my street's slow trickle pours into the going-to-work traffic torrent, I can see the rush hour rat race of people in their cars, bumper to bumper, glinting in the morning moisture. They don't notice me. I'm just some skinny 16-year-old nobody who secretly cuts herself, thin enough to disappear behind the cherry trees and the autumn mist. I could've crossed the road, could've hovered on an island, then proceeded to school to wince my way through the day, hoping Connie and Co. don't notice me.

But nah, I'm not doing all that. I'm not doing geography today, not learning ethnic folklore, not watching the clock while I poke my leg with a compass to stay awake, not wading through a choked hall of lookalike bitches. I'm walking a mile back down my posh, leafy street in the opposite direction from Girls' High. Where am I walking? God knows. All I know is I'm definitely skipping school.

That's me, yup. A total rebel. Princess Leia, Joan of Arc, Tay-Tay, Boss Bitch, fucking . . . Beyoncé. I'm turning firmly around and making a plan to go back to my parents' house. If Mum's car is unlocked, I can steal some of her parking coins and go buy cigarettes and candy and maybe a bottle of cooking wine if I show the clerk my pierced nipple.

All I need is to zig from tree to tree through the fog, zag between a couple of parked SUVs speckled with dew, and duck down outside number 1807 so Mr. and Mrs. Khan's security camera doesn't record me and tell my dad.

I start with a few steps. Them I'm fully in it. After five minutes, I'm a full-on ninja.

I scamper under the cameras and flagpoles and high gates of 1753, 1725, 1619, make it as far as 1609 when I realize the white shirt/green skirt uniform that looks like a mirage is actually—Oh, please God, no.

It's her.

Tsuru the Exchange Weirdo.

And she just waved at me. *Fuck.*

I know next to nothing about this goth/Lolita bitch, except she is probably a snitch, and I'm going to get found out.

I press my back against the fence of a property called Silver Lining Lodge which looms over a slim alleyway. I melt into the privet hedge and try catch my breath. Tsuru should literally not be here. Last thing I need right now is witnesses.

I hear the hoof of her black leather boots clopping towards me like a damn Clydesdale.

The clocks stop and she's there, in front of my hedge, wavering like a video game character waiting for you to hit Start.

I move forward out of my scratchy bush.

"Fuck are you doing here?"

"Hi," she says, shyly moving her hair behind one ear, and adds "Soo-sin," as if saying my name is a separate thought.

It's SUSAN, yo, I wanna tell her. Except I like the way she says my name delicately, as if the texture is fresh on her tongue. Soo-sin.

No one else says my name like it's special.

"I'm not—really, I don't—" I have no idea how to end the sentence. *I don't live here? I'm not really cutting class?*

I gulp, push my own hair back and go, "So, you going to school, or... ?"

Tsuru blushes, pours her face into her hands. Suppresses a snicker, a giggle. I can tell she's struggling to formulate an explanation. Bitch has got a naughty streak.

"You're cutting class, right?" I continue, painting over her nervous silence, making things less awkward. "It's cool. Me too. I mean, unless you're just late, or... ?"

Tsuru is nodding like a woodpecker.

"I guess we can hang, I mean if you're not, like, getting a ride or whatever."

Our bodies clearly want to walk somewhere; it's just that one direction would take us to school, the other direction would take us to my place. We hover on the lip of the alleyway. We have the mist to cover us, for now.

"You guys are at number 1400, right—the place with the little checkpoint control box guard-thing? Your family, um, fuck, what's the word . . . I don't speak your . . . listen, is your people's place safe to hang out at, or—?"

We talk it over and work out it's a No to Tsuru's house, and a No to mine, too. I can disarm the security system at my parents' place, but the problem is I can't erase the CCTV footage that gets fucking beamed to my parents' goddamn mobile phones telling them I'm being naughty.

A car comes, black and glistening, a Mercedes. I find my hand crumpling Tsuru's shoulder as I pull us into a closet of privet to hide.

We watch the car cruise past. Headed towards a purpose, unlike us. We haven't even thought up something to do with our day.

We need to think, plot, plan. Lay out a mission.

I guess we could call an Uber, except my dad pays my credit card bill so he monitors all my transactions, and I totally know he'll snoop.

Tsuru finally motions for us to scuttle to another alleyway between 1599 and 1601, an alleyway I've dropped many a bottle and butt in, though the problem is this alleyway goes past the house of—seriously? Please God, no—

The house of frog-throated property king Al English.

We don't have a choice.

*

His gate opens smooth as a fridge door, closes cleanly. His yard is all paving stones and bird baths and sculptures of white cherubs. A fountain, a pond, lily pads, a pergola with roses, a hammock... .

Tsuru has a cute backpack of that puffy panda/cat beast Totoro. Just past the gate she kneels, opens it, pulls out a pack of smokes, a stolen-looking bottle of brandy, some men's razor blades.

I spot a trio of comics in there. Bio-Meat. Ichi The Killer. Uzumaki, the one about the deadly spiral. Unless Tsuru's gone and shoplifted in my bedroom, I think this crazy bitch has got the same taste as me.

"We fill, yes?"

"What, fill your backpack with Mr. English's shit? Like, rip him off?"

Tsuru is nodding and about to blurt something when I spot Mr. English and stick a finger against her lips. Sssh. Time to roll the old rich fuck.

He's waiting at the top of the stone stairs. Must've seen us out in the alley looking directionless. He's stirring his coffee and finishing a conversation on his Bluetooth headset. Black lizard eyes under squares of uniformly-caramel skin like he's had skin grafts or plastic surgery. The hair on top of his cooked pink head is squelched down with some kind of sticky wax, though it springs out of his chest in fuzzy curls.

Sure, I'm concerned about getting tongue-raped and manipulated, but we have to be off the street so Truancy Services doesn't tackle us. Being in a rich guy's house with shag carpet and a dark-wood spiral staircase with a library and a drinks cabinet is relatively okay, I guess.

He presses the device in his ear, says "Girls, top of the morning to ya," as if it's totally not unusual for teenagers to appear in his front yard. He waves us in, walking behind presumably so he can get an eyeful of our asses. He locks and bolts the ranchslider behind us. We sit on his hard leather couch while he puts Pop-Tarts in the toaster for us. He mixes us a drink each in a martini glass. I'm bunched up against Tsuru, sitting so close that the barcode-scars on our thighs press together. I glance sidelong at her, sitting upright and anxious. Tsuru's lips are nervous, puckered pin-points. They need to be kissed, I think, weirdly.

Mr. English is away talking smack, roaming the parlour and kitchen, mentioning five or six times that we're welcome to help ourselves to the champagne he's put in the ice bucket on the coffee table.

The ice cubes in his glass clink as he paints with his hands.

". . .Aaaand that's when I realized the wisest thing to do is acquire tranche number three, considering the all-time nadir in volatility, you'd be an imbecile not to, know what I mean?" he says, settling into an armchair with his third drink, folding one knee over the other, adjusting his dressing gown over his fat thighs. "We all remember what happened to prices in oh-eight, obviously. But enough about my passion." A smile leaks across his face. His eyes crease until they're black lines. "Tell me, Ladies: tell me what gets you *off*."

Tsuru's eyebrows are so high up, I'm worried they're going to burst out the top of her head. She's been given a glass of stinky schnapps, but she doesn't know where to put it. "I am liking . . . swimming in the ocean?" she goes. "When this is warm water, is warming?"

"My daughter, Annika, she was swimming at Summer Bay four years ago and she—" Bent over, he's melting, warbling, warping, like water is falling through his body. Pinching his nose, bottom lips shiny with moisture . . . *Jesus*. The dude's crying! And rolling forwards out of his chair, knees on the floor like he's praying to Allah! What the fuck? I've only taken one bite of my Pop-Tart and already the day's an abortion.

I was hoping to get propositioned, kind of, or robbed, but here me and Tsuru are, side-stepping African statuettes and Javanese idols to get to an old caveman hunched over in a half-somersault to rub his back and cheer him up. Tsuru is murmuring soothing things to the creep. We share a gaze, then our heads turn mutually to the wine rack.

Tsuru unzips her backpack. I begin filling it.

After a minute, the drunk, hairy, dressing-gowned wreck looks up from his puddle of tears on the carpet, star-tled, shocked, seizes Tsuru's wrist as she tries to step over him and grab the champagne. "Take me to my room. Down those stairs. Please. You have to."

He snatches both our forearms. We have no choice but to park our bags of loot and help him up. The guy is shorter than me and his pale-yellow throat bulges like a fat frog. He says, "The Burgundy," turns and grabs a bottle of wine and a corkscrew and has a final glug of blood-dark stinky alcohol before we let him descend the few steps to his sunken bedroom.

Bronze wood panels. Thick carpet. Mirrors above the bed. Low ceiling, like we're on a yacht.

The sheets we peel off his California superking waterbed are rich black silk. We urge him into the sloshing bed, and he hands his Burgundy and corkscrew to Tsuru. She studies the objects she's been handed. She looks like she's never used a corkscrew before. Its point is so sharp that it twists into a needle then disappears.

"Cheers for having us over, I guess." I ask Tsuru a question with my eyes, like *Why are we still here, this guy's a drunken loser, what are you hoping for?*

"Tsu. It's first period. We've got to cruise. Right?"

Dumped on the bed, Mr. English is lying on his back, smiling, teeth sticking out over his lip like an alligator. He doesn't look upset any more. His eyes gleam in their wet pink patches.

I shouldn't be standing this close to his bed.

He snatches my wrist, crushing my white shirtsleeve.

"Nurse," he says, yanking. "You have to look after me."

I splat into his bed and the covers close on top of me, and even though he's shorter, Mr. English is twice as heavy as me, squishing me as he rolls on top, licking and nibbling and sucking my throat, pushing my hands against the headboard.

In the mirror on the ceiling, I watch the sheets slide off his furry black back as his legs push my knee-high socks out to the sides, starfish-wide, his arms mirroring mine, keeping my hands pressed away from his eyes so I don't claw him. I don't scratch or scream or bite. My brain's still half in the alleyway, stunned. Still thinking I can control what's going to happen in my day.

Mr. English pulls his lips off me, leans back, shrugging out of his dressing gown, tugging at the elastic band of his boxer shorts, revealing a stripe of veiny blubber as he begins to yank his undies over one leg. There is a pen in his neck, suddenly, a silver pen I've never noticed, or it's grown there just now, a pen or a torch or a crank, something with a black plastic handle, sticking to his froggy throat-sac with black paint, no, dark-purple blackcurrant juice that spasms, squirting across the room. Blood, dark as ink. Dripping down the cupboard doors thick and slow as barbecue sauce.

Mr. English falls backward off me and kicks, fingering whatever's stuck in his neck. His crusty toes bash my chin and I bite my tongue. I roll out of bed, clutching my school uniform against me like armour, too breathless to scream. Tsuru reaches to pull the corkscrew out of the man's neck. I slap her hand away, shove her towards the exit. We pause, turn, watch him struggle. Mr. English's legs push away from wherever he thinks the corkscrew is. He kicks himself off the bed, lands heavily on the corkscrew side. He speckles the carpet with a dozen dark puddles as he tries to stand, one hand on the flap of his dressing gown, modest. He gropes his neck but can't grasp the slippery corkscrew handle between his stained fingers. The corkscrew is deep, almost inside him. Buried.

"Ambulis," he croaks. Bending, folding, sitting on his butt in a pool of oil spreading so thickly there are little ripples and rapids in the blood. His eyes attempt to meet ours, but they're flicking in two separate directions.

"You fill bag."

While I've been frozen, Tsuru has gone up to the kitchen, brought down wine carriers and canvas shopping bags, as well as her fluffy Totoro backpack.

She dumps the sacks at my feet.

"HEY. Filling bag, NOW."

Mr. English gurgles, tries to crawl towards us through the red sticky swamp, hairy bum in the air as if he's pretending to be a worm.

"Ev-e-rything," she orders me.

"Is he—is he dead? He—he—he—can't be— "

"EV-E-RYTHING. SOO-SIN. BAG."

I scurry up to the kitchen. We open another liquor cabinet. I stuff two sacks with Bacardi, Jim Beam, VSOP, Courvoisier. I toss in a silver cheese knife, a mortar and pestle, steak knives, a candlestick, postage stamps, a restaurant voucher, a meat thermometer, think think think, girl, what's gonna make you rich? What do you need, what will you regret not taking? Thinking, grabbing, shit, um, this china plate, yeah, fuck, dropped it, pour out the parking coins from the fruit bowl, yeah, a metronome, okay, weird, car keys, a crystal ashtray, a letter opener, a butter dish, fuck—

I'm so busy stacking bags of loot by the ranch slider, preparing to escape into the alleyway, that I realize I haven't seen my friend in minutes.

I freeze. Cold shiver. Fuck was that noise? A hand cracking walnuts? No. Somebody ripping a fish in half? No. Water balloons smacking on concrete? Wet, tearing, dripping, juicy. Splatty-crunch.

I tiptoe down the three carpeted stairs to Mr. English's sunken bedroom. I peer around the corner. I see a pelican, yellow beak thick as half a kayak, too large for the room, hunched under the ceiling, pulling off chunks of red-stained robe and gulping them down. An enormous seabird, giraffe-sized, crammed in a tiny space, bumping its head, beak like two surfboards, eyes black frisbees. Its wings are white curtains stained grey, bunched, quivering. Its rear end spans meters, reaches into the en suite bathroom. Tail feathers big as paddles.

The giant bird twists its head to pull a chunk of flesh inside it. It has Mr. English's arm in its beak. A webbed grey foot like a rubbery stingray is clawing, holding Mr. English's body while it pulls him apart, beginning with his left arm. His free hand is trying to hold on to a bedsheet. He's looking at me with drowning eyes. The pelican-thing makes the choking, sucking sound of a blocked vacuum cleaner then gulps the arm into its mouth, sucking up the black silk sheet like a napkin, and Mr. English's head disappears. His shoulder blades are folded and squashed as he trickles head-first down its sticky throat. After his shoulders, it swallows his back and belly, his hairy butt, his butter thighs. I watch the shape of his body stretch the gullet of the bird.

Lastly, the cord of his dressing gown whispers, flaps, as if asking us to fetch help, then the slippers fall from his toes as he disappears.

The bird chokes, pulls, swallows, and when it has finished swallowing, it turns to me. Its eyes are my equal. It knows who I am.

Big Bird. Big Bird from Sesame Street. Big Bird with black eyes. Big Bird with a mouth of stiff plastic. That's what its beak looks like as it talks.

"Now you've seen."

The giant bird's cheeks flex. As it swallows, its eyes blink, huge and slow. Eyelids of skin from elsewhere. From a dimension of sea-bottom beasts asleep in the deep.

My scream tears the air in two.

The bird stomps, revolves, grunts. Its head smacks the lampshade. How—-how—how did it even get in? Pelican, yes? No? Heron. Stork. Swamp-bird. Eater of snakes and tadpoles and—sad—sadlonelydesperatedeserve—

"Susan. Promise you'll keep me secret."

"I pr—pr—promise."

I back up the stairs, leave my bag of kitchen loot. I rattle the ranch slider 'til I'm screaming and throttling and praying and the ranch slider handle breaks and I sprint down Mr. English's garden stairs, slipping on expensive white stones, gasping as I bump over a gnome and it shatters and I leave my heart throbbing behind me.

Tsuru appears from somewhere, dropping a computer monitor in the goldfish pond, her fingers tense like claws as she catches up and grasps my shoulder, sacks of loot rattling at her side.

My school bag, heavy with rattling metal and stone.

We sprint to my house, shower together, put our clothes in the washing machine, set the cycle for 8 hours and hide under my bed. We cry and bite our knuckles, weep into my mum's belly, watch my dad thump the wall and turn away, wait for detectives who never come, watch the news for reports of Mr. English missing, read his obituary in my dad's Property Investors Federation newsletter, slowly return to school. I have a skeleton of steel, now. A hardness in me.

I sit beside Tsuru every class and let her lean on my shoulder and whisper and when Ms. Bowker tells us to get a room, I tell her to go fuck herself, challenge her to a one-out. The same week, I push Connie into a pile of desks, hold a sharp pencil against Francine's eye, crush Hannah's scalp in front of 50 girls in the hall and scream in her terrified face, "I ain't afraid of nothing no more, specially not you, you bully-bitch-cunt-FUCK," laugh and pash, sip vodka from our drink bottles in the toilets, accept a bundle of correspondence school papers, battle my exams lying on my bedroom floor sipping alcohol and popping Prozac and bleaching my hair and listening to Baroque music and studying, sending secret forbidden texts to my BFF, and I realize, opening my university results one morning two years later, wondering how the fuck I got an A+ for accounting in the first place when I resent keeping records and remembering things, I realize I've drifted down a river of time far from where I used to be, and my counselor has taught me how to ground myself, how to stop letting people rock me off my perch, and I realize it's safe now; no more cognitive distortions, no more hallucinations, no more waking up at 4am whimpering. There is no monster chasing me, and there probably never was.

I can stop running.

2.

College is fucking lit. On our first night, the Finance Society puts on a Burning Man party with a scarecrow stuffed with straw. They light the thing up and all us accounting and commerce kids rip off our clothes and dance in our bras and panties, playing beer pong and chanting anthems and throwing coconuts full of beer, tearing up our student loan contracts, pashing strangers, climbing the registry building, pissing off roofs. We party and study and blow up condom-balloons and scream at the future We are not afraid.

Summer, we get a break, and my heart rate slows. A lot of the girls are off getting with boys, but I'm not really focused on cock, nor is my best friend. Out at the beach, me and Tsuru toss our clothes into the wind and stomp through bitter green waves, shrieking, nipples hard as marbles. She's still shy, still perpetually running away, hiding, retreating, and I tackle her from behind, force her into the dark sand, hold her down as an icy wave tosses pebbles over us.

In autumn there's Pumpkin Fest, and we dance on the stone bridge in the middle of campus 'til our feet ache. At night we watch speech bubbles of white emerge from our mouths, linger in the black, frosty, twinkling sky. There's a party in Hamilton Hall, and as we drunkenly stumble to it, I tell Tsuru "Wait—wait—wait!" and pull a mouthful of orange juice from her backpack and a mouthful of vodka and tell Tsuru that she is one Ooooooooorganized Bitch, Organ, Tee Hee Hee, Orgasm, Huge Throbbing Organs, and Tsuru rolls her eyes and marches up the stairs, and she's so pissed off at my rude Western white girl ways, she tries to get away from me. The bitch can't help but be polite, though, that's her DNA, silly Tsuru, all mild warnings and soft threats so she's knocking patiently on this party door and tapping her foot passive-aggressive until I catch up and begin massaging her shoulders, and I smell her mango-y shampoo and sneak a little drunken nibble of her earlobe, and she tilts her head left, inviting me to nibble again. The hall is ours, the hall is OURS, WORLD, SO FUCK YOU and I don't want any passengers sharing my drunken ship, but the hallway is spinning and the party door opens and we fall inside, and there's candles flickering by an open window and wavering curtains like ghosts and jazz on the speakers and an amaaaazing gathering of bitches, yeah, Thingie-Blue-Hair, the reporter from the . . . student newspaper . . . thing, and—and—and Kate, oh, Kaaaate, Kate Smirnoff.

Chertoff, she tells me. You're loaded, Suze.

Takes one to know one, I tell her.

Connie—we're friends now, fuck her, needy bitch—is whispering in Tsuru's ear over by the kitchen island. Tsuru is looking down in judgement, arms folded. Bitches are obviously talking about babysitting me 'til I'm sober, like I need their pejorative friggin–

Okay, okay. I'm going down. I'm letting them press my shoulders. Curtains drawn. Ring of candles. Dark, spooky room. Buttery flame between every girl's knees. They're folding me into the floor, and there's a circle of people around me, and Connie settles a plate of lasagne between my knees and gives me a fork, and I take a mouthful then jam my dirty fork down her cleavage and cackle so hard, I spurt up little chunks of meat and tomatoey onion and tell my friends this lasagne is like seriously sooooooo gooooooooood, you've totally gotta get some down ya.

They're not laughing, my friends, and they're not lit up much, either. It's dark as a cinema in here. In front of my toes is that thing from, like, that movie . . . Glaswegian—Weegie—a Ouija Board, yah, that's it.

"Urgh, your turn, I spose," Connie says to me, wiping between her tits with a piece of paper. "We've already gone. You ever witnessed the paranormal?"

"The paranormal," I go, and snigger, and gulp my Smirnoff and cheesy pasta. "Is that what—we're—conversating?"

"You heard her, byatch," one of my friends goes. "Slenderman? Some of us've seen him. And Mariam said she encountered a fucking yeti, like for real, when she was volunteering in Nepal. Chulani, she got her door knocked on by a vampire. We all told our spooky stories. You don't get to drunk your way out of this, girlfriend. Your turn."

I look over at Tsuru. She's too far away for me to grab her hand and squeeze. I can see her shrinking, folding, packing up her joy, preparing to skip town.

I swallow, drain a cup of mulled wine, crumple the cup, play with the squashed, cracked plastic then toss it into the dark corners of the room.

"You sure you guys wanna hear this? Cause it'll spook the shit out of you."

"Just fucking tell us."

The world is encased in ice. Our eyeballs lock for eternity.

"You can't tell anyone this. Kay? So, when I was, like, 15—I skipped school, this one day—and I had nowhere to go, like, I couldn't hang out at my mum and dad's place, but, like, there was this creepy lecherous kinda dude, and I guess I went to his house and—"

"And you fucked him?" Connie goes, grinning. "Did you suck his dick? OH. MY. GOD. You totally sucked his dick. Tell us how disgusting it was, eeeewwwww, did his foreskin have, like, headcheese under it from like the 80s and shit?"

"No, I was with—" I look over at the only person in the world who shares my secret. Silent Tsuru has tilted her head, so her hair has fallen around her face.

It's not a big deal, this thing. It's public knowledge. It was in the papers.

Bloody Crime Scene; Landlord Missing.

Day Ten Without Body—Police Halt Search.

Property Magnate Staged Disappearance, Police Believe.

"I—I skipped school and I was—I saw this—"

"Spill it. What'd you see?"

"This—I saw this guy, he was going to hurt me, then this, like, it—it came out of nowhere, it just sorta—and I promised."

"Promised? Promised what?"

"Promised I wouldn't tell."

Frozen clock. Everyone's eyes are paused, bodies still, ears pointed towards me. I'm watching Tsuru unfreeze, prepare to walk out forever. If I speak, I have lost her, and no story is worth losing her. I'm up, I'm drunk, I barge the hat stand over, I leave the door open; the girls complain and call me back, but I'm sprinting down the fire stairs and I'm catching Tsuru just before she gets in an Uber. She's slapping me, I'm touching my fiery cheek, she cools my burned cheek with her lips, then her tongue is on mine in the back of the Prius and her knee pushes into the cleft between my thighs, and we're glued crotch-to-crotch, cold noses pressed into each other's ears, we're waddling into the room we share where there used to be two single beds until tonight, and I'm licking every secret scar carved into her skin, working upward from her knee to her panties 'til I hit the sweet spot and we drink one another.

3.

Our love makes years melt and decades dissolve. Years of arms wrapped around Tsuru's waist at the kitchen sink. Years leaning into the cleft between her shoulder blades, resting my head there. Years cooling her down when Tsuru gets flustered with her hater-parents on Skype and slams the lid of the laptop down, parents who are all anti about her having friends, anti about her coming out. Anti-everything. I'm there when she's had a bad day, and we lie on our bellies in bed and sip sake and eat pistachios and gasp at our seinen horror comics and say Omigawd, check this out. I'm there when she wants to share the bathtub with the only human she trusts. I'm there to snuffle kisses from her throat down to her thighs.

When I'm not drunk on love, I'm drunk on tallying and reconciling and filing. Accounting is a sensible career for me. I've had more good luck than I deserve, and it's time I appreciated whichever god gave me my ally, my confidante, my co-conspirator, my secret wife at home. Well, a common-law wife since our marriage hasn't been planned yet.

Every night I start getting mad at my reports around 7 p.m., and Tsuru walks up behind my swivel chair, lifts my hair, kisses my neck. We make love in every room of our house. We cool down and let our hearts relax. We catch up on years we missed when we were afraid all the time, running from repercussions.

We want children, and we want to get married, though we're both not sure in what order we should get it all done. We go to see Fertility First, at that private hospital with the shiny tower. Our expert, Himesh, squirts moisturizer between his fingers then gets Tsuru to lie on her back. We hold hands with him while Himesh gets us to close our eyes and envision not the sperm and egg, not the birth, but the people we want to share our blessing with. One of the people we want to bless our child's birth is the sperm donor. This is the only thing that matters, Himesh tells us: how the story of a person makes you feel about them.

Go with the story that sings to you, Himesh tells us.

Choosing a sperm donor from a catalogue is quickly completed in ten minutes. He's chubby, he's a web developer, he's ginger, he's South African, he's terrible at stand-up comedy, his profile says, and he dresses up as Santa to make kids smile at Christmas.

He's nothing like the beasts we grew up with.

Within an hour we have our future planned.

Tsuru works from an office pinned to our garage. She scours internet auctions and old ladies' garage sales, buys antiques cheap, sells them online for a premium. She has an instinct for which things should be passed on quickly and which things must be sat on for years. In our spare room she keeps floor-to-ceiling glass cabinets, and in there, among the suits of armor and ebony carvings, are a crystal ashtray and a letter opener and a butter dish, objects with radiation on them, contaminated from some throbbing glowing chained-up locker buried under the back of my brain.

We put away savings, and we can afford to meet Tsuru's parents' idea of an authentic Shinto wedding, even though they mostly don't want us to marry. We find a pure white *uchikake* kimono for meek, secretive, demure Tsuru. As for me, it's agreed my *uchikake* will have a black stripe and an embroidered crane, a bird I've dreamed about for years. Connie can be the shrine maiden, the *miko*. She gets to pour the rice wine into our sacred cups. We sketch plans for our parents' *tomesode* kimonos in case they agree to wear them. We source wedding cake makers, a party quiz on printed cards, games of minigolf and boules, cake, karaoke. A place with a *tatame* room. Tsuru knows special corners of Alibaba. com where she can get nuptial silver cups for us to drink our sake in the ritual of *san-san-kudo*. Rings, hair, makeup: all efficiently organized in a file on the computer of my reclusive, thoughtful bride-to-be. My fiancée. My lover who falls asleep with me at the kitchen table, our foreheads resting on fancy paper stationery.

*

After years of worry and angst and secrecy, it's finally a week go 'til we tie the knot. HEN PARTY, BITCHES!!! Me and Tsuru and Connie, Francine, Hannah, Grant from Xero, plus a couple of buddies from the LGBTQ+ community who won't out us too much, seeing as Tsuru's family keep going on about *himitsu* when they tell her off over Skype at 3 in the morning, beaming in from Niigata. Himitsu this, mimoto that. I finally have to use Google Translate when Tsuru won't tell me.

Turns out *himitsu mimoto* means covering up who you are. God damn control freaks are obsessed with keeping Tsuru's identity secret.

We want to party the pre-wedding tension off, except Tsuru has a tiny shrimp-baby growing in her tummy, so we're definitely not taking her clubbing, not that she'd be brave enough for clubbing anyway. We decide to bring the party to her. Hen Night at our house.

Everyone—fucking EVERYone—gives us shit for having a hen night together. You're supposed to be apart, they tell us. There is affection in their scolding, though. Big Gay Grant pulls me into the laundry and laughs under the weak light bulb. Tells me he's honestly never met anyone in the universe that's as close as us two. How'd you get bound so tightly, anyway? Did you go through the trenches together or what?

"We ripped off this, um, like we didn't set out to steal his—" I stop. "Nothing."

"Ripped off what now? ExCUSE me?! Sister Steals, you got a dark side!"

"THE DRESS!" someone is chanting. Hannah I think, pulling us out of our laundry, "THE DRESS, YOUR KIMONO-THING! SHOW US!"

"Yah bitch!" Connie is going. "You have to, you have to!"

They're tipping out Tsuru's closet of wedding prep, upending her hat boxes, while she protests, wincing over her belly-bump. Tsuru has a whole closet packed with kimonos. Gay Grant presses one against his body and parades up and down the house while my flustered fiancée chases him. Francine, pouring whiskey into her mouth, pulls stacks of comics from under our bed, and she and Hannah and all the bitches decide they looooove Japanese horror, shit's soooooo seriously gross, ewwwww, specially the tentacle porn, hee hee, plus the myths and legends.

We settle into a quieter zone, resting our exhausted drunken chests on the breakfast bar while the MDMA wears off, turning manga pages absently.

There's not much conversation left when I finally pull down a bottle of sake and we chink shot glasses and toss fire into our tummies and go Mmm.

Everyone except Tsuru, who stands apart, hand on her pregnant stomach.

"So, that thing you were gonna tell us," Connie goes. "C'mon Suze. It's time. Fess up."

"What thing?"

"The thing that happened on the day you skipped school, dumbass. You've kept us waiting for, like, Gawd, how long?"

Spear in my heart. I stagger back an inch. The alcohol turns horrid on my tongue.

I haven't thought about The Thing in years.

There are eight eyes boring into me. Eight eyes across four heads.

Not my girl's eyes. Over against the wall, Tsuru's head is bowed. Crushed. Turned down. Ashamed, as if she's preening her belly-feathers. Typical Tsuru. Hiding secrets.

My friends have been waiting a decade for my story, though. They're important to me too. I can't let Tsuru guilt-trip me anymore.

I stare down the hydroslide, then descend.

"So there was this day I skipped school, okay? It was like all misty, like pea soup. This was high school, right, you guys remember Year 12, I was like 16, and—sorry, Tsu—I totally hated Tsuru's guts back then. She was like this hard-out preppy perfect."

Tsuru has drifted to the edge of the room, like she's about to leave. She won't meet my eye. Two hands cradling her belly. Pigeon toes.

I down a shot of fiery Sambuca and shudder and everyone smiles. Connie is about to say something smart-ass, but my words come out first.

"So here's me skipping school one day, Thursday I think it was—or Tuesday—and I'm dragging my feet. Y'know how it is? Like my parents were, like, super negative, and they totally wouldn't support me in going back to bed for a day. So, I'm like doing laps of my street, at a loose end, y'know, trying to think up a place to go and, like, self-harm. But who do I see coming up the motherfucking street? Tsu! 'Cause her family lived like half a mile down from me! And she's being a badass as well, which I didn't know at the time."

Connie slides another Sambuca along the bar top. It's my fifth, I think. Or fifteenth. Things aren't adding up, my eyes are lying, 'cause I could swear Tsuru was against the wall ten seconds ago, looking immaculate in silver and pink, sulking, studying us, and now she must be in the next room. Gone somewhere. Vanished.

"So, Tsu drags me into this, like, creepy paedo rich guy's house, and that's cool, kind of, 'cause we need a place to hang so truancy doesn't get us. But then he, like, starts feeling me up and pushes me down in his bed, and I'm like WHAT THE ACTUAL FUCK, and then he starts having a heart—"

"Suze?"

"His body was, like, jiggling, like electrocution sorta thing. Convulsions, y'know? 'Cause he got sta—I mean, he was gonna rape us and he, like, he fell on a knife, I mean, not even a knife, like those sharp things you use to open wine, it wasn't our fault, he—"

"Holy... Did you take him to the hospital?"

"It grabbed him. This thing, this *bird* did. Grabbed him with its, like, beak and it—I can't even say it."

I'm shaking so bad, I splash Sambuca up my wrist. The sleeve of my blouse stinks.

"I'll just shut up now. I wasn't supposed to tell. I pr—promised I wouldn't say nothing. I said I'd—I wouldn't."

"But you did." Connie looks like a judge, like a principal. There's no jokiness behind her eyes. "You told. How you gonna be faithful to your wife, Suze?"

"YOU PROMISED."

Explosions in the whitewall. Plaster dust in Grant's eyes. Knocked bottles. Screams. My friends duck under the table. The bird's wide wings scrape the edges of the hallway, knocking picture frames as it crunches towards us, crushing the floorboards. Its head bursts the lightbulbs in the ceiling. The bird fills the room, shunting our dining table into the wall, pulverizing pot plants, scattering cat biscuits.

Fishy rancid rotten seaweed breath melts my eyes. I'm looking into a tongue big and red as a steak, a throat as black as a sea cave.

Its beak is huge enough to swallow me in a single gulp.

"YOU PROMISED YOU'D NEVER TELL."

The crane pecks Connie first. Gobbles, actually. Devours. The crane gulps Connie out of existence, seizing all her body except her shoes. I can make out the shape of Connie's hands and knees and screaming mouth as she presses against a bulging blue throat-sack.

Grant dives into the kitchen, crawls like a cockroach, tries to escape out the cat flap. The crane steps on his left leg with its rubbery foot, big and webbed as a kite. It pulls Grant's leg from his hips with the sound of torn paper, leaving a hole, a circle of white bone and gristle hiccupping blood.

While I scream and weep and shiver, the bird gobbles up my friends, snapping and swallowing, shuffling awkwardly in the cramped room, its beak as long as a coffin, its vast bunched wings cracking every window it bumps.

Francine has a head one moment. Next, the beak snatches it off, then tugs her arms out of her torso. She smacks against the wall like a tossed banana peel, falls headless into the washroom.

The bird pulls Hannah to pieces in frantic, rushed snatches. Pecking.

When there are no witnesses left to eat, the bird takes six thudding, stomping waddles to adjust its feet in the too-small room until it is facing me. One black basketball-eye on each side of its beak.

It presses me against the wall. Hot intimate reeking salt-breath puffs out from its nostrils, steaming my face. Something trickling. Moisture in my eyes. Fish-stink.

The mouth opens. The tongue lifts and flaps like a flounder. The throat pinches as it struggles to form words.

"You promised."

As the bird lowers its beak and preens its belly, snuffling, mournful, I sink to the floor. As it rummages in its tummy feathers, my eyes wince and stretch and bend. It finds the spot where our baby resides, around its belly button. I pray for death. Get me out of this.

But I live. I live and watch her peck her belly 'til her flesh gives way and a torrent of pink water spews onto the floor. I watch her pull a tadpole-thing from her insides, hold the twisting fetus aloft as it spatters the ceiling fan with juice. I watch the crane bite our baby in half then suck the meat into its gullet.

The bird turns, waddles into the lounge, jams its beak into the French doors, shatters the glass and wood with a few flicks of its head, tossing the doors onto the lawn.

It moves out into the sucking cold air, the wet grass, green below, black above, lit only by light leaking from our kitchen.

Tsuru spreads her wings, rattling the apple tree, smashing the pergola.

Our wedding vows, our invitations, stacks of menus spin in a whirlwind. Each flap of feathers sends paper flying, our home tornadoed.

Then, she's gone.

CLUB HUNDRED

1.

Manu is at this party at the house of this environmentalist chickypie who knows everyone, like EVERYone. Manu barely knows her, and doesn't think he fits in. His All Blacks jersey is new and clean but he's still got his work boots on and he's got mud on the carpet and he's taller and fatter than half the people here so he keeps his hand over his oafish belly, trying not to be noticed.

The party is all fairy lights and djembe drums and Greenpeace activists wearing bamboo-fabric shirts and that whole gang who run that plastic-free whole foods store Manu's ex-wife shops at. He doesn't fit in with them, but stumbles into a pit of cool cynical people in the poker corner balancing crumbs of tobacco on their Rizzlas as they roll joints. Manu saunters over, half-looking away so if he ends up embarrassed, he can pretend he didn't even try. His wife called him a loser as she packed newspaper around her porcelain, told him he deserves to be alone, and Manu thinks she's right. He hasn't done that much with his life. Got a plumbing apprenticeship and a full-time job connecting pipes, that's about it. Not enough to impress folks at a party, that's for sure.

On the edge of the circle, Manu falls into a conversation about all the pot plants in the house and accidentally drops a *Predator* reference and this English guy with fluffy black eyebrows makes a *Universal Soldier* reference and that's them, instantly smitten.

Like long-lost twins, the chirpy English guy and Manu; after a couple of minutes of conversation, it turns out they're 100 percent into the same shit—EDM, jiu jitsu, home-brewing—Dude, they both root for Bayern Munich—and they get into the English joker's bus—yup, mental, right? He drives a 25-seat tour shuttle that he deals ecstasy out of—and he says his name's Jase and they do a midnight run to the liquor shop to buy smokes and bourbon then they spend the whole night doing loops of the city in the bus, laughing 'til they have to wipe the tears out of their wrinkles, filling up at Mobil two goddamn times just so they can continue talking movies and porn stars and pussy. It's love at first sight, honestly, and Jase doesn't make it weird that Manu is faded brown and Jase is burnt white. Drugs and chicks, that's their language. And being separated, too. Separated and single and torn off and reborn. That comes up a lot. See, Manu's been desperate for a new best mate. And Manu can sense Jase needs someone, too.

Next day, once Manu's had a feed of KFC to salt the hang-over, he checks and checks his phone until at last it pings; it's Jase saying *We ought 2 double date u randy cunt* and that warrants a whole 'nother cruise-around-town, they both take the afternoon off work and they idle through the docklands and stand under the sun-blotting cranes smoking a blunt and talk Celtics versus Lakers and Fat Joe versus Fiddy Cent and Tyson Fury versus AJ as they get the sunset stoned.

Being married was like walking through a prickly lawn barefoot, but this bromance, it's a relaxed thing. Easy and comfortable. Jase used to rave at all the festivals up and down Britain and he's permanently brain-fried from some drugs he took at Glastonbury one summer. Manu feels dazed most of the time, too. Dazed from his wife giving up on him as a father. Secreting their daughter somewhere. Sending him a cold, final text that Manu read standing over the Insinkerator.

They seal the deal in the smoky front seats of Manu's van. They shake on it. They're gonna get on the prowl together. Score some chicks. Manu needs a woman, and to get a woman, Manu needs a man.

2.

Hot gold wood, hanging steam, black ceiling, low yellow light coming up through the wood benches. Men in white towels against the wall, hands on their hairy thighs.

Jase leans through the sauna mist, lowers his sunglasses.

So, how many then, mate?

No question what the question is. The whole day, they've been planning sex, squeezing each other's knees, slapping shoulders. Jase's knuckles on Manu's scalp. It started with a mention of the size of the areolas of Jase's ex-wife while they were buying fishing rods and it snowballed from there. Sheena, Jase's ex is called. Then they got talking about the size of Manu's ex-wife's pussy lips at the shop counter, got into a debate about girls who spit versus girls who swallow as they were driving, then by the time they hit the gym, Jase was talking about the "undiscovered frontier" of cougars in their 50s and they couldn't stop bullshitting.

The concept of age has been making Manu wince, actually. Manu's just hit 30- years-old and he feels like a big baby; Jase is close on 40, though he parties like a younger man. He's had years to have sex with more women than Manu, so Manu would rather not report legit numbers when Jase raises the *How Many?* question.

C'mon pal. You've had yourself a baby so that's one shag. You do realize there are other vaginas in the world, do you not?

Manu's cheeks burn. He can't hide in the steam stalling for time. There is zero question that the code works like this: If you get inside a woman, from the front or from the back, that counts as a root—doesn't matter if you come or not. If she blows you, it's half a point. Any other stuff like fingering isn't even a quarter-point, it's worthless.

Every man knows the numbers he's achieved in his life. His stats, his acumen. His worth.

And Manu's numbers are pretty low.

Time's up, boy-o. Tell us.

Few dozen, Manu blurts, making the steam stir, Uhhhh, around the 45 mark, give or take. It's probably 50, if you round up.

50, okay, okay. Jase is nodding, eyebrows up. So that means 30, with the exaggeration tooken off.

But it's . . . but I'm—

Don't gimme the Scooby Doo face, pal. Everyone inflates 50 percent. Plus, we have to discard those pathetic fumblings you did when you were 13 and tried to stick it in your cousin, yeah, but oi: I'm in a generous mood, my friend, and I am hereby ruling that you have officially been laid with 10 different women. Correctamundo?

Jase has killed Manu's bluff. Seen right through Manu's exaggeration. Manu stands up, bumping the hot wood wall. If he had the guts, he would walk out.

Instead, he pours water on the plastic coals. Hiss and smoke.

He puts his arse back on the bench.

Well, how many girls you been with, bro? I'ma subtract 50 percent on your numbers too, Jasey.

It's not how many I've done already, he says, leaning through the steam. It's how many I plan to do. And that's a hundred. Cause you and me, sunshine: that's where we're heading this year. Club Hundred. 100 women, whammed and bamm'd. Starting from zero. We'll reset the clock. First to a hundred's a fookin' legend.

He prods Manu's big chocolate thigh, winks and clicks out the side of his teeth.

See you at the finish line.

3.

Manu pops by Jase's apartment on a Tuesday, 'bout 11. He's taken the morning off for a doctor's appointment and a haircut. If he can squeeze in a catch-up with the bro before getting back to the construction site, his day will be perfect.

Jase's apartment is a 10-story box beside a K-mart carpark. The building is new, tightly squeezed, the exterior white. Fancy thick modern windows. Manu has no idea what happened to the home Jase and his wife used to live in. Sold or given to her, or something.

Manu enters, climbs the stairs two at a time, excited to see the bro. It's cheap on the inside, smells of plastic and glue. He finds door 468 and knocks, waits, knocks again, then curses. He's digging his cellphone out when the door disappears. A woman is standing there with a towel painted around her torso. She's holding a copy paper box with pencils and photos in it, a snow globe, some paperweights, a papier mâché sculpture. It's Sheena, no doubt about it. Jase's ex. Psycho-intellectual; real head-case. Psychiatrist; obsessive mother. Wanted to send Jase's daughter to a weird school.

While Manu tries to explain the purpose of his visit, apologizing for spitting while he talks, Sheena turns her face like an owl. Manu wonders inside if Sheena has a god damn reason to be at Jase's place herself anyway. Her shoulders are bare. Her hair is black-wet and steaming.

Just tell him I came round to talk about the project, the mission, cheers, Manu tells her.

Oh, a mission? the woman in the towel says, her shoulders steaming. Her smile soaks up Manu's dorky words. Intriguing.

He'll know what it means.

You can tell me your secrets, Manu. Come inside me.

He gulps, says he has to get back to work. Jumps down the stairs three at a time.

That night, lying in his bedroom with the music up loud, Manu masturbates to visions of Sheena unwrapping her towel, tendrils of black muff corkscrewing around him like vines. Pressing Manu's face into mud-colored circles on her breasts which spiral hypnotically, her fingers pressing the back of his skull, his face dissolving in plump creamy flesh.

She's terrifying, Sheena is. Those 'Answer-me-now' eyes. The lizard grin, little teeth showing. The confidence to be naked in an apartment that doesn't even belong to her.

The dialogue comes back to Manu as he bends his toes and thumps his pelvis. She smiled and asked what Freud would make of Manu's lingering gaze, he remembers. She cricked her neck and her towel slipped. She rode a knee up the door frame.

*

Thursday, as they smoke and sip mineral water on a bench beside the basketball court with towels around their necks, Manu begins asking for stories about Sheena-the-ex.

Pfft, James spits. You want the bad parts or the worse parts?

Sheena was trouble, tormented, dark, dangerous, Jase explains, watching a ball roll off the court. A cock-devouring demon that one, he says, mashing out his cigarette. Nuff said.

Just wanted to find out a little more is all, Manu goes.

Why don't you tell me about that sheila you were married to, ya cheeky choirboy. Bet you didn't even pop your cherry, ya bufty. Did ya? Eh? Course not, pal.

Fuck up, Jase.

If you weren't gay, you would've denied it by now. So that's that settled.

Manu stands up to leave, but he needs a ride home from Jase in the bus. He puts his face against the cool metal fence, sighs and sits back down.

Manu, Jase says, zipping up his sports bag and slinging it over his shoulder, Quit moping. Main thing I'll say is I'm glad she's no more. All right, lad? Leave it be.

On the rare days they don't connect, the lads video call one another on WhatsApp, Jase strutting around his house with a Heineken in one hand, headbutting the camera. With enough beer in him, Jase opens up a little. He's gotten louder since he lost Sheena, Jase confesses, waving his phone's camera around his apartment. He needs his loud voice to fill the place. They used to own a home together, but that bitch took the china, the bedsheets, the curtains, shit, she even had the movers rip out the dishwasher—all this on a day when Jase couldn't help being asleep at Beach Bass 'cause some wanker spiked his acid.

Manu, pal, never get into a relationship again, mate, promise me, Jase pants into the camera. That Sheena, mate, the bitch was cursed. Literally cursed.

The house is cold. Manu feels tickling on his neck. He whirls around, lifts a curtain.

Ah'm serious. She's a succubus. Her mother was in a mental institution, grandma, too, in fact the whole lineage—Māori, all of them. Possessed, their whanau is. The whole lot of 'em.

Good thing, what happened to her, Jase adds.

Happened? What happened? What do you mean?

Jase shakes his hand. We don't need to go over it. Oi, though: that's by the by, Jase assures his friend. It's September and the first signs of spring are showing and they're on their way to a hitting a hundred girls and they don't need to worry about ghosts from the past.

*

"The System" is what Jase has called it. A system for removing panties with mere words.

Manu thinks about The System while he soaps his armpits, while he shaves his throat, while he adjusts his necktie and clips on his nametag which says *Home Appliance Guru.* He's quit the plumbing and is trying this retail thing for a bit. Less grubby; hopefully it'll get him laid.

He thinks about systems and patterns and hacks as he dumps a bundle of mail at his ex's house, plus a gift of water balloons and some unicorn comics for his daughter. Patterns, habits, traits. Manu won't get to 100 shags unless he has a system. He has the Mark Manson seduction book on audio, and the print book by Julien Blanc, and his mind is pinging with advice from the *How To Stop Them Saying No* video he watched on YouTube this morning.

He's concentrating so hard a Mack truck honks as he swerves urgently in front of it. Fuck. Didn't see it coming. Manu gets off the road immediately and sucks a ciggy and calms down in the parking lot.

As Manu hovers in front of a dumpster, panting, bleached with fright, his phone rings.

Jase? Is that you?

Course it's me. You ain't got no one else. Oi—want the news, pal? Course you do: I've hit one percent, I have. Scored the sister of one of me exes, ya poofter. All began with a coffee at morning tea, mate, that's when lassies want it the most, write this down, they're horniest when it's mid-morning and no one's home, mark my words. She was always eyeing me up, I do recall, and considering she was fat,

I'd filed her under Easy and didn't have trouble setting up a coffee date, going round to her place and getting inside her. Follow the system, pal. Go for the ones with a broken wing. The sad ones that've got the baby blues. Divorcees, they're always horny. Oi—no one said the whole hundred had to be beauties, mate!

Okay, Manu responds. He looks at his pink eyes in the mirror. Sniffs wetly, still spooked from the giant truck encounter.

One percent, ya cunt, Jase tells him. So, who was the first, then, eh? First ever, I mean. Who'd you lose your V card with, son?

Alison Greggs, Manu responds straight away.

Continue.

I was . . . she was like the yearbook editor. Real goody-good. Should'a seen her fingernails, man, her hair. The way she used to smile at me, like I was some big asset. Came from a perfect home and I was . . . I was in a hurry, you know. Tryna be like one of the jocks and shit. Fucked her and dumped her within, like, two weeks and. . . man. If I could take it back, bro. . . . But you went and got your second hole, didn't ya. And that's what counts.

Manu slaps his cheeks, shivers himself straight.

He opens the door, steps out into the wind.

I've gotta go to work, Jase.

Indeed you do, my friend. You get them numbers up, lad, promise?

Promise, bro.

*

The senior teacher at Manu's daughter's kindergarten, the frazzled one with loose wires of hair sticking out of her bun, she's always had a thing for Manu. Little glances. Extra teeth in her smiles. Noticeable lipstick.

He always had her mobile number on his phone in case of emergencies. Now Manu reckons it's time to cash it in.

This kindergarten teacher, he remembers, she's bookmark-thin and her collar bone sticks out and her lips always seemed dry. Bleached yellow hair, with black regrowth coming through. She's anxious and hungry and lonely.

Tasha, yeah, that's her name. It takes Manu an hour to track Tasha down, trawling through Facebook, getting a conversation going so Manu can message her to set up dates. There are three dates required, actually; a coffee date, an evening drink, plus a rockabilly concert at the pub before Manu kisses her in her tiny Honda and convinces her to let him stay at her place.

He spreads her across the bedsheet and pins her with strategic kisses. When he licks her wrist, he sees she has self-harm lines carved on her veins and bolts upright, scared. Just like on Alison Gregg's wrists, after what he did to—*no. Don't do that to yourself, bro. Be a man.*

This girl, he needs to work on her before he has sex with her. Go gentle. Manu sits with her through the night while she tells him everything and he listens and nods. She says he's the nicest guy she's ever met. Squeezes his hands.

At the ragged end of the night, as the birds are screeching, he tips her backwards, crawls on top.

As he's stepping into his pants in the morning and trying to ease out the door, Tasha the Kindy Teacher asks for another date—could do Thai food this time? And salsa dancing after?

Friday's no good, Manu tells her. Can't do Saturday, either. Booked out for a while, soz.

Her calls come every hour throughout the day. When he switches his mobile back on after 24 hours, he has to hold the phone away from his ear. She's finally understood that he saw her as a one-nighter. A single serving.

You're a filthy lowlife piece of shit, her voicemails say. I'm fucking engaged, you scumbag. He's overseas serving our country and he loves me. Don't fuck around anymore girls. I'll tell on you. Everyone will know what you are, you creep.

The last arrow finds a gap in his armor, lands deep in his flesh.

Everyone will know.

Except Jase laughs and takes a huge drag on his cigarette. They're watching a tugboat brush the water. So what? The whole town'll know you've got testosterone in ya. Fook 'em. Do you want one hole for the rest of eternity, or do you want to get to a hundred shags? You came for advice, mate, and here it is: Get back out there and put that ding-dong of yours in another pussy. Kappish?

The pussy of the plump, dazed-looking teen who used to babysit. She's next.

Third is an 18-year-old on Tinder. Dumb and confused and naïve. Doesn't even know how to drive a car. While Manu has sex with her in his bedroom under the framed Jason Statham poster, the girl watches a video messaged from her friend, sipping on a vape.

Number 3 of 100, Christ. Manu knows his numbers are not enough. Knows that Jase is beating him.

This whole thing is starting to feel like a straightjacket. Like a curse.

4.

They catch up at the playground. Jase spins his daughter Lola on a roundabout. He has custody of her this week, it seems—though didn't Jase have custody last week, too? And the week before? How come the mother isn't around? Sheena, that's her name. Sheena in the bath towel. Sheena steaming like a ghost.

Standing on white and red rubber tiles, Jase is sucking on a spliff and Manu's got a cigarette cupped under his glove. It's chilly and frosty-sparkly this morning and Jase squeezes droplets out of his gloves while he convinces Manu to put all his expenses on his credit cards.

Mate, it costs, getting laid, it does. Mostly alky-hol. Put all your vodka 'n cokes, your ciggies, your Ubers, your fookin' Durex condoms and hotel suites, mate, chuck it all on a big generous Mastercard and that's you sorted. You'll hit your hundy in no time. . . . OI! LOLES! OFF THAT BLOODY THING! Mate, without alky-hol, I wouldn't've scored that air hostess, the hairdresser, gee, and a good siiiiixxxxx . . . seven? Naw, six—six women from the bus. 12 out of 100, my friend, 12 out of a hundy in one week. Oi, 'ere, smell this. You smell that pussy-stink? That coming through your end?

Loud and clear, mate. Who's the lucky lady?

Rhiannon.

The one that was, like, Rhiannon that worked under your wife?

Indeed.

What Manu has been finding out over the past week, drip-fed during catchups, is that Sheena has, or had, bipolar disorder. Apparently, she forced her clinical supervisor at the hospital to prescribe her heavy meds. They both got in trouble. Sheena self-harmed. She had a demon in her, whispers say.

Funny woman, that'n, Jase goes, sprinkling hash into his spliff and licking the paper. Tortured soul, she was.

Her appearance belied it. Drastic boyish black haircut like Clark Kent; professional boss-type. Massive tits, twig body and a cameltoe pussy when she wears yoga pants, and that shimmering, twitchy unstable rage rippling through her, pulsating out from her dirty hairy black curly muff, seducing any man who got even close and wand—

Manu! Oi!—Manu! Marns! DUDE!

A few people have stopped behind him, tilting their heads like owls.

Lola is standing there, blinking her huge wet lashes.

Oh, Christ, Jase is going, clutching her face, moving over by the slide. You didn't hear me say shit about Mummy, did you, sweetie? We don't speak ill of the departed, do we now.

They move on to the monkey bars. Jase meditates over his spliff. When it burns his fingers and he has to flick the roach into the rubbish bin, he looks mournful.

He digs his hands deep into his coat. They watch Lola race around and around a pole which she grips with four fingers. Manu sniffs. His own girl used to do that. Run in circles through puddles, bright with joy.

You know I called her a succubus direct to her face, one time, Manu. Told her I'd done me research down the library and I was onto her. Seen a picture of hairy-hoofed succubi sittin' on a fookin' man's chest in a 1403 carving out of Wales and it looked exactly like her, it did. That blimmin' boxy, creepy haircut of hers that looks like Clark fookin' Kent. That's where the word nightmare comes from, did ye know that, Manu? Mara—the night woman. She slapped us for that.

True?

Ae. Mate, she got slapped herself 'n all, for dispensing anti-psychotic meds to herself at work. Got a final warning, she did. Here's Sheena at home, ra ra ra, cursing up the house, yelling and smashing things and wolfing down pills and bullying yours truly, and here's me, burying my head in books, right, obsessed with the research, fully. According to 15th-century Bishop Tostado, an incubus and succubus were simply two forms of the same demonic entity. D'you know that, Manu? Tostado theorized that a succubus lies with a man in order to collect his semen and then that very same seed morphs into an incubus to fertilize a female with the ill-gotten seed to produce Satan-kids. I apologize, mate. I'm ranting. Thinking about her, Sheena, the memories, it gets us, well . . . brr! Jase claps his hands and stamps his feet. Oi, listen: gotta dash. That lassie over there, the Irish-looking one, yeah? The ginger with the freckles on the bench? She's mine, she is. Mark my words.

Jase sprints over to where Lola is attempting to climb into a seesaw and barge boys off. He pulls his daughter down and settles her into a swing beside the supposedly Irish park bench sitter with puffy orange hair under her knit cap and begins talking until she doubles over. Jase has made her laugh hard enough to clutch his arm and he'll hit 13 women by the end of tonight, it's obvious. He's left Manu far behind.

*

Eventually, Manu finds a woman to get his Monday night numbers. She's had her stomach stapled so she is pillowy, uneven, her body like a waterbed. As soon as Manu comes inside her he rolls away, aghast. Hauls his bones out of bed, showers, and dresses. He feels like his house is melting. His skin is soaked in shame, falling off in rotten chunks. Manu's ancestors feared God. They kept their lips to the ground. They were thankful for the chance to court and marry a single special someone, and now Manu has disgraced them all.

He sucks a bottle 'til he's too drunk to sleep. Watches the ceiling spin. When it calms, Manu flicks through Tinder. Exciting red flame. Pictures of beaches and bikinis.

A lot of the women on his screen are dull, pointless to pursue. One who he's pretty sure is a grown-up Allison Greggs, decayed now, saggy, purple dyed hair, piercings. Fat and poor and living in a trailer, the pictures seem to indicate.

Then the app shows Sheena. His eyes widen. It's the actual real straight-up Sheena, yes siree, plain and true, staring at Manu through the camera. Sheena, divorced from Jase, separated, liberated. Manu rolls over, hugs his knees, plunges into shivering, tortured drunk sleep, imagining how terrifying life would be if he had to walk around with the guilt of having shagged his best friend's wife.

Still, he masturbates for the tenth time to the image of his fingertips stroking through Sheena's black curls. Unshaven, overgrown muff, stinky and wild. He holds her picture in front of his face as he comes, his toes twitching.

Manu gets up in the morning, changes the musty bedsheets, puts his nametag and work shirt on, arranges a new woman to distract him from his self-loathing after he knocks off shift at 5. Woman number seven is a chubby young bank teller, pale as a polar bear, with curly yellow hair and pimples on her chin and glasses to hide her shy eyes. She comes over as the black night is reaching around the edges of the curtains. Manu pulls her off the doorstep, guides her to the couch, opens wine. He spends three hours on the couch as she opens up about how her best friend is a bitch and people needed to appreciate her more because she is beautiful.

She pauses, sits erect. Asks where Manu's little girl is. She's kinda sorta at her mum's place this week, is the answer, but that's okay, don't feel weird. They watch a movie together, a Kevin James one. Laugh, unwind. Manu offers her a massage, just a small one, and she shrugs off her denim jacket and starts moaning as Manu squeezes the tension out of her shoulders. Manu puts in five, six, eight minutes of foreplay before he spins her head, aims her lips at his.

Her eyes agree.

It is nearly 2 a.m. when Manu ejaculates, rolls off her, scrubs himself in a shower that burns off his outer layer of skin 'til the water runs cold. She's still on the couch watching Netflix and he tells the girl he's going to bed and she can let herself out. She takes forever to understand, open mouth, astonished. Manu lies under the covers 'til he hears the door lock limply shut and he's alone with a full moon watching him like God.

Watching as he pulls his phone in front of his face and finds Sheena on Tinder and—typing fingers hitting the tent-sheet over his head—asks if she would like to get together for a cup of coffee.

Or something stronger.

*

1412 Hawley Avenue is an old blue weatherboard house behind towering weeds and long, bushy grass full of cats. The porch has piles of plastic-wrapped newspapers and circulars. Sheena is a dark shape coalescing in the cloudy glass door.

The door creaks as she opens it and beckons him in. No lights. No noise.

"I brought alcohol," he says, apologetic, holding up a brown bag.

We both know what that's about, Sheena tells him, smirking. It's okay. Come.

Between columns of boxes overflowing with psychology textbooks and DVDs and ethernet cords, there is a trail of hallway carpet. Manu follows her down, hoping.

In the kitchen, Sheena apologizes that the electricity's off. She's hardly ever home, which is why the place looks uninhabited. Leaves in the sink. Birdshit in the laundry.

They move to the lounge. The room is dusty and full of boxes and the curtains are torn and Sheena sits on the couch, which groans, and pats the cushion beside her.

Sheena bites the sleeves of her fluffy sweater as the ice breaks and Manu eases into a conversation with her. She won't have a sip of his Southern Comfort, but she tells him to go ahead.

They're soul mates, the two of them, Manu decides as he sips his bottle. Okay, that's impetuous, but there's definitely something there.

The conversation begins with Sheena's caseload, and the pressures of being a mental health professional, and coming home to a man who was very eccentric, as Jason was. Surely you'd agree, Manu?

Manu nods and shifts his butt off the loose couch spring. Definitely, oh yup, totally. Jasey's a lunatic. Are you still, um, still working, miss? It's just I heard, you, like you had some troubles at work and . . . and they chucked you on suicide watch and that?

Sheena sighs. We're not talking about me. We're talking about that ex-husband of mine, Manu. If he's not careful, that boy is going to get himself diseased. And it's not HIV that's the main concern anymore, Manu. Are you aware Treponema pallidum infection can lead to neurosyphilis? We're talking brain disease. BRAIN disease, Manu. In a nutshell, syphilis starts downstairs and ruins upstairs, it does. I won't use technical terminology, don't worry. And yes, I'm cognizant you're looking at my boobs.

What? Pardon?

You've been staring at my breasts since you walked in.

I was—I wasn't—

It's okay, Manu. You can't help yourself. You're a slave, aren't you. A slave to your desires. Even if they lead you into hell. Anyhoo, putting my doctor's cap on: syphilis begins with a blistery sore from the location the bacteria first entered you. Secondary stage gives rashes around anywhere saliva forms, mm'kay? Discolored rash on the palms and the soles of feet. Also hair loss, aches. Then tertiary syphilis begins rotting your brain. That friend of yours, my former husband. He'll have contracted it yonks ago, mark my words. Headache? Discoordination? Dementia? All symptomatic. Watch yourself, child.

Manu tries to come up with a line but he fumbles the words.

Sheena—boyish dykey short bowl cut, big breasts tucked under that turtleneck jersey, condescending smirk—runs her fingers over his shoulders, arches her eyebrows, asking a question.

Manu gulps.

"Thought so," she says. She pulls him up, guides him two meters across the floor to a stack of mattresses in front of the fireplace. She pushes him down, spreads his limbs. Manu pulls down her work pants, her knickers, begins entering her, heart spazzing, expecting to pump 'til he comes, but she rolls like a crocodile and pins Manu on his back and grinds and squeezes. Manu regrets the sex before he's even come, but she is riding him, crushing his ribs, scraping, clawing. Working on something.

He finishes inside her cozy pussy and she grins with fangs. She reaches inside herself, takes the come, fishes inside a sleeping bag, pulls out a doll and smears the come on it with two brisk wipes of her fingers. The doll—a featureless poppet —stinks of fragrant damp wet woody mushrooms. Sheena holds it to her chest like an infant, disappears from the room naked, bottom wobbling.

Despite the musty mildew ceiling, the peeling wall-paper, the rotting hallway, the weeds growing up through the floorboards, Manu lies on the mattress until his heart settles, happy he's got his numbers up.

*

Manu awakes on a rocking, swaying boat. It's night. Dark ceiling. Lights flickering from something electronic somewhere.

It's his stoned, drunken body that's rocking. He's holding onto the sides of the coffee table. He gets up, head rush, can't stand, can only sit up.

Jase leans away from the movie and stabs his finger at Manu and says there's no fookin' way. Nooooo fookin' way whatsoever.

Who's he talking about? Manu feels like he's come down from outer space.

Jase sucks his pipe and washes it down with a blast of whiskey. On the TV screen is *Under Siege* with Steven Seagal and he's rewound the scene with the stripper bursting out of the cake several times. Above his head, photos of Sheena on the walls with daughter Lola. Sheena stares out from the photo, watching him. Her hair is a thick, overgrown bowl cut and she wears dungaree overalls with nothing underneath but a bra. She looks like a simpleton. Or a mental patient.

Did I—am I—Jase, how did I get here?

Ah'm tellin' ye, pal, that slag'll do no better than me, Jase is yelling at the TV, And if she wants to be a FOOKIN' SLAGHOLE THEN FOOK HER!

The fizzing fog evaporates. Manu accepts he has slid into an alternative dimension. Like it's two years in the past. Except Jase's rant, continuing, indicates we're in the present. Jase, crushing his drink, is furious that a girl from Bumble walked out on last night's date, deciding she hated him.

That's a fookin' first, believe you me, Manu. 'Cause ah'm valuable, me. Ah'm platinum, mate.

Next in the story, Jase is following her home and blue lights are stopping him and police are putting a hand on his chest and ordering him to quit following her, as if he's some out-of-control stalker.

Me! *ME*, Mango!

It's Manu, man.

Jase takes another smoke and another sip of hooch. He's livid at Bumble, livid at this hoor, and furious he didn't get his drugs tonight. His hookup, Māori guy from Rotorua who dresses like Bob Marley, his guy promised Oxy but, in the end, simply told Jase no, and Jase feels, well . . . it's hard to tell. He's slurping back the whiskey and beer with tokes on his bong in between, occasionally kicking the TV screen with his toes as he rants.

"Fookin', erm, what was it? Oh yeah, accountant, shagged her, innit; fookin' librarian, she was an alright piece of erse 'n all. Had a good few come through from Bumble, the classy ones, Asians, all of 'em, and Badoo, scored on the old Badoo. Nearly blimmin underage, one of them turned out to be, the cheeky twat. And you, Mango, where's your numbers at, eh?"

Manu takes the bong and the bottle. He's thinking maybe this crazy competition ought to stop.

He's also wondering what numbers he can tell his friend. Because Jase and this competition are all he has.

*

Family restaurant. Giant wood barn with a hundred families in it, fifty hurried staff in cowboy hats holding plates of buffalo wings high above their heads. Cacophony. Children running and screaming. Eruptions of laughter from tables of cowboys in bluejeans. Arcade games, mechanical bull, huge bowls of wedges and nachos. Sour cream and steam and sweet chili sauce. Live band playing on a stage with hay bales. Noisy place for a double date.

Two girls are squeezed in the booth, one blonde with a nose ring, one strawberry blonde with blue ribbons woven in her pigtails. They're simple, both of them, special, dumb, deluded, raving. They mispronounce items on the menu like chipotle. They get distracted by Snapchats on their mobile phones, leaning across the table to see each other's updates, giggling.

There's real beer on the table, a pitcher of it, beside the pitcher of margarita. Jase has had a couple of pours, but he's far from drunk. He's intoxicated on something else. Jase can't stop sweating, forgetful, lost car keys tonight, lost wallet. Crammed in the booth, boxed in by girls, they're trying to talk about the rugby and Jase is forgetting players' names, and arguing with the waitress about whether or not he ordered those jalapeño poppers. He calls Manu "Moustril" at one point. Manu, strangling a napkin, wonders what the hell is eating his friend's brain. Jase is sweating, feverish, as if he has flu or Covid. His handshake was weird tonight. He seems to have hard little circles on his palms. An archipelago of warts.

Distractions save them from punching each other's faces. The blonde with blue ribbons is receiving a story from Jase about him being a widower, apparently, and Jase is milking it, talking about the loneliness getting to him, how he's been writing poetry deep into the night in a draughty apartment that could really use a woman's touch.

"There used to be a witch, there did, a witchy-poo sending me cuckoo, but ding-dong, goes my song, for the witchy woman is no more." Jase reaches across the table, squeezes the knuckles of Blue Ribbons, looks deep into her eyes. "I feel reborn, with you."

Jase hiccups then, and liquid pools around his lips. He excuses himself, crawls out of the booth to vomit.

Manu follows him towards the toilets, grasping his mate's shoulder.

"Dude. How can you say that stuff about Sheena? She's the mother of your daughter, man."

"Hands off the jacket, pal. Losing Sheen was the best thing that ever happened to me."

The droplets beading on Jase's forehead are about to fall off. As he stands there, waiting for Manu's big announcement, he shivers, twitching, scratches his chest. Manu can see black splotches on his chest and pink lumps on his fingers.

"I have to tell you something, on that note, man. Look, this Club Hundred thing? We have to quit, man."

Balls of fire light Jase's eyes. His eyebrows collide as anger ignites.

"Look, I'm like massively sorry but—we hooked up. Me and Sheena."

After a long wait, Jase says, "Very funny," and staggers drunkenly toward the toilet before Manu grabs him again.

"GET YE FOOKIN' HAND OFF ME. I'll not tell ye again."

"I'm serious. I feel terrible, Jase. You can hit me if you want."

Jase's brow smashes into Manu's nose, flattening it. Manu lies on his back on the polished wooden floor. He counts the crumbs under a table, a stray gnawed rib, a barbecue sauce bottle.

The girls aren't confused or upset about the headbutt. One is filming. The other is texting.

Jase squats over Manu and begins shouting.

"THAT DIRTY FOOKIN' HIGH-FALUTIN SLAG KILLED HERSELF TWO YEARS AGO THIS TUESDAY AND THAT'S A JOKE TO YOU, IS IT MATE? EH?"

"What—what are you talk—"

"I OUGHT TO KILL YOU, WINDING ME UP LIKE THAT."

"Bro, I'm honestly, like, epic-sorry."

"Fook your sorry. She was a witch by the end, that hoor. Fookin' obsessed, she was. Fookin' dreamcatchers, mortars and pestles and incantations, fookin' spells written with blood for ink. D'ye know there was a dead fookin' rabbit hangin' up in the laundry? Eh, Manuel? Told me she was cookin' up punishment. I caught the dirty sow rubbing me jizz into a dried-up voodoo doll. God's truth."

His breath reeks. There is black muck in his nostrils. His beard is frosted white. His skin is green, his tongue blue.

After this, after the girls' slack jaws, and the stunned waitress holding a birthday cake with sparklers in it, after the rubberneckers staring, after the fist hovering in front of his face, Manu will leave his burger on the table, escape into the parking lot, the streetlights melting, the traffic a blob of continuous color, fratboys on the zebra crossing saying *Step up and fight, faggot*, assholes in a pickup truck throwing a beer bottle at him, teenagers in the drive-thru biffing a burger at the dirty stained loser, after Manu has staggered through all this, he'll curl up in bed and count the girls and wonder if syphilis is stalking him too, but for now, Manu cowers under the shadow of his best friend, sure he's about to get another headbutt. His nose is molten, his teeth throbbing. "When the mental people rang me up and said Sheena'd been sectioned, told me she'd been put in a cell for her own protection, told me she fookin chewed her wrists open and painted fookin incantations on the wall till she bled out, d'y'know what, Mongo? Jase's breath reeks. His eyes are rotten. *"Best phone call I ever fookin' got."*

Then, lower, deeper: "Eighty-two more girls, mate. We're seeing this through to the end. Then we'll fookin' talk."

*

BLAM-BLAM-BLAM-BLAM-BLAM.

BLAM-BLAM-BLAM-BLAM-BLAM.

Early morning door. Sand in his eyes. Dressing gown with come and wine stains on it.

It's the police, a short black man and a lanky Aryan woman. Hats on, notebooks in hand. There's been a complaint, they tell him. Pause.

A complaint of a sexual nature.

They open the warm clean back of the car.

"D'you mind coming with us? You don't have to."

Manu makes eye contact with the male officer only.

"It'll make it easier if you tell us what happened."

"What girl said it?" Manu asks. "There's—there's been a few."

"You don't know how many girls you've been sleeping with?"

Manu shakes his head. "I don't—my brain's not—"

"Are you sick?" the male asks. "Tell us if you're unwell."

"Tell us at the station," the female adds, and Manu slides into the back of the cop car.

*

"So, how many?"

The short cop seems to overcompensate by writing notes extra-diligently. The female is a lanky blonde woman who's always been great at sports, Manu imagines. The woman yawns and sticks her hands behind her head. It's a tiny room with foam insulation to stop noise getting in or out. There is an old-fashioned computer with a box monitor and a squat hard drive and a small mountain of photocopier paper.

The ceiling is low. Manu feels squashed.

"Like, eight chicks? I didn't even get double digits."

Now both cops are looking up. "What proportion of the sex was non-consensual?"

"Zero."

"That's your final answer?"

"I mean, c'mon. Look at me."

"I am looking at you," the woman says. She brings in her tight cheekbones, cobalt eyes, puckered lips. "Tell me what I'm supposed to see."

Manu throws up his hands. "Like, specifically, has someone said something? 'Cause, y'know. It'd be cool if I could explain what happened."

"And what *did* happen?" Two scientists, eager for results.

"Nothing. Nothing illegal, that's what I'm saying."

"So not being illegal makes it okay?"

"Jesus, you guys, I mean, come on. There's no law against—like Jase, Jason Bolger, that's the dude you should be talking to."

"Except we're talking to you."

The woman pulls up her satchel, reaches in. She pulls out a thick clump of photos so fat that three prints spill onto the carpet and the wad still looks just as thick.

She *plaps* down the photos in pairs. First, a photo of a girl looking happy, surprised in a kitchen or patio, caught off guard, an intimate photo supplied by each victim (Jesus, man, they're not victims, come on.)

Second, a photo of each woman pulling her knickers on and looking shocked, or disappointed, or stunned, or surprised to be sent home by a man they expected to nurture them. Manu in the background with a bottle or a smoke in his fingers.

"How did you—who snapped these?"

"Tell us if you recognize the girl. Yes or no only."

After each couplet of photos, the police ask Manu if he recognizes the girl. There are thirty couplets of photos. Manu finds himself saying "Yes" to photos he doesn't recognize. Some of them just seem like girls he would have pumped and dumped this year. Photos from the next month coming up, somehow.

The last couple of photos begins with a picture of a brown boy with one foot on a soccer ball, his arms squeezing a giant bottle of Mountain Dew, Chupa Chup between his fingers. He's had a great game and he deserves a treat and Mama says that's okay.

Somehow, existing in some fold where two layers of reality overlap, this is Manu's child.

His eyes melt. He pours his face into his hands.

"Is this when—like, in the movies, this is when I ask for a lawyer and shit, right? Should I be asking for a lawyer?"

"I don't know. *Should* you, Manu?"

*

The street is heavy. Draggy. The air thick, sludgy. Like wading through quicksand. The car doesn't want to start at first. The world has condemned him.

Manu at last gets the engine running, switches on the radio, flips through stations. An irritating song about an unfaithful lover. A jingle about wandering eyes. Classic FM has a relationship expert on, Dr. Marisa Giarratano. She's explaining what could possibly have gone on in the mind of Guierlein, that cricket player-rapist who fancied himself with one too many women. It's right that the police were sent by God to hold him to account.

On the ring road running between the boatbuilders and cement factories, Manu sees a billboard worth watching. Actually, no. As he speeds closer, he decides it's watching him. A photo of Manu pulling up his pants, shirtless. Giant white letters on the picture. RAPIST LOSER. It darkens the sky.

At the lights beside the supermarket, a window washer notices Manu approach, throws down his squeegee and bucket. He squints, gawps, runs up and begins thumping the bonnet, roaring OUT, OUT, YOU SICK CUNT.

A mob of fratboys parading in the green part of town beside the university. Manu becomes caught in their parade. They sniff, sense, snuffle towards him. Wriggle their fingers in the gap between his window and the roof, try to pull Manu out of his car as it rocks and squeaks. Manu ducks, suit jacket shoulder pads concealing his head. He doesn't remember dressing up in a suit jacket for the police station interview. Everything is strange, dreamy. And in a passing bus window, the face of Sheena, lively eyes, watching, enjoying, leering.

*

Jase's apartment is a dump. A tipped-over mattress, clothes across the couch. A running tap. Flies swarming around a furry green pizza.

As he stands on the balcony, scanning the city, a number Manu has never seen before appears on his cellphone. Green icon. Incoming call. Hidden number. Looks suspicious.

He answers, anyway. Maria something. Journalist, she says. From that newspaper he sees around town all the time, the *Harbinger*. We're doing a feature on you, Manu. We're thinking the headline will say Police Stop Sicko, Maria Something says. Just wondering what you think? We've got this academic from the university to comment on the rot undermining relationships in 2021, and no doubt, Manu, you're suffering from pathological narcissistic obsessive-compulsive disorder with sociopathic tendencies.

Manu throws his cellphone into the street.

From the pulled-out kitchen drawers, he steps over a toolbox, spilling screwdrivers everywhere. He takes a meat cleaver. Goes to find his friend. To find him and finish this thing.

*

The house is abandoned. He should've noticed. Stupid douche. No way Sheena could have lived here if she was real. Rusting metal in the grass. Smashed pots. Ivy growing across the windows. Spiderweb on the door.

230 kilometers of driving around the city, thinking, cringing at billboards condemning him, then another six kays to get here, to push open the creaking door, duck the puff of wood dust and dead insects, then a final few meters until he hits the end of the hall.

In the master bedroom is Jase, sitting with his back turned. He's positioned on two rain-ruined mattresses. Hole in the skylight letting dusty sun through. Shirt off. Underpants halfway down. Turned away, caught naked. Focused between his legs.

"Must'a shagged her six hundred times in here, ah reckon. All it takes is one, though. One to put the curse on."

Manu lingers in the doorway. The room has weary sunlight coming through, though it's darkened with black mold. Detritus from floods. Sticks and leaves piled in the cupboard.

He lets his meat cleaver fall to the soggy carpet.

"Years, we had together," says the tired voice of the half-naked man with crimson bumps on his hands. "We done everything under the sun. Threesomes, orgies. Bum stuff. Cocaine. Home movies." Jase shakes his head wistfully. Still turned away. Still facing the stream of dusty sunlight. "She took me blood, mate. Hairs from the shower. Scabs, fingernail clippings. Me jism, though, that's what it was all about. Bottled it up. Collected it. On full moon nights, she'd go out back to the birdbath. She was talking to someone out there, but if there was a bloke, mate, I couldn't see him. Couldn't see most things. But I see it now."

Jase is sitting in a puddle of dark fluid, Manu realizes. A slow sludge is staining the mattress under him, oozing down into the carpet where it leaves a reddish-black pool.

Jase thumps his penis again. This time, Manu notices the yellow plastic handle of the screwdriver curled in his fist. Notices a squirt. Sees the shine of fresh dark blood.

Jase turns this time. Lets go of his weapon. Picks up a bottle of some sort of chemical with a large WARNING sticker on it.

Drain clean, it says. Active enzyme.

Time to cleanse ourselves, young Manu. For we have stained our bodies.

"We were just—just playin' a game—"

"Lie, lye, lie. Get it, do ye? Caustic soda, pal. Burns away everything." He puts on the mocking voice of a museum tour guide. "Been reading up, I haaaave! I've been looking for a way out of this. Sodium hydroxide is used in many industries: in the manufacture of pulp and paper, textiles, drinking water, soaps and detergents, and as a drain cleaner. Worldwide production in 2004 was approximately 60 million ton, while demand was 51 million ton, is that fascinating or what? Ah've been reading Wikipedia, I have. Done me research. Had to make sure this was the right decision."

"Jase, Jesus, don't—"

"You've been seeing her, you said. The witch. She reached out to you. She wants your essence. But we have to say no."

"Bro—Don't do this—"

Jase hefts the container of solvent powder. Opens the lid.

"Decomposes proteins at ordinary ambient temperatures, says here. May cause severe chemical burns."

Manu steps forward, preparing to tackle his friend. Jase gets off the bed, steps out of his bloodstained undies, backs up against the cupboard, his blackened penis wobbling and dripping, red droplets spilling down his thighs. He waves the lye bottle in front of him, sprucing the air with caustic powder. Manu has no choice but to stand back and watch it happen.

"BRO. YOU'VE GOT FUCKING NEUROSYPHILIS. YOU'RE FUCKED IN THE HEAD. I HAVE TO GET YOU TO A DOCTOR. GET IN THE CAR NOW, JASE."

"Mate—sorry for everything," he says. 'I'll tell Sheena meself."

Jase presses a handful of white powder onto his cock and balls. His pubic hair smokes and curls away. Manu gags on the white steam. The shrieks burst his eardrums. He has to back out of the room, cover his ears with a shoulder and a hand, phone an ambulance with the other. The screaming stops when Jase inhales his own burnt, blackened, sizzling flesh, vomits and faints.

*

The police want a great place to meet him. The hospital will do fine, since he's there, at Jase's bedside. They drop in for a brief chat. About that thing the other day? There's not enough evidence to proceed with a charge, they tell him.

"Must be proud of yourself," the female says as she's leaving. "Real amazing use of your life."

At night—jobless, aimless, fired, on the dole—he's been sitting on the edge of the bathtub. In the bathroom cabinet he's found a bottle of drain cleaner. He's been rolling it between his fingers. Considering.

They've tried to tell him in his ear that he's not innocent, it's just that they won't prosecute because there's simply not enough evidence.

Manu doesn't disagree. There is one other way to take his dirty skin off. One person who can help.

Her address is 1674 Missal Court. Manu slows his speed as he enters her neighborhood, turns down a crescent that twists through a thousand ugly shacks, hits the 1600s, begins counting. He's been told to look out for a trailer with three pink flamingos by the letterbox. Christ. It's not even a house. It's a caravan parked on a muddy lot. Manu kills the engine, takes a breath. Steps into a puddle. Aims towards fate.

Her dogs roar and snap. Bump his knees. Snuffle his toes. They growl. He smells wrong.

She slams her door against the side of her trailer, stands there in her lime dressing gown and flip flops, arms folded. Children appear on either side of her, peering past her hips, between her thighs. A baby bleating in the background, too.

Manu has told Alison Greggs he is coming, so he doesn't need words. He speaks with his collapsing body, his weary back, his cringing face. He speaks by getting down on his creaking knees, bowing over her exposed toes. Crusty toes, with crystals of hard skin. He puckers his lips, begins kissing. From one pocket Manu takes wet wipes. From the other, sanitizing gel. With his knees in the mud, Manu washes her toes while she smokes two cigarettes and drinks a coffee, standing on her porch. When he has finished washing her feet, Manu rolls over on his back, unbuckles his belt, pulls his pants down, adjusting his penis so it's ready for her. He stares at the honest, raw sky. Watches clouds ebb.

Alison Greggs yells into the trailer, asking her oldest child to hold her coffee cup. She shakes off her right flip flop, looms over Manu, gets her balance right so her foot is hovering directly below his belt buckle, and stomps.

UNDERGROUND

Black ocean, orange fire. Taxis beaded with rain. Bottles screaming as they smash in traffic. Droplets steaming on a pizza oven. Skinny cheekbones shivering in wool coats. Fog breath. Fedoras, vapes, black ties, white shoulder pads. Youngsters in clusters of five and six, arms folded, standing with you round StraightShooter under a heat lamp with people who aren't really friends, though they might become Somebodies in future, which is why it's essential to Friend them.

You laugh about the same shit, complain about the same shit, and when there's a thin spot in the conversation you rummage in your handbag, acting like you don't know how many tampons you've got in there. Your temporary friends, they all play in bands and this one girl has a necklace and brooch designed by the same Moroccan artist who does brooches for Azealia Banks. You follow six new people on Insta within 12 minutes, then when the conversation starts to get slightly weak and they look at you funny for guffawing at one of their in-jokes, you say, "Well, drinky time," and leave for the bar, imagining they call after you "Byeeee, Rachelllll." You're low on oxytocin. Low on vasopressin, cortisol. Low on alcohol. Same as everyone else out tonight. Needing peptides you can only top up by rubbing shoulders with the right people.

Your money's all gone on new tights and data for your phone and white menthol Marlboros and breath mints and

Lorazepam and all that's in your purse is taxi chits and free download vouchers and business cards of Somebodies and the asshole at the bar won't trade those for drinks, but you tell that dreadful bore Spittle, the rapper-slash-poet, that you like his hoodie and let Spittle wrap an arm around your neck and stare at your chest and as soon as he pushes a drink into your hand (oh my God that's refreshing, the sting of cranberry, the roar of vodka) you tell him you have to go to the bathroom and you've almost lost him when you spot— is that? Yeah, you're 99 percent sure—yes it fucking is, oh my God, James *Fucking* Murphy from LCD Soundsystem is at StraightShooter. Because your day job is all about handling the social media for people like James Fucking Murphy from LCD Soundsystem you know he's obsessed with vintage 80s Nerf water guns so you get talking about those and you hang just off the edge of his elbow until there's a break in the conversation then you have to drop in a mention that you're the Social Media Coordinator for a certain massive record label and that Somali girl who was in that Childish Gambino video crosses the circle and gives you a hug and says, "James Murphy said to give you something," and lets you follow her to the toilet and crush Tramadol and X on the toilet tank. It's funny to hear him called James because underground he is James Fucking Murphy, underground where you're safe and warm and protected, and as you're trying to hold onto the entire bar and tell the Somali model from the Lil Nas X video that James Fucking Murphy should never be referred to as James, Ashley Bradley Coyle arrives in your perimeter.

Ashley works in your office putting discs in digipaks and special editions, couriering flashdrives with album promos to influential people, copying autographs onto vinyl with a silver Sharpie. Your desks are across the room from each other. His wife and two-year-old kid come to pick him up sometimes, always looking needy, tired, waiting in the foyer, heavy and damp like airport luggage. They drain Ash.

He once told you he tried to make his baby watch *Marlon Williams Live At Burning Man* and his wife pulled the TV power plug out of the wall. He spends as much time being an indie rocker outside of family and work as he can, to revitalize himself. Tonight, breathing celebrity air, he's very nearly Somebody. Ash is like you by day—meditative, quiet, pissed-off, hungover, anxious—but tonight's Ash at StraightShooter (Public Ash, Look-at-me Ash) is huuuge on Bandcamp, not to mention he's got 2300 likers on Facebook. Ash—who's been tagged in photos with Macklemore and Q-Tip, and Lana del Rey—could really be Somebody if his stupid partner would let him. His band M.O.R., formerly Middle Of The Road, formerly the Ashley Bradley Coyle Project, opened for St. Vincent at the Powerstation one time. He's talented on the guitar and people adore his lyrics, which reference early 90s nostalgia.

You're trying to think up a way to talk to him when you lose your purse then someone hands it back to you, dropping some reference you can't remember sharing. Drugs are melting your mind, your thoughts have overflowed, trickled to somewhere you didn't want them, James Fucking Murphy's groupies are breaking up, there's that guy who everyone says is secretly Banksy in conversation with Del the Funky Homosapien, but now there's talk of A$AP Rocky getting beaten up at Calendar Girls and your team has to go save him and you link arms with that Peep Of The Week columnist and she asks you for a white menthol Marlboro which means an opportunity to jump in her taxi with the chain of Somebodies she's attached to—including Ashley Bradley Coyle—and you find a seat on Skrillex's cousin's lap and someone tells the driver to take you over to The Venue where Fleet Foxes are doing a private birthday party gig for 200 people only, but Ashley Bradley Coyle reveals in the taxi—with shoulders mashing his face against a tinted window—that he's Facebook friends with Billie Joe

Armstrong who's friends with Lorde and he comps you all into the private Fleet Foxes birthday gig and fuck, what's her name, from The Deliverance Project calls out "Oh, sup, Ashley," and in the part of your mind where you register people's importance, you make a note: Ashley Bradley Coyle just became a little bit more of a big deal.

When everyone spills into the convenience store to buy chips and smokes and hot dogs, you pay for Ashley Bradley Coyle's ridiculous bag of ironic 5 a.m. candy floss and he says Thanks and you register the thanks because when Ashley Bradley Coyle becomes huge in three years, everyone will need to know that one time he thanked you personally, but hang on, he's fallen on his bum and there's a bouncer standing over him with an afro and earpiece and you've got one of your high heels off and you're smacking the stiletto heel right into the bouncer's skull, hoping it connects hard enough to kill the bastard so you can be The Somebody Who Saved The Life Of A Guy Who's Friends With A Guy Who's Friends With Billie Joe FUCKING Armstrong.

*

Your feet are cut and dusty and cold. You've walked from the police cells straight over to work, a good two kilometers, maybe three. You make it into the office and limp to the lockers. Nobody's hassled you yet. Whew. You have more clothes at work than you do at home. A little foundation and some lipstick and mascara and you're good to go. You collapse into your chair, groaning.

Urgh: daylight. Too bright. Sunglasses on.

"Whoa," your manager says, leaving the web designers' table and approaching you. "Are you *okay?*"

"Yeah. James Murphy from LCD Soundsystem was like all over me last night. He's sweet but it was like, 'Gimme some space,' y'know? Like seriously clingy."

Your manager puts both hands on your shoulders. "I saw your tweet about— actually, you shouldn't joke about that if you didn't really go to jail. We thought you were locked up. You're two hours late."

"Lots of famous people get locked up. I'll stay late to make it up."

"But honey, that's the problem. How come you're wearing shades, Rachel? Are you... Is your health okay?"

You open Facebook, Instagram, Twitter, glancing at a queue of emails on the side, hoping something eye-catching sticks out. You search the list of senders' names, select the most important people to respond to. Email from Adele's agent. She needs you to try and find her a good Cambodian vegan restaurant in the city, somewhere small and dark where Adele won't get hassled by nobodies.

Halfway through the morning, you look across to the desk of the boy known by day as Ash. He's wincing. Seems like his partner is on the phone and he's in trouble for going out last night. Your eyes meet his. Having a family must be like wading through glue all the time. You invite him to endure yours with you. There's like this family lunch bullshit you're obligated to go to. He'll probably hate it.

*

Your fat, pink-cheeked, white-bred baggy pantsed untucked flannel shirt family invite you and Ashley to a Western all-you-can-eat feed trough place that's all ribs and chicken and salad bar and pretends to be classy 'cause it uses the word *smorgasbord*. It's between a water tower and a hardware store, for God's sake. You spend an hour messaging Ashley before you meet, apologizing in advance about the Daylight Dorks that are gonna seriously pollute his cool. Sometimes they wear denim with track pants, you tell him.

He responds saying you ought to treat the lunch as an ethnographic odyssey.

Ethnographic Odyssey=killa album title, you text back.

U serious?

Serious. Just go for it, Ash. Take a month off family and record it, you tell him. Get a producer to*DAY*.

He waits for a punchline, finally understands you're serious. You share his rock 'n roll delirium. He's shocked with happiness.

Your fat family squeeze into their chairs with wobbling plates of French fries and pasta and full-sugared Coke. Them being chubby and untanned is bad enough but the fact they have no ambition to be known underground is, well . . . It's disappointing. You love them all, their acne, their gross sweaty tits and shiny cheeks, it's just frustrating none of them consider being Important important.

The Family Stone was a cool family. The Wainwright Family was a cool family. Of all the things that disgust you about your family (apart from their boring Anglo names and their polar fleece jumpers and their melting fat faces) the worst has got to be the way they gather at LUNCH to eat, cousins and aunties and your dad loading up their plates when they've only been awake for five hours, people with skin the color of peanuts wrapping spring rolls they don't need in napkins and jamming them into their backpacks. *Blech*. Eating for recreation is greedy and dirty.

You excuse yourself, tug Ashley away with you, lock yourselves inside a disabled toilet stall. You hand him a bottle of nail polish and you each paint a picture of someone dead and happy on the toilet stall. Jim, Jimi, Janis. Kurt and Cornell and Chester, somewhere in the universe, together having THE DOPEST party in history.

You sit back down at the family trough and your dad draws his chair up close, tips his head onto your shoulder and tries to nuzzle you like a big cat. His bald spot has gotten wider. You give it a quick kiss to keep him happy. It won't even look good if he shaves his head. You have to have the swag of Kanye or Billy or Moby to rock a shaved head.

"So, is this here Mr. Right?" your dad asks, referring to Ashley.

"Or merely Mr. Wrong?" Uncle Angus adds.

Dad seizes the joke, smears his eyelids thin with his fingertips. "Or Mister Wong! Chinese Gweengwocer! Me so solly! Ah so!"

Dad's brother starts braying laughter and a little bit of fried cabbage hits the clean white plate he's lined up for his third helping. A line of uncles elbow each other. Your dad comes from a warm, secure position, third out of five brothers. They all do well-paying, shit-sucking jobs where they serve other people and get dissed by students and builders and quantity surveyors and have never had anything written about them on a website. They are teachers, heads of department, network administrators, building inspectors. None of them have their own brand. They all wear dated reading glasses from ten years ago. They have three cars, pool noodles, jet skis, boogie boards, family mountain bikes, freezers packed with meat, holiday homes, pensions, oodles of kids, kids running behind you, kids making noise, kids coming up and staring at your bony pierced chest and neck tattoo then giving you concerned 11-year-old nephew-y immature eye contact.

"Angelpuff," your mum is going, jiggling a toddler on her knee while the toddler chews on one of her earrings, "we are just SO proud of you."

"For what?" you snarl, turning your disappointing phone over. No new Tweets in ages. Piece of shit.

"Heard you're kicking gluteus max in the music biz," says Uncle Robert from across the table, balancing two nephews on his knees while they pull off his reading glasses and play with them. He bought the glasses from a fucking supermarket. "So, tell us already: you been schmoozing with Santana? Phil Collins? How about Eric Clapton? GOD I love me some Clapton. Fess up: So, who's the most famous person you've dealt with?"

"Depends," you go, and sense a vibration which may've been your phone or may also have been the brats kicking the underside of the table. No new messages. It was the brats. Fuck. "Doooo you consider playing Foosball with Sia's entourage conversation-worthy? God, ummmm, I did Zayn Malik's baby shower invitations the other week? He got some groupie pregnant in Sydney. They flew us over. You probably wouldn't've heard about it."

Something sickening in their smiles is saying that they don't envy you. They're grinning with pure love.

"Can you guys stop gushing on me? Seriously, the talent's right here." You elbow Ashley. "This guy opened for freaking Arcade Fire. I mean, seriously."

"But you must have a boyfriend by now, my little baby waffle?" your dad is going. "What intentions do you have for my daughter, good sir?"

Ashley pushes his sunglasses on and shields his brow. He doesn't do unironic people.

Down the end of the table, someone is laughing so hard they spill their wonton soup and someone else goes, "Taxi!" and Taxi is about the only sensible suggestion these howler monkeys have made all day because a screeching-to-a-halt Lyft car has two empty seats built exclusively for you and Ashley Bradley Coyle and it's roaring towards the cemetery corner of K Road and Symonds Street where rap-rant cross-over genius Streetcred is doing his EP release party amid the tombstones and there are only a few dozen people there and a generator, tiny amp, turntables, and a microphone but that's all that Streetcred needs, and he asks who you are as you kiss his cheek and it's okay if Streetcred doesn't know who you are right now because he will, soon enough. You and Ashley Bradley Coyle, the undiscovered element. He'll see you underground.

*

This little girl—she can only be about 19 years old, wearing sneakers under her work dress, for God's sake—she comes in saying she's got a package for Mister Coyle and he says thanks and opens the papers and it's about his separation and his pink eyes shatter and the manager's trying to tell him to please go outside if he's going to act upset and you know Ashley hasn't slept in 55 hours 'cause you went out with him last night and the night before. There was no fucking, just lots of photos with lots of Somebodies as you stretched your lungs and limbs underground. Ashley, looking like he's just been punched, says he has to get out of this mad place and your boss points to the stack of booklets on his desk, each of which has to have Action Bronson's signature stickman doodle put on them, because they're supposed to be Christmas cards from Action Bronson himself, and ABC tells his boss she's interfering with his creative satisfaction and he puts his fedora on and storms out and you follow him to the Cambodian vegan place, the place made instantly hip now that Adele's brand is associated with it.

You try to tell him about Adele's vegan mission and also how Kendrick Lamar wants an authentic *Tongan Pride* t-shirt from the Avondale market and how you have to proofread RiRi's Hall of Fame speech and send it back to her asshole manager by end of business. You try telling him about your manager's children running round the office playing with business cards and breath mints and lanyards and when your boss was pregnant how you spent like $300 on that CONGRATULATIONS ON YOUR NEW BABY JOY cake but you can't remember the fucking kids' names.

All good. You're in a laneway now, breathing smoke, chilling. You both keep your coats on and your satchels in your laps. You don't tell him he looks hot; he doesn't say he loves your labret piercing. Just two vamps who both want nighttime to last forever.

"I seriously don't wanna go home," he says, exhausted, slumped face melting on the palm of his hand. "My kid and Play-Doh and blocks and Dr Seuss and all that. . . It's literally depressing."

"Hang out at work, maybe?"

You each take out your packets of white menthol Marlboros and begin to smoke 'til you feel dangerous.

"Does daytime ever, like, piss you off?" he says.

Ashley Bradley Coyle has a bottle of clear Absinthe in his bag and after the waitress has given him water and he's thanked her in Khmer, which makes your blood pang with jealousy, he pours the Absinthe into water glasses and winks at you.

"You're right about the blocking and ragging and whatnot. This chick I married, she—" He punches his forehead and winces. "Fuck family. Austra, yeah. You checked out Austra? Let's talk about what's actually relevant." He tilts his wrist so you can see the cufflinks. "From Ontario, Canada? They're pretty alt right now. Austra gave these cufflinks to me. In the green room."

"Hang on. Lean in." You extend your phone and photograph the evidence. "I've been digging Austra for a while," you lie. "How'd you learn that Asian-y language, anyway?"

"Picked up a little Khmer when me and Sufjan Stevens did that thing together, that EP."

"I . . . I knew that. He's actually playing, tonight, up at the Biodome, did you know?"

"Pfft." Ashley Bradley Coyle smashes his cigarette to death in an ashtray. "That guy's like—he's like a stalwart these days, know what I'm saying? Like if you're gonna be a singer-songwriter, you've got to innovate, you know? Plus, he's a dick in person. He wanted me and Björk to do guest vocals on that side project-thing, The Treasury, but it was like Nigga, please."

Nigga. Khmer. Sufjan.

"I was just gonna diss him," you suggest, lamely.

"Hey. Oi. We were at school together, right? D'you remember when, like, everyone was watching the girls' soccer, like the whole entire school and we were like ten times cooler than everybody, all by ourselves in the music room trying to figure out how to tune Mr. Sipeli's bass? And you did that Sufjan Stevens cover with those lyrics about his wife and it was like—" You click your fingers to try and nab the right metaphor, which has to be floating around in the air. "People said you and I should've got married and shit. . . ."

You both slump back, push your seats out from the table a little bit. You write something on your phone, as does Ashley Bradley Coyle, but he finishes whatever he's writing first and stares hard at you.

"The fuck are you writing, anyway?"

"Just checking Weezer's social for them. You?"

He goes to the toilet, comes back, picks up his satchel, yawns. "Dan the Automator and Sampha are playing tonight down at Inferno, just so you know."

"I'm on the door already."

"No, *I'm* on the door. And I've also got work tomorrow. And my wife's got this— thing on. Coffee group for mums or whatever. I'm supposed to support." Ashley Bradley Coyle scrunches up his face.

You follow him to the bus stop. He keeps lighting smokes then crushing them.

Ashley is 26 and three quarters and he hasn't even recorded an album yet. A lot of his idols had already peaked by 26. We both need this underground thing to work out, else we'll be stuck up near daytime, frying in the sun. "I'll tell Dan the Automator you said hi."

He holds his head between tense fingers, shakes it, gargles air then stands up and declares no, fuck it: he's not going home. Let's have pre-drinks. How much money you got?

*

Inferno is a puddle of people pooling in a basement bar built from a multi-level underground carpark. Streams of people trickle out of taxis and down the stairs. You do a hip-enough handshake with the bouncers and they pull you into their chests and pat your shoulder with love. Ashley Bradley Coyle goes in for a Bro Shake. Good, Ashley. You're becoming Somebody. It's warm underground. Come huddle with us.

You yell in Ashley Bradley Coyle's ear that his family will always be there but fame is fleeting and he needs to network as much as possible. It's pointless—he can't hear you cause Lars Ulrich from Metallica is asking his opinion of *Infinite Jest* and Ashley Bradley Coyle is yelling in Lars Ulrich from Metallica's ear that *Infinite Jest* IS a magnum opus but it is SO overrated because EVERYTHING DAVID FOSTER FUCKING WALLACE FUCKING WROTE IS A FUCKING MAGNUM OPUS, DUDE, I MEAN WHO DIDN'T RE-READ *THE PALE KING* TO PICK UP THE REFERENCES TO 1970S MEXICAN SOAP OPERAS? AND SPEAKING OF MEXICO, DON'T EVEN GET ME STARTED ON ROBERTO BOLAÑO, and since Ashley Bradley Coyle is preoccupied you're free to get a \$15 cup of gin and ice shards from the bar.

Second level down there's Suzi Analogue having a hilarious jokey rap battle with Mike Patton from Faith No More and on the level beneath, past those stinky, smoky Wu Tang hangarounds on the stairs, there's the artist Algiers, who won't shut up about blood diamonds, cool, whatever, and someone's saying below on Level 4 where the ceiling's low and the pipes scrape your head there's this girl who was in a love triangle with Pussy Riot and Regina Spektor and en route to talking to her you get stuck in this HILARIOUS story with, God, what's his name, that guy from that thing, and while it's pretty interesting hearing about how Sam Smith is actually really fucking rude if you talk to him while he's trying to chillax in the sauna, on Level 5 you and Ashley fall into a game of Hopscotch with Nikki Minaj, who's like super sweet and actually rather immature in person, but that can only hold your attention for so long cause Paolo Nutini—who is obviously tripping, probably on shrooms—insists you HAVE to come and play naked ping-pong with The Flaming Lips and finally you get to the bottom and there's been this nagging, dragging sensation behind you, but it's only Ashley Bradley Coyle, his eyeballs bulging, and you notice the phone in his hand, and you know his phone is full of selfies that he's posting as he goes, and on the bottom layer of the inferno, where the lights and smoke machine make the air blue and white and violet, there's all the guys from Mastodon trying to get a sound out of a mandolin and Ashley Bradley Coyle approaches men who are pretty much titans to him and they hand him the mandolin and he starts jamming. You groove for an hour and it's perfect, deep underground in the bunker, everyone important is here, but now your new friend Aaliyah needs a packet of smokes and outside there's a limousine, yes, and Lil Peep is putting his pale yellow finger on everybody's lips and saying Seriously now, seriously, seriously, everybody shut the fuck up, DRIVER, FUCKING DRIIIIVE! and the limo lurches out into Ponsonby Road but there's a milk truck looming right over the limo so close you can see the driver screaming and thankfully, *thankfully*, oh God that was a close one, thankfully the truck has rolled right over your vehicle and you're all walking out of the limo, straight through the doors, shaking the cocaine crumbs out of your threads and laughing with your tongues to the sky as Daywalkers shriek and fuss and your troupe crosses traffic in Converse and Doc Martens and high heels and a bus honks at you and an Uber Eats boy on a bicycle with a basket knocks you into the path of a motorcycle with wheels which turn your clothes inside out and you're looking at the underside of a car that's come from nowhere, and paramedics are shining a torch into your eyes and they keep saying, We've lost her, she's gone and you get a glimpse of a—what's it called—stethoscope? Is that it? and finally you're up on your feet and amidst the billion people in the black-and-orange nightworld you find ABC sharing a blunt in Roundhead Studios with Proof and Mama Cass and Darcy Clay and Mac Miller has opened a bottle of VSOP and Aaliyah is trying to record her vocal track without distraction and she throws a coffee mug at the glass and everybody pretends to flinch and cower and she goes back to her recording and who's that on backup vocals—holy fuck, it's Elliott Smith, with blue blood coming down from his nostrils and staining his lips purple—and Elliott's and Aaliyah's saliva is hitting the same microphone and pooling before it trickles to the ground, and Ashley is taking out his phone and playfully shielding it from Big Pun with his rotting eyes and blowflies on his scalp, who keeps trying to snatch it, and you stumble into this gallery opening and that Basquiat guy with the real bad English is talking about his work and you're taking all the selfies you can and Basquiat tells ABC how he 'totally digs' listening to Ashley's music when he's composing art and ABC is so exhilarated – he's new to this underground thing, lol – that he spills taxi chits all over the floor and it doesn't matter because everyone's getting in the elevator to go 20 floors down where it's warm and orange, a sulfur mine, a glowing pit, further than you've ever descended, and who's that opening the doors, aw helllll yeah, it's Euronymous, the face of black metal, spreading his arms in front of the inferno and he greets you by name.

THE DEVIL TOOK HER

Put your fuckin' money away, Patrick. You think after all the shit I've been through chasing Melanie for you that it's still about money? It's about comPLETION, son. Finalizing. Putting a summary on, on, on something that's bigger than you or me or this whole so-called "real world" we think we live in.

What? No, I can't give you the short version, Paddy my friend. You asked me to find out what happened to your wife in my capacity as a private investigator, okay, so the least you can do is sit there and shut the fuck up while I report like a professional. Actually, fuck you: I could talk for two hours right now and that would BE the short version, considering the enormity of what I discovered for you.

Jesus Christ, I don't usually curse like this but the aggravation's not insubstantial. It's been, what, four months since you booked my services? Five? You shove a box full of papers and diaries and Melanie's laptop computer in my hands in the rain in a god damn alleyway outside a 7-Eleven and scuttle off and I'm supposed to pick up the pieces? For, what, two grand when it's been at least 300 hours of effort, Patrick?

The bridge pinch, they call this. I am pinching the bridge of my nose to signal to you that you're frustrating me right now. Typical client, never ready to actually handle the news you claim you wanted to hear. Pass me some of that water.

Mm. Better, now. Cheers, P. I'm cool now. ANYHOW, let's not focus on the money. Pay me after what I'm about to tell you—if your head hasn't exploded.

Because you see this? This brick of paper right here that I'm unveiling—I mean, fuck, sorry un*wrapping*, I know, I know, unveiling's what you do with a—

It's Melanie's journal, okay. Your wife's diary, her personal . . . God, call it a confession if you want. Did she do anything wrong? Have a read and make your mind up, although I'd say your mind's already made up, isn't it, Patrick. That fair?

I think when you engaged me, it wasn't just about breaking the encryption on your wife's emails so you could see if she'd run away to Timbuktu. Frankly, I think you wanted me to find her journal more than find her. Took forever to find that stupid hunk of paper, all across Cali. The journal that she obviously wanted someone to read after she was gone.

You were scared because what Melanie went through takes everything you know about the surface-level world and flushes it down the gurgler.

So. Ready to find out what happened to Melanie?

Here's her words. All you need to do is read.

January 8

It's raining outside. Then again, it's always raining, lately.

Seems as soon as I started the file on the Golden State Dementor, the clouds cracked open and dripped cold all over California. Like God was weeping, or trying to wash me off my research, or . . . I don't know what God's position on the murders is. God allowed it all, I suppose. If you realized the attacks across inland Cali were connected like I have, you too would wonder what kind of God's watching over. Not a God that cares about people's wellbeing, that's for sure.

All through Christmas, you've been inundating me with presents and glasses of red wine and slices of cheesecake and I've had to barricade myself in my study. You're like a giant puppy dog, Patrick, a husband that constantly needs attention, and as soon as I withhold a little bit of myself, you can't handle it. You say I'm clinically depressed, sure, but look at your neediness, Patrick. That's a sickness too.

'Golden State Dementor' isn't what the cops call him. It's just my private nickname right now for the killer. Kinda stupid, I know, but I'm the only one in the world who's spotted that these attacks near McDonaldses and Burger Kings and Jack in the Boxes in the central valley are connected, so it's fair to say I have a stake in this monster and I argue the media won't become interested unless we brand him with a catchy name. Seeing as the cops have barely given two shits about catching the killer, I feel I own him and the narrative. If YOU'RE gonna be the one to pursue this bastard, you can name him yourself. Until then, this is my passion project, and I'M in control.

Lol. I'm ragging, I know. My period stings. Guts feel like they're petrified. Maybe the anger's good. 25 days ago, when I last had my period, it inspired me to open this can of worms. It began with a provocative email I cheekily sent to Contra Costa County Police. It was just before Christmas, and I was pissed off that those assholes sent me a speeding ticket when I was on my way home from a shift in the newsroom in Stockton putting out stories singing the praises of law enforcement. I submitted a California Public Records Act request, personally addressed to Sheriff Livings, asking for a list of outstanding homicides. Pretty routine journalistic enquiry. I was going to publish a blog asking why there were eight murders yet to be solved while cops were wasting their time prosecuting a five miles-over-the-limit speeding ticket, except the CoCoCops—surprise, surprise—sent me back a brick of unsolved cases in a courier package the Monday after I put in my information request. Seriously, like one and a half reams of paper with a note saying "Dear Madam, we trust this information answers your query. Sincerely, The Office of Daniel Livings, Sheriff, 651 Pine Street, Martinez, Cali, blah blah blah."

A whole ream of data? Talk about overkill.

I went to bed with my brick of paper, laptop open at my side in the empty shell where you used to sleep before you stopped coming to bed with me, Patrick. I tumbled into my black, depressed, worried world of papers and stories and affidavits.

I got ready to laugh at the officiously written nonsense in each dense page.

Instead, my jaw dropped.

I read all night.

I read all day the next day at the public library.

I requested boxes of information from the county's repository. A truck had to deliver the files to my doorstep.

Because I spotted something. Something that ought to shock everybody.

You want to know why the door of my study is locked, Patrick? I can't have you walking in here and upsetting the way I've got the paper laid out on the carpet, wall to wall, all the attacks spread out in sequence.

Why?

Because it's only when the papers are laid out that we see how big this thing is.

February 12

It's black and chilly and I'm positioned between a cardboard recycling dumpster and a dumpster outside the McDonald's in Martinez, a brightly-lit triangular-roofed building on a street full of fish processing factories, squatting, waiting for someone to get attacked, notebook in hand, camera round my neck. Sunlit families disappeared hours ago, and the solemn lamps and bug zappers came on soon as night fell. This is a sad corner of America, like a sagging part of the tent-roof where moods are flat and the night is full of shame. It's a place for lonely folks yelling as they walk out of McDonalds' air-conditioned safety into the black, smashing their soda sippy cups on the sidewalk, heading up the street to make trouble or drive into the darkness, their voices echoing and fading. I'm wet from stepping in a puddle and my knees ache and I have my period and I tried to bleach the blood out of my favorite underwear and they got ruined, stained pink, and I'm inhaling the stink of chargrilled burger patties mixed with rotting deep fry grease. I'm suffering 'cause I'm desperate to string together enough words to sell a story to Rolling Stone magazine. If not Rolling Stone, then Newsweek, or Esquire, or Vanity Fair. Hell, maybe even the Central Cali Courier. Any place that'll pay me enough to leave my neurotic partner and go find my future in L.A. or New York.

Sorry, Patrick. Sorry to spring that on you. But being inside, comfortable with you? That ain't the real me. The real me is a dirty journalist, doorstepper, alleyway-lurker, carpark-conspirator. This is real journalism, this dirty dark dusty danger, so I'm not leaving this parking lot 'til I spot somebody getting attacked. I've spent three weeks reading up on the patterns of these inland Cali killings, muttering to myself on buses and in libraries and in the bathtub, reading old *San Jose Mercury* newspapers, psyching myself up to go out and confront the killer.

I swear this here and now: I am going to endure this dumpster-dwelling shit every month until I solve these killings. I am going to break out of reporting city council news and become a gonzo journalist. I'm going to go hungry for half of each week. I'm going to starve the fat off my hips. I'm gonna be Nellie Bly crossed with Joan Didion and Nancy Fucking Drew, and I don't need your approval, Patrick.

I work for the missing people whose identities have been forgotten. Well, forgotten until their names tumbled out of the police reports and gave me a reason to live.

Innocent names like Ruby and Maria and Sarah that belong safely in nursery rhymes. Names belonging to people dolled up for their school photographs. People whose eyes now reach out across time, wide and hopeful. Begging to be brought back. Recipients of the ugliest degradation, desperate to be treated right again.

I should explain what I mean by degradation, cause these girls suffered some truly appalling shit that didn't make the papers. Here are the attacks that I want police to admit are linked:

Aug. 29, 1996—Rancho Cordova, CA—Teenage girl found murdered 30 meters from McDonald's Restaurant. Trauma to the vagina indicating rape. Sharp torch-length implement inserted into the victim causing damage to the cervix, uterus, and bowel. Two liters of blood lost. Some unidentifiable numbing anesthetic applied to the victim by attacker. Analysis: inconclusive.

Sept. 4, 1997—Carmichael, CA—Nanny of prominent local banker raped behind McDonalds. Not a murder, just the sexual assault. No semen found, just tearing of the flesh. Choked unconscious then anesthetized and violently probed, with bleeding. Victim described a man in black and white cloth, like a chessboard. You ever see that old movie *The Invisible Man*? Yeah— wrapped up in cloth, like that.

Victim insisted offender was not Caucasian. The color of the night, she insisted, with skin of glass.

Oct. 5, 1998, Citrus Heights, CA—18-year-old student taken as she returned to her car opposite Kentucky Fried Chicken restaurant, 7098 Auburn Boulevard. Hood placed over head. Suffocated. Survived. Had her head bopped against the ground. Said afterwards that she felt the attacker 'put something up me.' Almost like she'd been stuck on a meat hook, or had a giant needle inject something cold and dizzying all the way through her loins and into her stomach. Actually, not a needle, the woman corrected herself in her statement, shivering under a blanket, nursing a coffee. More like a bee sting, because it was agony at first, then numb.

"You're sure you want me to write that?" the officer noted. "Numb?"

We're part of his collection now, the victim responded. She looked at the officer with eyes swimming with pink fizz. We're safe among the swarm, she said. The legion.

FACT: These attacks occurred around all-night fast-food restaurants spanning 100 miles of Central Valley in all seasons of the late 90s and early 2000s. The attacks were ugly stains on inland Cali towns known for orange groves and warmth and safety.

FACT: They hit the news, some of them. Carmichael police are reporting a woman was attacked as she sat in her car feeding fries to her three-year-old daughter outside a Taco Bell on Manzanita Avenue last night. The victim is reported as unidentifiable, having failed to attend the police station to complete the second half of her witness statement.

He (and it has to be a 'he', surely) is sticking some long, repulsive, sharp implement up these women. It could be some freakish mutated monstrous penis, okay, sure, but the damage to the insides of these poor girls—it's more like he hoisted them up on a hook by their nether regions and squirted formaldehyde in 'em. Put something in them that made them groggy and half-comatose and uninterested in complaining. Turned them into drones, slaves, sleepwalkers. Zombies.

March 1

Inland California is a beautiful place to go missing, Patrick. I wish you could see the romantic side of the horror. The communities these kids are vanishing from, they sleep at the foothills of mountains sprinkled with sugary snow. Cool streams flow through the vineyards. Boroughs named for apple varieties and morning views and desert plants. Safe, warm, trustworthy names. Crestview Drive, Pacific Rose Ave, Citrus Heights, Orangevale. Noble oaks on dry berms of county grass under the moonlit streetlights. Wide boulevards of fresh asphalt for kids to bike on, four abreast. Hockey on flat concrete driveways lined with perfectly mown lawns. Frisbee in the street. Schools with American flags and yellow buses. Except there's a problem, isn't there, Patrick, when the inland empire sprawls endlessly. When communities don't have walls and their highways and motels and power lines march into infinity. Youngsters mad at their parents, storming off, walking the boulevard 'til it hits the interstate and becomes the edge of an ocean of strangers. Twinkling lights that call to kids, run away forever and ever.

There's a line, I argue, between shallow night and something deeper and darker. Somewhere kids fall into and can't come out of.

The victims, they were all weak and upset when the Dementor snatched them. They all wanted to squeeze a little more meaning from the day by buying a treat late at night. Babysitters on their way home from another crushing gig, hugging their handbags, spending half the night's pay on curly fries and a strawberry shake, stupid financially but it brought these youngsters a few fleeting minutes of joy. They felt momentarily independent by blowing their dollars on a naughty sweet treat, too young to buy liquor and black out, too old to ignore the upset in their lives. Their Mom, back home, sobbing through divorce. Their school locker room contaminated with Crips and tag. Their alcoholic dads melting in armchairs in front of big-screen TVs.

These youngsters, they tried to find respite from all the ugliness with a tangy flame-grilled Whopper hitting their gums. Momentary delight.

He's pounced upon these women and penetrated them with, well – with whatever that tool of his is. When the penetration of these victims has failed, he's been killing them. Police have admitted in their reports they suspect the attacks across the hundred miles are linked— after all, that's why the CoCoCops dumped forty files on me. I think they wanted me to identify the linkage. But what confuses matters, though, is what happens after each person is attacked, because some victims live, some die, and some simply don't come home.

Parkwoods, 2015: victim is a 46-year-old prostitute and mother of five. She dies of bleeding, receiving tearing to the anal tissue, penetrated in a dumpster full of McCains cardboard fry boxes. Coroner believes something sharp went up inside the victim, presuming a stingray barb. Body tested positive for a neurotoxin, as yet unidentified. Witness at a Texaco observed an attacker wearing a "cloak made of Milky Way" with a gang of "black midgets" numbering as many as 40. Not black as in African American, the witness clarifies. Black as in "made of night."

Modesto 2016: Alexandria Manning, 12, disappeared, presumed murdered. The next night, same location, but the beast attacked a couple this time: Dr Luiz Offerman, 33, and his date, Charlene Lyman-Smith, 18, dropped their prescription glasses and asthma inhalers in an alleyway one block from a White Castle where they'd been seen having coffee before they followed what—according to security footage— appears to have been an impromptu parade. A column of black child-shapes spangled with stars, playing invisible flutes and cornets, flailing their arms joyously, following their leader, a half-invisible specter with flaps of fabric under his arms like a bat.

Offerman and Lyman-Smith turned a corner, where CCTV couldn't see them. The parade followed, like a current of night-water flowing towards them.

Offerman and Lyman-Smith are still missing as of 2020.

That's what's fucking me up, Patrick. All the variables, like as if anyone could be at risk. Some of these people have joined the night parade. Some have left cars running in parking lots. Some lost their keys and their driver licenses in ugly carpark puddles. Others never had a car at all.

Patrice Harrington, Keith Harrington—married, both 25. Davis, California, 2007.

Manuela Withuhn, 11—eleven, for the love of God!! — Ygnacio Valley.

Cheri Domingo, just 10. Taken while waiting for her mother to finish her shift at a McDonald's in Cockleshell Drive, Walnut Creek.

A dozen more—a baker's dozen, actually. 13 missing people whose lives have been packed into dusty evidence boxes. Swept like leaves into the corners of our minds at the end of autumn. Forgotten with the change of the season. Crimes made permissible when our community lets the slate be wiped clean because we haven't risen up and reacted.

Each person taken was miserable in her or his own way. Girls who stormed out on their parents and yelled they'd never come home. Couples trying to rekindle their joy. Co-eds who got too used to taking Ultram for a bad back and slipped down the slope into using raw Tramadol then Oxy then heroin then crack then found themselves wearing high heels on a midnight street corner.

I believe these people aren't gone forever. I believe I can find these folk, and if not, I'm going to confront their killer and ask him a question.

What are you doing with these people?

April 4

Last night, I saw him. After 22 nights in 22 ugly, stony, cold locations, playing a lonesome lottery, waiting in the black wasteland beside glowing drive-thrus with the crickets and moths, I finally saw movement in the night, and I knew it was him. Him and his followers, his parade.

I'm still stunned.

I'm not sure if I should put this on paper, actually. I sprinted after him—her, it, that, they, whatever gender it is—and he turned. Whirled, is more like it, because the night around him twisted like reality was made of silk. I'd been sitting on a barrel among a mountain of tires where Vroom Valley Automotive Panel and Repairs meets Burger King, watching an occasional teenaged slave drag out an armload of cardboard boxes for the dumpster, wondering what Patrick was doing, if he was sorry for changing the TV channel. Wondering if I was going to have to face the boss at work after I'd stormed out. I was reading on my tablet to pass the time. A Wikipedia entry about Baba Yaga took me to one about witches and child-stealers and after a few more clicks I was studying the legend of the enchanted man who leads the town's population away, one by one. All cultures have this legend, as if he exists everywhere, popping up in civilizations whenever it suits him. In Japan, the enchanted man manifests as *Fuefuki*, the frog who lets youngsters bounce on his throat before swallowing them. In Laos, its name translates as Moon-Father, the man who can turn his skin into blue night sky.

In the town of Hamelin in Lower Saxony, during the Middle Ages, the villagers struggled with a rat infestation problem and were desperate for relief. Legend has it a mysterious man in piebald black and white garb approached the mayor promising he could rid the city of its vermin, asking only payment of 1000 guilders. The mayor agreed, and the man played a magical pipe to lure all the city's rats to a nearby body of water, where the rats were duly drowned. When the Piper returned for his reward, the mayor refused.

Furious he had been cheated, the piper returned to the town on St. John and Paul's day. As the grown members of the town attended church, the Piper once again played his magical pipe through the streets, this time luring the town's children from their thatched homes, down the creaking stairs, out onto the muddy streets to frolic, lured one by one, at first, then trios and twins and siblings, first a dozen, then forty, curious, delighted, entranced, finally over a hundred in total, laughing, clapping, dinging bells. Every child in Hamelin. Tottering toddlers, large-headed six-year-olds, confident ten-year-old girls cartwheeling, callow teen boys jostling to be head of the queue. He led them towards his cave—various versions describe it as a sinkhole or mine shaft, like something a trapdoor spider would hide in—and none were ever seen again. The only child left was blind and could not see where the other children were going. When church let out, the blind little survivor told the townspeople what had happened, and the rest is histo—

Noise. Shatter-tinkle-bang. A commotion. Somebody startled, upset.

My eyes struggle to adjust. A shape in the black. There he is. That flicker, the ripple of pebbles that indicate where an invisible man is standing. Alive and real. He has encircled a fry cook in an apron carrying twin garbage bags in both hands. The boy has just left the safe security light of the Burger King and is about to cross the rubble and sling his garbage into the dumpster, except he's encircled. Surrounded.

I watch human-shaped pieces of night crowd the boy, who wears a startled face of surprise. They dart and nip like fish.

They bunch around him, the night-gang. Cookie cutter cut-outs made of moons and stars. One of them looks like Charlene Lyman-Smith. Another could be Patrice Harrington. I should know: I've stared at their photos every night for five months.

I wriggle down off the barrel and land on tingling legs made of pins and needles.

Smash, tinkle. Scrape. I've knocked over a soda bottle. The Burger King boy drops his load and sprints back to the loading bay where he pounds on the roller door, LEMME IN LEMME IN LEMME IIIINNNNNNNNN.

Me, I run. I get inside my safe steel car and drive twenty miles and park in the brightest, glaring-est Texaco gas station I can find. I locate my cellphone. I Google psychiatrist + Stockton + seeing things + am I losing my mind?

May 8

I'm desperate to bring excitement into my life. Last night I asked you, Patrick, to press a knife against my throat. I needled, whined, complained, followed you around the house begging. I HAFTA FEEL THE STING I screamed. You caved, finally, pinning me angrily against the wall, bumping the framed photo of us in our wedding dress. Your eyes flared red for a second. We were about to make love but you ran away, disgusted, just as my panties were dampening. You're useless, Patrick. Pathetic. Fixated on following rules. You lock the doors at 7 p.m. and draw the curtains. Afraid of what's out there in the night.

Patrick, babe: If we actually talked, if our home weren't built on an icy lake, I would tell you exactly what's out there.

Undiscovered species, that's what.

Guess I'll have to find excitement elsewhere. There's certainly no excitement at the *Mercury News*. God knows I've tried to get my editor at the *Mercury* to pick up the Golden State Dementor story. Tried to get the old lecherous motherfucker to pay me for the hundreds of hours of overtime. D'you know he laughed and returned to typing his email then looked up a minute later and asked why I was still in his office?

Because, I told him, if we're not going to write a headline confronting the Golden State Dementor, I'm walking out on my job. Today. Here. Now.

He told me to consult the Employee Assistance Program. You're creeping people out, Mel. This is why you have no friends. The company's happy to pay for free counseling sessions for psychiatric problems, he said.

Can you believe that shit?! Like I'm crazy or something! As if I'm delusional!

I certainly wasn't delusional when I dropped into The Stockton Hope Centre. Nerviest thing I've ever done, Patrick. The reason for braving a homeless shelter? Because the homeless are out there, at night, in the Dementor's territory, seeing things the rest of us are too clean and sanitized to see. I planned to ask certain questions which should set me on the path to winning the Pulitzer Fucking Prize.

The Hope Center was having something ludicrously called the "Stockton Hope International Culinary Festival." I nearly burst out laughing at the title—it would have been perfect for our "On a lighter note" section on page 28! My head was dappled with the bottoms of flags dangling from the ceiling, some still being put up by men whose armpits I could smell from meters away. Flags from the Bahamas, Thailand, West Africa, Syria, Indonesia, Haiti. My appointment was with the colorfully-named manager Armistice Brown, who squeezed my shoulder and led me to what looked like four kitchens joined together. Industrial grade equipment, giant tumblers and mixers and a wall of bagged flour. Armistice had told me I couldn't talk to any of the people "until you've put in your mandatory ten." She meant ten hours of volunteering in the kitchen. Customary for all outsiders, apparently—I was expected to glove up and cover my hair and squish butter into flour and ruin my best shirt for ten hours before I was welcome. Okay, I told myself. Think Gonzo. Think Pulitzer. Journalism necessitates getting dirty sometimes.

The first people I was paired with to create pastry were two guys from Vietnam, father and son apparently and both named Binh. It was almost impossible to hear them over the sounds of blenders and clanging pans. Some black guy elbowed through us with a scalding pot, crying, "Hot soup, comin' through."

Second day, I nearly cried. Squirting cheesy sauce into a thousand tubes of cannelloni—literally, a fucking thousand—gave me a sore rotator cuff in my shoulder and I growled at Armistice Brown and she told me Thank you for your service, smirking, basically pointing out I was equating myself to a hero for giving up one day of paid work to get dirty.

Fine, I decided, fuck it. I worked despite my agonized arm then went to the Chill Out room to find a bag of peas and rest my muscles.

A young male crackhead in a singlet—no, a woman, taut, muscular, white tank top, flat tits, pronounced biceps—was giggling at me. She looked like a white upper-class Valley Girl, but with platinum hair sticking out insanely like she'd been shocked, plus a big splash of pink over one of her twin buns. She had bright eyes with lots of mascara, though her voice was pure street.

"You's a trip, girl, you loco!" she said, and sprayed glowing fake teeth at me, "What's yo name?"

"Melanie. And you are?"

"I'm Callisto, babe. Whatchu poppin', Mel?"

"Pardon me?"

"What pills you have for breakfast, girl?"

"I don't really want to tell you."

"Tell me or I'll fuck you up." She smiled through all of this.

Callisto—not Calista, CallistOOOO, like the second largest moon of Jupiter—was completely unfazed as I explained why I'd been finding it so hard to sleep lately. *Late night after late night. Uncomfortable crouching in parking lots and grass verges. Grimacing, squinting into the inky black indigo, like working deep underwater. And when I'm not out on location I'm watching videos of women giving statements to detectives. Tracing their bloody thighs. Pointing out contusions around the vaginal area.*

Photos, too. Snapshots of horror. A picture of a victim's body in Oakdale, discovered as a leather skeleton under a pile of wood pallets where she'd crawled like a hedgehog, desperate to hide from something. Someone.

Callisto interrogated me about how much Xanax and Tramadol I had in my car and could I get prescriptions and whether I wanted to buy a rottweiler. She pointed her cigarette at me and said, "Ayyyy: so you wanna talk about the missing kids and the Stinger-Man who takes 'em dancin. A'ight. Let's talk."

I pulled the plug. Everything poured out. I told her I believed this thing, this Peter-Pan-Piper-Leader-of-the-Lemmings, whatever it is, goes back to the Dark Ages. Medieval Europe, Silk Road, East Asia. Villages whose teens were becoming sick with the Black Plague would send their young ones off into the woods. There would be entire tribes of lost girls and boys in the forest, living for weeks banned from coming home until they died. Free from school and church, free from rules. That's where Ring Around the Roses comes from, just as a sidenote, forgive me, Callisto, ha ha, too much education. A rosy rash was a symptom of the plague, and a posy of herbs in your pocket was believed to ward off the disease.

God knows what happened to them when these children were exiled to the woods. They died far from home, playing hopscotch or tag or jump rope, skipping and singing while they starved and suffered, desperate for an adult to lead them. To come play with them.

I imagine they prayed to a hundred gods. And I imagine in their desperation, someone unexpected answered.

Someone from a dark dimension. A man who promised he would shepherd the children. Take them out of their misery. All he had to do was put them to sleep first, and all it took was a little sting before the numbness set in and the children could play wayyyy past their bedtime.

Play forever.

Callisto was crying by now. Not so hard and threatening anymore. Crying and apologizing.

I asked Callisto if the people around here had seen anyone get attacked, or at least heard of attacks, or if they knew of people from the homeless community who'd gone missing, or been raped or seemed zombified, Novocain'd.

"Naw, nah nah nah, they ain't seen shit," she said, sniffing. "You're wasting your time, white girl. But I did."

Callisto led me out to the balcony, tugging eagerly while I watched muscles work in her bony back. She slammed the ranch slider shut, prowled the balcony, swatted everything metal away—a bean can with cigarette butts in it; one earpiece from somebody's headphones.

"Right over there," she said, tilting her forehead at a McDonald's. "That's where the choir was."

Choir?

"Like a whole song 'n dance troupe. Skipping in a circle. Ring Around the Rosy. Gahhhhhd, that brought back, like, schoolyard memories, know what I'm sayin'? You can hear 'em singing if you listen right. Choir ain't complete, though."

"You have to expand, I don't know what that means, Callisto, you'll tell me on the record, won't—"

Callisto smashed the Dictaphone out of my hand. It tumbled into the weeds below. "Means the bad man's looking for about another six or seven people before there's enough in the group."

I demanded to know how she knew.

"I's in the choir," Callisto said. "Ain't easy to get out."

Callisto opened her legs, unbuckled her belt. Showed me scars and stains in the veins and soft tissue where toxic acid wriggled around. Purple worms crawling up her stomach and away from her vulva where the poisonous sting had stuck her.

June 6

The devil took her.

The devil took mah child. Mah bubba.

That's what I keep hearing from these people's parents, as they fall back into their lace-covered armchairs with a lunchtime glass of whisky, numbing the injury.

The devil took my son. My daughter. My one and only.

They tell me this verb *Took, take, taking*. I counter with the word *dement*. He dements, he demented, he will dement— and then their spirits will detach from their bodies and they will walk into his arms. From the Latin *dementare*, meaning to drive somebody out of their mind. I ask the chain-smoking mother of Ruby Zhao, as we hang out her dripping laundry, if she has heard of *Ampulex dementor*.

What? she says, What's that got to do with my Rubes?

The Dementor wasp, found in the Mekong region of Thailand, will sting a cockroach or spider, any hapless bug ambling home, and release a toxin that goes directly to the neural nodes. The toxin will act as a blocker of the octo-pamine receptors of the cockroach. This leaves the victim alive, but without the ability to control its own movements. This allows for an easier capture. Control. As if someone has stuck a microphone deep inside your ear so they can whisper instructions. It causes the cockroach to run into a wasp's nest as if responding to a call or notion. To do the enemy's bidding.

This "devil", this "Pied Piper" is telling people to join its army of ghosts, a legion, as the Bible calls it, and I'm going to confront him. I'm going to bring them back—if I can. All the dead children.

I'm going to make the world right.

July 31

Oh . . . my . . . GOD it's easy to find him!!!!!!!!!!!!

As soon as I recognised the pattern, I had the bastard. The first time I spotted the Dementor, the Piper, we were both surprised, but this time, it was all planning. Strategy. And I know he respects that. He respects anyone who can catch him.

Okay, okay, let me dial it back.

I've used shades of black to code the date of each attack, then pinned each little shaded note on four A1-sized maps of California which I've stuck to the wall of our hallway (and fuck you, Patrick, for complaining about the damage to the plaster, this is MORE IMPORTANT THAN MAINTAINING THE SANCTITY OF YOUR WALLPAPER!!!)

Attacks that occurred in the first quarter of the year were coded full black. Attacks in the second quarter were semi-black. Attacks in the third quarter are a very diluted black, really gray, and the final quarter of the year's attacks I coded white. Placing the colored attack stamps on the map, the pattern is immediately recognizable. This Pied Piper, this Dementor, this Wasp-man with his paralyzing sting—he's circling. Is, was, will be. The first attack, in Vacaville, was like a 10:30 p.m. on an analogue clockface, like north-north-west. He then shifted northeast, like 2 p.m. on a clockface, attacking at Sacramento before going southeast, attacking at Vineyard which is 4 p.m. on the clock. It wasn't long before he'd gone as far south as Modesto before rising up again, heading north.

The clockwise cycle has then repeated.

Six attacks on six points of the compass—clock, whatever. Color-coded, we had the start of each year throbbing black, before the attacks went grey, like the color of 17-year-old Maria Lindauer's face as the blood emptied from her My Little Pony underwear and swirled around her ankles, dripping in the drain.

The last attack I can see is in Sacramento. He'll be headed south or southeast, coming down the 99 through the San Joaquin Valley, dipping his proboscis into the night, licking up lonesome kids in Elk Grove or Lodi in the coming month.

And when he comes, I'll be ready with my camera and my Dictaphone and a fistful of questions.

August 10

Some say the devil's dead
And buried in cold harbor;
Some say he's alive again,
And 'prenticed to a barber.

Some say the devil walks at night
With all the village children
He clothes them, feeds them, schools them,
They're grateful that he killed them.

September 11

Date of the big world-ruining explosions, huh. 9/11. When everything changed.

Everything's changed in my world, too. Yours as well, right, Patrick? You don't notice me hiding in corners, notepad and curled pen, camera on silent mode, observing you. I see you sneaking sips of wine at 11 a.m. I see you installing Tinder on your Samsung, holding your cellphone out at arm's length, trying to snap a selfie that doesn't reveal you're a 42-year-old balding midget with black hair on your arms and grey wires in your whiskers. Don't be hurt by this. Don't be upset. I'm just a mirror. I reflect.

My back crunches when I get in and out of the car. It's curling, my spine is, from the stakeouts where I crumple up in a dark dumpster, chin on my knees. Bending, wracked, and stressed. Panging like an alarm during the day, numb at night. Doesn't help that I'm hunched over my laptop all the time. Whispering into the ears of stepmothers with lost daughters.

WHEN did you say you spoke to her that night?

WHAT was she pissed off about?

Hold up—skipping you said? S-K-I-P-ping? Your daughter *skipped* off into the night?

That was just how she walked, you tell me, gulping. Even when she was mad, she skipped. A little girl carving out a tiny piece of joy in a harsh world of arguments and slammed doors and curfew. She skipped out her window, Ruby did. Skipped away into the night.

It's the vibrations that get your children snatched, I tell these wrought mothers and ruined fathers. A trapdoor spider hides in a black burrow. Its ears are attuned to patterns of noise. Vibrations that tell it a 90-pound girl is skipping through a vacant lot of glass shards and poison oak and rubbish and ragweed. Vibrations tell it the girl is carrying warm chicken tenders and a sweet Coke, looking for a place to go and eat and forget the world is unfair.

That's me, I've realized—well, it can be. I can dress up like a child to lure the Dementor out. I can tie my hair in pigtails, wear my tiniest dress. Put on shoes with bells on the buckles. Sing Ring Around the Rosy as I dance around the parking lot with my little bag of deep-fried joy. Extend my fingers, close my eyes. Wait for a warm hand to take mine and carry me into the stars.

October 22

I met him, Patrick. I had to. Your wife Melanie, the forgotten woman, the depressed friendless headcase who sleepwalks through the day and thrives at night—she got the exclusive. The scoop.

And to do it, I crossed into his realm.

I know you're probably reading this and I'm gone or vegetated or comatose. I want you to take a deep breath and just chill. It wasn't *bad*-bad, the meeting. It was a wake-up, actually. An electric shock. A squirt of adrenaline that left me exhausted and wanting to cry. What I learned is the Legion has a life force. A pulsing heart. At the center of it, a father. A leader.

It's children that he wants, you see, well, mostly. The doctor and his wife, and that 50-year-old in Modesto—just collateral. People who got in the way. This is me speaking on his behalf, though, because the Piper didn't explain all this. There were no quotes, no words. He has nothing to say. All he does is hold out his hand.

We met when I was spending the night in the hedge beside a White Castle in Elk Grove. I crouched for nearly five hours, past 10, past midnight, on across 1 a.m., 2 a.m. Finally, at 2 : 16, with creaking knees and blaring thighs, I got up. The moon was wide awake, spread-out, yellow. Moonshadow fell under my body on the cyan sidewalk. I stood in the middle of the road, placed my right foot in front of my left, bent my knees, let my eyes drop two tears.

It hurt my back to get into position. And it embarrassed me, being alone in the night.

But I began to skip. Toes tickling the air, knees up, butt straight. I danced with the passion of a child.

The streetlight moved, bending. Little flints of light solidified into eyes. I found myself encircled as the cookie-cutter kids joined hands around me.

One child taller than the others. Black and pied with white patches, like a chessboard.

Except he was no child.

He was Leader.

He took my hand.

I let him lead.

November

Ring around the roses
A pocket full of posies
Atishoo, atishoo
We all fall down

Vanished in the night-wind,
Daughter on the breeze
Skipping with our master
One, two, THREE!

The man, he lost his maiden
the husband lost his wife
The Blackness put a ring on her
Bride of the night

The robin on the steeple
Is singing to the people
Its lungs are bloody treacle
Falls underground.

My daughter went away with him
Mama knows she's gone.
Patrick fluffs his wifey's pillow
Please come home.

*

There is nothing for December, Patrick. No entries.

Pages empty, my friend. Empty as the rubble beside these burger joints where people drop their trash.

I don't know what to tell you. This thing, this journal of hers, it was incredibly hard to find, man. I had to drive all across the San Joaquin Valley, midnight after midnight. That's how come I wanna charge you for 300 hours. I sniffed, essentially. Sniffed all of these towns. Using my senses to get a feel for which midnight McDonalds looked the saddest, the loneliest. Places where people would go if they needed cheering up.

Elk Grove, I found the journal. Still had a pen pinned to the cover. Stained with rain, browned with sun. Found it in a hedge full of wrappers and cups and paper bags, Patrick. A little cleared circle where a person's bum or a pair of feet might have rested while watching folks collect little brown sacks of happiness from the drive-thru, staring, obsessed. This person – a woman, I'm guessing – left her little nook eventually. She heard some signal, some calling. She got up to stretch and see whether she'd had a sighting. Heard a chorus of kids start singing a song on every side. Took a warm hand, joined the circle. A smile spread across her face. Calm. Blissed out. I'd say she got stung, then. Injected. Drugged up on toxin, I suppose she did something, kind of— kind of wild.

She started skipping.

She'd found friends, Patrick. A community.

For the first time in ages, she wasn't alone.

FAKE ID

1.

I meet Matt McAnulty under the willow tree by the science block out the back of school. The branches drizzle droplets round us like a screen of freezing water. It's just us and an ocean of wet grass and a sky bruised with cold rain.

It's Friday afternoon. Start of the weekend, pretty much. Everyone has gone off to their cabins and cottages and penthouse suites to get the fuck away from school.

Me, I'm staying right here and getting lit. I don't care how cold it is. I've dressed up especially. I'm scoring me a sweetass fake ID and I'ma get me some cans of Cody's bourbon and coke and relaaaaaaax, yo. Be drunk in the alleyway by dinner time if everything goes to plan. My parents run my life like a prison, plus everyone at school thinks I'm a noob. I need to get out. Need some electricity in my gray Friday. I need a new life.

Matt McAnulty isn't up on my vibe, even though it was his original idea to push this fake ID on me. He's a senior, 18, ancient compared to me. He's seen a lot. He wants to take my desperate money quick then say something mean and slink away. He's cold and cautious and disappointed on the best of days and today, his jaw is like a hunk of wood. No chewing, no swallowing. His eyes are unblinking balls of white glass. I guess he's wary cause he comes from a vanilla home and both his parents are, like, neurosurgeons that teach at the medical school, or they were before his dad got forced out or whatever. Becoming a badass gangsta for Matt McAnulty means selling fake stolen shit and fucking up his grades and getting in trouble and being mean to younger kids like me and breaking his parents' hearts. He's working on it.

"Fuck's up with your faggy-ass clothes?"

I've got a white church shirt on and a tie, the only tie I could find. It's got Snoopy and Woodstock on it. "Thought I'd, y'know, look like I'm old and stuff. Make it easier to get the alcohol bought, know what I'm sayin?"

I press two twenty-dollar notes into his hand for my fake ID. He one-eighties, moves under the darkest bough of the willow tree, turning his back completely, counts the cash while I shiver and stamp my feet.

Finally, Matt McAnulty spins back around, holds out a little rectangle of plastic, and I take his driver's license. He'll tell the feds it's stolen and get a replacement, easy peasy. This fake plastic me, this Matthew Laurence McAnulty in the ID photo, has paper-colored skin, blue irises fizzy with pink. Looks vaguely like me. Could be a cousin, if you squint.

The real-world Matt McAnulty is pulling the white hood over his red NBA cap and backing away. He's preparing to gap. Steam comes out of his mouth as he gives me instructions.

"Oliver, kid: don't tell people I got you this."

"I won't, I promise." I put the fake ID in the chest pocket of my corny white church shirt with my alcohol money.

"You people'll say anything while you're having a spaz though, won't ya?"

He's making fun of my condition. My disorder.

"D'you even take your meds today? 'Cause I don't want people seeing my name on your card and thinkin' Matty McAnulty's some disabled faggot."

"Totally, bro, I took my pills, straight up."

What he means is I have this glitch in my brain called epilepsy. Kids at school don't think it's massively weird if they've grown up with me. People just think having epilepsy is the equivalent of having jug-handle ears or something. They're random-as, my seizures, like I'll be riding my bike home with a box of Chinese food and the world will disappear in white and I'll find myself on a tractor beam pulling me up to the clouds, except when bystanders roll me into the recovery position and I wake, I'm actually on a roundabout with foam bubbling onto my chin. I have these partial seizure things too, like I won't realize I'm taking my shirt off and sitting on some random kid's desk and drawing concentric circles and they're, like, What the actual? It's electricity zapping your brain, that's all. I have these meds called Levetiracetam that suppress the seizures, except I've been selling 'em to Matt, hoping it'll make him respect me.

If he does respect me, he ain't showing it. Matt McAnulty has a kitchen knife—the same Ginsu that my mum has, actually—and he's stroking his finger along the blade, as if he's thinking of siccing it on me. It's still got orange rind on it. Musta borrowed it from his parents' kitchen. Considering they're brain surgeons, he could've borrowed something sharper.

"I ain't goin' to jail for fuckin' sellin' fake IDs so jus' . . . jus' don't do anything retarded while you're being me."

"Hundred percent."

"Promise?"

"I promise, man."

Matt puts his knife away, jams his hands into his pockets, shoulders hunched, takes another step back then looks around. He wants something from me, before he goes. Like as if dumping his ID on me is dumping his actual identity, and he's anxious about saying Laters to it.

"Just, like, off the record 'n shit, what does it, y'know, *feel* like?"

"Oh. My epilepsy? Thanks for asking, Matt, um, I guess it's like this glowing white fire so bright that it, like, rubs out everything, like that Batman eraser you biffed at me that time? Then I wake up on the ground with a sore neck. Your muscles tense up real bad."

Matt's jaw still doesn't move. He shifts away a few feet, leaves a trail in the dewy grass.

"There's partial ones, too, where it's like I can see that my body's doing spastic stuff but I don't control it," I tell him.

"My old man's into that neuro shit, so . . . I dunno, bro. He'd love to get his hands on you." He pulls his white Ecko hood up further. The hoodie looks brand new. His rich surgeon parents must've paid for the threads. He fiddles with his hood one last time, pulling it down, and takes a quick side-to-side glance to see if anybody will notice him being nice to a loser. "Your seizures is your temporal lobe fuckin up. Problem's in your hippocampus 'cause that's like your control switchboard." He spits, grinds the spit with the toe of his puffy skate shoe. "Brain stuff, G, s'just dinner table talk where I come from, know what I'm sayin?"

"You want me to come to your house for dinner, Matt?"

"Whaaaat? Shit no. You don't wanna meet my family, nigga. Anything happens with your fake ID," he begins, then searches for the ideal words. He's about to tell me he'll be there for me, just give him a text and he'll back me up. "Anything happens, you don't know me."

He runs towards Mrs. Hamilton's fence, which borders the school, vaults the fence and disappears.

I want to do the exact same—shit, it'd be awesome to follow Matt McAnulty's footsteps, live his life, be his twin—but I wait 30 seconds so I'm not walking up his ass.

I take the route out of school past the special needs retard unit, past the short bus, past the lemon bushes and neatly mown Bermuda grass. I mosey down Taradale Place, connect with Lincoln Road, suck a breath of air and tell myself You Got This. I position my legs to take me east up Lincoln Road to buy some liquid happiness. Melt away all the stress and frowning and mean-ness I get from my depressed dad. All the failure from my fingertip-nibbling mum, hiding behind piles of laundry.

I begin walking the 3.1 kilometers up the road to my destination. To the magnet on the horizon: Liquor Boss. Navy blue building, with big white and red stripes, throbbing among the tire shops and warehouses. Powerful American colors. There's electricity inside the store. Naughty thrilling intoxication. Magic potion to take me out of my lame-ass life.

I duck inside the first bus shelter, outside St. Ninian's church, push against the wire mesh, go behind it so I'm as far away from traffic as possible. (Is that my dad in his Kia? Is that—no—yes? —Matt McAnulty's old man driving by? The fuck?) I press my back against slimy fences and dripping walls and hedges, kicking a sack of rotten McDonald's out of the way. Bushes hang low over me, camouflaging me for hundreds of meters. I stay almost invisible. Forgotten. I take the long route behind a rubbish bin and a discarded fridge. I hop between islands in a puddle large as a lake. I hold my tie against my chest, so it doesn't get splashed.

C'mon bro. You got this. Here we go. 2.0 kays I've travelled so far, my FitBit tells me. Alright. 2.1 kays, 2.2. I'm outside Sunnyside, the mental hospital. 2.3 kays. Here's the dairy, here's that place that sells balls of wool yarn. A chain of old villas. Traffic is slurping past on a conveyor belt. 2.8 kays, 2.9.

Close, Oliver, close. Hold it together. You're dressed like a door-to-door Mormon. No one's going to question you.

Three kilometers covered. Whew. Liquor Boss is right here. I'm on the lip, the edge. Look—customers are crossing the concrete forecourt, coming and going with their paper bags of liquid party.

Swallow, Ollie—no, *Matt*, actually. Yeah, Matt McAnulty, that's me. Got the driver's license. Swallow, Matt. Ground yourself. You're a young professional with a tie. Just goin' about your business, legit. Two minutes and the deal will be done.

I'm advancing, crossing the forecourt with some hard strides and—

Holy shit.

Hovering outside is a fancy-ass black Mercedes. License plate reading MATTHW.

It's them.

Thunder. The roof rattles. My eyes match the driver's. A speccy man whose blond tight sheep-curls have faded whitey-platinum, sitting with the steering wheel in his lap. A woman beside him.

Matt McAnulty's parents.

I sprint so fast inside the store that when the sliding doors close behind me, I can hear myself panting.

I straighten my tie, look around. Pretend I know what to look for in this dim palace of bottles and boxes.

In the dark end of the fishbowl, some woman is buying a whole basket of wine. I observe her actions, mimic her, turn to the shelf in front of me and select a bottle of hooch. God it's heavy. Polish vodka, this shit. Silver label. I heft a bottle of cognac, and some stuff called VSOP brandy with gold foil. I pretend to weigh a pair of Bombay Sapphire blue gin bottles, two for fifty bucks. Ruby red port. Shiraz wine.

I simply need to find my Cody's bourbon 'n coke and gap. Cody's is the only alcohol I can tolerate to get me fucked up. I've had the stuff just once, at this party at Glenn Ogawa's place. It was sweet and jagged and hurt my throat like toxic waste but it got me out of my head. Away from my identity as a crippled loser.

The clock is ticking, Ollie. Some sort of alarm is gonna go off. Get the merchandise and get the fuck outta here.

I know the Indian dude at the counter is watching me. He's pressed a button that's lowering the ceiling panels, I'm pretty sure. I search the last few shelves, merlot, no, absinthe, looks poisonous, crème liqueur, scotch whiskey, Irish whisky. . ..

"You are lookingk for somethingk is particular, sir?"

I'm staring directly into a name tag which says Aruneshwar. He's sidled up beside me. Above the name tag is the face of a student-looking dude who can't be much older than Matt McAnulty. Big round pumpkin head on a pencil neck. Tons of pimple scars. Total noob. But I need him.

"Cody's?" I gasp, "it's, like, um bourbon and coke?"

Aruneshwar guides me to the prize. It was in the beer chiller this whole time. I squint against the cold and take a six-pack of Cody's cans, dark and golden as bullets. I'm trying to read all the information on them. Aruneshwar tells me there's a discount plus a free t-shirt if I buy a case of 24. I almost say yes, except I'm down to my last twenty bucks, plus I have no way to carry that much alcohol around.

He leads me to the register. I'm positive he's going to handcuff me to the counter then call the cops. I slide a twenty dollar note across the divide. He looks at the cash like it's a dead fish.

"You are havingk ID, sir?"

I swallow. Dry throat. Search my right pocket. Nothing. I search the left, and my back pockets.

"I—I thought I had—"

"Forgive for me saying to you, sir, but this is in your. . . ?" Aruneshwar is tapping his breast. He's telling me I need to check my white chest pocket. The dude's right. My church shirt is so thin and flimsy you can see the ID from outer space.

I slide it across the counter. He picks it up, almost sniffing it.

"I'm Matt," a voice blurts. My voice. Fuck. I didn't tell my body to say that. Matt's identity is taking over.

"Havingk you a good night, Matt" Aruneshwar says, smiling, and takes my twenty and hands me back four dollars change.

The glass doors slide apart. I'm baptized in the air outside. I can breathe again. I'm in heaven.

Where to go now? Back to school, yeah. The retard block is the nicest place to hang. I can play with the plastic trucks and wood blocks while I drink my six gold cans. Lie down in the sandpit when I get too drunk. Think about how I'm like Anne Frank or something and everyone's mean to me and they'll regret it when I'm gone. Maybe I'll leave a diary.

Under the overhang, I hear thunder stomping the earth. Birds scatter, flapping for somewhere sheltered—but it's cool. It's an omen. It's the world clearing its throat to say it's ready for me. Old Ollie reborn as Gangsta Matt: hard drinker.

I step out from under the overhang of the liquor store, scope the street, and take a single step back towards school.

I'm blocked immediately.

The Mercedes drifts in front of me. They were undercover, the people inside. Feds, narcs, without a doubt.

A man who looks like Matt McAnulty, plus 30 years—drained, baked, bleached, tired hair with filaments of silver—reaches from the driver seat to the back and opens a backseat door.

"Hop in, son."

Before I can tell them that I'm not their son, or ask how they think they know me, or swear I'm just a faithful missionary going door to door, I'm trapped.

2.

Two grown-ups in the front. Matt's dad driving. Matt's mum with her hands in her lap, admiring the view as the car hoovers up Lincoln Road, sucking each wet meter under the front.

I bury myself in the velvety upholstered darkness in the back, clutching my precious cans as if I could possibly come up with some explanation for the alcohol.

They're driving me to the police station, I guarantee it. They'll frisk me. My fake ID will get me in a shitload of trouble. My life is totally fucked.

Except they're super-mega-nice. Teeth and shiny lips and eyes creased with joy as they give me a lift home. They're bursting with conversation and asking me what heat setting I'd like the air conditioning on and it's making me awkward as fuck.

I'm nervously half-listening to Matt's dad talking about the roadworks, and when the council are going to trim those poplar trees brushing against the power lines, then he's going on about his career and how much he loves "My dear Lynne" and how they fell for each other at medical school and shit.

". . .so that was us, married her on the spot, give or take three years of angst!" Matt's dad is going. Pretty damn cheerful for a dude who apparently lost his job at the university hospital for malpractice or something? I could've been wrong on that count though. "Anyhoo, young child, pray tell: You've got your supplies. Where's the party at tonight?"

"Wish we could come!" the doctor mum adds. She does a little clap like a bipolar street corner nutcase, so enthusiastic that she bumps her own glasses off her nose. Are these jokers in a cult or what? So fucking cringe. I tumble along the rapids with these guys, lurching against the seatbelt as we slow for orange lights.

"So, you guys are like doctors, eh?" I ask the front of the car.

"Past tense," Matt's dad goes, "We *were*."

"Understood," I go, not understanding.

"Weeee've arrived at the end of our subservience to the medical establishment," Matt's mum says, staring hard into the rearview.

"Free to do as we wish these days," the dad adds. "Every man's dream, eh?"

"Totally."

My hood trickles by—Best Burgers, Hillmorton High School, my street. I'm expecting sirens, handcuffs, a SWAT team hard-stopping the car, except we've turned into Jacaranda Crescent, which glows briefly orange as the dusk burns out, and we slow down in front of a big empty bush-leafy park with a path, except it's not a path, it's a driveway, these guys' property is so vast that it disappears from the street.

Everything is blue, now. Night is falling.

There's a full 30, 40, 50 seconds of bending up the driveway before we slow outside some mansion in the middle of nowhere and Matt's dad yanks the handbrake up.

"My good sir," he goes with that fake phony upper class cheeriness, like he's performing on stage in a musical, "I do believe we have arrived."

They split open this big thick pane of frosted glass. Turns out it's a door. The place opens up. Their house is so big there are, like, six different directions my head wants to turn. There's the marble foyer, with its lake of thick red rug and carpeted stairs. They have an alarm with, like, a facial recognition thing. They have framed photos of Matt McAnulty on the wall. Him at five, blond, freckled, on Santa's knee. Matt aged ten, almost as tall as his dad, the three of them in a shopping mall photo booth. Framed snippets of Matt's athletics results from the school newsletter. Ink prints of Matt's baby feet. Photos of these guys' careers, too, stethoscopes on their necks; blue gowns and face masks and goggles. A picture of Matt's dad graduating, robed in black. A picture of Matt's mum with some medical-y type people in front of the Sydney Opera House. A photo of Mrs. McAnulty shaking Barack Obama's hand, even.

They seal the door behind me. It feels final, like the outside is never coming back. My dick has retreated up into my tummy. Where the chandelier light doesn't reach, the house is black.

Matt's mum's hands land on my shoulders. Soft fingers. I realize the mum is short and dark, almost black, like Indian maybe. She can't be Matt's birth mum. Maybe the dad killed Matt's mum early on or something. She has black hair, eyebrows like dark smudges, but she's got nice bulgy curves and I like the way her hips bump into me as she licks her finger and wipes some goo off my forehead.

"Dinner's ready and waiting, my love."

She tugs me through this room with paintings all over the wall and into a kitchen with copper pots dangling over an island. They've left the oven going while they've been out (cruising for kids? Picking up random dudes like me?) and Mr. McAnulty is rising from floor to island, putting down another steaming tray of gold with his oven mitts. The dude's put an apron on. His spectacles fog up. There are glasses of wine in these guys' hands all of a sudden, and they're smiling down like angels.

Makes sense, 'cause I've arrived in heaven: the island is overflowing with golden salty fried crispy deliciousness, fingers of steam swirling into the blackness of the ceiling. In front of me is a dish of chicken nuggets, a pan of beer-battered fries, a platter of epic mouth-drooly fried chicken. Tater tots, chicken tenders, barbecue sauce, Thousand Island dressing, sweet chili sauce and—oh my God, literally, you can't be serious—mini corn dogs: my favorite.

I eat like an octopus, reaching across with my right arm while my left snakes under it. Two sides of my body, each at work. I'm filling a white plate with brown crispiness while at the same time I'm pulling the deliciousness directly into my mouth to get as many calories down me as quickly as I can. Thank heaven, God, Buddha, the Jewish God, whoever, man—at home, this would be like eight different treats across six months.

I'm wiping my mouth and accepting the knife and fork that Mrs. McAnulty is handing me when I finally catch my breath and go, "Sorry, you guys. Just hungry is all. My olds kind of don't remember to save dinner for me sometimes 'cause they're breaking up and stuff."

"Don't apologize, son."

"Sorry, Mrs.—"

"Hush, now: it's Lynne. Or Doctor Lynne!"

"Sorry, Doctor Lynne."

"Here. Let me help you with that. Doctor's orders. I insist."

She's talking about taking my alcohol. While I've been scoffing, I've been clutching my cans of sweet bourbon. The bag's really crumpled and the cans are close to falling out. Mr. McAnulty is squeezing my shoulder and I'm yielding, I'm letting go, I'm coming undone and my precious cargo is sliding into his soft warm dad-hands.

"About those drinks of yours," he begins.

My mouth goes dry. I'm about to get massively told off. Detention, grounded, cops, juvie, anything could happen.

"It's beer o'clock, hm?"

The world unpauses and instead of narking on me, Matt's dad cracks a can open with strong fingers and pours the stinky coke into a glass. It fizzes and reeks like a recycling bin. "You've earned this."

"Un assaisonnement petit?" he goes, pulling a pill in half and sprinkling the grains into my drink. He has the orange half of a digestible pill casing in his right hand, the white half in his left. His wife leans into him, caressing him and staring down like they're admiring a new Labrador. Apparently I'm the fuckin' Labrador.

"Drink up," Mr. McAnulty goes, lifting my glass to my lips. Mrs. McAnulty rubs my throat as they perform their two-person act and I'm so woozy I don't even notice the drink disappear down me.

After shoving more food behind my teeth, I realize I'm drunk, drunk off just one sip. I've been standing half-off my stool, leaning over the fried food, but I'm getting dizzy and fat and full and heavy, and the stool pulls me down and everything is weighing too heavily for me to stand up and fight gravity.

"I got ebilebsy," I blurt. My words are meltier than usual, like my lips are heavy. "Sorry, just fort I should zay."

"We know," the mum goes, beaming down, her eyes half-closed with contentment, like she's drifting off to sleep. "We've done our research. You're truly special, child."

"Ever heard of Roger Sperry, son? No?"

"Wuzza? Sberryson?"

"We'll talk once you wake up," Mrs. McAnulty goes, tiptoeing out of the kitchen. "I'll fetch you a pillow, child."

I reach for a chicken nugget. It recedes into infinity like it's caught in two elevator mirrors facing each other.

They catch me as I fall towards the tiles. Four surgeons' hands, firm and caring. I can feel marshmallowy cotton absorb my head as they shove a pillow under.

Night-night.

3.

"Dr. Sperry was the best mentor a young man could ask for, when I was just getting started at medical school. Well before you were a twinkle in your father's eye, I expect!"

There are thick black tendrils around my hands and fore-arms. The tendrils flex and pull and tighten when I wriggle. My butt screams. I'm sitting on something hard, and my spine wants to shift but it can't.

Chair with rails . . . dining table . . . soft lighting. As I look around, the colors dribble like a picture on a broken TV screen. I'm on acid, I think, or drunk, or having a fever.

We're in some lounge-parlor in front of a fireplace. A room with books and some dinnerware in a dresser. I'm sitting up straight. I can sense the kitchen behind, though I'm facing away.

I'm tied up in front of Matt McAnulty's smiling, angelically lit parents. Their faces melt, detach, float around like balloons then find their place again.

". . .found was that Dr. Sperry was the first to identify the corpus callosum as the region of the brain dividing the left from the right hemisphere which was, of course, monumentally influential, wouldn't you agree, honey? I mean his work really did shape the course of both of our careers."

"Without it, you'd have one brain," Mrs. McAnulty says. "But you don't. You have two, child."

"I have. . . two chilze?"

Mr. McAnulty turns his head away, laughs, returns. "This is challenging for you. Frankly, I don't even know why I'm telling you the history of . . . I suppose it's because our son never listens to us."

"I fink I'm sick."

Silence. My own protests, echoing.

"Lemmego, I goh geg, gog, gotta, gotta get back to—"

"Get back to where, exactly? You're in no state to go home, drunk as a skunk. Unintelligible, frankly."

Mrs. McAnulty crosses her arms and crumples her face. "Shame on you, Matthew, really."

"If you'd cast your attention this way?" Mr. McAnulty's eyes are wide with delight. "I promised I'd regale you with the saga of one Dr. Roger Sperry."

"I wan' go hobe." I try to move my forearms. The tape feels stronger than ever. My neck aches. "Plis. Plis lemme . . . lemmego."

"Now, I met the man who was to become my mentor when he was close on retirement, we're talking 1982, '83, but back in the 1960s, Roger Sperry – Rodge, to me – performed experiments to study functional differences between the two hemispheres of the brain so he really was extremely radical, yea, cutting edge, if you will," Mr. McAnulty continues. "Rodge's point of difference was that he became focused upon a certain bundle of neurons people had long ago named the corpus callosum and what Sperry—he related this in the most enthralling lectures, to which mine pale in comparison—what Sperry, dear chap, did was he severed the corpus callosum in cats and monkeys to study the function of each side of the brain, you see, as any of us would."

Two faces of Mrs. McAnulty detach from the walls on the left and right side of her. They float through the black kitchen, past a dresser of fancy dishes, past the espresso machine and the vase of plastic roses, and the two faces re-enter the room and settle on the front of Mrs. McAnulty. "It's the split brain, that's what Rodgey articulated," she tells me. "It's having two independent brains in your head. Two! D'you see?"

"The split brain enables mammals to memorize double the information," Mr. McAnulty goes, looking at me hard. His jokes are gone. "Surely you see how significant his advances were, son?"

"A visionary, he was." Mrs. McAnulty is preparing cups of tea now, setting saucers and teaspoons and a sugar bowl on a tray. Choot choooot. We're on train tracks. A locomotive is coming—no, a fountain—no, steam, a train. Or the kettle is boiling.

"Realized a wee nip-tuck on the old corpus callosum could ease epilepsy for folks just like you, he did. I mean, doesn't this blow your mind, son?!"

"Nodyor . . . I'm nod your son. . . ."

"He found the hemispheres in human brains have different functions. The left hemisphere interprets language, but not the right. The right is for imagination. Theorizing."

"Matthew, you have your left brain to thank for logic, language, reasoning, science, math," Mrs. McAnulty goes. She's leaning off her chair now. Her colors don't melt and warp and ripple as bad as before. "A child who'll meet the STEM needs of the future. That's what we need."

"Mad," I go, "Maff, Maffew, MadMcAnulty, he's got my . . . my idenna...tee."

Mrs. McAnulty bends down, puts a kiss on my cheek. "Hold still."

Mrs. McAnulty pulls a paper mask over her mouth. She's staring at my hairline. She presses a needle into my scalp. My head was throbbing before. Now it lifts off and floats away.

Mrs. McAnulty is squirting oil on what looks like an eggbeater with a circular sawblade on it. She flips a button. It hums. "We'll make that nasty old epilepsy a thing of the past, dear."

Mr. McAnulty's hands go somewhere above my head. The patch of wall I'm facing stays steady as Mrs. McAnulty runs her eggbeater slowly along the side of my face above my ears, thub-thub-thub. When the bent-over position hurts her back too much, she moves around about two feet. Pink icicles form above my eyes, drop and splash. My eyelashes shake. Something purple squirts, hits a wall, trickles down onto the armoire. Then I'm seeing Mrs. McAnulty upside down on my left side, standing on the ceiling, and so is Matt's dad, they've swapped positions, and finally she's in front of my eyes, switching the eggbeater-saw off and resting it on a metal trolley.

"Easy peasy lemon squeezy," she tells me from the ceiling, warmly. "Halfway there. Hang tight."

With Mrs. McAnulty lifting on the left and Mr. McAnulty lifting on the right, they remove some annoying thing that's been sitting on top of my head. It's an eggshell with bluey pink squiggles on the white inside and lots of spiky blond hair that looks like mine. I think someone put a bicycle helmet on me that I'd never noticed.

Mr. McAnulty smiles as he crouches in front of me, placing a rubber ball under my chin to hold my head straight.

I'm feeling air riffling through my hair. Light summer crickets. Relief.

"Thangs guyz for takey off."

"Stay as still as you can," he tells me. "Mum-mum'll look after you."

Mrs. McAnulty's tongue is sticking out the side of her lips. I'm surprisingly high in my chair and she has to stand on tippy toes to reach in with her cutter. There's chewing gum in my hair, I think, maybe? Or she's just giving me a haircut?

"It was controversial, of course, what our Rodgey did, but what better way to establish which eye talks to which hemisphere, I mean, for Pete's sake!" The dad is roaming around me, doing laps while his wife operates, almost shouting over the squishy, crunching sound. "Now, our illustrious doctor started with split-brain cats. He taped shut one of their eyes and presented them with two different blocks, one of which had food under it. After that, he switched the eye patch to the other eye of the cat and put the food under the other block. The cat memorized those events separately and could not distinguish between the blocks with both eyes open. Rhesus monkeys followed, naturally, and the split-brain monkeys memorized two mutually exclusive scenarios in the same time as a normal monkey memorized one, proving conclusively two brains were operating. Of course, he had to progress to clinical trials! I mean, wouldn't you? He had to . . . pursue greater *challenges*. Surpass boundaries. Roger Sperry moved on to human volunteers, as any of us would. . . ." He pauses.

"Sever the corpus callosum and you've got yourself sharper focus, fewer neuroses, anxiety completely cut out. Returning the brain to the way it ought to be, if you ask me." Mrs. McAnulty leans over. I see a blue electric flame hover in front of me. It smells of propane gas. "And the grades you're going to achieve now you're able to focus better?

Equally groundbreaking as everything our Rodgey achieved, we like to think." She squeezes my knuckles. "We're just *so* glad you're staying with us, child."

I'm in Las Vegas. Teleported. Arrived in front of slot machines with spinning wheels that deposit images in two columns in front of my eyes.

One column, on the left, is Mrs. McAnulty reaching into my hair with a gleaming steel butter knife, steadying herself with her left hand.

Second column, right—Mrs. McAnulty holding her gleaming steel butter knife, placing it back in a little kidney dish on her trolley.

The blue flame has disappeared.

"All done. Attaboy."

Mr. McAnulty squeezes my wrist. "You'll be a terrific son for us, Matthew. I've got a feeling about you."

"I'mnotta . . . not a son . . . I'm not MaMcAnulty I'm . . . pleazlemmegohome."

Mr. McAnulty is embarrassed. He chuckles once, looks at his toes, looks away. He reaches into my chest pocket and pulls out a small pale rectangle, wiping a spot of blood off it. "You look like Matthew Laurence McAnulty to me. Though our Matthew usually has a little bit more on top, of course." He reaches up to tousle my hair then yanks his hand away, sucking a little blob of crimson from his knuckle.

"I carn feel my hairses?"

"We'll fix that right up for you." Mrs. McAnulty pulls on fresh gloves. In her right hand she has a mug of steaming cocoa with marshmallows on top. In her left, she has a porcelain bowl, like a giant white tennis ball cut in half. Shaggy yellow hair hangs off it. My hair.

She flips the bowl over, reaches behind my head, positions it gently with two hands.

Mr. McAnulty fetches metal plates, screws, a stapler.

4.

I can't remember some parts. Nobody can remember coming into this world. You just wake up and there's your family and you have a life in front of you.

I study. I do my homework. I talk a bit fonny, but I'm a good boy. I put my clothes away when Mum-mum says I oughta. I eat my carrots. I can trace a circle with a compass, can you? My hand is seven inches long from top middle finger to bottom of my wrist. What about you?

I'm not allowed to go out and play with friends. Don't need 'em anyway. A boy's best friend is sposda be his mum and dad. This kid, though, this pale, grumpy-lookin' kid stops round at my house to pick up some clothes. He has cool puffy shoes and a cool tattoo on his neck. Looks kind-of familiar. I reckon I've seen someone just like him in a photo pinned to the fridge. As he carries out his clothes, he looks at me with my hovering spoonful of Fruit Loops, shakes his head, walks out. Mum-mum says he's going flatting. Needs a small microwave convection oven. A cordless phone. Some ethernet cable. A box of Mum-mum's groceries. Mum-mum talks to him on the porch. She leans in to give him a kiss and a hug, but she leaves a distance between their feet. Not too close. He ain't family.

My dad plays catch with me in the yard. He can hit a softball to the moon. Can your dad do that?

He rustles my hair like he's wiping a window clean. What about your dad?

I like my name. My name is Maffew. Maffew McAnulty.

I'm safe in my room, did you know? Mum-mum and Daddy trust me to study. Don't need a curfew, don't need to take medicals. Sometimes when night is falling my Daddy takes me down to the park and pushes me on the swing. We walk past the bulletin board outside the shop. There's a Missing Child ad for this kid Oliver who's about my age. The poster's whited-out, bleached by sun. Old news. I feel sorry for his mum. I don't fink the kid is comin' back.

THE STRANGE PAPER

1. A thin veil draped over reality

When I was 15, my father grounded me for two weeks.

If I wasn't at school or saxophone practice, I was supposed to be in my bedroom. And that was okay. I didn't ask for food or juice or candy or TV or computer time or my scooter. There were 64 pages in the latest edition of *The Strange Paper*, and I let my eyes crawl over every damn word.

God, I loved that magazine.

While rain dragged on the windows, I would hold *The Strange Paper* against the ceiling, blocking out the light, the wind, the weather, reading about suppressed science, conspiracies, cryptozoology, puzzles, pyramids, psychics, UFOs. My magazine of mysteries blocked out the door, blocked out my dad dissing my mum, blocked out my mum howling on the phone to her sister in Ireland. *The Strange Paper* blocked out my computer, my phone, my cat, casserole dinners. Hockey practice and collecting for the blind. Blocked out that girl Shiori Koizumi from Music Club with the weird tooth who always passed me notes in class.

I didn't want a girlfriend. I wanted to read the unexplained and feel a tingle of excitement.

The Strange Paper became the screen through which I saw my world. Its articles were radioactive, caustic, searing. Ideas lost in time and rediscovered. Horrors stretching across governments, wars, epochs. Behind a thin veil draped over reality lurked awful conspiracies, the stories taught me. Out in the world was wickedness barely disguised. Sinister plots to undermine our organized world. One cover story looked at the abduction of a girl in Kamagasaki by a malevolent Japanese spirit known as a yōkai. Elemental traces of the phantom were discovered by psychic researchers. Another issue evaluated photos apparently showing the Nottingham Forest Troll and the article determined it was likely to be either Yallery Brown or the Green Man of English folklore, or even Puck, the fawn-inspired legendary halfling. Behind every bafflement which appeared paranormal was verifiable science. Proof. *The Strange Paper* showed me the mystical world was real, and that the "real" world was bullshit.

As school ended, so did my faith in the superficial shopfront world. I read about sonar evidence for the Loch Ness Monster while my friends were pouring bottles over their faces at Joel Chad's Yearbook Party. I pressed my face against a story covering the Cottingley Fairies during the prizegiving for football, where they called my name twice before I zombied up to the podium and accepted my award, trying to read while I walked. I couldn't explain *The Strange Paper* to my friends or teachers. Partly they wouldn't have believed it; partly I wanted each revelation to be mine alone. I needed a conspiracy.

I graduated school and emerged from my exams resolving to enroll in whatever courses would demystify the world. I enrolled in Advanced Biology, Introduction to 20th Century History. Courses on psychology, geography, journalism, evolution. A paper called *Examining Claims of a New World Order.*

I ambushed each new copy as soon as the delivery truck pulled up at Baxter's Books on the second Wednesday of every month. I devoured my magazine on buses, roller-coasters, rides home from school, taxis, family vacations. I read it in a tuktuk in Thailand while my dad tried to convince Mum to love him again. I read it in a toilet stall at Changi Airport where I could pull my face mask down and breathe without being watched. 17, 18, 19, even when my parents were groaning about me rolling out of bed at lunchtime and how I oughta get my own place, I was learning about what really mattered in this world. Hoovering up information from *The Strange Paper*'s print pages and website, eyes darting left and right. Typing, tracing, drinking pages of text and video and parsing scores of comments. I slouched on my computer chair, lay on my back with my phone above my eyes, hanging upside down off my parents' couch in the living room, hair scraping the carpet, pouring content inside me. *The Strange Paper* Issue #417 was a scoop about a sighting of Wuduwosa, the Sasquatch of Suffolk. Issue #390 looked at the Mandela Effect causing the public to mis-remember CIA cover-ups. Issue #248 discussed how the cure for cancer, discovered in a Jordanian laboratory, was destroyed thanks to Israeli-US-Soviet Cold War machinations.

While my friends had moved on to university and beer pong and road trips and skydiving, I was reading the letters to the editor, the contents, the legalese, the briefs, the advertisements, every inch of *The Strange Paper*. Every conspiracy I read about, I frantically Googled for extra info once the story ended. I obsessed over the editorials, too, pressing my nose against the editor's ever-changing photo, always different each time I grabbed my brown paper-bagged copy from Baxter's.

See, there was a pledge made by *The Strange Paper* in each editorial: *Everything published here was reported to us as true.* And that promise had a man standing behind it: editor Maxwell Winkle.

The only thing constant in Maxwell's photos was that he was white, aged about 50, and he had a punchable, sticky-outy chin and a boyish grinning face like Boris Johnson. Some months he had fuzzy yellow muttonchop sideburns. Some months he was clean-shaven. There was a summer where he wore dark-purple smoked glasses and his Dennis the Menace-ishly blond hair was a tight ponytail. One issue, there was a photo of him at the marble tomb of Charles Fort, the chronicler of Fortean phenomena and the first Westerner to begin systematically compiling reports of the unexplained. Issue #318 had Maxwell diligently scraping soot from the wall of a supposed gas chamber at Auschwitz, which actually turned out to be a facility NASA used to dispose of extraterrestrials. Issue #333 saw Maxwell with a measuring tape tracing the pentagram carved into the plaza outside the presidential palace in Astana, Kazakhstan, headquarters of the Zionist Occupational Government. Each photo usually showed half a face and one ear. Always his head was tilted towards some distant calling.

My old friends fell out of my peripheral vision and the only person left who made the effort to ring me at my parents' place was Shiori, the girl with the dorky tooth. She'd talk a little about the restaurant she helped her parents run and the battles with the council's food department and Trip Advisor and fussy tourists. She'd try and frame questions about *The Strange Paper*—which I'd sent her several copies of—though she was usually behind in her updates, still thinking that mammoths were extinct, for example (audio recordings from near Lake Baikal had proven their existence). Still, I appreciated her trying to match my interest, and when I'd get absorbed in tab after tab of Wikipedia and Reddit and Culture Wars, and a bowl of soup proffered under my nose would snap me out of my trance, it was always Shiori holding the bowl.

I worked at the community pool as a lifeguard over summer, reading aloft on my high chair, trying to keep the sun off my flabby freckled chicken-skin. Then I got fired because a child swallowed too much water while I was engrossed in an article, and plus I wouldn't keep my Covid face mask on. The article was about fluoridated water, which it turns out is tons worse for you than drowning, so one life was actually saved that day – mine. I stepped down anyway and wondered where I would go now. I couldn't do life-saving, couldn't do university.

I read my *Strange Paper* on my handlebars as I cycled back to my dorm room. I read while I applied for unemployment relief on the government website. I arrived at my 20th birthday living in my own box with a slanted ceiling under the stairs in my dormitory hall. I was merely visiting my parents' place for Sunday roasts by this point. Shiori was driving me everywhere and doing my laundry, and when my parents asked Shiori if she was "keeping that man of yours in line," I had to sigh and concede she'd become a girlfriend. Accepting Shiori as a paramour meant it looked like I was doing something about my depression so my parents would stop sending me to see a specialist. Urgh.

Shiori was a tolerant girl, though. Lively and humorous and affectionate. Warm in the bed, like a hot water bottle. Plus it felt good to explain stories to her and watch her nod. None of *The Strange Paper* articles I read her resulted in disbelief. She took long, deep nods, absorbing everything without judgement.

On my birthday, after a few begrudging kisses and hugs turned to full-on sex, Shiori reached under my crumbly mattress and fished out a white envelope as the locomotives in our chests slowed to a stop.

Within, a birthday card.

"You're going, I've arranged it," Shiori announced, her chubby forearm wiping sweat from her brow with a handful of bedsheet. "This Thursday, I sent him an email. To meet that man you're always going on about. Manuel?"

"Maxwell . . . wait, what?!"

Within the card, a ticket to the remotest part of Auckland. The windblown peninsula of Beachlands, where the city tumbled into the expanse. An Uber voucher, too, with directions written on it for the driver.

589a Beachlands Drive. A modest converted garage office, her Google Street View printout showed. A building larger than a shed, smaller than a strip mall.

The office of *The Strange Paper*.

2. Let's talk about why you're here

Maxwell Winkle was standing over his computer desk, his bum out of his chair, growling at one of four monitors. I interrupted his trance, and he looked up from his screen at the jangling doorbell. Hot, alarmed, wild, darting eyes. He'd just shaken a tablet from a small brown pharmacy bottle, and he put it in his lips and sucked it down with a swallow of Heineken.

"Enter." There was a twang in that first word. Maxwell Winkle was American, it seemed. Exotic. Brought in from outside. He was like a giant boy, hair so white-yellow it was almost silver, and a wide, smiling face, all cheeks. He wore a black leather jacket with a Led Zeppelin t-shirt and blue jeans. Snakeskin boots on his feet.

"Who sent you?"

"I'm—I'm just—I'm nobody, I—"

"Relax, son, relax. I'm trained in krav maga—top level martial arts, reserved for Israel's most elite soldiers. Nobody's whacking out this guy."

I reached across to shake his hand. He left me hovering.

"You been jabbed? Hope not. Better not be bringing that vaccine shmaxine shit in here."

"Like, coronavirus-jabbed? Nah, people my age, I don't think we have to um, mandatorily, um, sorry, not sure if mandatorily's even a word... ."

"Fucked if I know. Never been great with spelling. That's what's interns are for. And you know what, Mister Potential Intern: ain't no such things as coincidences in this world."

"I just love reading your stuff and, like, m-my girlfriend, she arranged for me to come and—"

Maxwell held a *Ssshhh* finger up, then removed it. "You'd better not be reporting back to anyone."

He typed a few letters, thought deeply, deleted something, tucked his t-shirt into his jeans.

"My son was a spy," he went. "Ex-wife used him for leverage. Got him to snitch on me, report back to her leech-of-a-lawyer. Haven't seen the boy in fourteen fuckin' . . . Anyway: Let's talk about why you're here."

Maxwell put all his work on hold for me that afternoon. I sat in a leather chair, mesmerized, picking at a thread, too enraptured to concentrate on the hot chocolate with marshmallows he placed on the coffee table for me. My mouth hung open so long it went dry. I drank my tenth-ever beer that afternoon while Maxwell told me the history of the magazine and its spinoff DVDs and YouTube channel and internet radio station and podcast. His dad and him had taken over *The Strange Paper* after the old man joined INFO, the International Fortean Organization in 1979. Maxwell was in the United States at the time, at a university in the eastern realms of Oregon, 'top of the river' he called it, chuckling as he recalled him and his mates pouring two industrial barrels of LSD into the Columbia River water station to change the mindsets of the concreteheads downstream. "Can't say I didn't drink a fair bit of it myself, woo-whee!" Maxwell told me, chuckling and patting the round belly under his black t-shirt. "One only sees things clearly after a year on acid. We woke a lot of people up that day, yessiree."

He finished his beer and shook another pill out of his bottle as he continued to reminisce, placing his right cowboy boot then the left on the table, tilting back. "Best not discussed where the feds can listen in. Long story short: I've taken her over from the old man, financed her, turned her around. I've never had an assistant that's lasted more than a week, but if you want to try work for me, kid, shit—here's a start." Maxwell biffed at me *The Strange Papers Volume One 1980-1989*—a thick hunk of fluffy newsprint paper the size of a phone book. It fell open at a story about the unexplained deaths of those skiers in the Dyatlov Pass incident.

He took his feet down off the desk. "Bring it with you. We can talk internship on the road. We've got a meeting to get to. Get in the car."

3. They Wear Our Skin

We passed gas stations and billboards and siloes and cornfields and brown rivers and green peaks. Maxwell drank Monster Energy as he drove, and popped at least four different kinds of pills, crushing one type of pink gel cap into powder and rubbing it into his gums. We passed caravans full of children staring out the windows, raving as we raced them. We overtook on bends. We undertook cars. He blazed past petrol stations. Passing a sign for Rotorua on the 'Taniwha Expressway' got Maxwell ranting about crytids and covered-up species and lost tribes like the Anasazi and he pointed out the Illuminati symbolism of the street names in the new subdivisions we passed in Te Kauwhata and Pokeno. Maxwell would talk for thirty seconds straight, take his eyes off the highway, gaze at me then re-focus just as he was drifting off the road. Maxwell pressed his Mustang to drive over 200 kays an hour. The government's little speed camera surveillance system couldn't photograph vehicles driving faster than 199, Maxwell explained.

It was hard for me to read back issues of *The Strange Paper* with Maxwell driving so crazy, but I opened and closed the compilation in a few places and got the gist of the magazine's history. He used to work under his dad, then the dad dropped away something like 2002. There was a whole series of interns, I think, but no record of them, cause unless Maxwell cited the original writer of whichever piece he published, "by Maxwell Winkle" was the only byline.

I worked out that interns had to've done a shitload of work for him, though, cause Maxwell reviewed a different drug every month on page 44, and wrote the drug stuff himself, and you could see how fucked-up his English was without a proofreader. I wondered how long it'd been since the last intern and what had happened to them.

After five hours we squealed through Rotorua, then Taupo, then 30 minutes later coasted into the gravel parking lot of the Turangi Baptist Church and spurted to a stop.

"I thought we were heading to Hamilton for this thing?"

"So did the NSA, son. That's why we don't go blabbing about all of our plans. Write that down."

It was dusk when we got out and walked across the gravel of the church parking lot. Inside we could see a circle of old people listening to somebody leading a meeting.

Welcome to SITU, Maxwell said. "The Society for the Investigation of the Unexplained. They're not exactly friends. Currently."

Maxwell skipped up the wheelchair ramp, pulled the door open and walked right into the middle of the meeting.

"Ladies," he grinned, flashing a smile yellowed from cigarettes and coffee. An old Indian guy with a cane and thick glasses was midway through delivering a presentation, but a dozen old ladies and men with thinning hair turned to see the arrival.

Maxwell was important among these people.

They rose to greet him, to touch his shoulder, to press their books into his chest and ask his thoughts. Maxwell was a celebrity, it turned out, and I was his shadow.

"Nice of you to show," sneered a purple-haired hippy woman with a jade locket and a rainbow vest and a name tag saying *Vivian Thonger-President*. Her Covid face mask had a big Q on it. "We've actually already commenced."

Maxwell snorted, shook a few hands, exchanged a few updates, and when, after a couple of minutes, the presenter tutted, he sat down and swiveled around to face the front and let him continue. The presentation turned out to be about ancient Celtic fairy people. Called Patupaiarehe, or Turehu, they hide in bushes, according to the presentation, sneaking out to bewitch trampers and infiltrate the gene pool. As the presenter was talking about fighting the government to get it to release Official Information Act reports about loggers on Crown forestry blocks encountering the fairy people, and the coverup thereof, Maxwell leaned over and whispered a correction.

"Infiltration yes, forest-fairies no." His eyes locked with mine. "Organized infection of the human race with alien DNA through mandatory inoculation. Not bloody Tinkerbell. Do you disagree?"

"No sir," I whispered.

"Then say you fucking agree."

"Honest, Maxwell, I agree."

He nodded deeply. "It's all about infiltration, that's what's going on. They invade the gene pool, you know. Johnny Government squirts 'em inside you, yesiree, that's what you're getting when you think you're getting a so-called Covid so-called remedy. Big old dose of deoxyribonucleic acid from the inhabitants of the Draco constellation, son. They wear our skin, y'know. Look just like us. This so-called woman here, Vivian? Case in point."

The hippy woman wearing rainbow took control as the elderly Indian man bowed and went to leave. Her snarl showed her teeth.

"MAXWELL. Have something to add, do you?"

"Matter of fact I do, *Mizzz* Thonger." He got out of his creaking folding chair, walked around the crowd and in front of the projector screen and took over the podium. A big man in a tiny church prefab, the room seemed to shrink around Maxwell. "Every incident this old fart's just mentioned comes back to forced inoculation on a scale not seen since Nazi Germany, my friends. So-called immunization with so-called vaccines. Now, you're an intelligent lot. Deep down you know this already. I'm Maxwell Winkle, folks, and for those of you who haven't heard of me, I'm the publisher of *The Strange Paper*, okay, and you need to know I stand opposed against bullshit, and I'm calling bullshit on your presentation, sir."

The Indian presenter-guy put his hand on his chest, hurt and shocked. He found a gap beside the Vivian-lady and dropped out of view.

Maxwell looked hard into the eyes of every person in the room then crossed the floor, studied the parking lot, eyes thinning, and pulled the blinds shut.

"I'd like to posit a theory to unite everything discussed tonight. And I'm going to repeat this all at Armageddon sometime soon. We're talkin' *THE* biggest conference in the country. I know many of you'll be there and I thank you in advance. Ready, are you, I hope? Vivian—Madame Thonger? Patricia? Lionel's been waiting for it. Jessica, I know you have, too. Mrs. Flax, I can tell you're ready and waiting. Here we go."

What Maxwell revealed that night in the church lounge changed everything. Maxwell linked Madame Blavatsky's Secret Doctrine with dragon-men with Lemuria with the ascension of Vladimir Putin and the so-called Queen Elizabeth Windsor. Take the skin off her face and we would see the lizard underneath, he promised. The Illuminati-slash-Lizard People would, of course, frame any whistleblowers as unhinged; they'd campaign to withdraw advertising from *The Strange Paper* were any of this to be printed, oh yes, predictably so—but every dismissal of the Lizard People simply proved his case.

Maxwell leaned down over the podium.

"The threat is real. We need to begin opening the books to*night*."

The Indian presenter-man exchanged a joke with the Vivian hippy woman, and they giggled. He put his hand up and asked a mock question.

"Not enough people opening your books, I take it, Mr. Winkle?"

"I'LL OPEN YOUR FUCKING HEAD, PAL. SEE IF YOU'RE ONE OF THEM."

Maxwell was about to cross the room and punch the hippy lady when a woman rushed up and thrust an album of photos at him. Distracted, Maxwell let her pull him to the rear of the room while he glanced grumpily over his shoulder.

"Iiiii believe we can conclude the evening on that exciting note!" Vivian announced, laughing, brushing her purple hair out of her face and pulling her Q mask down. "Let's have a bite, shall we?"

Somebody wheeled out a trolley of biscuits and cake, tea, and wine with a sloshing, steaming urn and twenty cups and mugs. Everybody took their Covid masks off. Some people put them in the rubbish bin.

I endured a cup of tea poured slowly out of a huge teapot, with wood-hard gingernut biscuits. People asked me what it was like to have the privilege of working with Maxwell. I blushed and reported what I could. Somebody opened a bottle of red wine and put a glass in my fingers. I stood in a circle and got drunk with people who'd written their theses on astrology and spontaneous human combustion and the clock crawled. They pressed me for gossip and I couldn't find a reason to say No. The circle sucked up my anecdotes about Maxwell, whom I'd only known for, well, a matter of days. Just a single day, really, if you added up the hours. The only person who wasn't enthralled was the smug hippy Vivian lady, who appeared to have agreed to walk down towards the river for a private conversation with Maxwell, pulling up her Q mask as if to keep Maxwell out of her mouth.

Just before he walked out with her, Maxwell shoved a wineglass at me with something fizzing in it. It looked like a vitamin. "We'll catch up in a bit. Drink this, for now."

"I will, I promise, sir."

He clawed the back of my head, pulling my ear down beside his gritted teeth. "Drink. It. *Now.*"

I tossed it back, belched, apologized, continued the conversation without my boss in the room until the ceiling swooned and I asked to lie down in the coat room and—.

*

I awoke inside Maxwell's cozy Mustang, thrown against the doors with each twist and turn. Little glowing blue lights on the dashboard, while outside everything was black as a mine. The headlights burned through the night. The time had to be, God, 1 a.m.? 2? I'd gotten drunk and passed out after, well . . . I only remembered one wine, but it felt like I'd drunk ten. My bones ached. My mouth tasted like sherbet.

I asked Maxwell what had happened with that Vivian chick while I was asleep.

He sped up to 180, took his eyes off the road and stared at me hard.

Maxwell was now wearing brown leather driving gloves and crushing the steering wheel.

"If I told you, I'd have to kill you."

"DUDE. SERIOUSLY. THE CORNER. PLEASE SLOW DOWN."

"So, you withdraw your question?"

"Okay, okay okay, forget it, pleasejus. I don't wanna die."

Burger King in Taupo, 24-hour KFC in Rotorua, 3 a.m. coffee in Hamilton, breakfast platter at dawn in Auckland. We said nothing to one another. The question hung around us like body odor.

The silence was so awkward, I was relieved when he dropped me at Shiori's flat. I stood outside the driver window on the street while the Mustang murmured. There were some strands drifting in the breeze at the back of the Mustang, like a fringe or tail hanging off the back. Like he'd stuck purple streamers on the back of his car, or someone's purple Halloween witch wig was caught in the trunk.

"Diiiiid things go okay with that Vivian lady?"

"You can stop thinking of it as "Vivian," son. That was never its real name."

Shiori waddled onto the doorstep, hugging the flaps of her dressing gown, smiling at me.

Maxwell tossed his gloves out the window into the gutter, u-turned and sped away.

4. Uncover everything covered

As head writer, my job was to bring Maxwell's Unifying Theory into every story that we paid for or copied or stole or borrowed. He had this kinda dyslexia thing and his Unifying Theory thoughts kept pouring out like when you pull endless tissues out of a Kleenex box. He dictated a lot, and on top of ghostwriting and spellchecking, half the time my job was to find primary sources to prove what he was saying. We devoted a double-page spread to the Unifying Theory, then four pages, then a centerfold which readers could lift out and Blu-tack to their walls. If Maxwell didn't stop getting himself excited, the Theory would take over every damn page. Maxwell's ideas were unstoppable, though.

We began the work at 9 a.m. on a Tuesday, aiming to work "late," finishing around 6 p.m. Instead, we worked 'til 7, then got curry delivered, ate 'til 7.30, promised to wrap up at 8 p.m., then found ourselves at 2 a.m. slurping Monster Energy and espresso while Maxwell rattled the back of my seat and dictated. It was hot and pressured in his office, and the windows were black and close. Every corner I looked, Maxwell was there, ranting, shaking books, cutting things out of the newspaper. He'd had assistants in the past, but they hadn't kept up, so he was used to calling the shots over layout, copy editing, advert placement, colors, covers, social media, and managing subscriptions. He paced, snooped, and sampled his medicine, some colorless vinegary concoction apparently called GHB or Fantasy that he reserved a space in the magazine to review for his monthly drugs bit.

Maxwell forced a squirt of the stuff in my mouth, lifted my hands, put my fingers on the keyboard and said, "Write this down. You ready?"

He busted out a rant about Putin's Russia acting as a bulwark against the Reptoids from Draco and proof that the Russian sleep experiment had ended with Draco infiltrators outing themselves. He talked about how the Dracos polluted everyone close to him – his old man, his interns, his ex-wife's brain. He asked me if the GHB was working or not and said Gamma 4-Hydroxybutyric Acid originated as an approved therapy for alcoholism in Italy because it puts people into a 24-hour sleep so they miss opportunities to drink. GHB is the antidote that clears your mind, so you see the real world, Maxwell said, then positioned me in front of my computer monitor.

"Needs more, this series does," he said. "Readers want it linked better, too. We need to work on your segues, your continuity. Unless you're intentionally handing in sub-par work. Is that what you're up to?"

"No, man."

"You selling this story to anyone else? Eh, dipshit?" He slapped my right ear. "*Nexus? Unexplained?* Answer me, you little trickster."

"No sir."

He didn't breathe for 30 seconds, 40. His eyes tunneled through mine, ate a hole in my head, and emerged out the other side. "Righty-o," he concluded, grinning ear to ear. "On with the job, shall we?"

We used InDesign to expand our eight-page special on the Unifying Theory to 16 pages, then gave it half the magazine, plus an insert letting readers know to watch out for Maxwell's ex-wife. We put a big profile photo of her and description of where she worked, her measurements, and her schedule and routines. Birds were waking up by now. An orange glow diluted the dark-blue sky. Maxwell brought me an espresso with something bubbling on the surface, some kind of sugar, presumably. He pressed the cup against my lips and rubbed my throat. "Drink, drink, drink. Attaboy."

I tasted that Fantasy crap on my tonsils, looked into the bottom of my empty espresso cup, then the lights went out.

5. A War Is Coming

We hit the Information Liberation Expo in Christchurch. We did Melbourne's Vax Attacks alternative health expo. We drove and flew and beamed in to conferences in Perth, Sydney, Kuala Lumpur, Dunedin, Palmerston North. We joined conferences led by semiotics researchers, 5G experts, anti-genetic modification activists. People with proof that vaccines give kids autism. People with proof of a pre-biblical flood in the year 8,000 BCE. Every time we traveled and toured, we got more and more audience, and Maxwell got more restless, more frantic and irritable, as if he was running out of time and he had to force the end.

I didn't pester Maxwell for an apology for sharing his medicine with me without my consent. I knew his intentions were noble, and he was trying to cool me down from being overworked and, uh, not exactly paid apart from being allowed to sleep and take showers at the office and eat pizza and glug Monster Energy. When he was in a good mood, he would blurt out unexpected compliments on my writing and buy me burgers and books and brunchtime shots of Absinthe and bottles of beer, and he tousled my hair, pinched my cheeks, and that was compensation enough for him making me take mandatory naps with a sip of Fantasy. On the balance of things, it was a privilege to be doing my dream job. To be living under his wing.

Our Unifying Theory scoops pushed readership up on every level. Reptilian saboteurs from the Draco constellation were behind most of the world's setbacks and advancements, our stories revealed. It made so much sense that there had to be a force leaning on not-altogether-stupid governments around the world, pressuring them to push this vaccination scam. *The Strange Paper* subscriptions hit 2000 a month; online readership passed 400,000, then 500,000, then surged up to the 750,000 mark. I achieved full-time status, with a hundred bucks a week all of my own, though it wasn't about the work. I would've written for *The Strange Paper* for nothing. I got up at 7 a.m. each day and worked according to his whims—writing reviews, spell-checking, processing adverts, replying to queries. Helping with accounts, subscriptions. Pasting stamps onto envelopes. He was half-boss, half-father, Maxwell was. Fun, exciting, always random, spontaneous. Better than my real dad.

I worked mornings, evenings, late nights. It made sense to take a break from Shiori and move into his garage and be with him all the time.

We managed to prove a link between freak hailstorms in Haiti and crop circles in Florida and the Bosnian Pyramids at Visoko, which bore a map of the Alpha Draconis star system whose population had emigrated to earth 3000 years ago.

We connected more and more dots with every issue. We covered the Dracos' injection into royal bloodlines—the Merovingians, the Bushes, the Rothschilds, the Windsors – based on actual DNA analysis of relatives who swore they'd witnessed their family getting stuck with needles over the years. I wrote an exclusive revealing the precise date Fidel Castro was replaced with a lizard as part of the New World Order. We published an exclusive showing that Iraq was invaded in 2003 because Saddam was poised to hold a press conference denouncing the Dracos. I had an expert from INWOS, the Institute of New World Order Studies, contribute exquisite diagrams showing the chain of transfer during which Draco DNA is injected into human children during Covid vaccination and how autism naturally results from our immune system's pushback against the alien DNA. Atop a surge in subscriptions, we followed it with commentary from an expert who proved that Draco DNA was to be found in the crack cocaine the CIA pushed on black communities during 1986.

People from *Natural Health* magazine and *Nexus* and *Unexplained* came to knock meekly at the door and pay homage to Maxwell in his office while he cracked beers and leaned back in his leather jacket and jeans and put those cowboy boots up high on his desk. Occasionally Maxwell went and spread the Unifying Theory overseas, too. He wouldn't always say where he was going, but when I packed his bags, he would have me add a ski mask or swimming trunks, as if he were going somewhere snowy or somewhere tropical, plus I noticed spikes in subscriptions from Russia, from the UK, from Sweden, South Korea, the Philippines. Orders of t-shirts and coffee mugs. There were overnight conferences, too, on Microsoft Teams and Zoom and Google Hangouts. I was shut out of some of those. Door closed.

I envied these people and their private time with the sage, the guru, the master. Meanwhile my so-called peers sent me invitations to their weddings. Talked about me in a high school reunion group on Facebook. Showed off the babies they were squirting into the world.

Somebody asked if they'd seen me lately, caught up with me.

Nah, the bro's an anti-vaxxer now, they said. He drank the Kool-Aid big time.

They posted a photo, too. Me standing on the corner of the Auckland War Memorial Museum steps, gazing admiringly at Maxwell commanding the megaphone in this epic Down With Lockdown rally last month. Me and Maxy amongst 20,000 protestors who'd had enough

I had no place amongst the high school homogenized sheeple. I deleted my Facebook. If people wanted to reach me, they could go through Shiori. I was dedicated solely to investigative journalism now. The lonely, sacrificial life of a Samurai. I came off Prozac at the same time as Maxwell. He was supposed to be on these mood stabilizers called Depakene for bipolar people, but they weren't worth the trouble. We couldn't have Pharma controlling our thoughts anymore. We wouldn't let them lower the guard of army veterans or invalids or even dogs and cats, so I guarded the door of the garage, parading with one of Maxwell's 7mm Remington rifles each night while he conducted research on the best ways to check how bad the problem on infiltration had got. Maxwell had caught this affectionate tom cat that was using the cat flap way too often. He tranquilized the feline and looked under its skin. He determined it was a well-grafted fake, extremely convincing and lifelike. It's not until you fully remove the epidermis that you can spot the real from the fake, he explained.

Maxwell stood with me outside the garage. He had a stain on his forehead and scratches on his nose and hands that he was dabbing with a handkerchief.

"Did you, um, find more than one way to skin a cat?" I asked, cringing.

"This is nothing to joke about, son," he told me. "A war's coming. We have to get inside the invaders. Peel 'til we see the real." He lit a cigarette and snorted at me. "You need to undertake some actual skinning. Prove you can stand up for this team. I have to know you're loyal."

"I am loyal, Maxwell. Honest."

"So you say. Then you'll need this."

He pressed a scalpel into my hand and pulled me inside the garage to the work bench. A Labrador was strapped down with bungee cords and electrical cable. It looked up as I approached, stuck its tongue out and wheezed hopefully, its neck tag tinkling.

"It's just practice, it's not Lassie here we're concerned about, really," Maxwell said. "Now glove up."

6. *Conspiracy's evrywhr. Help.*

Maxwell veered hard right. An oncoming truck honked. We were one foot away from getting totaled when he settled in front of the motel and yanked the hand brake up.

"You and me need to talk."

"Fuck, Max! Can you just drive normal? That was close!"

"Too close for anyone to have followed us." He snorted, hopped out of the car. "Guess you've never shaken a spy off your tail before, greenhorn."

The motel was three stories tall, a tablet of white-painted concrete rising out of a tiny parking lot. It had Christmas lights wrapped around its balcony, a cigarette machine, and bags of garbage around the drain. Disgusting as the motel was, it was nicer than the parking lot, which had protestors in it, sleeping wrapped up in their flags and banners and tents, plus a dumpster dribbling waste grease from a fried chicken joint. And what really mattered was it was straight over the road from the stadium where, tomorrow, the big event began.

We were in town for Maxwell's presentation at Armageddon Wellington, the pop culture convention where more and more presentations from the intellectual dark web were appearing each year. We'd bartered for a low-paying advertising deal, running a mixed bag of print, digital, and social adverts for Armageddon in return for them letting Maxwell deliver his big Unifying Theory lecture at the expo. This was the capital, and people had been doing sit-ins on the lawn of parliament against the Prime Minister's mandatory vaccines. Historical stuff was happening. Maxwell Winkle had to be at the centre of it.

We checked into the motel, got our keys and were about to enter our room when Maxwell put some hard fingers on my chest.

"Massive day tomorrow," he said. "Pretty major revelations in my lecture. You're aware it's copyrighted intellectual property?"

"Um . . . I guess."

He slammed me against the wall and scrunched my collar. There were tiny white bubbles on his angry lips. "TELL ME HOW YOU FOUND OUT ABOUT ME."

"I saw *The Strange P-Paper* at this, this, um, this bookstore? When I was a kid?'

"Name the shop."

"Buh-buh-Baxter's. Baxter's Books?"

His eyes flicked from left to right and back again, like blowflies inside his eye sockets. "He's one of them. Baxter. The bookshop bastard. A shifter. A deep-fake."

The darting eyes settled on me. Finally, I said, "I agree, sir. Totally. Can we g-go in our room now?"

Soon as we sealed the motel door, Maxwell turned the TV volume on as high as it would go and checked under the beds for listening devices. I texted Shiori.

Maxwell's losing it, I wrote. *He's seeing conspiracys evrywhr. Help.*

While Maxwell was running a loud shower, Shiori responded sarcastically, *He knows da truth lol.*

One of us is a shifter?

Ur wordz not mine;0)

"Talking to your handler, son?"

Maxwell was standing over me, blocking the light. A phantom of steam rose off him. He had a towel around his hips and his belly was bulging over it like pizza dough.

"Nothing." I tucked my phone under my thigh. "Just messaging."

"Who?"

"Just my friend. . . ."

"You don't have any friends." He waddled to the blinds and twisted them to block the light out. "They can read remotely, you know. I can read, too. I can read minds. And I can tell you're full of shit. Show me your phone."

I gave up my cellphone. Maxwell ruminated over my messages to Shiori. I'd told Shiori that Maxwell was bombarding me with text messages constantly. I'd said Maxwell was pressuring me to take a helicopter up to study contrails and I didn't like it. I'd confessed I spent Christmas with him dipping a ladle into Auckland's water supply to get samples we'd send away to test for extraterrestrial DNA.

"You can have this back when I trust you," Maxwell decided, frowning, holding the phone out like it was infected. "She's not who you think she is."

"Are you mad at me, sir?"

He looked like he wanted to reach out and squeeze my hand. Then he shook his head in disappointment.

"I care about you, son. That's all."

He went back to the bathroom, slammed the door.

7. The Horror Underneath

Armageddon was erupting, boiling over, buzzing, humming. Outside, police with hands linked like cookie cutter gingerbread men were trying to maintain a human rope to keep Down With Lockdown protestors from crashing the conference. Inside was only room for elbows and hips and everyone was battling to be heard through their facemasks, mouths muffled with cotton. Balloons everywhere, speakers, coffee grinders, people selling comics and posters at tables, artists holding Sharpie pens signing chests and foreheads, VR helmets, bodybuilding supplements, vapes. Banners with giant portraits of The Witcher and Jon Snow and Black Widow. A life-size Millennium Falcon, big as a blimp, blocking out the skylight. I passed kids from high school dressed up, safe in young good-looking packs, joyous, chattering, tight skin, eyes stretched into squints from laughing. They'd taken buses and trains to dressed in furry Pikachu costumes. They were Spock and Pacman and Goku and Gandalf and Pepe the Frog and Tyrion. People were laughing and calling and holding hands. Balloons, confetti. Everyone having an ecstatic time, and here I was, struggling to haul a trolley of boxes across 500 meters of carpet to the Hilltop Room. Ground Zero for Maxwell's Big Reveal.

The room was as small as my parents' lounge, just about. A fraction bigger. The Hilltop Room—flat, windowless—didn't have a stage, just a sad skinny black microphone plugged into an amplifier.

"This'll be us," Maxwell concluded, unboxing his laptop. He stroked the walls and put an ear against the plaster.

"Can I go see the Bitcoin thing?"

"Shut the fuck up. You're here to work." His ear was interested in the heat pump remote control. He rubbed it against his face then tapped it twice, then four times, hoping to find a listening device. "If you want to be known as disloyal, go ahead and be disloyal. That's on you. They're doing jabs in the lobby, I heard. Go get yourself a nice juicy vaccine."

I kept my mouth closed and helped him set up.

We had a single pull-up banner with a picture of our Real Independence Day special edition, and that was our only visual aid, as far as I knew. Apart from a laptop, Maxwell's presentation was mostly in his head.

An hour before he was due to go on, a producer girl, with sexy hipster glasses and freckles, informed us there was a special appearance by The Dora the Explorer Experience at the same time. We'd lose most of our crowd to a child with a monkey.

"Ummmm, sorry to be a pain but one last thing – d'you guys reckon you could put your masks on?"

Maxwell made a fist and thumped the wall. He towered over the producer girl, pushing her out with his belly.

"Tonight'll be the last night we ever hear about masks, honey. Mark my words. Better get onside today. Word of warning."

The girl disappeared. Maxwell took his vial of some chemical from his pocket, jammed it under his nose, snorted, turned, and pointed his finger at me.

"Go. Get me. A fucking audience. NOW."

I pulled the sleeves of a couple of cheerleaders in Spandex. I bailed a trio of Hobbits up against walls. One fat nerd dressed as Wonder Woman squirmed through my handshake. I gave him twenty bucks to promise he would scrape some people together to attend. All my week's pay was used up bribing people to join, but finally I had a make-shift audience.

The presentation started off in front of thirty people in costumes and black t-shirts, people who rotated in and out, some tugged away by their friends to watch the Dora puppets, others who needed to play *Magic: The Gathering* or *Pokémon Go*. Maxwell began reading from a printed script before sliding it to the floor.

"Ladies and gentleman, EVERYTHING out there, the shiny lights, the Star Trek hacks, the phoneys from Hollywood: they're all distractions. After this here today, you'll see everything for what it really is." He searched the distance with his eyes. "Scratch the surface of this world. Beneath, you will find those waiting to harm us. Conspiring. Plotting. Organizing." His eyes roamed the room, settling on a fat man with a ginger beard wearing a suit jacket, a pair of Lolitas, a news photographer who he pointed his finger directly at as he pulled out his cellphone with a free hand.

"Eyes front. This is important."

Maxwell jabbed a button on his phone and his laptop made the projector burst into life. The image was a big square of blue with the Samsung logo which quickly became white, then a loading icon, then an image of pure horror.

Behind him, on the wall, blown up to nine square meters, were the freckled arms and legs and shoulders of a woman duct taped to a chair. Everybody in the room held their breath as Maxwell scrolled through a sequence of pictures. The first photo showed a hooded man approaching the tied-down woman with something small and shiny in his hand. The second photo, lines drawn professionally on her skin with a marker, as if she were about to get plastic surgery.

The third photo made the room roar.

First, we saw the hooded man dragging a scalpel from the woman's temple down to her jaw. As he peeled her skull like an orange, we could see brick-colored muscle and a hint of white eyeball ringed with blue vein.

"HOW DID YOU GET THOSE PHOTOS?" demanded the bearded man, "WHAT THE FUCK HAVE YOU DONE?"

He tore his *Strange Paper* in half and slammed the pieces on the floor.

"Intern: lock the door."

Most of the herd surged out before I managed to lock the room. With half a dozen people left, Maxwell flipped to the last few photos, nodding. The five who remained took it all seriously. They sat on their butts like kindergarteners. Eyes front. Ears keened. Dedicated, hypnotized people who looked like they would go out and tell their contacts across the world to do whatever Maxwell said.

"This is it, my friends. Underneath those we least suspect: Definitive proof they've infiltrated the human race. You see it, don't you? Tell me you're seeing it."

Woman's body sitting at the head of the table, topless, arms the color of timber, navel, creases of belly-fat, slumbering old breasts with streaks of stretched fat, strands of purple hair on the body's shoulders. Above her collar, where a bloody ooze was trickling through her cleavage, the pink-splashed lightbulb of her skull was covered in liver-brown flesh with accents of salmon and blue and red. In her former face, black holes where her eyes had been before Vivian had been skinned.

8. Ready for the end

Traffic was tense and frightening. Maxwell drove insanely close to the far lane. Protestors were hurling bottles, marching across the blacktop, stopping cars, burning banners, chanting. The entire city honked at him. He turned the stereo up so loud it smashed my eardrums. He made me shake a little foil of white powder into a cartridge in his vape and he sucked it and said, "MMMMMM, them's good apples" and swerved and veered. He ordered two drive-thru meals in an hour. He sniffed and snorted and smoked and punched my knee whenever I didn't respond to his rants quick enough.

We were high on Armageddon. Excited by the big announcement. The end. High like magicians, like circus performers who'd revealed something extraordinary everyone would be telling their friends about.

We veered into the motel so hard and fast I was sure Maxwell was about to collide with the building. The brakes stopped with a squirt of stinking rubber. Maxwell got out of the car so fast he left his door open, as well as the front door of our unit. I tidied the car and closed the door after him.

"Peeling the layers, like an onion, thasright," he ranted, pacing our motel unit. "So, are you an onion, yeah? Or a spinach? Lettuce?"

I sat on my single bed, exhausted, embarrassed, disgraced.

"Or possibly a pod-person. Speak up, Planty Boy. Because you're definitely a plant. Fucking infiltrator, fucking ratboy snitch, fucking undercov—"

"Dude, seriously, you're starting to freak—"

"A mole. Designed to invade and undermine *The Strange Paper*. Like that little Yoko Ono of yours. D'you know she was a plant from none other than Mossad? Designed to have the Beatles change the outcome of the 1966 election, yeah? Didn't know that, did you? But your little geisha girlfriend knew it. She told me the whoooole lot."

I tossed my hands and shoulders to either side, slung my backpack over my shoulder. "I'm going to get some onion rings, man. Text me if you want anything."

"Don't you want to see photos?"

"Of what?"

"Of the truly repulsive being with its fake veneer taken off."

I took one stride toward the exit. Maxwell took four, crossing the room and burying his thumb and forefinger in my throat. I pushed back. He twisted his hips, slammed me down on the bed, put his second hand on my Adam's apple and squeezed. I scratched at his eyes. He pressed his 110 kilos into me, squeezed and crushed while a sleepy smile oozed onto his face. Shiori was in the room, calling to ask what flavor of milkshake I wanted. My dad was above me, telling me to make my bed properly, army-style, with the corners folded like so. Flocks of Pikachus and princesses from Armageddon were passing through the room, clutching candy floss and balloons. The air tasted of bitter raw dirt and earth and tangy blood. Just as a black filter was darkening the ceiling, the crushing boulder-man took a few kilos of weight off before his hand returned.

He held a water bottle, jammed the plastic hard against my lips. He was giving me a . . . drink? Of something bitter and delicious and fizzy, sugar and vinegar.

The black filter descended from the ceiling. Darkened my eyes. Heavy eyelids.

Sleep.

Something hard burrowing up and out through my back. I could see a fragment of the corner. Motel ironing board. Patterns of fluffy moons and smiling stars. I jerked upwards an inch. Something stiff pulled me back. I was tied to the ironing board on the bed with extension cords. There was a white pillowcase between my teeth and twisted round the back of my head like a rope.

The room appeared empty, though the TV was on. Al-Jazeera news, the only channel Maxwell believed was untainted, pure, trustworthy.

I heard rattling from the kitchen. Bottles chiming. The chink of somebody rustling through the cutlery.

"It's a day of reckoning, today is," Maxwell said, appearing with a gleaming shard of stainless steel. He was holding a steak knife in his right hand, tapping it against his left palm. "They're having the masks pulled off, all around the world. Biden's aide, that bodyguard second from the right, there? You see that thing? It's the blackness of the eyes that gives it away."

The light in Maxwell's face went out.

"Same eyes you've got, come to think of it, son."

Maxwell kneeled on my shoulders while I moaned and choked and bit into my mouthful of fabric, tasting every dry fiber. His hand on my brow was warm, tender. Almost gentle. He licked his fingers before pushing my hair away and slicing through my scalp. I bellowed and shook with the burning electric shock as the hard cold blade cut into my skull, brushing bone, setting off wildfires of agony. He brought the knife up again and went over the same line.

A probing finger of light speared through the blinds, painted the wall, then disappeared. I screamed through my cotton-gag, tears pooling. Volcanos of bubbling foam erupted around the corners of my mouth. My eyes rippled and blurred and trickled.

Maxwell saw the light, stared hard at the source outside our motel room, then returned his attention to cutting off my face.

"Sorry about the blade, she's a dull one," Maxwell said. "A dullard! Yes! Exactamente!" He giggled, leaned off me, stuck his nose into a teacup of cocaine, grunting contentedly as he licked floury snot off his top lip.

"Ready for the end? Here we go."

Maxwell twisted away from me, pushed the TV volume up to maximum, and pulled from my face a flap of skin as big as a postcard with a gap in it where he'd carved around my eye socket. The skin was saggy and translucent as a condom, wobbling, jelly-like, as thin and full-of-holes as a slice of Swiss cheese, and bright with blood. He grasped my chin, his fingers slipping in the red juice, then squeezed tighter and pushed the hard knife down.

"I was right about you, son. Who you are. What you're doing. Just like my previous so-called son. What I'm looking at is truly monstrous."

The room exploded with light. Noise outside. A humming, whirring drone.

A UFO. Or a car loudly reversing.

"It's time," he said, blood dangling like wet red icicles from the tips of his fingers, and took his weight off me, rolling off the bed, taking three cautious steps to the door, knife in one hand, my jelly-cheese face in the other. "All around the world, you know. From Auckland to Sydney to London, dear boy. Washington, Cairo, Kiev, Vancouver, Berlin. Hong Kong, Taipei. We're seizing the reins. Rising up."

I watched through a twitchy screen of speckled pink, my eyeballs spasming in agonizing dryness as the muscles searched for eyelids. It was impossible to look away from the TV, where Al Jazeera was running remembrance clips for the high-profile people they were announcing as dead. Leaders from Warsaw, from The Hague, from FIFA, from OPEC, from Tesla and Google and Amazon and Amnesty International. A worldwide purge. A pandemic of assassinations.

Hillary Clinton critically wounded in Manhattan apartment bombing. Narendra Modi, beaten down by a mob and skinned. The president of the International Cricket Council, burned alive. The Russian ambassador to Turkey kidnapped and flayed.

The Riyadh palace of the Saud family, stormed and sacked. The Dáil in Dublin, torn apart by the 99 percent.

Mobs had poured into the European Parliament in Strasbourg, the New York Stock Exchange, the United Nations General Assembly. Protestors with flags and paint and glitter bombs had scaled airport control towers, Big Ben, the Statue of Liberty.

Maxwell tossed his keys playfully in the air, blew me a mock kiss, went out to see whoever had brought their vehicle to the door.

I raged against my straps, twisting, then froze, listening. Maxwell cranked the Mustang's engine, those 12 cylinders that purred as they rattled, low and confident. His car beeped as it reversed. Our motel door was red with his alien lights.

From the trunk of his Mustang, Maxwell pulled a maroon-colored mannequin, still wrapped in plastic which was spotty with some red industrial dye. He brought the thing inside, lay it down, and on the motel unit's cheap beige rug, Maxwell injected the mannequin with an Epipen shot. Adrenaline? It had to be.

Through watery, stinging eyes, I watched down the length of my prostrate body, trying to control my panicked breathing. Woken with stimulant, the rust-red mannequin sneezed then rolled on its side and vomited on the floor. Lidless, the eyes were bright ping pong balls popping out of the flesh, the irises lolling in different directions, exhausted, dry, mummified. Maxwell wiped the thing's lips then pulled it upright, propping it against the back of a chair. Its skin-less flesh was raw and dried and hardened, cracking into tessellated maroon tiles gridded like plates. Scaled like the creature from the Black Lagoon.

Like a red lizard in the shape of a man.

I called its name. The skinless reptilian thing.

"Shiori?"

YOU DREAM OF JAIL

1.

One of the so-called Crips crouches over your hand and bites your knuckles.

"Fat cunt, aintcha?" he's going as you hiss and relinquish the door frame. "Skinny fuckin' legs, though, ya ginormous cunt. Need a fuckin workout."

With nothing left to hold onto, they drag you to the top of the stairs. The polished concrete floor is too slippery to get up. They put their fingers inside your armpits, tug you upward, tip you over the rail, shake your body.

"WE WILL DROP YOU, CUNT. WE WILL TERMINATE YOUR FUCKIN—"

You wake, gasping. Heart smashing against your chest, trying to get out. The room is blue and your knuckles are pressed into your skull.

"Kase?"

Kasey is bunched away from you. Her body is trying to escape your gravitational pull. You're a giant unit, glued to the mattress with sweat. A dugong in pajama pants, twice the size of your wife. Your so-called half of the bed is really two thirds. You're a failure at losing weight and a failure at the job you have to get up for in a couple of hours.

"Kase, I dreamed about jail again, people were, people were beating me—Wake *up*. Hey. KASE."

You shake her shoulder. Her nightie is silk, thin and papery. You tug the duvet back. The nightie reaches her hips only. You don't remember her buying it. You don't remember falling asleep at your PC five hours ago, either. You haven't been mindful, lately. You nearly fucked up the conference you've been producing. The Biotech Canadians threatened to pull out. You had to beg them to remain committed. Had to prove your mind was focused. The problem is, dreams have been leaking into your day. You're becoming paranoid, flinching. You drank chardonnay from the bottle on the drive home this evening . . . last night? Fuck.

You sit up and blink into the thin darkness.

"KASE. I have to tell you. I was in this, like, cage—is that what you call it?"

"Cell, Henry. Cell." She smacks her lips, buries her shoulders under the blanket, snuggles into her slice of mattress. "That prison dream again? Back to... Back sleepy."

"Be serious. Oi. Support me on this." You jostle her shoulder. These prison dreams are becoming alarming. You need her support. "So I'm in this, well, it was like worse than even that shitty hospital we went to that time in Laos. So, I'm in the sick bay in some kind of jail, a real prison, y'know, and these two, like, goons, these ape-men are yelling around the doors. Calling, hooting, sorta like, I dunno, howler monkeys? They wanted to beat me up. Smash me, kill me, toss me over the rails, hurt me for something. Dunno what I've done, though."

Kase is still turned away. Still eyes closed. "Must've been something," she grunts.

You put your feet on the carpet, release the covers, ease out of bed, and stand in front of the full-length mirror.

You jiggle the blubber around your big hips. Six feet and three inches, towering over most folks in the office. You're a big cuddly bear, if people would just be a little more patient with you—except every day, smaller people push you around. Their criticisms carve scars. Your company—which used to create conferences for the public good—is going corrupt in its pursuit of revenue, accepting money from dirtier and dirtier partners. Tobacco makers, arms manufacturers, bankers from Panama City, climate change denial outfits, multi-level marketing, payday loans leeches, dirty biotech, and here's your boss, Warner The Apologist, telling staff that paying a yoga hippie to deliver stoic mindfulness meditation once a week during lunch breaks will stop staff having anxiety attacks.

"Babe, do we have to seriously solve your problems at— what time is it, 4.30 in the friggin'—" Kase has been shielding her eyes with a pillow. Now she hurls it at the curtains, gets up, crawls behind your expansive back, massages your shoulders like she's rubbing seasoning into your flesh. She gets a long yawn out of the way, so wide it splits her head open. "Get this month's conference done then bail. You can line up other work, right? You can get out of there?"

"I don't . . . I'm not positive. I'd need a letter of reference, I suppose, and I can't get one of those unless I . . . I'm just trapped. I can't get out of work."

Kase goes cold. You're looking at one another in the mirror opposite the foot of the bed. She's giving you a hard verdict, a test result. "Insurance comes out this month. It's eight-hundred dollars, Henry."

"What was that thing in that book they sent you home with? *Twenty-First Century Stoic*? How it says you're supposed to imagine you're in a shittier situation to appreciate the things you have?"

Her words sound like she's giving up, but her actions say love. She abandons your warm pigsty in the bedsheets, pulls the tallboy open, tosses your clothes on the end of the bed.

"We can't afford you calling in sick again. Do whatever it takes to get through the week, Henry. Use your imagination."

2.

Stripes of yellow through the slats of the blinds. Ripples of light behind the water cooler.

You're the first one in the orange dawn office, not that you're proud of it. Kase was nice to put cream in your coffee, and she let you have salmon on your bagel. You couldn't really afford the cream or the salmon, though it started the day with a smile—except the smiles seemed to end as soon as you pulled out of the garage and joined queues of metal and glass on the motorway. Rubber, exhaust, overbearing billboards, honking, intimidating motorcycles whooshing by, all topped off with the yoga hippie's annoying podcast on Bluetooth. God, you can't believe you let the boss convince you that you could meditate while driving.

Agony. Unfairness. Stuck in mud. Paying for petrol to drive to a job you don't want to drive to. Gulping two fattening sugary drive-thru McMuffins to distract you from your unhappiness.

The chair complains as you collapse into your cubicle and tuck your legs under your desk. The computer is cold. It hums loudly as it wakes, disc drive groaning. Fuckin' old hunk of junk. The Conference Company used to be a market leader, back in 2005. Today it needs everything updated. The carpet is grey and pilled and ugly, the computers are three years too slow for virtual machines and the RAM-suck of the marketing videos you're supposed to be publishing. Even the staff kitchen dishwasher ought to be sent to the dump.

Once the computer has loaded, you squeeze out a quick prayer—well, not a prayer, just a "postcard to myself"—going over the things you're grateful haven't been taken from you.

This is what the Stoics did, the skinny yoga twerp with the manbun taught you. The Stoics envisioned themselves in adversity. They imagined losing everything.

You find a circle of calm in the middle of the hurricane.

Then you open your inbox.

You're hit with 14 emails from the BioVentures Québec guys who've flown down from Montreal. Any emails that aren't from them are from Warner instead. Warner, your manager, a dude even more depressed than you. A little fellow who has aged a decade over the past year, crushed and flattened, stooped posture. Stones on his shoulders.

Everything in the biotech guys' emails is full of bold and underline and exclamation marks. The biotech bullies talk of sponsorship, but they've come in and more or less taken over the place, and a buyout is probably coming. It's not sponsorship – it's an invasion. They need your company to hustle their product for them at supposedly non-partisan conferences. They seem to think they can bully everybody 'til the shareholders let them take command of the company, which they almost can, to be honest. They've seen what happens when revenue is put in front of Warner, seen his head flinch like a cat watching a mouse on a string. Many of the 14 abusive emails are pretty much implying the Canadians want each conference to become an advertisement for their pharmaceutical products. They want control.

Last week, The Conference Company accepted two hundred kays of investment from these guys to "support" your *Re-envisioning Biotech Contracts* conference. Ostensibly it was a sponsorship deal to sell the drug Strensiq. Realistically, they want to sell their product through your conference, and the next conferences too, and now you're expected to peddle lies to fill the seats to help their sales. The self-entitled suit-wearers from the big bully continent expect you to bend over and get fucked up the ass, you, and the other conference creator schlubs tucked into booths like lab rats.

You've witnessed Warner's armpits turn black with sweat when he shakes the sponsors' hands and tours them around the building, desperate to make them look on us favorably. Desperate to reverse the company's losses.

Part of you wants to make them welcome. You can be a team player, surely. You want to let the Canadians know you're a money guy. That the F column on your spreadsheet can in fact add up and create a profit return. That you can forecast $1000 of expected advertising returns around each of the 900 delegates you're aiming to get through the door—general practitioners, surgery specialists, nurses, healthcare assistants, clinical managers.

C'mon, man. You'll do this for your family. You'll persuade delegates to list Strensiq as a favored supplier so your monthly report proves you've created a million-dollar conference so these investors get a dividend. Problem is you're hollowed out, right now. Scraped empty with exhaustion. Dreading another 9-hour day in your prison cell-sized booth with photos of Kase tacked to the walls. Last night's dream was the eighth this month. These visions are becoming more regular. Anticipated. Dreaded. You're expecting to dream of jail every night, now, and sure, there are benefits to being reminded of what life would be like if you were in prison—it makes you appreciate your family more, no doubt about it—but these are violent dreams. Screaming-Lemme-Out dreams.

The minutes from 6.33 to 7.33 are spent with the rising sun streaking through the blinds, heating the piles of doughy flesh on your back while you lean into your computer monitor, your nose nearly touching your spreadsheet.

At 7.45, the door erupts. A squeak of surprise escapes your throat. He's standing there, black rings around his eyes, looking frightened.

"Warner," you blurt, "didn't expect you, man. You're in early."

"You're here," he goes, "you're working," looking so pale and sweaty it's as if he's been soaked in cold water. "Good. Goodgoodgood."

"I couldn't sleep. I had a bad dream."

"We need this. You have to save this conference."

Or what? you want to ask, *Or the company's going to collapse? We'll all lose our jobs?*

You may as well ask if the sky is blue. The answer is that obvious.

Warner slumps across the office from your booth to the booth of desperate skinny mop-haired graduate Sean Cross, that little bastard who puts memos reminding everyone to join him for Social Soccer on Wednesdays after work. Teambuilding? Bullshit. Distractions, all of it. Fiddling while the Titanic sinks.

Warner bends the blinds, peering down at the parking lot. He's hovering. Worried about when the suits are walking in.

His voice is tinny as he speaks, facing away. Depressed.

"They'll be here in, like, an hour, Henry. Man, you need to give them something. It's not just my welfare, or the company's. It's yours. Just compromise, will you? Let the Canadians take over for a bit. Don't be a martyr."

Right-o, you tell him. I'll make some adjustments.

Except adjustments aren't enough. It's about total control.

Warner gets up after a while and beckons you into the board room. He's printed your marketing copy and he arranges it like a periodic table. Stable elements on the left; liabilities pushed to the far corners.

The way you've written the sales text, your "easily accessible" conference will only entice a couple hundred delegates. The Conference Company will lose investor money on this, Henry. Warner says his back's against the wall. How the fuck am I supposed to pay for my daughter's dog when it needs to go to the vet? You've got to get a thousand people through the door, Hen, and you've got to push them on Strensiq, man. Push 'em real subtle. We can't have that university egghead telling delegates that a cheap, equally effective alternative to Strensiq is going to be widely available within the next two years at all clinics and hospitals to treat people with osteoporosis, shit no, Henry, that doesn't help The Conference Company at all. Get an expert on stage to tell 'em Strensiq is the only way. Please, man. Tell everyone in the audience to register Strensiq as a supplier. I need you to do this for me.

He's out of his seat, looking energized. Happy to forget he's got a target on his own back so long as he can aim a gun at you.

Look at Sean Cross, Warner continues. He's a team player. That guy's conference on keyhole mining has a sweet half a mil sponsorship from Rio Tinto. It *balances*, man. Look at the climate change conference Rafiza Sultana banged together for us. She has Monsanto telling the truth about glyphosate leachate entering the ecosystem—well, I mean, telling their perspective, I should say. It's about keeping us in the black, Henry, Warner is trying to explain, bending over more and more. His hair, frazzled white curls, is almost hanging over his eyes, his spine stooped, worried fingers fumbling with his wedding ring. It's not gaslighting or greenwashing or any of those buzzwords, he continues. All we're doing is giving a platform to some honored guests so our delegates can get a balanced picture of what's available for them to procure.

"Just feels dirty," you say at last. "Some of this stuff they're asking—"

"Hey: you wanna be a lone wolf, go be a lone wolf. Good luck surviving without a job." He looks at you with a face that's been blasted with a firehose for an hour. "You don't have to go out like this, man."

Sigh. Fine. Comply. Your computer chair complains as you dump your bulk back on it. You find the biotech bullies' website and copy their marketing text, which claims Strensiq is the only option for people suffering osteoporosis. Prescriptions are costing consumers $200 for a pack of eight tablets. Delegates don't need to know their patients can get a 15-dollar alternative. And university egghead Dr. David Hanmer doesn't need to know the reason he's been cut.

You can send him an email right now, do the deed. Cut Dr Hanmer from the speaker line-up and the Canadian bullies will be happy. They'll spare the ax.

Except you don't.

3.

You hit the concrete hard. They've dragged you off your bunk bed, two pairs of python-arms around your ankles.

NO NO NO. STOP STOP STOOOOOP, YOU GUYS, DOOOON'T.

They're little guys, these two attacking you, not quite brothers, but styled the same. Vicious white gorillas with glinting eyes and skin the color of biscuits. Too dumb and cruel to have the sophistication of a person of color. They're from the hopeless projects, rumor has it. Expelled from school after school, their ugliest bullying impulses never corrected. Some ugly banal faction called the Peckerwood Cripz, they've been moving through E Block like Remington clippers, shaving away strays and stragglers, harrowing everybody. Choose Killa Beez or choose us. You ride with us, you're getting jumped in, and if you don't ride with us, you're getting stomped all the same.

Whatever you do, white boy, do not get caught on your own.

One of them is pinching your knee. The other is scraping your trouser leg. Sitting up on the concrete floor, wincing, you're trying to stamp the attackers off you. Still, they drag you like a rolled-up carpet, and they get 90 percent of your body out of your cell. Your fingers embed in the metal frame around your door, then one of the Cripz crouches over your hand and bites your knuckles.

"Fat cunt, aintcha?" he's going as you hiss and relinquish the door frame. "Skinny fuckin' legs, though, ya ginormous cunt, ya. Need a fuckin workout."

With nothing left to hold onto, they drag you to the top of the stairs. The floor's too slippery to get up. They put their fingers inside your armpits, tug you upward, tip you over the rail, shake your body.

"WE WILL DROP YOU, CUNT. WE WILL TERMINATE YOUR FUCKIN ASS."

Officer Getachew is in the corner, tickling his elbows, worrying, skinny and tired and nervous in his thick green prison jersey. He comes from Eritrea, originally, you've learned during sensitive snippets of conversation. Getachew's always seemed nervous, always bitten his lip, expecting uprisings, anarchy, backstabbing, self-defense. Never comfortable when the floor is silent. His uniform is light-green pants, dark-green jersey, shoulder pads. Soft woolen armor. Pointless, all of it. He's fingering the radio on his stab-proof vest. He sees the pair of bullies are about to drop you, but he won't intervene. He values his job, his residency. With his back against the wall, Officer Getachew radios the command center and asks for backup.

You know what this is about. They want you to murder a prison guard to empower their gang.

One of the attacker-apes is a fraction more communicative than the other. Through his teeth, he growls in your ear, "Jus' whack him out, make everyone happy. What difference does it make to you?"

"ICAN'TICAN'TICAN'T!"

"C'S UP!" The bullies are screaming like jet engines in your ears. "RESPECT. SALUTE, CUNT, SALUTE."

"FINE, FINE, OKAY, I SALUTE, LEMME GO, LEMME GO, I SHOULDN'T BE IN HERE, I SHOULDN'T BE IN HEEEERRRR—"

"FINEFINEFINE, okay, I salute, lemme go, lemme go, I shouldn't be in heeeer— "

Kasey is in your eyes, shaking your shoulders.

"Wake up, Hen, wake up." Kasey pushes a tumbler of water against your lips. "You were screaming."

You gulp the water, roll into a spare patch of bed. As soon as you've caught your breath, the tears spill.

4.

Warner clings to the edges of his lectern in the grand meeting room, rocking it a little. It's as if he doesn't control his hands. Control emanates from the Canadians, looking like twins in their charcoal suits, sitting closest to Warner, pinning him with their eyes.

After Warner has been through an update to the health and safety and cyberbullying policies, he mumbles his next announcement.

"...very privileged and honored to have Hamilton Bollinger and Guy Le Blanc with us—am I pronouncing that correctly?— all the way from BioVentures Québec. It's really special that they've freed up the entire week to lend their steady hand to our Re-envisioning Biotech Contracts Conference, which— provided our producer Henry plays his cards right, ha ha—should really help us meet the one point four mil increase in revenue we've forecast in the annual report which, ha ha ha—the shareholders will presumably welcome!"

No response from the room full of silent heads and neckties. On a Skype screen in the corner, shareholders in Toronto and Montreal are watching. All they want is to hear that the new sponsors have confidence.

"Anyway, everybody, without further ajew, ha ha, not that these guys are even, um, Jewish, that's a little joke, I'd like to welcome Guy and Hamilton up to speak. Round of applause!"

Nobody claps.

Guy Le Blanc takes Warner's place behind the clear plastic podium. Hamilton Bollinger stands at his side.

"Merci beaucoup," the twin on the right goes. "Er, je m'appelle Guy Le Blanc, Directeur Général de BioVentures Québec." He seems humbler than his twin. Guy Le Blanc is the smaller, more thoughtful one, the charmer. Clean and slick as a cobra.

"Et je suis fatigué, pardonnez-moi, le voyage ici a été très long. J'aimerais vous présenter mon partenaire, le président des ventes, Hamilton Bollinger. Hamilton?"

As if your ears were gently lowered into a bath, you realize Mr. Le Blanc has been speaking French. His partner takes over the lectern. You're at the front of the table. Beneath the bombast. You can feel the nervousness of your colleagues behind you.

Hamilton Bollinger looks furious. Impatient eyes, displeased face, skin the color of cold metal.

"Frankly, I don't have a lot of time to dance around the obvious," Hamilton Bollinger says. Unlike his delicately spoken partner, Hamilton has an acidic American twang. "Life is short; I'm not going to lose one second of sales by being polite. The fact is, your boss has let me know that you guys are not pulling your weight. And when YOU don't pull right, *WE* don't pull right. You understand me? We will take two million out of this company by ten o'clock if you continue to dick around. You think I'm joking?"

Hamilton Bollinger slaps both palms on the tabletop inches from your face. His breath tickles your lips. "You. Big man. You're the one that's not getting your fucking job done with Strensiq. Harry, is it? Henry? Yeah, I thought it was you. I don't mind saying it in front of all these people, *Henry*."

His eyes are black and fierce, and you are the focus of his hatred.

"What, you want me to pull up your stats in front of all these losers? I don't care if some of these speakers on our wishlist aren't saints. You'll bring in the speakers that WE tell you, you'll hit the delegate revenue WE need, you'll get your speakers to market Strensiq real subtle, else I will beat your fuckin' skull in. Understand me?" Hamilton Bollinger leans back, snorts laughter out of his nose, adjusts the lapels of his suit jacket, extends his elbows 'til they crick. "Lesson for all of you," he continues. With his partner mirroring him on the far side of the table, he circles the edges of the room, his voice buffeting everybody from behind their heads. "Shareholders want reSULTS. Me? *I* want results, too. You want us to invest in you, we expect you to do your jobs. You need to be getting every single fucking delegate at your fucking piece of shit conferences to be ordering at least ten grand of the right product if you want a job by the end of next week. Now get the fuck back to work. Go. GO."

Warner puts up his hand and begins saying, "I just have a little, um, quest—", then lowers it.

A tide of shirts and neckties and black pants flows out of the boardroom.

"How you say, you do not fail, you do not fucking this up, yes, Henri?" Guy Le Blanc says, squeezing your shoulder as you try to leave. "We shall be, er, assisting your decisions you are making."

Inside your booth-prison with its furry walls and pictures of Kase, the biotech bullies drag their chairs up against yours, barricading you.

From 11 'til 5, they tell you where to click your mouse, who to call, what to type. They press their ears close when you call people. You're forced to invite a speaker with a history of sexually harassing women at his pharmaceutical buying agency because he'll bring with him key clients who will likely purchase product from the Canadians. You're forced to let in Philip Morris, who will sell IQOS vaporizers to keep people hooked on nicotine. You begin sniffing unstoppably around 4 p.m. By 4.10 p.m., you're sweating into your keyboard and the investor-thugs are shaking their heads and leaning back in their chairs, arms folded.

You've brought in the business; now the numbers are crunched. With an injection of morally dubious but persuasive presenters included in your conference, you'll have an extra 180 people attending, including those key clients BioVentures has to sell to.

They squeeze your shoulder, tell you you're doing a good job, and don't fuck it up again.

5.

Keys clanking, chinkling.

Crisp footsteps on polished concrete. Endless grey walls with nothing but fire extinguishers for color.

Getachew arrives at a mark on the polished floor five meters from the bullies' cell and shrugs.

He nods, indicating you need to go in and talk to these guys. You can't get jumped and stomped again. You have to play politics if you're going to survive in prison.

"Just feels dirty," you say, killing time. "Some of this stuff they're asking. . . ."

"Whatever they say, Henry, you are doing it. We do not are needing blood is spilling in here."

Getachew's English is off by a little, and his skin color is extraterrestrial. He's from a planet you wish he could take you to.

"THEY WANT ME TO HIT A FUCKING GUARD, MAN! Doesn't that scare the shit out of you?"

"So, you are doing the hit." Getachew was lucky to get into the country. Now he's terrified of disturbing the peace. His hair is limp black curls almost hanging over his eyes. His spine is stooped. His worried fingers fumble with his wedding ring. "If I were being in your boots, Henry, I am would doing this for them. You have years to go in here."

"Getachew, mate, c'mon man, let's sneak in a game of chess and—"

"HEY! Hey! Henry: We are not befriending. You think I am being your friend because I am trying to stop you get keel? Hey—you want you be lone wolf, go be lone wolf. Good luck surviving."

Taking those last stubborn, sticky steps and standing outside the beasts' lair is like walking on the moon. The Peckerwood Crips emerge immediately after Officer Getachew has gone, pale and acne'd, yellow hair sweaty, sticky with gel, faces polluted with dark green tattoos. They slump against the rail, the walls. They leap for the ceiling. Baboons. Animals. Bouncing and barging and sniveling.

They pull you inside the cell.

"So, which, um, which guard do I have to, you know. Hurt."

"That nigger friend of yours. That's the one."

"Need you to hurt him, bro."

"Fuck him up epic. He's a nigger. S'all good. Black Power's boughted the hit."

"Blacks own allllllllll the niggers in here," the other Crip says, eyes wet with happiness, fangs creeping over his raw lips.

You gulp. The smaller of the Crips is almost girly, a little feminine when he stops moving. His gelled mullet spills into piles of curls around his shoulders that would be beautiful and delicate if he weren't doing all this. Someone told you in the lunch line the dude was a tae kwon do champion as a teenager. Slim, bendable, twisty as a bookmark, he likes to knock down big men with a heel to the head.

"So, you're gonna go out there and you're gonna use this, oi."

The rougher, heavier Crip lunges forward, pushes a flannel into your hand. Inside is a thick syringe with the plastic handle of a trowel welded to it.

"Sidle up to your bum-chum and stab that screw in his fucking nigger screw-neck. Else you're gonna die in here."

Outside of the cell, you turn and cast your drowning eyes down towards the Pigeon Nest, a little one-guard chamber that's occasionally manned.

Getachew is standing outside it, craning his neck, trying to see what's happening. He has to ensure you're alive so he doesn't get told off by his bosses. Plus he seems to care about you, a little.

"DON'T YOU FUCKING LOOK AT HIM."

"GUARD!" you shriek, uncontrollable, terrified, "RUN, MAN! EMERGENCY."

"*FUCKIN' FAT BOY.*"

They seem to have eight arms each, these monsters. They're grabbing your ears, your nape, your scalp, your shoulder, bending, twisting, jumping up to punch the back of your big skull to force your head over the rail. Then they have their arms wrapped around your thighs and they're lifting, pushing, tipping.

Twelve meters below, a metal dinner table with a chess set. It reaches up through the vertical space, taunts your brain. One rook is lying on its side, rolling. The players have knocked it over while abandoning the table. They've heard your screams. They know you're getting dropped

At 7.01 a.m. on August 12, as men are leaving their cells to waddle like penguins in a line through the mess hall to receive a bowl of porridge and cup of coffee, there is a womanly scream. It's the scream of a big heavy male flapping in the air for three brief seconds before his 121 kilograms of meat and cotton and rubber flip-flops destroys the chess set, crushing pieces, wrecking the board, and leaving a bowl-shaped dent in the metal table.

Chess pieces roll across the floor in demented semi-circles, then stop.

Everybody, stunned, watches the man crawl off the tabletop and roll onto the concrete. His skull tonks on the unforgiving floor with the sound of pipe tapped on stone. He collapses on his face in a sickening angle.

It is 10 minutes before the screws decide no one is going to angrily avenge the dropped fat man. 15 minutes before the riot squad is stood down. 20 minutes before they confirm it's safe to call paramedics. An hour before the body is lifted onto a stretcher.

6.

The doors of the Copthorne Ballroom open and the first suits and dresses and black polished shoes walk in, each with a branded lanyard on his or her chest. Coffee in paper cups, trays of pastries. You talk to the nerdy AV tech from Vladivostok, of all places, and although you have a headrush and swoon and grasp the wall and have to sit suddenly, the morning goes well. You reside in your corner caressing the keys of your laptop, setting up access so BioVentures can use your company's confidential customer contact list to sell Strensiq.

Reenvisioning Biotech Contracts 2022 sees one bony-necked bore after another trudge to the podium and recite a presentation with predictable slideshows of stock images and graphs. While the bores preach, Hamilton Bollinger and Guy Le Blanc pace the edges of the room, assessing the reactions on the faces of the delegates. Rows of 80 people, 12 deep.

Nearly 1000 guests in all, distinguished only by how close they each are to a table piled with samples and pamphlets and free flashdrives with the Strensiq logo on them. The BioVentures bullies come over and take nibbles of conversation, nips, snatches, tugging you aside every ten minutes to remind you how you can contribute towards sales growth today. Go hit this old moron, sell him on a two-year subscription. Go convert that bitch in the purple suit. They're almost-mafia, almost-owning the conference. You cower and crumble and shrug and let them shake your wrists and speak firmly in your ear, holding your quivering fat head away like a pumpkin wobbling on a broom-tip.

You thank God for the lunchbreak. Kase walks over from her building to meet you and you stroll through the gardens outside the conference chewing a croissant and commiserating. She asks a lot of questions, though. Questions about how much each of the delegates paid to be here. Questions about how much each attendee accepts from the sponsors. Questions about how much control these new, aggressive, imperialist colonist sponsors have and what it means for this family.

Are you being colored, corrupted, helped, coerced, bribed, taken over, co-opted, or what? If it's not that bad, then just do what they ask, Henry, God. Why you have to be so stubborn? So what if there's an academic they don't want speaking. Just whack him out, Henry, make everyone happy. What difference does it make to you?

You're sitting on a cube of concrete surrounding a fountain with a hundred other over-educated neurotics in blue suits, hunched over, hands between your knees when she slaps you. You're twice as large as her, still you fall to the side, catch yourself with your elbow. Instead of rubbing your cheek or asking her what the fuck, you find yourself checking your watch. The only thing that could make the slap worse is if it makes you late.

A tear cools your hot cheek.

"You need to seriously get back in there and suck some dick if you wanna keep your head above water," Kase is growling. "You should've taken the deal. We have bills to pay." A new hardness in her voice.

Your lunch date is over. Kase straightens her miniskirt, fixes her hair. You sniff your armpits to assess how badly your nervous sweat stinks.

Back to the sham-conference, where people are being marketed to against their will in a coliseum of plush carpet and soft croissants and intoxicating coffee, where lifesaving drugs are overpriced to make a few people happy while tens of thousands suffer, where the only ray of hope seems to be the slender, grey-bearded Dr. David Hanmer of the University of New South Wales, whose presentation is about alternatives to Strensiq, which Dr. Hanmer tells nine hundred influential people is not that great of a drug, and here's a chart showing price compared to effectiveness, and did you know there's a cheaper alternative that your patients will thank you for?

Dr. Hanmer is squeezing the edges of the podium as he says this, looking content. Looking like he's not used to getting this opportunity.

Medical professionals applaud, then rise one by one until the room is deafening. A standing ovation is happening. Everybody is overjoyed at the good news.

As Dr. Hanmer ducks the spotlight and looks down into the blackness of the crowd, it seems like he's making eye contact and smiling and whispering, "Thank you for including me."

You're smiling until you pull your phone from your pocket and spot eleven missed calls from Warner. Hamilton Bollinger is pinching your ear and marching you out through an emergency exit and opening a coat locker and shoving you inside and holding up his tablet where there's a break-down of forecast profit from today's conference and the numbers don't look good and under the drone of applause in the background Guy Le Blanc has your employment contract held up like a fish while his eyeballs bulge and he's tearing it up and telling you to pack up your shit and leave, and you're lucky it's not fucking worse, and you slam headfirst into a hard surface.

7.

Corrections Officer Getachew Mariam strokes the grid of screens where the monitoring station watches the sick bay. He hopes his fingers reach through the screen and caress the brow of the sweaty sack of meat with the white marble face and clenched eyes and wincing teeth. Through the TV, through the wires, through cinderblock walls and plasterboard, Henry Avery lies on his right arm in the Convalescence Ward of Northern Regional Corrections Facility. Before he got himself in jail, Henry Avery worked in sales and marketing for some company that sold information. Hated his job. Had a bottle of wine on the steering wheel on the drive home. Made a wild U-turn because he realized he'd left his wallet at the liquor shop. Smashed a skateboarder on the overpass so the kid was flung over the railing and fell onto the motorway and died.

He's alone, now, this Mr. Avery, except for the angel hovering over him, painting foundation on his face to cover up the purple.

Getachew walks two hundred meters through concrete tunnels, opening and closing ten gates, then joins Sister Cadence in the sick bay. Sister Cadence is a registered nurse. She began with Nga Whaea Atawhai o Aotearoa, the Sisters of Mercy. First year's work placement, she asked to be given the hardest assignment: prison. Male prison, specifically. Mean people who hit at the walls. People wearing faded skin. Creased faces. Black eyes. Hope extinguished.

Sister Cadence has a warm sponge and she's cleaning between the rolls of fat on the back of the comatose Mr. Avery. Henry, he should be called, if he's to be prayed for. He's been here a week and the sweat that gets trapped in his fat-folds is problematic. If he gets an infection, and survives, he could sue—sue if he regains consciousness, that is. This is the limbo week. Henry rolls between life and death and back to life again. His head crushed and smashed, his liver punctured, spleen split, his body struggles to repair.

"I am tellingk heem," Getachew explains to Sister Cadence, 'I am tellingk heem, you need to, how you are sayingk, suck some dick if you are wantingk to keep your head above water in this place, yes?"

"Charming," Sister Cadence says. "Look, I mean, I agree, he could've . . . *not* let this happen to him, he could've compromised, but this is . . . just look what they've *done* to him."

Officer Getachew squeezes Sister Cadence's shoulder, and they pray.

After three minutes of silent breathing, she tucks in his bedsheets, cleans the dead skin cells off his body, pours water into his mouth. His tongue struggles like a beached whale, blocking his breath, too hard and thick and stubborn to shunt back down where it belongs and let air in. His head looks like the Northern Lights, covered in purple and green. His hair was shaved off to allow the doctors to remove a tile of skull to ease the pressure on his brain. His eyes—when the heavy lids have lifted—gaze out on the electrocardiograph. Officer Getachew Mariam ordered the thing be switched on and properly used by the nurses the day the big fat cowardly man was dropped over the rails by the pair of ratboys who wanted to scare their rivals. Two so-called Crips too cowardly to go into the cage of the Killa Beez and fight man to man, they decided they needed to prove their toughness either through forcing a patsy to whack a screw for them, or simply beating up the patsy. They chose the easy route. Destroy the straw man. The fall guy.

Dumb-stupid mjinga-pumbavu, thinks Getachew Mariam, furious at Mr. Henry Avery for allowing himself to be exploited. He ruined his chance to get clique'd up. Branded himself fair game. Now his head's smashed in, and he lies on his side like a log, two wires plastered to the curly hairs on his nipples, staring at a machine, barely able to move, unable to stop his flannel-moistened eyes reading the microscopic words stamped into the plastic casing of the EKG, words seared into Mr. Avery's retinas as he vegetates.

Manufactured by BioVentures Canada Limited™. Made in Québec.

Sister Cadence leans close, puts her ear against his lips. He's dying, this one. His brain is bruised, swollen to 120 percent its normal size, pushing hard against a too-small skull. Forcing blood through the parietal lobe. Blowing fuses. Wiping out tiny villages of neurons, synapses, astrocytes, oligodendrocytes, microglia.

Sister Cadence wonders what he's dreaming of, this hurt man. Regretting that he didn't participate in the politics, perhaps? Sailing an ocean of pride for saying no to unethical actions? Dreaming of somewhere safer than this place, hopefully. Dreaming of everything he needs to feel safe. A home, a bed, a job, and someone who loves him.

I CAME TO SAY SORRY

Glowing pearls on cream necks, black drapery, crystal chandelier, bottles of alcohol-free champagne, pink ball gowns, white tablecloths and beehive hairdos and gold shirts and black bow ties and Kristina is nervously waiting in the corner for me to take her hand and lead her out onto the dancefloor, except I'm not gonna do that.

It's prom night and it doesn't matter if Kristina Kerschbaumer is secretly my high school soulmate: she could ruin my cred.

Here's what's up: I've quietly promised her a one-to-one dance, except tons of kids are watching and I can't be tied down to her 'cause, man, me and Kristina may be an intellectual match but I need a vagina match, okay, and if a real premium 8 out of 10 chick sees me getting with a nerd girl on prom night, I'll be consigned to the nerd dating pool forever.

I move over and mingle with the boys around the bar, sipping mocktails and taking selfies, keeping my back to Kristina's needy gaze. Me and the Lads have all got on cheap plastic tuxedos, neckties with pictures of Homer Simpson and 2Pac, wraparound sunglasses on our spiky bleached hair. Hopefully a cool chick will match with me while I'm surrounded by people who endorse me. Me and the Lads, we're a tight unit, best buds, solid, and they've never forced me to admit why I skip out on the occasional wrestling practice or half-court basketball to go talk Tesla and Kafka with geeky European perfect Kristina.

I'm not dissing Kristina unfairly or nothin', I acknowledge she's got a crush on me and we ought to have brain sex, it's just the point is we connect on an intellectual level, okay, we share feelings and quizzes and test each other's spelling and I help her prepare for Debating Club meets, okay, we don't swap dicks and clits even if she is petite with eyes like blue flame and a concave tummy. If they do attraction different in Baden-Württemberg where she comes from, fine, whatever—but this ain't Germany, this is my country, and if people think I'm gonna sacrifice my social progress to publicly slow-dance with some foreign exchange student with a corny accent and braces on her teeth and lipstick that's way too red, forget it. I'm protecting her, actually. I want to spare her from the Darwinian harshness of the bitchy people at my school who—if they catch her fucking up my chance at getting laid—will diss her 'til she's dead.

There's a pretend fight breaking out in my group of goons. An explosion of laughs and jeers goes off. I dive into the noise, pushing and joshing, slaps and shoves that turn to bearhugs and shoulder massages, lads kissing lads, girls kissing girls, holding out their selfie sticks. We're all glowing from the buzz. Tonight, it's cool to tell people you love them, it's cool to kick the air recklessly, cool to throw fish sticks across the dancefloor, it's cool to let ecstasy flow through your elbows, so long as you're part of an exclusive circle, keeping the losers out.

If you're not in with the winners, sorry, but I can't help you. Kristina The Wallflower doesn't seem to get it. I can smell her confusion as this second prize-chick Justine hands me a suggestion written on a paper note and I follow Justine to the backseat of her limo. She's not the hottest, but she's got her cool credentials and so long as I fuck her in her car, I can carry on being normal.

Tonight is prom, and prom night cannot be squandered on someone who doesn't play the game. You have to get laid. Kristina, babe—I'll apologize for walking out on you, okay, I'm a jerk for walking a meter past your face, leaving you looking like a stunned possum. I'll make it up to you, I promise. Just not tonight.

*

We're meeting for our date-that's-not-a-date inside this giant amethyst geode in the museum. The geode is big as a coffin, so large two people can fit inside—lovers, usually. Or two dorks pretending not to be in love.

I steal glimpses of Kristina when she's looking away at the planets painted on the walls. She has a boyish undercut, heavy sand-colored fringe that shields her eyes. Rucksack with a picture of Albert Einstein on it. Shy sunken shoulder blades. I snap photographs of her knee-high socks, her childish blue dungarees. Kristina is lanky and awkward and dorky and wears a critter cap that looks like a cow. She's had a cushy life up in a mountain castle with rich parents and private tutors and nannies and she's never had to force herself to dress in FuBu or Adidas to get popular.

Though she looks like an overgrown ten-year-old, Kristina is eighteen, same as me, we're both Sagittarius, even, and we have our in-jokes and our secret meetings and our private chats. We have our own universe, pretty much. Until she goes back to Europe in a month, that is.

We giggle as I complain about crystal spikes in my butt and adjust my position, my chest brushing hers. She tilts her head, flutters her blue German eyes. She's made a joke about me taking my pants off before they get holes poked in them and we're both blushing. Being secret best friends, she expects to see every neuron light up in my brain when I have a private thought. In one of our first conversations, up in my bedroom, with a suitcase full of novels against the door to keep Mum out, we played Two Truths and a Lie, and Kristina described herself as a sapiosexual, then tried to claim she'd translated it wrong, in that stiff robotic accent of hers. We blushed into our hands and looked at our Casio watches and commented about needing to get home, head off, wrap up.

Except we couldn't wrap it up. We passed notes in history class. We hunkered inside her locker in the hall for quick exchanges of Monty Python jokes. French cinema, strolls in the park, hours playing with her telescope and doing online quizzes and playing Trivial Pursuit, swapping idioms in German and English, sharing a pair of earbuds, and I hugged the tender white pellet against my ear with my shoulder and she paused the iPod every twenty seconds, describing DJ Deichkind's Krautpop lyrics to me, *Löschen Sie das Feuer / bevor es das Dach erreicht, Colin.*

Put out the fire before it reaches the roof, Colin.

Awkward in here. The cramped space is making us desire each other. Time to move to another part of the museum. She gets off the sharp purple triangles first, turns, extends a hand. I take her fingers, savoring the texture. We move on to a world-globe which takes two of us to spin. It's as tall as a phone booth. She asks me if I even know which part of the globe she's from, dares me to find the crazy little Black Forest mountainside village she arrived from ten months ago, but my finger settles on the wrong spot on the map and she mocks me, I am not comingk from Liechtenstein, *dummkopf!*

I'd love to check out your place some time, I tell her. Doubt if I'll make it over there.

I would liking that very deep, she responds. Very liking.

We check out the Steampunk exhibition, the continental drift simulator too, plus the nature photography. There's this touring exhibition on extinct birds I've told Kristina she totally has to see before it goes and she asks why I don't bring my "cool" friends, doing quotation marks in the air, and I shake the jibe off and she doesn't press the point about me ditching her on prom night and I go and wait under the pteranodon skeleton while she takes another hundred photos to show her parents. Parents she answers to like they're her boss, parents who puppet her with phone calls and Facetime and email every evening, parents who want to comment on every decision she makes. Parents who try to guard what she lets into her heart.

Hovering on the edge of the museum lobby, close to ending the afternoon and going our separate ways, Kristina looks at her wrist, says it's time for *Mittagessen* and she's desperate to get "fucked up" on the excellent organic gluten-free gelato from that food truck by the Court Theatre, And you are comingk, yes? She thinks she's being hip, street, gangsta by saying "fucked up." I'm twenty percent hipper than her which gives me the confidence to press my fore-head against her big, tall chin, shake her shoulders and tell her yes, sure, of course, totally—we've got to get in the joy while we can.

While we can?

Shit. I've given a name to the ice we walk on. I've reminded us both that she is 29 days from boarding a jumbo jet that'll take her to Frankfurt and she'll be unable to scream and beg the pilot to go back to Hillmorton High School. Kristina will be locked in Europe, barricaded behind Alps and oceans and impenetrable woods and snowy valleys and realistically, it would take some miracle for me to see her again.

We'll write, sure, we'll share intimate photos taken on carousels and ice-skating rinks, and obviously we'll talk on instant messenger, maybe even video chat, but everything reminds us we're coming to an end.

It's a religious thing, deep down, I guess. You meet the perfect person, your dream, your ideal match, but God has no reason to give you more than you deserve.

God, actually, is the reason I'm thinking of letting the guillotine drop as soon as Kristina packs her suitcases. We'll promise to be friends forever, we'll write that our friendship crossed continents and cultures, we'll say we were meant to be and comment about how if we were born just one year different, she might never have come here and met her soulmate, and I'll find it impossible to tell her I'm too much of a coward to come to the airport and say goodbye in case someone sees me.

We sit on the edge of the Remembrance Fountain and dip our toes and suck spoonfuls of gelato. It's good, the sweet dessert. It occupies our tongues.

My *Mutti* and father, she says, they are wantingk to speak to you again.

Maybe . . . I guess, if it's part of the culture and stuff.

They are loving you. Not this English love, this, this . . . what is better word for love?

She's reaching into the ocean of language to describe what it's like to take a chance on the boy your daughter is smitten with, but there's no better word for it, Kristina. Love is love.

*

A thousand of us schoolkids are nesting like seabirds across a cliff of blue plastic stadium seats, squawking and partying. There's a thousand heads and drink bottles and sun hats and spotty shoulders and there's a Mexican wave going 'round and kids are throwing paper darts and apple cores and whistling through their fingertips and it doesn't matter if you go down and do the long jump with your friends or save your strength for the 1500 meters. Sports Day is a party day for every kid. Every clique gets its own row of seats—and my clique shows its power.

Three things make the day joyous. There's my friends, firstly, the Lads, Diz and Macca and Screech and Sixty and Natey Potatey and Big Jono, Domes and Kingi and TJ and Fatfuck, and we've each got a fangirl that's been assigned to us, girls who sit on our laps, girls that bring us energy drinks and rainbow popcorn from the canteen, girls that grind their tits into our necks when they hug us. Rich girls who've been allowed to drive their jeeps here. Devious girls who sip vodka through their drink bottles. Girls we can walk into a room and be proud of.

Teach hassles us, and me and a couple of lads trudge out onto the field and do our mandatory minimum. I heft a couple shotputs, run the hurdles, do a couple dozen high-fives then settle back into the seats for some goss and a sneaky cigarette and some making-fun-of-Fatfuck. Only when I've put in the Being Ordinary work do I sneak away and find Kristina up in the drafty top corner of the stadium where pigeons shit. She's in a bloc of Korean math nerds and she may as well be coming out of solitary confinement, that's how pleased she is to see me. She steps over her loser friends and we hug and clink cellphones and I make a joke about Bayern München that only Kristina would understand and she retorts with this line about Fermat's last theorem that's a total killer and I feel a pulse of appreciation for the single most original friend (and soulmate, and alternate reality lover) that I know.

After exhausting the last few Big Bang Theory references, we go silent and sit without speaking under the pigeons and steel beams and vast, sky-blacking roof, staring down at 1500 teachers and kids and security. Everyone down there is oblivious to the inferno of unsayable feelings going on in this windy corner of the stadium. I haven't seen, before, what a sports bra does to her chest. How creamy her thighs are now that she's in skimpy running shorts.

For a silent hour, we watch the Year 10s pole vaulting, the Year 9s squealing over a rope tug-of-war, the Year 13 lads undertaking some serious 100 meter sprints. Loudhailer PA megaphone robot-voices floating on the air. Distant screams and cheers.

Finally, a call comes in and she holds her phone, waggling it, excited as if it's a box of candy.

Vati und Mutti, they are hoping to speak to you.

I roll my eyes. These calls have been increasing, the closer Kristina gets to going home, as if her parents want me to get down on one knee and propose marriage to her before she leaves or something. It's midnight in Bavaria, but I can't detect sleepiness in Herr and Frau Kerschbaumers' voices. Controlling their daughter keeps them wired, I suppose. They lean so heavily on Kristina, ringing her every day, using up like twenty bucks' worth of international calling just so they can force her to recite her homework essays over the phone. They're stalkers, if you ask me. Like they want to put their hands inside Kristina for total control. She's told me they're old school Lutherans, always worrying about keeping God's grace on their side, and they own a massive estate near the Swiss border and have inherited titles and buckets of money they cling to. They're superstitious, fearful of imps and witches and monsters they lock in the cellar, protective and they've never let any *Außenseiters* into the family. The word means outsider, apparently. It's stronger than *Auslander* and sort of means misfit, deviant. Interloper. Someone who trespasses.

I'm not really ready to talk to your parents, man, I tell her while she waggles the phone at me, wishing the roaring sports crowds would interrupt and save me from the cringe right now.

It's not like you and I are fully . . . you know.

She pulls her tendrils in like an anemone, hurt and scared, and says something flat and fast into the phone. Reporting that I've been a jerk, I'll bet.

Fuck.

I rip it out of her hand, accept a quick chat on the phone, hoping to make them like me.

Mein Sohn, Kristina's father goes in a deep, careful voice. Tell me everythingk.

I blab about how sports day is going, comment how summer's coming up and it'll be a shame to send Kristina back into winter, haw haw. Tell them my mum says hi and she can send you photos of her garden if you want. They make me pledge to give their love to my dad, which I find weird. One of their customs or whatever. They ask me my favorite sports, favorite football teams, even my favorite hamburgers, whatever that's all about. They ask me if I'm allergic to any foods and whether I prefer to eat at 5 or 7 p.m. for supper, as if they're planning to have me as a damn guest, even though I'm half a freakin' world away!

You are a trust this man, Kristina's father tells me over the phone. His English is just as mutated as his daughter's, like 90 percent normal, but deranged. Like a broken robot.

I am thinkingk young Kristina, she is wise choosing, you are understanding this?

Kay, I say, lamely, thinking "Choosing?" *Dude*, I'm bursting to tell him. She can't choose me. I'm married to my clique, man, we are NOT lovers and I am NOT committing myself to your family. You're on the far side of the world and your status has no effect on me here.

So, we have an understandingk, you and I, yes? Herr Kerschbaumer continues, You intend my daughter, yes? You are liking?

I guess, man, she's dope, I tell Mr. Kerschbaumer. But, like, we're not actually an item.

But you can promise not to breaking my daughter her heart.

Kristina yanks the cellphone out of my hand and ends the call with a few quick snapped words.

She swallows hard. Types a text message. Shoves it in my hand.

What happening prom night to us?

She's leaving in six days. This is the only chance to explain. We might not breathe the same air for years, despite what we've been pledging on instant messenger. She has been drip-feeding me German lessons, "For ven you are coming to Europe," but last Wednesday I gulped and confessed I'll probably never come to Europe, cause most of the others from my group are doing that personal trainer course, it's only 10 months, plus Stretch and Sixty are gonna ask if I can be a volunteer lifeguard with them, so that'll be me. Safe in the pack. Head down. Feelings packed into storage.

Catch up! I say to Kristina, miraculously chirpy, totally fake.

I stand up and pretend I have an important phone call coming through. I whistle then wave at the Lads and jump down a couple tiers of seats, stepping over some goths before plopping into a seat beside Fatfuck and accepting a slurp of vodka from LaTonya and taking a Sharpie that's being passed around to sign Sixty's plaster cast.

The Mexican waves are deafening and the Lil Wayne song is thumping way too loud from Screech's speaker and a girl with cold sores is whispering flirty shit in my ear but all I hear is the dumb fake words echo in my skull.

Catch up!

Two vague meaningless words to keep her confused because I've promised her I'll be at the airport waving goodbye. But that just ain't true.

*

I'm at Heathrow Airport ready for my big exciting Overseas Experience except I'm sobbing into the collar of my t-shirt because I've been pulled aside and bullied by two grumpy black customs officers in thick wool jerseys and bulletproof vests who've found a weed pipe in my bathroom kit and I'm begging, guys, BEGGING them to believe that it's not my fault and my dumb friends dared me to take it and please please PLEASE give me another chance.

Your friends are dumb, you say?

They're SO fucking retarded, I'm sobbing. Like they weren't even there when school broke up and everyone turned on each other and Janelle got pregnant to Nate except it wasn't even Nate's baby, it was TJ's, and TJ and Nate refused to be in the same room so like NO ONE went to polytech to actually do their personal trainer course and we missed the boat on studying and they all turned out to be retards who just wanted to live off their parents' money or the dole and just ride their cars up and down the strip every Saturday and no one's doing anything except having babies and doing drugs and hating each other and within one week Christchurch became a pimple, a blip, an unimportant fly speck and all the real world action is in Europe and I'm sooooo so literally sorry I didn't see how big and important Europe is and I've come all this way to England to get away from the aimlessness of it all and I'm begging you, you HAVE to let me through.

Actually, mate, we don't HAVE to do anything. We're letting you go this morning. But can I suggest you get yourself some better friends, yeah?

I'm about to tell them I do have better friends, well, one friend, who I haven't seen in years, but they won't believe me. They'll think I'm making her up.

First party destination is Cardiff. Pints of stout; somersaults into the river with drunken Aussies. Picking apples in an orchard; losing my passport. Sleeping on the street outside the embassy. Then Albifeira, Portugal. Salt crystallizing on my skin and cheap Portuguese tequila in a bucket that you guzzle and I'm making out with a girl from Finland and waking up in Rotterdam, getting an overland train along this river valley that looks like a picture off a calendar, then it's vineyard work, mostly, picking grapes and pouring bubbles for rich Germans in Esch-sur-Sure, this town in Luxembourg that has a river with glacier chunks flowing through people's backyards, dipping in and out of Belgium on weekends with hard-partying Kiwis to get fucked up on X and bang girls from Serbia.

It's going well, I'm doing lots of Facetime with the family back home, I'm telling people I'm happy, I'm settled, then I get this Russian girl pregnant and her brother drives like 2000 kays across Europe and she's giving me daily updates about how close he is to kicking my ass and my work permit is burnt out, anyway, so that's me, 100 euro left, playing this online roulette game thing with Aer Fergus that gets you discounted tickets. I pick up a flight from Brussels to Madrid for 10 euro, seriously amazingly cheap, and the Kiwis I'm drinking with in this Roman ruins-slash-museum bar thingy convince me I can totally join their crew in some part of town called Retiro selling books of coupons door to door and we knock on like 200 doors a day and my mate Jaime gets his cheekbone broken by the cops and we all have to run for it, none of us have work permits, and we fill up a backpacker hostel but this clique of Somalis staunch us out, slapping the manager, tipping our Kathmandu rucksacks upside down and chucking our shit off the balcony and I just grab my passport and sprint, bro, sprint, and here I am, Kristina, stuck in Spain.

I'm writing to you from this internet café just off the Plaza Mayor. I know it's been like three years, maybe even four but I'm down and out and I don't speak the language and I have like 15 euro and I don't know how I'm going to stay alive 'til I get a job to get money to get fed . . . so here I am.

Begging for a chance to reconnect.

I'm pushing in my chair, stretching, throwing up my hands, giving up, when I see movement on the screen. A line of words has arrived, top of my emails. Holy words, beamed down from on high.

It's you, Kristina, checking your email on a Sunday at lunchtime when every other kid is out doing something cool, it's you it's you, after nearly four years it's YOUUU.

You've written back instantly. Instantly! You're saying in your shitty English that forgiving me is, "As good as Heisenberg's uncertainty principle," and that's it, indisputable, pure distilled Kristina. Genius sublime witty sassy wisdom.

What you're saying is you forgive me, but if I attempt to pore over it, study it closely, it'll dry up, retract, move away, disappear.

I'm nerd-laughing into my screen, my eyes wet with relief. I don't care about the stray dogs coming into the internet café, the gypsies begging for euros, the dust on the keyboard.

We spend all afternoon emailing while my stomach growls, but she's on a train, she tells me. Just count the hours and I'll be there. She'll pick me up in two days, she says.

Pick me up? I jest, Like I've dropped into some low place?

Akkurat, she tells me.

I get an Uber to the airport at Barajas and I sit on an ocean of carpet amongst a bunch of Albanian losers.

When she arrives, dressed in an old lady's tan cardigan and ridiculous polka dot pants, with the same old Totoro backpack, she sticks out her shaky hand and says, formally, "Hallo, Colin," though she can't stop the smile splitting her face open.

I squeeze her hard. I feel our hearts thump together.

She buys us train tickets. Tells me I'll be staying at her family's home 'til I'm back on my feet, except Kristina stresses that her folks "are wanting of the blood" and they'll expect me to grovel. I can cope, honestly, I tell her.

"You are confident," she laughs out of the corner of her mouth. "They will expect you to give, how you say, a pound of flesh? You will, er, you will giving a part of yourself?"

We turn the phrase over, play with it, laugh it off.

I'm not giving anything, Krissy, I think. Crocodile tears, babe. You'll give me a few bucks, I'll eat your meat and drink your beer then I'll be on my way again. Catch up in 2030. No way am I stickin' around. Don't get your hopes up.

But there's no way to tell her that without breaking her heart again.

*

I am havingk so much to tell you, Colin!

Kristina weaves her fingers into mine and tugs me into Europe. She's excited, childish, girly, full of helium and light. Kristina wants to play. She leads me over the Pyrenees and the Dordogne and the northern Alps and I feel her staring not at the scenery but at me and every time I turn to catch her there's a sudden turn-away. An embarrassed look-at-the-floor. We get off the plane at Baden-Baden and rent bicycles in Freiberg, pedal through dappled shade under elms and pines and oaks and hop off in a resort of log cabins and hot springs. The foothills of the Black Forest.

I can't believe I ever thought Kristina was something to be ashamed of. Kristina Kerschbaumer ticks all the boxes, man. Those so-called apex predators at my school were lowlifes, I see it now, everything turned to infighting soon as we left school and we all got an apartment together but we got kicked out by the Tenants' Committee after our flat warming party and Nate got Janelle pregnant and there was that court thing and Chantelle hired, like, half our group for her start-up and she got fucked up by Inland Revenue 'cause she wasn't paying people's income tax and everything's inverted, everything about our dumb privileged under-prepared group was soooo fucking childish, and here's you, Kristina, the girl dissed for being quiet and cautious has got a degree and her own cottage in her parents' estate plus a huge allowance. *You, Kris!* A university degree—a whole degree! So young, while all us kids who burned through our lives too fast got scorched fingers.

The farthest I can get from my old stupid self is the summer waters of Lake Schluchsee. We rent paddleboats and trickle out into an expanse of milky coffee water, lily pads and geese.

Kristina fills me in on the past 1233 days as we bob in the middle of the lake. She clears her throat then tells me, like she's delivering a diagnosis to me in my hospital bed, that I broke her heart by not turning up at the airport.

I'm about to deny it, make a pun with her words, but I shrug and go You're right. I was a dick, I know. Lay it on me. I can take it.

Colin, you are lucky my family they have thought about you very much, you are understanding? Kristina tells me. You are beingk lucky that my father, he has the power to forgive. She goes on to say if he was poorer, more desperate, less afraid of going to jail, he might kill me.

Seriously? Literally?

Oh yes, she goes. Herr Patrick is a Kerschbaumer, as you know.

Actually I don't know, Kristina. I know zilch about your people. Didn't you tell me I'm a—what's that word— Interloper? Intruder? *Außenseiter*? I'm here with an open mind as to exactly how old fashioned your folks are, okay, and I'd be delighted to meet them and slip in a quick apology about not honoring your hymen or whatever the hell they want from me. Okay? Deal?!

Kristina reaches across her oar and squeezes my kneecap, gripping the sides of the boat while the water grumbles and mutters and we scare a gang of ducks and I'm standing up and shouting as if I'm in an old-timey movie, IS THIS ATONEMENT ENOUGH, EH?! and diving into the caramel water and Kristina is pulling her dress over her head and below the stripe of fat from hip to hip I spot her holy, never-before-seen pussy for a nanosecond before she's in the water, sucking my lips, trying to push me under, and we're laughing so hard we nearly drown and the world's most exhilarating "Just Friends" week begins.

On our first magical perfect day, in this village called St. Blasien-Menzenschwand, she pays for us to visit this Tolkien-y slopy-roofed bunch of wood/log houses sprouting red geraniums with a water wheel in the center of town, wood pails, milk jugs, wild flowers, fir trees and goats. It's the location that inspired Hansel and Gretel apparently. Gangsta. I take photos, conscious to keep her out just in case I need to tag the Lads sometime in the future.

Next, over a magical, blessed, sent-from-God, better-than-drugs divine awesome orgasmic ten days that I WISH I could rub in the faces of my old crew, Kristina (well, her parents' credit card) pays for us to take a chairlift to the top of this go-kart track at a place called Hasenhorn so steep it feels like we're going to fall off the edge of the earth. The chairlift stops. Kristina doesn't like heights. She squeezes my hand. She buries her face in my neck.

We stroll forests, lakesides, meadows, vineyards, lost in a fairy tale. We laugh and weave in and out of sweaty fat Ukrainian tourists in khaki shorts eating waffle cones and giant pretzels. The sun is close. The trees are noble, old, carefully grown. The forest is birch, larch, pine, tangly roots, waving vines, earth so dark it seems black.

Fat British families with cotton candy, jacket-clad Japanese on bicycles, towering redwoods, glinting mountain peaks. Kristina checks us into this hotel called the Feldberger Hof. It's at the base of Mount Feldberg and looks up to cable cars and stony peaks and eagles. The hotel has an indoor play area, buffet meals, daily program of fun games and singalongs. Painted on the walls are gnome-like creatures and their dwellings. Some creepy Catholic art, too—demons, devils, postcards from hell. They're rednecks, up in these hills, this drunken skank from Ireland informs me. People here carry grudges so fierce they span centuries. They'll caress you with one hand and crush you with the other, she goes, spilling her champagne in the spa. Only people to ever defeat the Romans, the Germans were, she says. Careful who ye mess with, pet.

Whatever, lady. I could beat up Kristina's corny old parents with one hand tied behind my back, I swear.

I'm in the midst of shooing away the Irish skank when Kristina waddles up nervously, wrapped up in a towel tight as a burrito. I can see fragments of a virginal white bikini under the burrito-towel. It illuminates a new dimension of her. Tall, blonde-ish, sparkling eyes, rich. I was an idiot to ever look down on her.

In the spa, I make up for lost years. While she's raving about The Big Bang Theory, I put my lips on her ears, my tongue in her teeth.

Hey, I ask her, you still got room on the Visa, right?

She nods once. Her eyebrows are worried. I pat her cheek. Awesome.

We giggle in the elevator. She breathes hard on my neck. I bite her earlobes, guide her back, opening the hotel room door, pushing a wineglass into her hands, undressing her.

On the bearskin rug, I become the first man to ever enter her. After, as she plays with the curls of hair on my chest, she tells me tomorrow is a good day to drive up to her parents' place.

We have to going, she says. My parents are very . . . how you say in English. . . ?

Kristina is making a slicing motion on her hand.

Exacting?

Kris, like—you haven't told them we're together, have you? 'Cause it's not quite . . . it's not like—

You are on Easter Island? she snaps. You are on the moon? You are with Janelle and Nate? Huh?

No. . . .

So, you are here. You are with Kristina Kerschbaumer. So, we are together. Dispute this, hmm?

Nah, man, I guess we're together, I tell her, to calm her down. No dispute.

*

The doors of the castle split open and Kristina's *Mutti* spreads her arms wide. Kristina puts her shoulder in and they kiss on each cheek. We're nearly 2000 meters up in this range of mountains called the Scarplands that are like foothills to the Swiss Alps. It took 2.5 hours of winding, cliff-edge roads and switchbacks before this massive meadow split the mountains open and there, between two tarns, was Hohenbaden Castle and under it, the Kerschbaumers' stone palace.

Burg-alt-Eberstein is 182 years old, Mrs. Kerschbaumer tells her daughter to tell me, on account of their shitty English and my shitty German. It was owned by Reichsfreiherr Kristofer Kerschbaumer and passed down to Freiherr Kerschbaumer, who was the great-grandfather of Kristina's dad's dad. They used to get their money by making serfs pick turnips. Today they hire out equipment to festivals and builders—fencing, portable toilets, turnstiles, kegs, speakers. Some of it's kept in the old horse stables around the estate.

Whatever, fine, okay. This isn't the Floating Fortress Armageddon Pool Party in Ibiza but it's a trip, it's cool. I'll let Kristina show me her childhood bedroom or whatever, then get the hell out.

While we're standing in the pebble stones, the doors open again and we all turn to face the father. Hans-Peter Kerschbaumer only comes up to my shoulders. Instantly I feel impolite for having the guile to be lanky. I scratch my biceps nervously, put out the wrong hand to shake, and say *Guten Abend* instead of *Guten Tag*. The mum looks to Kristina for permission to laugh, which they both do. The dad tuts and clears his throat and adjusts his posture, raising his heels, refreshing his legs in his tall leather boots.

Wofür is er hier? the dad asks his family. I sort-of understand. He's asking what brings me here.

I came to say sorry, I tell the dad, Like, to catch up, with your daughter and shit, I mean stuff, sorry... . I wince. The parents aren't laughing this off. The dad sighs, tilts his head. He's short, over-dressed and unimpressed, but politeness is massive in these people's culture. We'll spend a couple awkward days. Maybe if I visit again in ten years, things will've thawed.

I follow him into the castle and the doors close behind.

*

There is a suit of armor at the head of the table. Its gleam matches the gleam of the axe, the battle staffs, the sword collection, the crossbows, the Thuringian shield. The dining hall has banners and silver cups in a glass cabinet and chipped axes from ancient wars.

Kristina, she's relaxed about all the pompous shit—gold crucifixes, crystal chandelier. Weapons and jewels and carved wood and wrought iron everywhere. A stuffed bear towering over the dining table, high as the ceiling. Her *mutti*, too, and the dad, all bunched together on one leather couch as we watch a huge TV after dinner. Me, I'm in a leather armchair, legs tucked up under my chin.

Coming all this way to say sorry makes sense to me, bitches come and go in my world, no biggie, but Kristina's family chew over my one-word apology a lot—as in whispered discussions, knitted brows. Secret giggles between mum and daughter that make Kristina's mum snicker so much she has to dab her eyes with a handkerchief. Then the calm voices. The flat negotiations.

As I attempt to help scrape the butter off the dishes, the parents mute the TV. They interrogate me as to whether I'm here to marry Kristina or not. I'm surprised, and I splutter, and I have to double-check that things have translated properly. Kristina steps in, turns her secret pretty head towards them and confirms Ja, I'm understanding correctly: her folks are bamboozled that I would have come all this way.

Tell 'em we've got a cultural misunderstanding, I say to Kristina, laughing and slurping a big can of Pilsner. Moving things a little quick, aren't we?

I can see Kristina doing the math. Five years, actually, all up. *Stupid, Col, stupid.*

The dad, standing up and pacing the lounge, pauses under a huge dark thick beam to ask a question, which he speaks into Kristina's ear while eyeballing me.

Kristina pulls back a strand of hair. When she listens to her parents, she bends, stoops, lowers herself, bows down. She nods, understanding her short-ass Napoleon-ass father, then bears the news to me.

My father, he is wantingk to knowing if you are having the intention of I am becomingk your vife?

Krissy, man. You know I can't do that.

She leans into her father and injects the news into his head. He looks at me hard then walks through to the kitchen

I already said sorry, you guys, for not taking her to the prom or whatever you're mad abou—guys? Frau Kershbaumer?

The mother says something to Kristina then departs.

Kristina drops a translation then follows.

My parents, they are sayingk sorry is not enough.

They leave me to put myself to bed in a room I can hardly find amongst the other 30 rooms and I wake at 7.30 and clop down the stone stairs in the slippers they've given me and I'm gulping a milky spoonful of muesli when a sack is pulled down over my head and I'm up and fighting, my knee goes cold as it's soaked with milk, and I hear the fruit bowl wobble and spin. Knees on my back. Something hard and pointy like a fire poker whacking my head. Dizzy, I drop, unable to walk, but the kidnappers are under my arms, standing tall and dragging me through the house while I beg and command NO-NO-NO-SERIOUSLYYOUCAN'T-NO-NO-NO and my words echo, at first, then thud to the floor because I've been shoved into a cramped dank, stinky space and there's a thump and the light is gone.

*

My head has been split open. Air stings my skull. It's black in here—well, dark watery thin grey air. A little light coming from somewhere through some kind of blue plastic walls. Just enough to see the pictures of Kristina glued to the wall of this—

Portaloo? Chemical toilet? Thank fuck, I've just fainted while taking a piss or something. Glastonbury? This is GlastonburNOOOOOO.

Belgium, Spain, fucking . . . Where'd I end up... Lotta good times on Kristina's Visa and Ohhhhhh.

Black Forest. Kristina's parents' castle.

HELLLLOOOOO? LEMME THE FUCK OUT.

Why is the outside light fuzzy greyish-indigo? You wouldn't have a chemical toilet indoors unless it was in, like, a shed or a storage locker or something?

I rattle the plastic lock, finger the four walls, just three feet apart, four at the most. Put the toilet seat down, sit on it, get up, stroke the ceiling.

I KNOW WHAT YOU GUYS ARE DOING AND IT'S, LIKE . . . JOKE'S OVER, OKAY? I'LL TAKE KRISTINA OUT FOR SOME DATES, I PROMISE. KRIIIIIS? TELL ME YOU CAN HEAR ME. YOU HAVE TO LET ME OUT. DU MUSST . . . fuck . . . DU MUSST MICH GEHEN LASSEN, okayyy? Guys?

Silence.

BITTE LASS MICH RAUS, babe. YOU KNOW THAT FUCKIN' TRANSLATES, IT'S . . . it's . . . 'kay, sorry for yelling, all right, but you can't keep me here. I have rights, look in the, um, Universal Declaration of—of, um. . . .

I give up, sit on my potty for a while. It's brand new, though it stinks like farmyard horse shit. I pick hardened drips of plastic off the bottom of the toilet seat. I fantasize about crawling through the sewer pipes beneath—if it's even connected to the sewers.

Don't burn yourself out, bro. Patience, man. Kristina's a good girl. She owes you one, doesn't she? Or you owe her, or something.

The toilet door seems pressed against a wall and I think I can hear a chain tinkle every time I try to force the door open, as if they've padlocked me inside like I'm Houdini.

You're gonna be here a while, Colly Flower. Time to sit here and figure it out.

*

Every day I wake with a gasp on my toilet seat, ass-bones burning, butt cheeks leaking blood and clear plasma from pressure sores. I rise, stretch, attack the door keeping me in here, pounding and bawling. Frau Kerschbaumer clears her throat as she guides breakfast through the little feeding-slot and I claw at the plastic and bellow that you have to let me out, YOU FUCKING DINOSAUR BABOON NAZI FUCKIN' HORSE-FACED CUNT I'm sorry, I'm sorry, *mein*

Frau, bitte lass mich raus, okay, you must make me free? Yes, you hear me? I'm a New Zealand citizen, okay, I have protections, like laws, I have people looking over me, the police, all right, I'll be missed, they'll wonder where I am, if you can just lemme go that'd be reeeeal sweet, I'll pack my stuff and gap out the window, Frau Kerschbaumer, you can tell your husband and Kristina, honestly tell anyone that I was just gone one morning, okay, literally gone, plea— PLEASEPLEASEPLEASEYOU CAN'T LEAVE ME HERE. I KNOW YOU'RE LOCKING THE DOOR, IT'S—

BITTE LASS MICH RAUS.

FOR GOD'S SAKE, SHOW YOUR HUMAN SIDE.

Every day it repeats. Same cycle. No way out of my plastic prison. I've positioned myself upside down and kicked at the ceiling. I've dived into the black toilet, trying not to vomit from putting my face beside my own mummified shit and piss and I've groped around for a subterranean way out. I've kicked and scratched and bit and pawed at every aspect of my little box. Ingested the stench of hay and oats and manure, filled my stomach with it. I've read the boilerplate info on the wall printed by the Romanian manufacturer over and over. My eyes are black from weeping. My fingers are thin and sharp, squeezed into cold hard claws as I drag them down the plastic walls. I can barely sit down, can only sleep on my back, legs up against the sides. My bones throb and push out of my skin and, to dilute the pain, once a day Mrs. Kerschbaumer pushes two tiny tablets of Tramadol through the slot. Well, it was two at the start. There's been an extra pill each day. Yesterday I got ten pills. They made me woozy and happy. I stopped nibbling the hair out of my cream-coloured skin. I'm all slippery and leathery now, skin gone all hard since I bit all my fur out. Hairless and shiny as a snake.

The first week, every day I fight on the hour, and every half hour too. In between deafening myself, I make friends with a weevil, a spider, and a needle of light that only pene-trates my prison around 12 p.m. each day (I assume it's 12, because that's when that CUNTSLAVEMASTER tosses my peanut butter sandwich into the air vent in the ceiling. The first two days, the food splatted on my head. Now, I'm trained. The three meals a day, I catch like a frog tongue grab-bing a fly. Each meal comes wrapped in something recyclable or compostable—a page of *Bild* newspaper, occasionally a brown paper bag. A banana leaf, a couple of times. Once—oh, so memorable—my dinner arrived in birthday wrapping, the color of Scottish . . . neenish? . . . tart. Tart? Custard tart. My thoughts ripple, move to the edge of consciousness and fade.

I am mindful. Deeply mindful. My mind is the shelter within this prison. The place I retreat when I suffer panic attacks and hyperventilate.

When I'm out of my shell, two things keep me alive: food and Her. Every small stick of pastry filled with fruit pulp I divide into 20 patient nibbles to keep me from going insane, and I sniff the surface of each apple and admire its Milky Way of brown speckles and wonder about the apple's life. My bottles of Evian water are a swirling delight of wonder.

Each meal comes with a picture of Kristina taped to it, though. Printed snapshots of Kristina in her church confir-mation robes; Kristina at her 6th birthday party, dressed as a cowboy; skinny awkward Kristina standing age 17 in a hall of mirrors at Puzzling World Amusement Park in Wanaka, New Zealand, light years away from the high school bullies. I tear the first few photos up, furious, then decide it's bad luck. Soon these pictures have me begging and clawing all over.

The first couple I shredded and swallowed—the ultimate rebuke of the Kerschbaumers and captivity—but the next twelve photos come with a small rectangle of double-sided tape. Now one wall of my Portaloo prison is a grid of photo-graphs. A shrine to Kristina Maria Kerschbaumer. I love it when the midday bullet of light hits the pics. I watch it move down them one by one. As each picture is highlighted, a slideshow of memories plays inside my eyes. Her sheepish look at prom when I turned from the pack to catch her eye and saw her pleading. Kristina turning from the front of math class to see me at the back. How she stared at the empty seat beside me, begging to be teleported into it so she wouldn't have to do the walk of shame to ask if I was cool with her sitting beside me.

And there is a photo of Kristina stroking a horse's mouth. After twelve Tramadols I see it, like SEEEEEE IT-SEE IT, really deeply see through it, and I know it is the stable I am imprisoned in. Locked in a Portaloo in a stable in a locked, barricaded building until I choose to love Kristina Maria Kerschbaumer and it's IMMEDIATE LIBERATION!!!!!!!!!!!!!!!!!!!, ohmygodohmygod, why did it take a mountain of food waste building up around my legs to realize, yesyesyesfreedom, I will marry her, that's what I'll do. I'll marry Kristina. Make babies with her. Babies'll set me free, they have to, ha HA, ha HA, so simple, God!

I think about it all night, chewing the bloody meat of my tongue with a little seasoning of Trammy-Tram to make the blood taste good.

Nette Frau, Nette Frau, I squawk as Mrs. Kerschbaumer opens the hatch the next morning to toss my breakfast in. Mrs. Kerschbaumer, I'll marry her, cool, got it, agreed, done, we're done right? I'll take her out, I'll treat her honorable, yeah, z'that cool? We're cool, right, yeah, we cool, it's been nineteen days, I've learned my lesson I promise, I promise, umumum, er, Ich verspreche, ah, dass ich gut zu deiner Tochter sein werde, okay? Frau Kerschbaumer, ja?

Every day until now, Mrs. Kerschbaumer has disappeared as soon as she's tossed the food and painkillers into my cage.

Today, she stays.

She pours my food through the ventilation slat—and adds a single word.

"Promisingk?"

*

The blessed union of Colin Harper and Kristina Maria Kerschbaumer takes place in the foyer of the Kerschbaumer Estate, under the ivy-webbed stones of Hohenbaden Castle in the Scarplands of the Black Forest.

My arms are straitjacketed and my brain tipsy from the powder they rubbed on my tongue but Herr Kerschbaumer has quietly, patiently wrestled a black jacket onto me and pinned a single rose to the lapel above my concealed elbows and my hands are pinned to my shoulders so it's hard to hug the man, but the shrunken old count embraces me, bends his moustache into a smile and tells me, *Pass auf meine Tochter,* yes?

Look after my daughter, Colin my friend, he's saying, tilting starboard, then port, because we are on a sailboat across the Bildersee and everything is rocking. Viel Glück, mein sohn.

Good luck.

I step past the man, wobbling, drunk on today's dose of fizzy water (THEY KEEP ME CALM, THE PILLS, KEEP ME FROM RUNNING, KEEP ME OBEDIENT, YES, WELL-BEHAVED, I'M A GOOD BOY) and under the stone arch, there she is, the May Queen, the Princess, the Bride in her cream dress, the Pastor in black at her side, and Frau Kerschbaumer, the SAINT, THE ANGEL WHO FED ME IN MY CAGE, KEPT ME ALIVE, NURSED ME, STEERED ME TOWARD LOVE, the tight four, they're all here, grinning so hard their eyes are thin black smears as I step up to marry the woman I nearly lost, but naughty me, I'm desperate for a little air, too, so I shouldering past her, headed straight for a 200-year old stained glass window, thin single panes, and ramming my head into it and my body is flying out the window, too, tumbling like a rolled-up carpet dumped off a balcony, hitting the ground real hard, whump.

*

THEY KEEP ME CHILL, CHILLS, THE PILLS, THE THRILLS, QUIET MY ILLS HEE HEE HEE, I RAN, ONCE, BURST OUT THROUGH THE RAINBOW TRIANGLES OF THE STAINED GLASS WINDOW IN THE CHAPEL, HEE HEE, LANDED ON A SOFTY TUFTY HAY BALE, hee hee, bale smale kale, stunned momentarily, drunk on the fresh air, wasted on adrenaline I sprinted to the stream, snowy tufts, thick white ocean frozen sharp cut knees please ease wheeze misty breath, I fainted in the river, yes, that's what *Mutti* tells me, they found me crumpled against the base of the stone bridge, skinny and weak and bent as a dropped doll, my skin purple, my willy shriveled to a tiny acorn.

They upped my dosage because I was naughty. Trammy-Trams to flatten the man. Make me walk all pins-and-needley. I must learn my lesson. I now have fizzy tablets in my break-fast coffee, my lunchtime soup, my afternoon hot chocolate when my wife and I come back from our stroll. Fizzy Wizzy Makey Colin not naughty anymore.

My medicine is essential, the tablets keep me obedient, good, shepherd, pastor, control, dog, yes, Colin is a good boy, wood toy. My medicine, it keeps me calm at the wedding reception as we all bite cheese and clink glasses, as the after-noon dissolves in champagne bubbles and helium balloons and a slideshow of photos of Kristina and me at school, at the prom, in front of a waterfall. My chill pills and my strait-jacket and my ankle bracelet, they're important to keep me being a good boy as I go to bed with Kristina and she chains me down and puts her *muschi* on my penis and grinds, hands against the wall while I suck her nipples and stare at the painted ceiling and wonder how many people have died in this manor. They weren't good boys, no, not like me. I'm a good boy who cleans and scrubs and hauls bags of charcoal and helps Frau Kerschbaumer with the firewood to keep the house warm because we can't have our Krissy getting cold, no no no, she is precious, one of a kind, and if you wrong Krissy, you will receive a Time Out like I did, locked away in a potty, a Naughty Potty, because I'm a good boy, and I came all the way to Kerschbaumer Castle to tell the people who've been so good to mee that I'll never be a bad boy again cause I'm veeeery very very sorry.

MENGISTU

The curtains are sealed. There can't be people living here. Yellow 50s bungalow; lawn unmown. The letterbox is leaking paper. Still, the African kid cruising beside you on his bike—no helmet, no shoes—says it's the right place. Bike Boy is chirpy and has red cheeks. Bike Boy loves to help. He follows like a goddamn Disney critter. White people hardly ever come into this hood.

Trudging through the long grass of Mt. Roskill to teach English to refugees: it's a cushy sentence to receive for pushing over the bookcase in your supervisor's office at university. Cushy because you were going to be charged with assault if you didn't beg for diversion. Your parents wrote these totally emo letters to the judge and Mum cried in court and you pleaded it down so teaching ESOL is your punishment but honestly: you feel you should retain the right to kill annoying people. And you could, if you wanted to.

That whole court charade, all that fake contrition? Lesson learned? Pfft. Crocodile tears.

You knock on the door then stand back in the overgrown grass. No one appears for ages. Finally, an African woman opens. Ethiopian, she looks. Ethiopian is what you've been told to expect, anyway. She has these big pretty white eyes bulging out of her cheekbones, that's the first thing that strikes you. The black braids, the black lashes, the stark eyes.

"Heyyy, have I got the right, is this. . . ?" You introduce yourself and pull out the sheet of paper Ruth from Probation gave you, with the lads' names. "I'm here 'cause the court ordered me to teach ESOL to your kids or something?"

"My nephews. They mother, they father, he is being dead."

"Condolences, man . . . er, anyway, I'm here to see . . . how do you pronounce this? Neb-Yacht?"

"Nebeyat," she says quickly, as if the name's only one syllable, and shifts her body so she rests on the other side of the door frame. "He is inside. Come, Keee-vin. I am Shewaynesh. They are aunty."

Inside the air is brown, dark. Every window is covered by a tablecloth with Ethiopian Jesus printed on it, keeping daylight out. This East African Messiah is bearded, with white robes, walking through lush tropical valleys.

The house gets darker and darker until you find yourself in a simple square lounge, five by five meters, with a cold fireplace with some chunks of broken pallet wood and a two-seater couch occupied by one boy, or man. Someone very large yet young-looking. There's another, smaller male on an armchair in the corner. The two guys are watching—seriously? —MTV Africa, according to the logo, playing on a tiny 32-inch TV connected to a small computer with a desktop background picture of what looks like soldiers. The screen shows some kind of Senegal pop music with slutty dancers and playboys in racecars weaving through the crowded markets of Dakar or Lagos or wherever, throwing fistfuls of bullets into the crowd like a lolly scramble.

The larger boy is wearing black sunglasses, camouflage-fatigue pants and no shirt. Torso covered in black notches. The way he sits upright, he looks like some sort of a king, or dictator. He's patting a knife on his thigh.

"'Sup, guys, I'm Kevin. Guys? Guys!"

The younger refugee leans around his cousin. "What you like, Mr. Kevin?"

"Listen, I got some books here in my bag, see? B-A-G. *Bag.* This book's pretty choice. WordFind. You guys do many of these back home, or. . . ?"

The smaller boy offers you a packet of wafers. "You like snack?"

You chew a wafer suspiciously. It dries your mouth out so you crack open a Red Bull. The boy's eyes widen as you drink it.

"What's your name anyway, dude?"

"Rrrred Bool," he says.

"Oh, cool." You search your backpack for a second book of word puzzles before you click. "Hang on—no, YOUR name. YOU. Who are *you*, dude?"

"My name, it Berhanu Ammanuel Fisha Belachew."

"And your bro?"

The younger boy is smacking the butt of the can, patting the last sweet droplets into his mouth.

"Your brother, dude. I can't start the lesson 'til I'm 100 percent sure of his name. They gave me this little attendance register I'm supposed to fill out. Yo! Older Bro! Are. You. Neb-yot?"

"He cousin, not brother," young Berhanu says quickly, lowering his can and glaring at the couch-king.

"Right. Hey, listen, we need to crack on with this learning-English shit else my ass is headed to jail." You flick a light switch on.

Instantly the older boy, Nebeyat, is on his feet. He leans his forehead into yours. This guy is huge. Even though he's slim, his gravity bends the air. Big shoulders. Knuckles like walnuts. A fighter's body.

"I no am want light on this Oromo people, this child," he booms, pointing at his cousin. Then he thumbs his chest and says, "THIS man, me? This man Amhara."

"That's your name, or . . . I don't understand, sorry. You're saying you two are different tribes or something?"

Before the older one flips the light off and returns to his dark couch, you're left with a final impression that he doesn't look much like the other dude at all. He points to the youngster. "Russ-i-a is him," he says, "and America is I am. Oromo he; Amhara me. Amhara like Mengistu!" He thrusts a brief fist in the air. Beneath his sunglasses, his cheeks bend in a smile.

"Are you sure you wanna call him Russia, though? Aren't Russia and America almost at war?"

"WAR *IS*, YAH!" claps the couch king, then he points a finger right in front of his cousin's eyeball. He's chewing something which stinks and makes his lips red. "Is war, yes!"

You lay photocopied word-finds in front of both dudes. Only the smaller boy attempts to complete the literacy exercises. He's grateful, engaged, willing to learn.

The older one, Nebeyat, just stares at his music videos with his sunglasses on, sitting in that king-pose, muttering criticisms. He's not like his little cousin. He's not like anyone.

*

You can't stab people directly in their faces, but you think about it a lot. You don't start the day angry, it's just that people irritate you and the only tool you have is a crafty brain. Uber drivers, students in your ANTH309 tutorials, old neighbors peering over the fence as you use your samurai sword on a dummy swinging from a tree in your back yard. Irritating homeless people at the bus stop. Neighbors having noisy parties you aren't invited to. People on Reddit who disagree with you. It's hard to contain the rage.

You reluctantly go to this student social club party on New North Road hosted by this Somali chick called Awane—wait, she's Ethiopian? Somali? You've never been sure where she's from, she's just always in the student mag for winning scholarships and internships and for protesting. The party is held in a special room within the city council building and it's full of pretentious alphas from the student social committee and the deputy mayor's there in the corner, schmoozing, and it's so hard to keep a clean façade that finally you have to leave before you burst. You find a drunk, camp, skinny boy with big hair in the lobby, invite him to come have some private fun. He thinks you're going to smoke something. You lead him down the steps and away from the music. You move through a dark cleft between buildings, cleaving through alleyways no one knows about. The two of you sprint along a wall, then it's a shortcut through the park before you boost the kitchen window of a house with nobody home. After, when he's lifting his body up the fence to escape, you pull him down, wrap your arms like pythons around his shoulders and collarbone and skull, apply pressure to the chokehold to the count of 100, put him safely to sleep. You've done it twice before. Afterwards there was nothing in the paper about someone dying. Usually, they wake up unharmed. Usually.

You return to the party, return to the people in the button-up shirts, the women in golden hijabs and dashikis. You endure the difficult conversation, put on your normal mask. Know that if you wanted to badly enough you could execute everyone.

*

Aunty Shewaynesh explains more and more each time you enter the house on Saturday afternoons for another slow lesson in a hot, sticky curtained room with Ethiopian Jesus watching over. "Welcome you to us, Kee-vin," she always says, making your name sound exotic and spicy. She shucks corn cobs over the sink, carves up big hocks of beef imported from Yemen. It's nice to see more and more photos on the fridge each time. Looks like she's been going to church with

Berhanu. They're building a family. Nebeyat is not in the picture.

The third time you visit, there's a photo on the fridge of little Berhanu with large eyes in a rumpled uniform that's far too big for him, standing in some smoky camp of tents. Hard to believe that little enthusiastic teen in the lounge with the bright eyes, the dude sharpening his pencil in excitement over your visit, used to be a child soldier. There's a dude in the picture dressed in military fatigues holding a Kalashnikov behind his head and stretching—a dude who looks a lot like Nebeyat. You open the curtains to let a little light onto the photo. Hopefully today you can take down a Jesus or two, illuminate the boys in the lounge, get their eyes off MTV. Shewaynesh comes up beside you, tapping the old photo and says, "Rebel, Berhanu, he rebel, he have to be, Mengistu kill his family. His mother, she is my sister and he KEEL her with he machete."

With that, she yanks the curtains shut so no bullets can find the boy. Nebeyat watches you in the reflection on the TV screen.

Fourth Saturday, you lie on your belly on the floor with Berhanu and explain why C is sometimes a 'suh' sound and sometimes a 'kuh' sound, writing *circus* and *circle* in big plain letters for Berhanu while he copies notes, using his Hello Kitty eraser with pride. You tell them about the word *cicada*, apologize for the vagaries of the English language, try to stir up some laughs.

Nebeyat has spent the entire lesson with the shades over his eyes aiming his fingers like a gun at the TV screen and chewing something. When you press him to tell you what the digraphs *Ch* and *Th* and *Sh* sound like, he stares at you vengefully, still tapping the knife he cradles like a kitten. Still shirtless; still wearing camo pants and dog tags and those immovable black glasses.

"Guys, how would you feel about doing a mock interview with each other, to practice your English so you can get jobs?"

"I have job!" Berhanu pipes up, squeaky and enthusiastic. "When I not am study, I am make for Domino pizza!" He rises a little bit off his chair as he mimes his job proudly, showing his gums as he grins, stretching his arms as he tells his excited story. Nebeyat balances this by staring at you cold and hard. He seems to think Berhanu's enthusiasm is pathetic.

"How 'bout you, Nebeyat? Did they give you a job at Domino's too?"

Berhanu makes a loop-the-loop motion with his finger on his temple. "This manager, he say Nebeyat, he no work. He too anger." Nebeyat snorts. On the screen is another surreal African gangsta music video. Gleeful soldiers with bandoliers of bullets, men on chairs half-buried in jewels. Nollywood music on autotune. Little kids shooting Uzis at each other.

"This is me am work," Nebeyat says, lifting his huge sockless size 13 foot, toeing the TV screen. "Soldier: this Nebeyat work. Him pizza, him Domino? Is work for woman."

Still seated, still patting his knife, he speaks more words than you've heard him say so far put together. "Here is person," he says, indicating Person A with his left hand. "Over here is money." Money is his right hand. Then he puts his hands between the money and the person. "But here is applicashi-on, here is passa-port, here is visa, here is fucking, how say, fucking tunnel. Is TUNNEL. And not fit. Big man NOT down-he-go, not crawl for tunnel. Big man should, should, should tunnel come to HE." He points his sunglasses at you and stares hard. In four weeks, you have never once seen his eyes. Nor have the curtains been opened.

"Hoop is what you wanna say, dude, jumping through hoops, not tunnels—but I feel ya, I feel ya." You stick out your hand to high-five Nebeyat. He examines your hand, lifts it up to see if there's something underneath it.

On screen, some kind of Big Man dictator on the back of a pickup truck is driving down a dusty main street under palm trees, waving at admirers. The Big Man dictator wears a beret, medals, thick black impenetrable aviator glasses.

"*Fssht*, they are dream to be warrior." Nebeyat thumps his chest. "Nebeyat: HE warrior."

"What, you got combat experience, dude? Oh! I almost forgot." You rummage clumsily in your backpack for your print-outs. "I was reading about your country on Wikipedia and I was like Holy Shit. About motherfuckin' Mengistu. The Butcher of Addis Ababa, eh? And people said he had a zār, right? Like an evil spirit that's real contagious? And it gets passed from dictator to dictator?"

Little Berhanu gasps and looks away, muttering a prayer, making the sign of the cross.

"Am I saying it right? *Men-gis-tu*? Zār spirit? Like a demon that's contagious?"

Nebeyat grins from the couch, scratches a shirtless armpit. He even lowers his shades a fraction.

"So, you had like the nationalist guy Haile Selassie, the rasta guy, then this fella Mengistu Haile Mariam comes along? And he's like a Communist and real repressive and shit? And he got revenge on the other tribe, eh, the Oromos? And they called him the Butcher of Addis Ababa? Sounds epic—no offence. What side were you guys on?"

Berhanu covers his little mouth and shakes his face, mumbling "Not-not-not."

Nebeyat leans back cockily, laces his fingers behind his arrogant ears.

"Says in the thing I read online that Mengistu overthrew the palace of Haile Selassie, eh. Like, that hippie kinda emperor who founded Rasta, right? And Mengistu asked Haile Selassie where the crown jewels were hidden and the emperor spat in Mengistu's face and said he wouldn't speak to a slave so Mengistu put his hands on the dude's throat like this... . " You tickle Berhanu's throat then squeeze harder. Berhanu shakes and wriggles, battling your strangling hands. "Mengistu totally choked him out, I read. Crushed his windpipe. Like choked him so hard his thumbnail went right into the dude's throat."

Berhanu breaks out of the strangulation, attempts to run.

Nebeyat reaches out from the couch and seizes the boy's shirttail, hauling him in.

"Sorry, um, anyway, guys, we just got another three minutes before my time is over—"

"Your time is over saying who?" Nebeyat gives some growled instruction to the other kid, leans over the far end of the couch and slaps him.

Berhanu rubs his sore cheek. "He want to know who are telling you orders."

"It's, God, it's . . . this is hard for me to say: It's Corrections, okay? Like, probation? Police, judge—they tell me to come here and when I'm sposda leave."

Nebeyat snorts and smirks and claps his hands and knees. His large white teeth and pink gums are exposed. "You are creemenal, is excellence, is good," he says at last. "Tell Nebeyat your creem. I have cut off man ear and feed him ear, he eat him ear," he says. "Tell Nebeyat."

"Just assault, man. Common assault . . . with a blunt instrument. But I got diversion."

"Instrument? You keel him with guitar?"

"A bookcase. I pushed it towards him. Smashed up my supervisor's office a little bit."

A white smile spills on his face and leaks from chin to ears.

"Bookcase, heh heh. Keel with him book, yes." He claps his hands decisively, gets up and starts pacing. "Meester

Job, Meester Domino manager of pizza think he big man: I want KEEL him. I want CHOP de face. This why Nebeyat no servant. Nebeyat, he is. . . God?"

"God's not quite the correct English, bro, that's sort-of like a reserved word"

Nebeyat is still searching for the right word when Shewaynesh knocks on the wall and says the lesson's up. She invites you to share a cup of sweetened condensed milk and some biscuits. You turn the biscuits over in your hands, standing awkwardly in the kitchen, Shewaynesh and Berhanu grinning every time your eyes meet theirs, anxious for conversation.

The eye-shaped glass bead above the fridge catches your attention.

"What's that evil eye thing, anyway? Isn't that to keep away people that can change into like hyenas and stuff? I read that on the net."

"Buda," Shewaynesh says as she walks you to the door. "Buda, it is an eye. Buda keep away spirit of the bad thing. The zār, the spirit of the wolf, it ees, how you say—it is sickness, is corona-the-virus. Mengistu, he have this."

"The eye doesn't spot evil if it's already in your house, though. It said on the website."

They say goodbye and you step out into stunning daylight.

Behind you, Couch King Nebeyat appears on the top doorstep. "Nebeyat is God. This is the word."

"Right. Awesome try, bro. But God's more if you've got the power of, like, life or death and smiting someone?"

Nebeyat smiles at that. He smiles like he's smiling in that computer desktop photograph. A photograph of Big Uncle Mengistu with his hand on the neck of young soldier Nebeyat and Nebeyat folding into him.

*

Job interviews make you want to strangle, choke, kill, burn. They make you want to throw acid in a man's face, like you saw in that Uganda documentary in ANTH304. You feel like melting off your parents' faces, too, as they fill your wine glass with trembling, liver-spotted hands and tell you which job interviews their Probus Club arranged for you this week.

You do your best to interview well, but the nicely presented Perfect People seem to sense the frustration in you. They can call it evil if they want, but you think of it like this: you won't have to bring the pain so long as these people show you fealty. Respect. Deference.

You get calls every day to tell you you've made it to the shortlist for some job that would've been lucky to have you, but unfooooooorunately, another candidate was just that liiiiiiiiittle teency bit more qualified, at least according to Candy from Manpower. She personally phones and gives you a cruel spark of hope before taking a full 70 seconds to draw the let-down out in a gentle decrescendo.

By the tenth rejection, you're mad enough to put hits on these people that doubt you. "Y'know what, lady?" you rasp over the phone at Jasmine from Jobsource.com, "I got a friend who could make you eat your own ear if you ever, EVER fuck me again."

It's days like this you need a little perspective. You need to hear about the place where if you want to take the life of someone who's wronged you, you can go ahead and do it.

You don't even realize you're stomping round to Nebeyat's place 'til you're on the doorstep, late on a Thursday. He nods as you come in, like he's saying you've chosen correctly. You bring him a gift: *Grand Theft Auto Hit & Run*. Nebeyat, looking pleased, points down towards the PlayStation, ordering you to get the game going. Berhanu skulks in the corner buttoning his Domino's shirt, getting ready for work, looking uncomfortable as his cousin runs around Vice City bashing in heads with his virtual baseball bat. Berhanu seems to have looked up to you as a mentor, but this is the way you feel about Nebeyat. You wouldn't have even had to take the risks you've taken in your life if you had a brother as bold as Nebeyat.

He *Hit & Runs* a man's skull into a signpost so hard it bends the metal, and your hand reaches out to Nebeyat and he slaps your palm in solidarity. The two of you hang out late into the evening, drinking Red Bull, then you return lunchtime Friday and play *Postal* and *Fortnite* and *Jarhead* for hours, and *Sniper Elite* and *Dead By Daylight* and *Bulletstorm* and *Hemorrhage*. Saturday afternoon, while Berhanu quietly lies on the floor, scrawling childish letters in the workbook you're supposed to be helping him with, you and your new best bro are laughing at *Inglourious Basterds* and throwing popcorn at the TV. You watch *Natural Born Killers* next, then *Sin City* then *Reservoir Dogs* after. Nebeyat loves the bit where they cut off the guy's ear and he drags the couch closer to the screen and points at Berhanu and makes a scissor motion with his fingers and the two of you cackle together.

As the credits roll, you notice Berhanu behind the couch, crouching in darkness, outlined in white TV glow. You're chewing this peppery *khat* weed Nebeyat has given you. It makes you impatient and you find yourself snapping at Berhanu to bring you a drink and a smoke.

"*T'et'a, wisha, t'et'a!*" you snap at the boy and you both laugh. *Wisha* means dog. T'et'a means Bring me a drink.

"MM! MM! Almost forgot! Look what I picked up from Camo & Ammo!" You unzip your bag as fast as you can and pull out the army uniform. Sure, it's mothballed surplus from the 70s but it's dark green and it's got patches sewn on the chest and brass buttons and it's crisp and pleated.

Nebeyat's teeth and gums take over his face. He hoists the uniform up to the light, lays it down on the couch, waltzes around the room with it then promises he'll be back. He trots away to his bedroom to dress up.

When he returns, clad in green fatigues, tall and noble, he is wearing brown boots. His chest is puffed up like a pillow. His black plastic eyes point proudly at the ceiling.

"You look ready for war, bro."

Nebeyat agrees and presses a fresh chunk of khat into your lips.

You march down to Domino's, Nebeyat's boots thudding on the pavement. The sky is overcast, far too dark for Nebeyat's shades, but he won't take them off. He struts past the laundromat, past the Western Union and the dole office and the Hindi spice shop and the mosque and Lamb Traders towards Domino's. Shop owners look out as he passes. They tut and point and make calls on their phones.

The manager on duty at Domino's looks African—Ethiopian, then? He knows the score—or he ought to. There's something expectant and fearful about his body language, the way he tucks the other couple of pizza guys back into the kitchen, arms himself with a rolling pin. He seems to have been expecting this.

White tiles stretch ahead of you. Your penis tingles. Everything goes silent.

"You hold heem, Keevin," Nebeyat finally decides, and you reach across the counter and try opening the little locked gate to the kitchen. The manager bops your hand with his rolling pin, and you gasp and suck your knuckles and Nebeyat uses this as an excuse to attack, vaulting the counter and yanking the rolling pin out of the manager's hands. The third time the rolling pin comes down on the manager's head it breaks, and the man shrinks onto the tiles and hugs his legs. Nebeyat leverages himself between the wall and the till, raising his body off the ground to allow himself to stomp the manager's head more effectively. When he's done smearing the guy's skull, Nebeyat pushes khat onto a piece of pizza and munches it.

You grab Nebeyat's sleeve and yank him away.

*

That uppity piece of ass Awane, the one who's always putting on socials and protests, the one with her face on all those student council election signs? The one who loves following rules with the perfectly braided hair and the gentle voice? Turns out she's Ethiopian and she suddenly comes into focus. There's been war in the news again and you want to know where she stands. You walk into the student break room as she's making a coffee and she gasps as she spots the t-shirt you're wearing. It's got Mengistu printed on it, waving to a crowd. You found the shirts on eBay, so you bought you and your new best friend matching Mengistu gear. Berhanu and Shewaynesh were shocked speechless and Awane's having the same reaction as those two cowards. You try shut her up, explain that you've been volunteering on weekends to teach English to the refugee community from her fascinating country, so she should be happy.

She waggles a finger. "Not all aspect of my homeland are thees fascinating," she says, sternly. "Thees Mengistu, the Red Terror? He name is being obscenity to my people. A sacrilege word. A phrase we say only when spit."

"Who are your people, then? 'Cause my mate reckons Mengistu's all good."

You realize Awane's friends are staring at you. The devil's name has made them prick up their ears.

It looks like Awane's mouth is full of wasps. "Oromo are my people. You meet any Ethiopian person; chances are they're Oromo. Oromo suffer. Oromo in exile."

"Not my mate Nebeyat that I'm tutoring. You should meet him. He's Amhara. He reckons they're the best tribe."

Some of the Model United Nations Council cats have their mouths hanging open and they're tilting their heads forward, hanging on her words. "This is Nebeyat Fisha, you're talking about? That's the guy, hm? You have no idea who you're dealing with, Kevin." She beckons you into the corridor. "We'd heard he sneaked out of the country," she whispers, glancing over her shoulder. "We have a list of people, people we're concerned about. They've, they've . . . *infiltrated*. Contaminated the quota of refugees. People wanted for war crimes."

"What do you mean, list of people? What, like you're Nazi-hunters or something? You mean this guy's like some kind of bigshot?"

Awane grabs both your shoulders and aims her forehead at you. "Just a kid, same age as me. But a bad one."

"We insist he be deported," interjects one of Awane's friends. "We shall contact the police this very night!"

"Nebeyat Fisha, he be-a the HENCHman, the Devil," adds another. "He has the sickness. The contagion."

Big man NOT stoop, not crawl for tunnel.

"Do not let yourself be deceived. He is older than he looks. Ten years in the worst refugee camp in Zimbabwe. That's where Mengistu escaped to after he was forced out of our country. Sadly, the zār cannot be killed. Nor can Mengistu. He's approaching 90, now and, well." She dumps a huge sigh, heavy as the ceiling. "This is where Nebeyat has been trained. Exposed to the curse. Groomed, you are saying? I've lived here half my life, Kevin, and I tell you thees: there be nothing *good* about the government putting Oromo and Amhara together in the same house. Nothing *good* about giving amnesty to murderers just so they can say they've filled their refugee quota. Disaster, this is! If you had seen the things Mengistu's hyenas did to my people, to the Anuak, to the Ogadeni, to the Omo. But most of all to the Orom—" She bares her teeth, shakes your hand off hers. "To my family."

You think over this stuff for the last few hours of the day. The afternoon drags and you can't concentrate on your lectures. This thing with Awane, telling you she's on the opposite of Nebeyat and his army? It's a good thing. It's cards on the table. Least we all now know now where she stands. She's basically admitted there's a target on her head.

You vault the turnstile to get your train, tap your foot impatiently all the way, leap out as soon as the train stops and scuttle to Nebeyat's house as quickly as you can. Disney Bike Boy approaches, says Hi, dings his bell, sees what you've got in your hand and cycles away.

Shewaynesh opens the door, steps behind it. She's wearing the door as armor.

You've picked up a long hard bottle of wine on the way and you pat it against your leg as you search the house for your man.

"Tell me where he is."

"Nebeyat, he Immigration they come, in white car, with police."

You walk hard at Shewaynesh until she can't back up any further. "SERIOUSLY. I want to see my friend."

"HE NO IS HERE! HE DEPORTING! HE PRISON!"

The house gets increasingly dark as you move through until you find Berhanu in the corner of the lounge, holding his pencil case and *Hooked On Phonics* book.

Left for you, folded neatly on Nebeyat's knife are the black aviator glasses. You lift the glasses, push them on your eyes. You can feel the greasy warmth of Nebeyat's nose.

"I am so happy this danger man he gone," Berhanu says, his pencil case and workbook clutched in his fingers.

You shut the door of the lounge and adjust the shades. The world is dark.

You pick up Nebeyat's knife.

"You sure he's gone?"

TEST OF DEATH

1.

My best friend doesn't want to die but his cancer is irreversible and the sky is black and booming so I'm swallowing three of his Tramadols with a nip of eighty-dollar cognac, back turned, hovering shamefaced over the armoire where Jarrod keeps his dusty trophies and awards and un-drunk alcohol. I'm a shitty nurse, I know. I don't know what else to do except stand around and take his possessions and watch him die. I'm his oldest friend. He tells me to do stuff, I do it for him. He tells me to give his suits to the St. Vincent de Paul, okay, I do it. Give his Hot Wheels cars to my nephew. Throw out his trophies, fair enough—it's not as if I deserve one. I haven't done anything to slow down his cancer. We're supposed to be high school teachers, supposed to act brave in front of 200 kids every week, but Jarrod is behind me, watching TV slumped on his side, melting into the couch, and I can't face him.

Because tumors are devouring his insides and he's told me to help myself to anything in the house—his drugs, his booze, his washer-dryer, his vinyl collection, his Star Wars figurines—I'm filling a laundry basket with precious things, heavy with shame. I throw in a letter opener, a scented candle, benzies, opioids, all his pills and die cast toys and rare albums, sniffling while I work. I've moved the washer-dryer into the laundry, along with a suitcase of Jarrod's shirts.

I'll come back with a trailer and take the vinyl, though I'm scared of what'll happen after. Removing his possessions feels like pulling a plug out of a bathtub. The dregs of his life will swirl away. If I stop packing up his life, will it even slow the cancer? I don't know. People are coming round for a dinner party tonight everyone assumes will be the last. That's pretty final.

Jarrod is snapping his fingers at me from where he's splashed on the couch. The clicking thing is rude, though he gets a pass. Rudeness and gloomy sodden days are all we have. It's May 14 and the rains are coming every day and we don't expect him to last through the southern winter.

I creep back to the couch and settle down in front of him a glass with his morphine tablets crushed up in water and a long circus straw which he can sip without adjusting his body.

Since he's sold his armchairs and his rug that he brought back from Egypt, I find a space for my butt on the couch edge. It's gross, having a dead man near—okay, he's not dead yet, it's just that Jarrod sees himself as nearly dead. Jarrod embraced his bowel cancer in Feb, expected to die by the end of March, and started getting really black in April. What hurts him now isn't the cramps or the beetroot-colored poo or the burned skin. It's the uncertainty, the pointlessness of his days. He wants either a miracle extension of his life, or a death date. Fuck the in-between.

Jarrod extends an arm, his skin the color of mashed potato, straining, and the blood flushes out of his face as he points out this goof in the DVD extras of *Lord of the Rings*.

I try to have a laugh, agree with the prick, then clear my throat.

"You've been indoors for, like, a week, man. We should go to Burger Fuel or something, like old times. Get you refreshed before the dinner party tonight."

Jarrod rolls his eyes without looking at me. He's too weak to waste energy turning his head or sitting up. Chemotherapy eats up your insides and leaves you a bag of empty skin, your muscle melted, your skin burned and bumpy.

"Fine, man. We should at least stretch our muscles. Get the wine glasses and plates from the garage; open some Christmas crackers for the guests. C'mon dude. People wanna say goodbye. You have to, you know . . . dress the place up a bit. Put up some bunting or whatever."

"The thought is father to the deed," he says. "So go do it."

Jarrod unpauses his Blu-Ray, slips back into his sulk.

We barely speak for the next hour. I remember I haven't raided the bathroom. I go and take his fancy soaps and his razors, hating myself. He tosses his phone at me, and I read out the new messages on his Facebook for him, reciting the support and love and prayer while Jarrod snorts and rolls his eyes. He's always taught computing, always loved machines more than people. He's about to leave this world with no missus, no kids. A bit of money from life insurance, a pension from school. Jarrod has three hundred thousand bucks, and all he wants to spend it on is time.

Finally, the credits roll and that's his entire DVD collection over. He's read all his books, watched everything there is to watch. Clocked Skyrim on X-box. Unlocked every easter egg. There's nothing left.

Rain sprinkles the deck. A gust of wind tips a bucket over. His wind chimes tinkle.

"We'll get through this godforsaken dinner party tonight then we'll move on with our lives," Jarrod sighs. "Well, you'll get on with your life. I'll get on with my death."

"Bro—"

"MICHAEL." The sky booms. The roof rattles. "We can slow it down, granted. But we can't stop this thing."

*

At 6.29, just before people file into Jarrod's house for what could be our last dinner party ever, Jarrod and me hover in the coat room while I dust off the backpack full of drugs me and Jarrod used to take to festivals. There's molly in here, MDMA, enough for a little lick each. The corner of his mouth twitches, almost smiling for the first time in a month. Then he sees Sarmila and Kiran are here and he turns to his audience and hobbles over using his cane.

"Get your photos in," he says, bent, cynical. "This time next month, I'll be worm supper. Hopefully."

Sarmila bursts into tears. Kiran rubs her back and looks at me. I carry on putting out plates and silverware, breadsticks and pâté, camembert and olives.

Jarrod was an autistic unsmiling asshole even when he was healthy. He's not going to suddenly become sensitive in his last days.

Jarrod wheels his chair over to the door when the Milners enter, saying, "Come in, don't be shy, you know what to do." All the folks here are teachers, mostly. Tall and unimpressed, in thick coats and pointless scarves. Short and nerdy and Europolitan, in shoes they picked up in Florence or Buenos Aires. Jarrod plays dictator for the evening, sitting at the head of the table in an office wheely chair with arm rests. He dismisses or hisses or snorts at just about everything anyone says. I watch him while I serve soup and arrange cubes of cheese and pour cocktails. These people have their degrees, Jarrod is thinking, but all they know is life. They know nothing of the undiscovered country Jarrod is about to go to.

I serve roast lamb with mint and rosemary on it, torn off from the untended garden which has been creeping up to the house. After it's been eaten and praised, I slice up a thick chewy moon cake Lisa's mother imported from Taiwan, and Abdi shows off his Chinese. Initially when I check the time, it's 7, and Jarrod's conversation is confrontational, insulting, the guests clamming up, rubbing their wrists, looking at the tines on their forks. Next time I check my watch, it's almost 10 and the windows are black, and somebody's just called the deputy principal a cunt, and everyone is drunk and leaning back in their chairs, playing with their wine glasses. Someone finds a wrapped box of Cards Against Humanity. By 11.30, Jarrod is slurping whiskey out of the gold-painted plastic cup his students awarded him that day he took them bowling. Usually, Jarrod has three naps a day. Only the molly is keeping him awake. I pour wine into Jarrod's gold goblet while his face slumps and collapses on his fist as he rests his flabby melting skull on his knuckles. He's sitting at the head of the table but there are three conversations going on at once and now it's midnight and the table's a dump of torn garlic bread and glass and saltshakers and bones and corn cobs and quinoa on dirty plates.

We've all had a snort of molly and sucked tequila shots with lemon and salt. The Milners and Ahmed leave together, hugging and kissing Jarrod and taking a farewell selfie with him, kissing Jarrod's bald dome before bursting into tears while Jarrod rolls his eyes.

Next, it's 1 a.m. and even the storm has gone to bed. There's only one conversation going on. Rico is trying to tell us how he's been inspired by this Tibetan monk guy on YouTube who reckons death is nothing to fear. It's like a second life.

"You're giving me advice on death, Rico?"

"Dude, nah, no offence, I just mean, like—Tukdam, Jar. You've never heard of it?"

Jarrod looks at me. My eyebrows narrow.

"I suppose I can tell you a story, this thing I read," Rico is going. He looks over his shoulder warily.

His silent sidekick Stacey, or was it Casey, squeezes his arm.

"I don't know if I should. It'll freak you out, Jar."

Jarrod thumps the table. Everybody jumps.

"Do I look like a man with time to waste?"

Rico gets his phone out, clears his throat. "I warned you, okay? This story, it isn't—like, you shouldn't follow it. Don't do what these guys are doing. You're positive you want this story? Came from *Nature*, like the journal *Nature*? Listen. Here we go."

Tukdam, the Tibetan solution to death: science or supposition?

Tukdam appears to be an occurrence in which a Buddhist monk passes away but there is seemingly no physical decomposition for as much as ten to fourteen days. Dr. Richard Davidson of Wisconsin Technical College, whose doctoral thesis looked at the meditation's effect on bodily systems, studied the phenomenon at the Deer Park monastery, west of Ann Arbor in December 2019.

The monk that Davidson observed, Ongdurje, was aged 84 and suffering from advanced heart disease. Davidson documented the subject tidying his bedroom in the barracks, arranging a disused room, clearing the room's boxes and cobwebs, preparing only a cushion, sitting down, and entering a silent, eyes-open transcendental meditation which lasted two hours initially, then stretched out to three, five, and then 24 hours. Silent meditation was all that was required—no chanting, no recital of prayer. The subject simply focuses on walking through the tunnel of death and emerging instead of surrendering, I was told. During this time Ongdurje's pulse slowed to a marginal rate before dropping to zero, though the time of death was impossible to determine.

Davidson told Nature he wanted to create a model predicting the onset of an intertidal zone for subjects whose heart rate slows so much during meditation that it eventually ceases, even while the brain continues to emit gamma waves.

To find out how long life could last after death, Davidson was granted permission to attach electrodes to Ongdurje's temporal and occipital lobes, along with a heart rate monitor, to chart the descent into death—and potentially beyond.

"You walk into the room, what these guys are doing, it's indistinguishable from deep meditation," Davidson said. "Like a deep sleep or a coma. Zero difference. For this guy, for Ongdurje, his chest wasn't even rising and falling. I was there for research interviews; the other monks, they didn't blink twice about Ongdurje slipping away. They didn't consider Ongdurje to have died, actually; they didn't have a plan to ring a funeral director or anything. While we were waiting to see if, you know, if Ongdurje was going to be—if there were going to be any further developments—they took me to this courtyard, this separate area, in the south wing. This garden full of fuchsias and lilies and vines, kind of neglected. And they were in there. The guys that had done it, before Ongdurje. And at first, I thought they were statues. Like 'cause, they were blue statues, the people in the bushes, like Krishna? In

Hindu paintings? Cause they'd just . . . put them there. Left the monks outside in the bushes to sit forever. Exactly like statues. Four of them, I counted, between the bamboo. Sitting cross-legged, lotus-style. So blue that they were black, in the cracks and crevices, like around their armpits and where their heads had sunk into their collars. One guy, I don't know if I should say. It's . . . like, rats were all over him, yanking at his lips like fish nibbling bait. And he turned— just a smidgen— turned and tilted his head. Nodding. Like saying hello. Real calm. Real beatific.

"That's when I got the hell out of there."

Rico finishes. We all look up.

I yelp. Something is crushing my arm. It's Jarrod, looking more energetic than he has in weeks. Black rings around his eyes.

"You have to get me this Tukdam shit."

Rico has shifted over to the door. He's reaching into the arms of his coat. Stacey-Casey is tightening her scarf and looking anxious. The black world is closing in. It's almost 2, now. The bottom of the night.

Rico hovers, half-turns around. One last look at Jarrod.

"Why would you want to go through Tukdam? It's not something you can, like, do a weekend retreat on. Forget that Davidson professor guy, anyway. Fucker went crazy, I heard. Made all these weird-ass recordings then *voom*. Up and vanished."

Jarrod flings a glass at Rico. It splinters on the wall. Stacey-Casey ducks, screams, opens the door and escapes.

"GET ME IT." He turns and puts his force on me, eyes narrowing. "Michael. We have to try."

2.

Waking Up. That's the name of the app I download. This American-Vietnamese doctor guy, this philosopher, Thich Nhat Hanh, he's the narrator, except he's so robotically calm and quiet and so uninterested in making his English sound normal that you barely recognize it's a guy narrating until you're minutes into it.

Me and Jarrod, we're sitting with our elbows on the kitchen table, hunched over it.

Episode 346 is a conversation with that Richard Davidson guy, the doctor, the expert, on the topic of *second* life. This is what we've been waiting for. Except when Thich Nhat Hanh talks and talks about spiritual planes, and we realize Davidson has hardly said anything, Jarrod goes to the window. It's agonizing for him to stand up, and he hobbles, shudders.

"Davidson," Jarrod tells the storm outside. "He's the one we want. He has the answer."

"I already Googled. Plus, I emailed the university. They sacked him, I think, reading between the lines. If he's published something recent, pbbbt . . . God knows where. The dude's a ghost, man."

"Even so," Jarrod says, 'You need to find him."

*

It's on a Friday after-school drive home to Jarrod's, when the sky is purple, lit by white veins of lightning, and everybody is racing towards their weekend plans, that I decide to try Reddit. Google hasn't helped, nor has LinkedIn or Facebook or the White Pages. But I have a feeling.

I pull over under a service station awning and type Dr. Richard Davidson's name into the Reddit app on my phone.

Just a single reference appears in the results. In the single page, a single line.

On a subreddit called r/lifeafterdeath.

A whole discussion board. Someone is getting tons of upvotes. They've pointed to a *Scientific American* article. It says in the natural world, the less something moves, the longer it tends to live. Bacteria thrive on coral for 1000 years in oxygen-low waters. Seeds and spores—practically immortal—can have life spans of thousands of years before rising after a drink of water.

Redditor Friedman69 has an opinion:

You guys read that thing in Nat Geo? CPR = miracle yo. Ask Gardell Thoms, 7 years old. Kid fell in a frozen pond in Amish Country. Didn't breathe for 200 minutes. Pulse returned after they squirted warm fluid up him. You have 2 re-introduce oxygen slowly. I did pre-med at uni. Breathing. That's where we've been going wrong. All this time. Oxygen is a paradox. Take oxygen down to like 0.1 percent, you can keep nematodes alive for a thousand years.

Then there is PneumaTool16.

U guys heard The Blackness Then The White? Audiobook. Banned in 80 countries. U have to get it. Tells u how you can do that Tibetan tukdam thing extend life after death. Last copy of the recording = Pirate Bay but go thru TOR b/c they are watching. It's there. All the instructions. Every other platform dropped the podcast after u-know-what. How the thing took ova him. Shit got real.

I surge out into traffic, push my car through screens of stony rain and race up the motorway.

I burst into Jarrod's home and shake him awake.

"Jar, man. I think I've found it."

3.

The garage. That's the place for it, for us. A concrete bunker with a steel door where skeptics and critics can't get in. The place for this whole project to begin. Operation Tukdam.

I push boxes of framed photographs and certificates against the walls. I shove skis and a paddle and hiking boots and 200 sci-fi novels in a wheelbarrow into the corner. I brush the floor clean.

We each position a cushion in the middle of the floor, tighten our wool coats and scarves. I sit easily.

Jarrod packs his painful body down like he's easing into a hot bath, hissing teeth bared.

"You ever meditated before, Jar?"

Jarrod shakes his head. "Pseudo-science, it always seemed to me. Quackery. Hot yoga mumbo-jumbo. Nevertheless: Here we are."

We drum our fingers on our knees. Jarrod is wearing a white t-shirt. His armpits have leaked dark juice into it. Sweat, mixed with something awful and cancerous.

It's raining again today. We can smell it, sneaking through tiny cracks. Relentless drumming on the roof.

I lean forward, position my portable Bluetooth speaker between us. I hold my cellphone in front of me, get ready to push play on a recording that will change Jarrod's life.

Change his death, rather.

For the first time in years, Jarrod looks at me with beseeching eyes.

"Michael. D'you think . . . d'you think it will, you know. Happen . . . immediately?"

"I don't know but, like, you should probably text your dad, eh. Say goodbye."

There is a small window looking out into a chrysanthemum hedge. Jarrod stares at it, then back at the speaker. Jarrod's old man was a lot like him. A robot with as much heart as a calculator. "Just get it over with. Press play."

"Our existence is not a toggle—on for alive, off for dead," begins a slow, plodding, raspy voice. A tired, patient voice. "Think of our existence as a dimmer switch with which we move through shades white to black."

After a pause, we descend.

'They didn't want me to record this. They wanted me gone. Silenced. But you cannot terminate a dead man.

'This lesson, this sermon, this is my gift to you. You, with multiple sclerosis and 100 pills of paracetamol you're itching to swallow. You, with silicosis and agony in every breath. This is for the crippled. The tired. For everyone who has had enough of life.'

There's a moment's hesitation, then the sickly, crunching sound of a snail being stepped upon.

'If you've ever been diagnosed with squamous cell carcinoma, you'll know the first questions are all variations on *why*,' continues a voice which bubbles and pops. A sickly voice. Slow and crusted and scabby. A voice trickling with fluid.

'Why are the gods displeased with me? When did I go wrong? Can't I go back and atone? And your doctor, she's young. Embarrassed. Inexperienced. Turns away on her swivel-chair. Reads the script on her screen.

'If you've ever been diagnosed with a cancer of the lungs which feels like you have damp sawdust at the bottom of your throat. You'll waste money on therapists and self-help books and inspirational calendars. You'll watch your colleagues hug the wall to avoid brushing against you in the corridors of the faculty office where you once had value. You'll get used to the disappointment of your manager as you take off mornings and afternoons so slim doctors with good skin can pass magnets and radio waves over your body while you lie on a table and imagine what it's like to be a corpse. You'll burst into Deer Park Monastery distraught and drunk with vodka steaming out of your pores at 10 o'clock on a Wednesday night and collapse at the feet of the only people who understand. Tell them you want to do this, this tukdam thing. This letting-go. Beg them to let you die here. They'll rub oil into your head, give you a last bath with menthol and incense and the next morning, after a final meal of dhal and rice, they'll guide you to a private room. There is a cushion, and there is you, and there is infinity.'

A pause, now. No breathing. Low slurping sickly breaths, like the dregs of a milkshake sucked through a straw.

'In his seminal 1994 text, *Erasing Death*, critical care physician Sam Parnia reminds us death is a process – not a moment. It's a whole-body stroke. The heart stops beating but the organs don't die immediately. Organs can be harvested hours after the heart stops. They continue for quite some time indeed. So consider this, you, out there, lonesome, afraid. When a liver is rushed across the country to be put in the body of a needier patient, is this not death giving life?'

I open one eye. I'm surprised to see Jarrod staring directly at me, though he's not looking at me. His chest is barely rising. Jarrod is entranced.

'You're listening intently, I know. You're getting ready for the second phase. You're looking down a black waterslide.

Child, this tunnel into which I beckon you. It has an end, you know. You needn't be afraid. At the end is light, refreshing light – a gentle grey light which twists and swirls, like wading through fog. Your eyes will be dry as onion skin. And you will blink in the new realm. And you will notice an eyelash twitch and wriggle. You'll pick twisting grains of rice from the rims of your eyes. These things, drinking your juices. They are the children of flies. They are life renewed.

You'll creak and groan and slosh and you push yourself to a standing position and wonder what day it is. How long has passed. Two weeks, perhaps, or maybe three since you passed over. Feels like an eternity, does it not?

You'll stagger to the door, the hallway, the foyer. The brothers in the monastery, they'll nod as you pass, because they understand.

You'll put two hands hard against the very front doors, beside reception and the giftshop where postcards and gum and bonsai trees are sold. You'll notice something sprouting on your knuckles. The green mould that grows on bread.

Twin boys on tricycles will see you and drop their ice creams and shriek. The blue man, mommy, is is is – he's blue -

You'll push the glass doors open and here is the world. You'll put a hand in the centre of your rib cage. Your heart should be pounding.

4.

During lunch breaks in the steamy staffroom, I try to do my research. I try to listen as Davidson bores through a tunnel of answers towards the ultimate question. I keep headphones pressed against my skull while the teachers chatter and gossip and spray chewed-up sandwich, elbowing me to get my input on the new timetable. They want me to cover a sport for Athletics Day. They want to know what I think of that little fuck that got transferred from Marist. I make my excuses, abandon my box of papers. I leave a stack of unread memos in my pigeonhole. This daytime chatter, this babble and fuss, it's a waste of life. I just want to be beside my friend as he passes.

It's been eight days of meditation so far. Eight days out of a final ten. I don't think he will last until the weekend.

Jarrod has eaten nothing. I've pushed a sip of water into his lips and not much else. Any afternoon now, Jarrod is going to push up from the garage floor and declare this whole silly experiment a waste of time. Then he will die and I will shove his clothes into a giant steel bin beside a Korean barbecue joint. Place a notice in the paper. Meet with men in suits.

He appears dead, when I walk in, though sitting upright. A concrete man, heavy. Centre of an empty cement garage. Wind whistling at the door.

Jarrod's eyes are becoming dry and matte and I have to brush my palm against his lashes to make him blink.

In today's sermon, Davidson's plodding monologue tells of how he had to remain unresponsive through examinations by the monks at his monastery while they murmured and poked and looked at him hard. They tested for three cardinal benchmarks. The Tests of Tukdam. The tests of death.

Davidson describes the tests. I ask Jarrod if he has a pen and paper somewhere around here.

Jarrod says nothing. Jarrod is somewhere else.

*

In the grey, bruised hour before my lonely microwave pasta at home, I take my friend outside and commence the tests of death. The wind nips, yes. My skin and Jarrod's are studded with goose pimples, okay. But the cold will preserve him, I decided on the drive over, stroking the shelves at the pharmacy, wondering if I ought to turn back.

Through the house I drag my friend, from garage to hallway to the thud-thump-thud of the steps from the sunken lounge-pit up to his porch. His ankles scrape the carpet. His head smacks a corner.

On the wet slippery wooden slats of the deck, I use scissors to hack off Jarrod's t-shirt—stiff and brown—and I pull his right arm until it snaps into place. His eyelids riffle in the breeze, and a cockroach runs out of his armpit, but apart from that, Jarrod doesn't flinch. I find a vein, pull the pharmacy syringe from my pocket, unwrap the thing, screw the needle onto the pump, shake up a bottle of Betadine and inject 80 milliliters of iodine, then another ten. 90 mils. A huge dose. Jarrod told me to, in the instructions he gave me on a Google spreadsheet, before this whole unreal thing became real. Iodine slows oxygen metabolism, he insisted, clutching my collar. My heart needs to sip its oxygen, Michael. Tiny gasps.

Need to get him cold now. Rip the cotton off his saggy tits. Expose him to the wet wind. Slow down the movement of free radicals and hemoglobin in his cells. I bend him backwards, roll him onto his side, fetal. I take a curtain from the linen closet, spread it over his Pompeii-stiff body, hunched, awkward.

"Jar. JARROD, MAN. You can't hear me. Right?"

The wind answers, speaking through the plastic roof gutters which drizzle a screen of freezing rain. The lawn is soaked, bleeding mud. Brown puddles.

The first test of death is determining whether Jarrod will drink. I cup a handful of rain, pour it in his hard, rubbery purple lips. The water spills out onto his stubbled chin. Jarrod's tongue doesn't move.

Next, I wrench Jarrod's left hand away from his lap. I push back the watch they gave him for 20 years' service at school. I take from my pocket a thin plastic case the size of a business card. A selection of needles I've stolen from the sewing department at school.

I extract the longest needle, hold it up to the wan light. I mutter sorry for what I'm about to do.

I prise the fingernail back off the skin of the index finger of his left hand (long nail, needs clipping). I jam the needle into the soft sensitive nailbed, hissing and whimpering on Jarrod's behalf.

Thunder booms like falling logs.

Jarrod doesn't flinch.

Next, I cup another handful of water. I attempt to pour it in his ear. Most of it sits like a pool. A single bubble gurgles to the surface.

And still, Jarrod doesn't move. He is a hunk of defrosting meat.

I set the podcast on the deck to continue playing. I know he's dead, and my eyes are wet, but it feels right. Davidson's voice. It's Jarrod's guide.

As I walk away, I hear either the wind murmuring under the overhang, or I hear my friend call out. I don't turn back to check.

I run.

I open my door in a hurry, stagger towards the shower. I warm my skin 'til the hot water runs out and my teeth have stopped chattering. In bed, I swallow three zopiclone sleeping pills with a slug of schnapps. It's a gift bottle with a note thanking Jarrod for taking the kids to that hackathon in 2014.

I turn the lights out, study the backs of my eyelids.

I wonder what's beyond the blackness.

5.

"Jar? You here, bro?"

It's been a week and I've been flopping between druggy daytime sleeps and all-night paranoid Google searches. There are laws requiring you to report a person's death, Reddit tells me. I'm sure I've broken those laws. I've spotted police cars on my drive over here. More cops than normal. They'll be coming for me.

". . .broken light grey zone . . . calling . . . forest tunnel."

"Jarrod? It's me, man. You here?"

I finally locate the voice on the deck. The podcast is still playing through the speaker I've left plugged into Jarrod's phone. 24 missed calls. Richard Davidson's voice is melted and crusty. Exhausted and melting, like a Walkman with dying batteries.

But no Jarrod.

"Dude? You here? I'm sorry about all . . . I'll call an ambulance or something."

"Kitchen." A voice low and raspy and moist, like a bubble of words burping out of a washbasin.

"Dude!"

Beside the dishwasher, a single leg sticks out. Suit pants, rumpled as a used condom. A foot. Toes that twitch.

I fall to the lino, crawl to him. He's fallen like a frail old granddad needing a hip replacement. Like a pile of dropped laundry.

Most of a suit is on Jarrod's body. There is a clean white shirt over his distended belly. His arms are inside a black suit jacket. The pants, he must have tried to step into while standing. He's lost his balance and collapsed, unable to bend his stiff body. There is white foam crusted on his lips. His dried-up eyes point in wildly different directions.

"I'm late,' he says, 'Have to get to . . . wurg."

The head speaking to me is lavender. The color where pink bleeds into purple and cools into blue. Where the skin bunches around his neck, the folds are deep indigo. Blue, too, are the veins snaking across his flesh. Thousands of streams and rivers and tributaries choked with unmoving cold dead blood cells.

"Dude, I don't think you should . . . School, they're not, like, *expecting* you to work, know what I'm saying? They've pretty much written you off and said goodbye, so the whole suit thing is. . . ."

"They thingb I dead." That mushy throat again. Hard lumpy sticky words. And eyes that roll in their sockets but can't focus. They're cracked eyes, hard and varnished over, chipped like cue balls dropped on concrete floors. Jarrod is trying to look at me, but something dances on the edge of his vision. As if he can see midges flitting around me.

I pull him to his feet, guide him to the couch.

I put on those *Game of Thrones* episodes that he loves, Season 4, episodes 2 to 5, specifically, which he's always told me are the height of the show. I position him upright on the couch. As I'm sweeping cobwebs off the ceiling with a broom, I hear his body slide and thud onto the carpet. I drop my broom and rush to help.

He's on his side, after that. Back to the fetal position. No catching up. No reports from beyond. He's a baby again. A pet rock.

But he's still my friend. I can get used to this. We both can.

I will walk with him.

*

A knock at the door wakes me. I've slept in my work shirt and tie on Jarrod's cold carpet.

It's a real estate woman, carrot-haired, tight belt. Fuckable, gorgeous—but she's trying to peek around the door.

She slides a brochure at me.

Lost a loved one? the brochure says. *It's time to sell.*

I throw the door at her, put my back against it. Listen as her high heels clack on the path. She's phoning somebody. Some boss or authority or stakeholder. "You guys said he was dead though, right?"

A noise comes from Jarrod. I rush to my friend, check he's okay. It's his stomach. Something is shifting in there.

Around six, I insist on getting pizzas delivered. I forbid the Uber Eats guy from coming to the front door and wait outside on the street for him.

When I stagger in the door the next day, exhausted from the all-staff meeting, the pizza appears alive, bubbling and roiling and squirming with black jellybeans. Blowflies. They rise from the pizza, do a dizzying spin, and settle on his nose, guzzling the stream of brain fluid that flows through his nostrils and pools above his lips.

The pizza is not the meal. The meal is my friend.

I try to bathe him, on the fourth day. To get him to move, I have to stand under him, and juices and scabs stain my tie and shirt. I tip Jarrod into the tub, pull his underwear off. Maggots around his cock. I begin with a blast of warm water until Jarrod's purple hand reaches out and squeezes mine.

"No," he gasps. Melting, rotting, weary voice. "*Cold*."

*

Jarrod—the new Jarrod, the changed Jarrod, the passed-over Jarrod—cannot comprehend time. I put on another of his favorite films, *Dune*, a miniseries, and after the four hours has passed and the credits have run 'til the end, he remains staring at a black screen. The flies return, big shiny jelly-bean-sized bluebottles, drinking his eyes while he gawps. Later, when I haul him off the couch and we stagger to the bedroom, I observe a pool of maggots in his wake, little wriggling yellow grains of rice that fall around his ankles. I clean his socks in the sink, though the smell is impossible to conquer. The salty stench of rotting shoes pulled from a muddy river.

Mornings, I sit him on a backyard bench to watch birds. I give him a log of luncheon meat. He chews, pulls the soft pink meat into his decaying throat. I hear the meat roil and churn in his belly, which has become a swollen hump, pushing out against the depressing wool jersey I've forced on him. On a Thursday, I race to his place from work and walk in and have to stride to the kitchen to turn a tap off. An inch of water has pooled in the kitchen, the larder and laundry. He's been leaving lights on, too, as he lurches up and down his house, haunting rooms, leaning against walls for hours, leaving sticky smears on the wallpaper where juices leak through his back, soaking the pathetic suit jacket he wears for a job he'll never attend.

Then the power company shuts the power off. No more lights or warm water. No more DVD marathons.

After ten days, we walk to the park, me with a hand around his squishy shoulders, urging him like an old man. Spring is coming down. The wind nibbles with gums instead of teeth.

On a bench looking through the roundabout and bark chips and rope cage, we gaze toward the brook. A girl comes up the grass slope, clutching a fistful of broken-off bulrushes, babbling Hotdogs, hotdogs, getcha hotdogs.

Her eyes lock with Jarrod's. She trembles, begins rocking side to side. The girl's pants are yellow at first. As she takes in the horror on the bench beside me, her pants turn black.

The pier, the week after. Slapping wind, blades of sun. Wet droplets in the air. Seagulls circling.

"Bad here," Jarrod is mumbling. "See them waiting. End of the pier. Mouths. Tails."

Jarrod more inflexible, harder to lug and heft, his legs stiff as glass.

"What's waiting?"

"Them. Swarm. People . . . black. Devils. They want me. To join."

Jarrod's foot comes down in a crack. He twists. I hear his tibia snap. He bends, wobbles. Falls over on his back, his foot upside down, twisted as a fettucine noodle. Seagulls immediately bomb us, nipping, tearing, squawking. They land and begin gobbling mouthfuls of meat from Jarrod's snapped-off foot, a white bone oozing purple blood in a leg that's blue.

As we run toward the car, a rottweiler wrestles out of the grip of a woman on rollerblades and bounds after Jarrod. I manage to get the car door open just as the dog bumps the side, arfing.

I drive us home. There is a long sleek brick of a car in the driveway. A black hearse.

Behind it, an ambulance, and a skinny police officer, all uniform, neat shaven head, blue hat, notepad. I keep the car running, idle past, sure I can see in the rearview the funeral director stepping out onto the street with a paramedic beside him, pointing as I disappear.

I'm in trouble. But I want to protect my friend.

6.

X-Base Backpackers on Queen Street. A place we last came to when we were 19 and ridiculous. We take a dorm room. Downstairs, breaking glass and shouting. French girls chanting. Relentless nightclub unst-unst-unst.

"It's over, Jar," I say, sniffing the disgusting hostel pillow. "We gotta face it, dude. If there was a way out, a shaft of light or something, you'd've said so, right?"

I'm pacing wall to wall, peeling awful green leaf-patterned wallpaper, dark and hopeless and depressing. I pace because I think I can walk out of all this. Walk 'til they forget, at school, that I abandoned the job. Walk 'til the police and health services and coroner forget that a man died at 2289 Mairangi Drive and his body disappeared, parts of a foot later discovered at Murray's Bay Wharf. I pace and peel wallpaper and Jarrod lies a meter away on a tomb-sized bunk, two arms and 1.5 legs, as if practicing for his coffin.

His stomach is slopping and rippling like he's got hunger cramps, so I sneak him down the fire stairs and drive us to Burger Fuel. Our old favorite. Our routine.

I pull up in a disabled parking space, right outside, where tarmac meets concrete curb meets linoleum.

It reeks in the car. I open a window.

"Hungry," Jarrod gasps, drunk with death, hair trickling down his skull, head lolling and wobbling. "Hung—hung— you've . . . you have to—"

From his mouth blurghs a river of yellow fluid, sickly thick custard. As he's beginning to say sorry, fumbling to open the car door, a second torrent of maggots pours onto my lap. He's vomiting so hard he's pushed back. He squeezes the door open. Jarrod, puffy and blue, falls out onto the tarmac, begins to crawl, toward Burger Fuel, away from Burger Fuel. Anywhere. But he cannot walk with just one foot. He can't even get on his feet. Instead, tearing his knees open, he crawls.

A family tips over their table and runs as the blue lumpy creature in a torn black suit reaches out, begging for a helping hand to pull him up. Panic. Spilled chips. Overturned burgers. Screams and roars and me, cursing Jarrod as I wrap my arms around him and haul 80 kilograms of meat toward the tarpaulin-lined trunk of the car that's just big enough to fit a man, except his head is sticking out. Hanging over the license plate and the towbar. I can't cram the corpse any further into the trunk and the Burger Fuel manager has a cellphone against his ear and he's slipping on squashed chips, asking police to come imMEDiately, and I have to get the trunk closed so I slam it right on his neck and blurt SORRY, JAR, OHMYGOD I'M SO SO SORRY and I crouch and catch the blue squishy coconut as the last flap of neck-skin detaches and it falls to the tarmac.

Catch my friend.

Catch his head.

7.

South of Auckland is Pukekohe. South of Pukekohe, the expressway lets us drive at 120 kays an hour. South of that, back-roads through Limestone Downs. Green wilderness. All valleys and castles of rock. Hedges and fields of waving corn. There are surprises over each hill and corner, and eventually, warm signs counting the kilometers, then Te Awamutu, and Smith Street, where I ease back the throttle as the orange empty light comes on.

I phoned him last night. While Jarrod slept. Had a talk on Skype, actually. Richard Davidson wouldn't say which country he was in, but I've got a theory. I think it's Bhutan. I think he's high up in mountains where the air is cool. In the snow, maybe. Refrigeration.

Davidson—who took a hundred emails and seven phone calls and a ton of private Reddit messages to track down—contains himself in a hoodie and says nothing. His face is darkened. I'm not even sure if there is a human in there. I can tell he's in a tent, talking to me. He listens as I tell my story. We've been winning, I argue, we did okay. We got through. But there's not much left of my friend. And I don't know where we're going.

The man in the tightly drawn hoodie says little. It is only when the sleeping back he's rested his laptop on shifts and catches fresh light that I see a snapshot. That skull, from the Misfits logo. A skull with eyeballs in it shrunken like marbles. That's what's inside the hoodie. A skull without eyebrows or sideburns or nostrils or lips. All bone and eyeballs.

Finally, a noise comes out of him.

"Wish I had a fren," the skull says, "Fren like you."

A bone falls out from under his jaw. He is reaching for it and pressing it back into his throat when he terminates the call.

*

The woman behind the reception counter looks like she's been tumbled under a truck. Violently bleached hair with black roots. Rubbing a keycard against her hip, standing up, suspicious.

"You ain't got much luggage."

We're at the two-star Pirongia View Motel. Hardly an establishment to fight over. I tell her I just need a room. Farthest from the road. No windows, I don't care. We just need shelter. And she has to let me know if any cops come past.

"You can wash that, you know, your towel," she says, leading us across the gravel. "We got a laundry. What you got in there, anyway—bowling ball? Me, I love to bowl."

"Totally," I say, shifting the big round weight from the crook of my right arm to my left. "Bowling, right."

The windowless motel cube we hole up in feels safe. It's our bunker, our fortress. There's unlimited SkyTV with all the American channels. A block of showers and sinks. Fish and chips over the road, not that Jarrod will eat anything.

After dinner, we kick back on the bed and watch *South Park* and I guffaw 'til I cry.

Jarrod's eyelids are half-down. He looks sleepy.

This laundry the hag at Reception mentioned. I'll be needing it. I'm almost ready to think of tomorrow. Depends if tomorrow comes or not. Because if I do wake tomorrow, I'll need to do intense, heavy, hot washing. The bowling ball bag is so saturated with juices that it drips. And I'll need to get the bloodstains out of the sheets before the motel asks questions. He's leaking, Jarrod is. Soaking through the sheets. His cut-off neck oozes endless fluid, much of it blackish-purple blood. Other fluid is clear stuff with pink veins in it, like crab guts, that cascades out of his nostrils like a sticky moustache, pooling on lips that he struggles to lick. It's the frontal cortex of his brain, putrefying.

We watch silly shows 'til midnight and I even pop out for a bottle of wine and come back and ransack the cupboards and find a plastic sippy cup. I pour wine into my friend's lips, and it gushes through his jaw, fingers of wine and blood trickling across the bedspread, but it's okay. I believe Jarrod appreciates the gesture. His eyes have shriveled to nearly nothing, now. Like lights switched off, with just a little afterglow.

Me, I turn the motel lights out and crawl under the wet covers, wriggling 'til I find a dry spot. I roll on my side and stroke my friend's scalp. I have to halt the stroking every 30 seconds, wipe off chunks of skin and sticky hair.

In the blue hour before dawn, we listen to trucks rumble past. Hear a fight, broken glass somewhere. A cat's claws on a steel drum.

"Goodnight, Jar. Love you, bro."

In the blackness, I see two teeth appear, pale blue, as his lips pull back and his cheeks fold.

A smile.

ITCHING

Stop sucking?

Shyeah, that's about right, Warwick. It says STOP SUCKING on the label and it's aimed at you.

You fully SUCK and this girl's gonna make you stop SUCKING by pouring bitter-ass poison into your pretentious almond milk.

We have a communal kitchen at Code Academy. Usually it's the chill-out zone me and Jerome and Sarah and Danni-Lee hang in to play chess or swap code or borrow a tampon if our student allowance hasn't come through. But my friends are at their seats right now. Scared to leave else the instructors will tell them off. This is the only moment I have in the kitchen alone.

STOP SUCKING—written on the bottle in scary capital red letters—is the bitterest stuff you'll ever taste. One dab on my little girl's thumb before she went to sleep and her thumb sucking was all over, rover. I had a teeny taste one time and my lips tingled like I'd blowjobbed a lemon. Head Asshole Warwick Yang is good at sucking, so I hope he enjoys the fifty mils I pour into his too-good-for-you milk. It oughta screw up his mouth so hard it'll suck his whole face in.

It's just balancing, I tell myself, scampering back down the hallway to coding class, cause Warwick has unbalanced everything. We were meant to work together. He tutors, I pass my coding assignments and make him look good then leave for an internship and never look back. Graduate and part ways. Except he had to get all Nazi on the deal. Yesterday he hauled me into the principal's office while winter lashed at the foggy windows and they told me I was gonna get kicked out of Code Academy if I borrowed code again. All 'cause Sarah sent me some lines over Messenger, and these dicks considered it plagiarism. From the chair beside me Warwick turned—just his head turning, robotic and cold, so I got half a face of the bearded wizard with his hood pulled up—and he said, "Private communications aren't as private as you think."

Haunted me all night, those words. Filled up my dreams.

So now I've poisoned that wanker-of-a-tutor's almond milk and I'm scampering back to my chair, clearing the adverts that have popped up while I've been away from my browser. Warwick's gliding over to the kitchen as I'm settling into my seat, sweeping my purple fringe over my eyes like a shield. I hear our instructor-in-chief opening the fridge door. Hear the rattle as he yanks his box of seven-dollar milk free of its shelf and grinds beans for a perfect espresso.

Perfect apart from your poison, cocksucker.

I'm shunting my chair in under the desk, clicking the X to close an ad for a poker website, another ad telling me there's a one-day deal on Nikes, plus a weird ad which says, 'Itching powder—the ultimate practical joke!' with a picture of a Grim Reaper scratching skin off its leg with five bony claws. Eew.

I get rid of the pop-ups and I'm getting on with styling my Jamstack so the spacers center the content for mobile. I'm picturing my grades moving up the alphabet as I code. I got threatened with a D yesterday 'cause I borrowed Danni-Lee's code but today I might finish with a C-minus, hopefully even a C. Get something passable handed in so I can get out of here at 4 and pick my babygirl up from BrightSparkz daycare. Finish the damn course and move to a city where people are warm. No more miserable Wellington buses, wet wheels, umbrellas, foggy windows, old dusty cold buildings.

Reflection on my screen. Frowning robotic stiff-shouldered face. Warwick's coming back. I pretend to work on my script. Pull my hoodie up over my ears. Typey type type.

Warwick's entering the room, and everyone glances at him with one eye. Body like a surfboard. Black vinyl hair tied back in a topknot. Long-ass boss-beard. Cold dark Chinese eyes.

Every footstep is measured. Same 13 strides from door to desk. Warwick hovers over Sarah with his coffee, reading her code. He does it to all of us, ten times a day. Nods at line 38 on her Javascript.

"You sure you want to do that?"

Sarah, honey. Take one for all of us. Give him something to fuss over. Don't send Warwick my way. I can't be near him when he spits his coffee out.

The itching powder pop-up bursts onto my screen again. I click it six times, battling to hit the X and close it. The ad evades my pop up blocker, mutates, shifts to an amateur, mutated knock-off of Ali Express then a checkout, pretty fake looking, then it's saying *FREE—PAY LATER!* with some strange currency symbol I've never seen and it's telling me my saved Mastercard has not been charged but the seller has been instructed to ship the goods to my saved address and I'm like What-the-actual-fuck and I'm about to open Task Manager and eradicate the sticky pest-of-a-pop-up when Warwick arrives at his pretentious standing desk, feet close together, posture like a general, blowing steam off the top of his drink, extending his lips to sip and—

Omigod. He actually DID it!

From across the room, I see his lips snarl. Eyes twitch. Throat shudder. Foam at the corners of his lips. Duuuuude . . . I think I've broken him. He's trying to stand stiff like a border sentry, studying everyone, but his gums are stinging.

He coughs, catches something with the back of his wrist. Hoooollleeeee shit. I think he's swallowing a throatful of puke.

The whole room begins to notice. Everybody turns to watch the monk lose his shit.

"*Garkgh.*"

He fights to place his espresso cup down without spilling. Slops three awful droplets on his pristine white Apple keyboard.

Shudders and swallows.

Pours the coffee into his wastebasket.

My vag tingles and tightens.

Silence, for ages. Twenty coding kids duck and hold their breath.

Warwick looks for someone to punish. Selects a paper from his In tray. Taps it on his hip. Marches over to me. Arrives behind my shoulder.

"Install that Express package?"

Warwick's not going to admit a little liquid fucked up his day.

I turn slowly, pretending I haven't watched him creep up.

"You wanted your grades back. Here."

He puts my grade paper by my mouse.

Beside where it says Jasmine Tauariki ID391034327, beside *Assignment 19 Jamstack Jekyll integration* are twin numbers like stakes in my spasming heart.

4 and 9, the numbers say. 49%. A *D* grade. D cause I'm a Dumbass compared to Warwick Yang who's done nothing since age 10 but code.

D means a fail. The eighth, so far. One more and I'll have to re-do the semester. My student allowance runs out shortly and if this fuckwit fails me, I can't pay my rent. I'll have to go live with my mum or go homeless. No daycare for my daughter.

Too softly for anyone to hear, Warwick pokes the results paper and goes, "Just something to sip on."

He spots another kid to crush, turns and walks on.

*

I wake at six. Dream of an Indian beach and bliss swirls away. What day is it? Tuesday. Shit. The days've been all fucked-up since Warwick the Wizard-Wanker put me on probation two weeks ago.

Black outside. Beige polygons. Façades, rectangles of sidewalk outside my apartment window. Red dot eyes of trucks in the winter morning mist.

I have a quick smoke and a coffee and quietly take a dump, sitting on the toilet lid while it flushes so Saffire doesn't wake. From 6.18 to 6.48 I get in half an hour of dishes, watching the storm out the window as black sky melts into blue, chopping carrot sticks and looking at my friends' happy lives on my phone before Saff calls my name. I get my babygirl's lunch packed and raincoat on and switch the baby monitor off so I don't have to pay for new batteries. I know she's too old for it, really, Saff's two and a bit, she's way beyond a baby, but she's the center of my everything. I have to hear that she's safe, even if it means clutching my phone all day long in case daycare calls about some crisis.

I wrestle gumboots onto her feet and pick up some courier package on my doorstep and shove it in my handbag and we get out the door to catch a 7.26 bus to beg for a good grade so I can makeover my life.

Saff's hair looks crazy and she won't let me brush it, just tie ribbons in it, pink and yellow. Our bus gets immediately frozen in honking traffic. Frantic windscreen wipers. People stuffing broken umbrellas in rubbish bins. Long awkward seconds getting out of the bus on Courtenay Place with a skateboard and pram and across the whitewater churning in the gutter. I get in the door of BrightSparkz and they ask how my course is going and I say Awesome, thanks, this bitch has almost graduated, ha-ha, and Saffire cries and clutches and guilt-trips me and I can't skate away soon enough. Nine precious private quiet minutes on my board, skating up the street.

Maybe my daughter knows I'm lying. Maybe Saffy knows we're about to go hungry if I let Code Academy flunk me.

I get drenched running up the winter Wellington Street, dodging people in soaking suits, and I burst into Code Academy seven minutes late with Warwick Yang tapping his watch and I'm panting and dripping. They have this culture of Sprints here at school and you're supposed to sprint every day 8 a.m. 'til 1, then have a massive rest with yoga and meditation then do another sprint at home, like 6 'til 8. I drip on my keyboard, and somebody tosses me a towel and I open Visual Code Studio and pull my hood over my ears, ducking my friends, and try to code.

If I can catch up and get my stack running without bursting into tears, it'll be a miracle.

Make my script display on test browsers—doable. Get the error warning to fuck off—also doable. C'mon girl, you got this. It's 8.07 now. I can get my code passing individual unit tests. Not my fucking fault if SEVEN FUCKING MINUTES INTO THE DAY MY STACK REFUSES TO LOAD ON THE BROWSER. Fuck my life so much right now. I just know tonight I'll be sobbing on the phone to my mum, begging her to clear out the garage so her failure-of-a-daughter can move in.

I totally know a certain tutor is circling the room and any second he could slide right up behind me and point out like three characters of incorrect code that are fucking everything up. Ruining my assignment and my hope of graduating.

From 9 'til 11, Warwick stalks past every desk in the room, arriving behind our chairs and watching silently, muttering some stabbing words, or moving and turning like a heron. He points out an update on Express that's not compatible with Jerome's stack, helps Sarah incorporate Hugo and he even explains the difference between yml and yaml to Grace.

When the prick comes past my desk, Warwick just snorts. Tiny little puff. A *Hmph. What's the point of you being here?* the puff says. *You're this close to failing. Then you'll owe six grand on your student loan for nothing. Plus, you'll have to repay your student allowance to the government. Go home with your daughter, Failure. Move into your mum's garage. Be an unwed single mother. It's your destiny.*

Warwick's got nothing to say today beyond the Hmph, though. Probably his lips twinge, knowing I'm associated with a bitter taste. Leave the skater girl alone, let her code, his lips say.

I rise after hours, needing to pee. 11.45, now. Almost lunch. Nicotine time. I'm three quarters of the way out of my seat when there's a chime as an email notification appears. Management's name on the sender. Oh God.

The email says if I can't make my API run, I'll have to do a whole 'nother semester here. And what it means is I'll be moving in with Mum.

My eyes moisten. My head folds. Danni-Lee tries to meet my eyes. I leave the room, close to bawling. Deep breath, Jas, thassit. Attagirl. Chill for a second. Serve some revenge on Warren Fucking Yang for negging you towards failure? Maybe. FAAAAARK. I dunno.

I piss and dab my eyes. Carry my handbag down to the carpark for a smoke. Stand in a concrete basement by the roller door and suck and puff and read the dwindling digits on my vaporizer.

Only three mils of juice left in my cartridge. Those cartridges are seriously expensive, like thirty bucks. And I've gotta get new panty liners and some mascara and there's like

290 bucks owing at daycare for Saffire's hours and I've spent my last ten on batteries for the baby monitor 'cause I get paranoid at nights and I'm rummaging in my handbag cause maybe, mayyyyybe there's a fresh cartridge I've forgotten about, pineapple, my favorite, and . . . what the—?

A package. But I didn't order any cartridges off the net, did I? While I was blazed, maybe? I've been smoking weed every night, I guess, trying to blot out the stress with a fog cannon. . .

The package doesn't even have a sender on it.

I tear it open, shake the contents out.

Itching Powder. In a flimsy cardboard box, small as a deck of cards. Fuck's sake—if my credit card has been charged it'll put me in overdraft and I'll get a penalty and I'll lose my frigging mind. That dumb practical joke pop-up—it was just spam. I closed the thing down, didn't I? Blocked its ass. Guess I might've accidentally hit Enter and it would've populated the order form with the credentials saved in the browser. Yeesh. I'm glad this is a one-time mistake.

I tear the Itching Powder's wrapper off, lock eyes with the cartoon figure on the box. An Asian-looking boy with bulging brown eyes, looking down in horror at the claw marks on his legs with little black fleas jumping off. In the background of the airbrushed illustration, black figures snicker, biting their fingertips. Creepy demons. Sniggering shadows.

I shake out the packet inside. Just corn flour, probably. Or fiberglass powder. That shit itches bad until you wash it off.

I trudge up the stairs, put my forehead against the fire exit door and melt. I want to be somewhere else. I want to be in an episode of *Girls* where there's laughter and hope amid the ruins. I want the lights of Hollywood to burn off my rainy Wellington reality. Steam it away with publicity.

But this girl's got to get back in there, haul one zombified leg after another across the floor 'cause if I don't, I lose my three hundred bucks a week, and I lose my lease, and if I can't feed her, I lose my baby girl.

As I hit the frosted glass swing door and force a fake smile onto my teeth, I pull the itching powder from my heavy handbag.

A wool coat is hanging from the rack, buried amongst twenty other steaming, dripping, soggy, smelly coats. It's a double-breasted coat with Primaloft insulation. Charcoal color, inner pockets, collar. Lots of nooks and crannies to shake the itching powder into. Soft wool that drinks the itching powder as I rub it into the fibers.

Warwick's coat.

*

"Varrick, he is unvell I am afraid to say," Johannes is telling our circle. "Tonight, ve are having Code Academy cleaned for fleas. Ve believe dere is a flea problem here, considering de itching."

Johannes is the kinder, softer tutor none of us want as a reference on our CV when we apply for internships. Much as we hate Warwick for being a bully and destroying our confidence, his name is known to the coding gods in San Fran and Sydney and Singapore.

He plays computer games regularly with these gate-keepers. They've all worked together, all been friends back when they were nobodies. Shares memes with them. Makes deepfake animations of Elon Musk and that Twitter guy saying dirty shit to amuse the world's most influential coders on Reddit. Rumor is that his stainless steel drink bottle was a gift from Mark Zuckerberg. Warwick's job reference will feed our families. That's why I can fuck with his milk and give him a little itch, but I can never question him to his face.

"You know this, ah, this rash, this ailment of de skin. He has the de eczema, soooo—Varrick is verking from home today. But he has assured me he will return tomorrow. Questioning?"

There are sighs from deflating chests. We can let a little tension out.

After a morning sprint to break the backs of our assignments, I stand in the kitchen with Jerome and Sarah talking smack. They've been inching close to getting internships with Xero and Oracle. Me, I'm still walking on a razor. Hoping another few weeks of effort will persuade Warwick the Great to let me pass and get out of here.

I guess I need him back to mark my assignment, though it's nice to have a day free from the prick.

We pour coffees and Jerome pretends to reach for the almond milk and we all laugh. The milk box is still on the bench where Warwick left it.

"I would pick it up and throw it out but Warwick's probably gonna forensically test it to see who fucked with his milk," Sarah says.

"So Jazzy, darl, since he can't hear us right now," Jerome goes to me, "fess up: you poured that shit in his drink. Eh."

I sip my chamomile. "Don't know what you're talking about."

They slit their eyes and scan me, top to toes.

And that's when we hear Johannes's dumb cheery voice.

"Oh, heyyyy, I am hearing you are unwell, you are coming into the building?"

Down the hall, where we can see a rectangle of classroom, twelve heads turn.

Something with a black hood, shuffling in slowly, stiffly. Like a robed old man.

We feel Warwick before we see him. He's—ohhhhh-mygawd—rubbing moisturizer into his skin from a squeezy tube.

Warwick senses something he dislikes in the kitchen. Turns, strides towards us. Face still buried in the black hood.

"Could you excuse us?" Warwick says as he arrives in the kitchen. My friends dissolve and wash down the hallway.

Warwick is not a smiler. He positions himself at the far end of the kitchen island.

The grin is gone in half a second.

As he speaks to me, Warwick reaches down into the cutlery drawer, pulls it open. Takes out a serrated knife—the type I use to fillet feijoas to slide into my babygirl's lips—and Warwick pulls the sleeve and cuff of his black cotton hoodie up past his left arm then begins scratching with the knife. Deep fillets, powerful scrapes. From his knuckles to his wrist bones, up the forearm and back again. I can see his fingernails are no good – they have chunks of pink debris under them.

He does it with the left arm first, as he talks. Then the right. Itching deeply, methodically, leaving deep gouges. Like the itching is part of him now.

Eternity passes with his eyes hooked into mine.

At last, I blink.

"Johannes cannot be allowed to mark your work," he says. "I'll be doing the marking."

"How—how come, Warwick?"

I'm immediately thinking of deleting my Chrome and going from Firefox to Brave private browsing with Tor, so I don't leave a trace of any conversation with my homies. 'Cause I know Warwick's here to find out who made him itch. I just need to type the final fifty lines of my stack and hit Save and push back my chair and leave. Take my baby and move away.

At last, Warwick's face emerges from the hood. He looks like a turtle rubbed with sandpaper. Skin yellow, decaying. Jaundiced, with deep lines etched in it like he's been counting fives. Lines which begin up by his scalp and carve runnels from brow to beard. Lines which show layers under his skin. All the way to the bone.

Scratches.

*

SHOCK YOUR FRIENDS!
  INFLATABLE PROP!
The pop-up bursts into my webpage. Like an airhorn blasting my face.

It hits me on a Friday. 9.05 a.m., as if the pop-up's in a hurry to fuck with my life before the weekend.
STINK BOMBS! 3 TO A BOX!
USE INDOORS OR OUT! CLEAR A ROOM IN SECONDS!
REALLY STINKS! BE THE FUNNIEST AT THE PARTY!
I don't have a choice. I don't even click. The screen throws up a thank-you message and tells me my order is on its way. Cool, okay. I'll use the prank, sure. But it's not my order. More like something's ordering me.

Funniest at the party? Pfft.

Monday and I'm feeling more like a used shovel than the life of any party. Warwick has this thing about kicking off his shoes when he comes in at 7.30 every morning.

7.54, I jam a couple of stink bomb vials in Warwick's slippers. I get half a meter away when I'm like, Hold Up. He's always gonna feel something with his toes.

So, I pop the tops off the vials of stink juice. Pour the juice into little twists of cling film and bind the stink juice bags with dental floss. Rig the jellyfish-sized stink bags inside Warwick's shoes. Then go to my computer and wait.

It's an amazing morning, actually. I containerize my stack, upload it to the cloud, pull it down for testing. I build in some structured query language and get it searching my database smoothly. Then, just when I'm getting engrossed in the coding that I supposedly hate, I notice the Grim Reaper flailing and kicking. Whirling, flicking its toes. Billows of stench wafting up as he kicks his slippers off.

Warwick drops his black espresso, staggers around the coding room, clawing his arms, scratching deeper than ever, leaving strings of clawed-up scab on the carpet like paper trimmings. We pinch our noses and someone cries, "Bro, rotten eggs!" and we're all giggling, clutching our ribs.

Warwick runs out of the room screaming. Two hours later, as we're sailing gusts of enthusiasm towards completing our assignments, he marches back in. He's changed his hoodie and he's sellotaped paper towels over his torn-up arms but we can still detect a pong and we're all pressing our brows against our monitors, pinching our noses and giggling, pointing at our keyboards across the room, *"Yo, G, you got a message,"* sending secret snides and stink emojis.

We have power for the first time ever. We've put a thorn in the shoe of a Titan. Probably sometime soon the Titan's gonna tumble, gonna crush me, so all I can do is try get my assignment handed in and pick up my daughter and scrape out with my qualification before I'm crushed. . .

. . .Except before I do, another pop-up interrupts:

BOYS MAKING YOU SICK, JAZ? WELL, SICK 'EM RIGHT BACK!

Surprisingly personal, that advert.

As if the advert read my mind.

The pop-up is hovering like a dog that wants to be walked. Like it needs me. Or I need it.

BUY NOW! PAY FOR EVERYTHING LATER!

Warwick's been avoiding almond milk—been avoiding most of us students, actually—but he'll die without water. Dude has to drink, which means an opportunity to punk him again.

The order form populates. I hit enter and wait.

The next pop-up prank to appear says *TRY WHOOPSTER 3000, MAMA—THE ULTIMATE WHOOPIE CUSHION!*

Mama? That's weird, that's extremely personal, like as if the Grim Reaper behind the advertisement knows me, but of course I click yes and after a couple weeks of scarves and umbrellas and zombified morning toddler and puddles and buses and car horns, and my cheap-ass skateboard swelling with damp and my keyboard getting ruined with rain dripping off my shoulders, the Whoopster 3000 arrives on my doorstep and brightens my month.

One Wednesday, we sew it into the foam padded stool in front of his standing desk, me and Danni-Lee, giggling. Everybody sees us. Well, when I say *we* and *us*, I mean my classmates stand there and tell me, We're not sure you oughta do this, Jaz, don't you think you've gone far enough?

'Cept they don't stop me. Because they've been bullied, too. They watch as I zip the case off the top of the stool and slide the whoopie cushion under it then zip the seat case back up. We scamper back to our seats. Wait as Warwick-the-scratching-skeleton finishes up the Zoom conference he's doing with San Francisco over in the next room—just audio these days, of course. He's massively disfigured. Can't face anyone. Wears a mask on his face, a bandana and gloves up to his elbows. Lumbers across the floor on legs striped with ripped skin, every movement agonizing. Pulls the chair out. Sits down.

The padded stool explodes in a puff of fabric and foam. Belches, erupts. Bursts air up into Warwick so his hoodie ripples. Warwick grimaces, trying to contain the geyser under his ass. Knocks his stainless steel water bottle across his desk.

He lurches. Rubs his butt, which is now stained red as if he's been sitting on strawberries. Stares at his blown-up stool. Sizes up what's happened. Why his anus has been ruptured and he's collapsing into the arms of Johannes who is dialing an ambulance.

When he comes back ten days later—after I've rejigged my Python assignment, getting my average up to 70%, hopefully going to graduate—I get him with some of that ipecac

I've ordered. It's this clear liquid in a little druggie glass phial that makes Warwick Yang hemorrhage everything in his stomach over his screen and keyboard, soaking a whole roll of paper towels, evacuating the entire room while somebody mops up the vomit and digestive acid and paramedics guide the wiggling pink top section of his stomach back down his throat while Warwick, doubled over like a pretzel, claws at his abdomen.

They carry him out like a rolled-up rug.

Me and my friends high-five.

The pranks have made us even. Nah, actually: better than even, cause unless Warwick has got some massive reprisal in the pipeline, I have won.

3.

We're up on the overhang smoking a blunt, watching the spring sun appear then quickly set. Winter has finally ended. It's me, Jerome, Sarah. Even Danni-Lee, with two vapes because she likes to mix honey and licorice flavors and you can't buy 'em together. It's 3.51 and I get to pick my daughter up at 4.30. The next 40 minutes feels like a festival. As if it's summer.

The cold will be over soon; the sun lasts ten seconds longer than it did yesterday. It's a gap in the rain, that's all, and you can still see the storm frothing the harbor white. But—because Jerome's got this app on his phone totaling the labyrinthine fucking grades, and it's indicating he'll get an A-minus and Danni-Lee will be a B-Minus and Sarah will score a B, we treat it like we're on vacation. Me, I'm a C-plusser, and that's cool. I actually have room to slide back to a C-minus if I want.

Get my qual, get my daughter, get the fuck out of here. Move to Auckland. Move to Melbourne, maybe. London, who knows. Silicon Valley. It's hinted in the orange melting 'round the side of the building. Orange like beaches and gold and warmth. Tanned white-smiling people a million times warmer than the black, white, and silver I put up with downstairs. Directly under this roof.

"I'll bet fuckin Warwick's at home right now, deepfaking this, making a video, Photoshopping himself into it," Jerome goes. "'Cause he ain't got no friends, feel me?"

We all snort and laugh.

"Jaz, babe," Sarah goes, squeezing my shoulder. "You okay now? You even? For what he done to you?"

Everybody's quiet. Finally, I tell 'em yeah. We're even. Then we get high and make a Top Ten Biggest Warwick Dick Moves list. We name 30 or 40 times Warwick acted like God. Soooooo pompous and cunty. Like a Star Wars villain. After, my abs sting. I've hardly laughed all year.

We clamber back down the fire ladder. Only eight days 'til we graduate. The ceremony's going to be basic as fuck. A few awkward nibbles in the kitchen. Fake champagne. Flimsy paper certificate from the Code Academy directors who spend most of their time in Hong Kong. Warwick—if he's not too embarrassed to show up—will have to shake my hand. I'll rip my god damn qualification right out of his bony fingers.

There's an exodus at 4.31pm. Everyone's amped-up. Some kids are lighting up joints or taking hits from their pipes in the doorway. A couple have cracked open cans of fruity vodka.

4.32, as I open my board and touch its wheels to the ramp, I take a last glimpse at my enemy across the room, buried in his hood like that evil old man on Star Wars. Former enemy, that is—'cause we're cool, now. He's been stripped to bare bones. Put in his place.

It's over.

Saffy-Girl is in my arms before 5. I don't have the money for McDonald's, but I buy her a Happy Meal anyway. I'm feeling chill. Protected. It's drizzling and the sky has returned to the bruised color of doom. But I'm feeling grateful. Exhausted spiritual buzzyness. I've got my family and I've got a plan to get out of here. There's the Oracle tower on The Terrace, up by Parliament. Huge and black and sparkly. The red-eye O is watching me. Saying, *Bring your skills to us here, Jaz. Graduate and gap.*

"I promise," I say, cutting carrots into shapes for my girl.

Saffire turns away from her cartoon and coloring book. "Who pwomise, Mum?"

Roundabout 6, I'm lifting some tubes of pasta into a dish while Saffire watches *Frozen*. After I've tucked Saffy in at 7, I pull open the sliding door, smoke a cone on the balcony, watch brake lights wince and flicker eight stories below. Listen to street fights, clattering cans, chinking bottles, karaoke.

"Mama?"

A voice on the baby monitor, on the table behind me. Kinda sorta Saffy's voice, but something must be wrong with her throat. Through the wall, in her black bedroom with the dinosaur nightlight, she'll be having a nightmare, I'm guessing.

"JAZMINE."

Demonic. Deep and rough and evil. What the actual?—

"CHOKEME. KILLME. FUCKME. RAYYYYYYP MEEEEEEE."

It's ten meters through my tiny apartment to my baby's door. I sprint every step, cringing as I hit her door. Sparkly letters spelling her name.

Shouldering it open. Squinting so I don't have to see the demon in the corner covered in—

No demon. Just laundry. A purple stuffed teddy bear. A stack of Dr. Seuss. Giant Jenga blocks. Hover over her.

Frantic. Stoned. Terrified. No problem in there that I can see? It's dim and tranquil. My babygirl's thumb in her pursed lips, shiny with—

She's sucking again. What'd I do with that sticky lotion stuff, Stop Sucki—

"KILL ME, MUMMY."

Oh. Ohhhhh. No no no. Nonononono. The baby monitor.

Back to the kitchen, the balcony, the sliding door. A howling wind ruffling papers on the breakfast bar. The wind lifts up the Vodafone bill, the water bill. WhereisitwhereisitwhereISIT. Stacks of docs from courses where I can get an internship if I jump through misogynistic hoops and—

"I FUCKED HER UP THE ASS. I'M FUCKING HER RIGHT NOW."

Found it: Square speaker, white plastic, emitting the most horrible, heinous, hideous–

"FUCK YOUR DAUGHTER FUCK YOUR DAUGHTER FUCKFUCKuckuckuck—"

I hurl the baby monitor off the balcony, 38 meters down into traffic. Eight stories ought to smash it. It's been hacked, contaminated. Crushing it under the wheels of a truck should put an end to that.

Back against the wall. Slithering down like slime. This is some bastard's idea of a joke. Kids have hacked into your monitor, that's all, Jaz. They're probably on the floor below you. It's the internet of things—you did your second assignment on it, remember? Anyone can hack you from anywhere. They'll be just down the hall. Those Vic Uni computer science incels who steal your wifi, girl, that's all. Nothing personal.

I smoke another cone. Cry and text my girls. Unplug the modem and router, my gaming computer, my phone, my Kindle so the internet can't get me. Even the fucking toaster.

I switch off the mains. Sit in the blackness and cry, ass against the skirting board.

Cry and pray.

Dear Warwick, I begin, and nearly ask him to spare me from another revenge prank. He's done one, okay, now we should be even.

I stop myself. Slap my face.

Prayers are strictly for God, Jaz. Don't let Warwick have that much power over you.

*

We party in the car park. The directors, they've said it's all good. Hot storm outside, so we try to dance it off. Rain leaks under the steel roller door. A window shatters and water sprays the kids at the back, extinguishing cigarettes as we laugh. Thunder pounds the roof and the lights shiver and we all whoop. Just eighteen of us in total, including a couple of 23-year-old boys that've already graduated but have come back thinking they might get to hook up with Sarah or me or Danni-Lee.

Johannes is doing an upside-down keg stand. Jerome is throwing up a quick gossip app projected on the wall. He's called it Ofice Goss, spelled wrong like a typical hasty coder, and everyone's got their phones in their left hand and their glow sticks in the right as we tweet on the app about gossip and crushes and rumors and blessings and groove to the DJ on his AirMac, carving neon paths with our headbands and glowsticks of pink goo.

I'm swinging from hug to hug, overjoyed. Liberated. My babygirl's at my mum's place up in Petone, an hour away by car and a world away in terms of anxiousness. I'm about to declare this the funnest night of my life—GOD! Throwing off that fucking course! Totally done!

And then my phone vibrates.

I find a couch with a Code Academy banner draped over it. Remove a Jim Beam bottle. Open a TikTok that's arrived on my phone. It loads for two seconds. Rich message, okay. High resolution. Chewing up a lot of data. This better be good.

First image: She's on her back, my girl. Tied down. That's her little tummy. Those are her ribbons, her knees. Writhing, struggling. My angel.

Second, a big polygon. Gleaming, pale gray. One of those silver metal rectangles on a wood handle. A cleaver.

The hand with the cleaver hovers over my girl. Her eyes twisted, screwed-up. Mouth puckered and howling. Just six little teeth to shriek Mummayyyyy—

The cleaver slams into her left arm. It falls away like a doll's limb. She's free of the ribbon tying her to the wooden board, though, and she turns, her body desperate to cover the raw wound which sprays the camera. The cleaver's more like a hammer than anything. My little girl's arm has been splintered and there are shards of white. Blood becomes thin brown tea as the camera light passes through it.

The cleaver returns. Slams into my girl's mouth. Her black grin widens, ear to ear. Huge howling smile in her neck that fills with blood, thick and syrupy and bubbling and—

Wonk wonk wonkkkkkk.

Waggling finger. Taunting grinning cartoon meme face.

The animation ends.

Fake, the entire thing. Synthesized. Days of work 'cause someone hated me enough to fuck with me with an animation so convincing it's made me piss my pants.

I'm pretty sure I know who did it. He's in every device. Everything electronic.

*

I shiver as I collect my diploma. Glee mixed with a chill on my back. A goose walking over my grave.

I hadn't spoken the word CAREER until I took the elevator up into the Oracle tower. 33rd floor. The view made my pussy clench. Exhilarating up here.

"How do you see your career progressing if you were to begin as one of our team?" the Bangladeshi woman is going. I can see the lock screen photo on her phone. A little grinning brown girl on a see-saw. Shit, man: this is me. Ten years from now.

"Um, like, I kinda wanna start anywhere," I tell her. "Like, mostly I'm just getting away from Code Academy, so I don't have to jump on another course."

There's a pause. I wet myself a little bit. Then I save my ass.

"Psych," I go. "Guess I sorta . . . like I do pranks sometimes. Practical jokes."

"Oh?"

I'm flailing in the deep ocean my big mouth has pushed me into. "What I'm tryina say is, like, I'm just fun. I'm just chill, y'know. I keep it real, I guess."

"And how would other people describe you?"

Vengeful. Coward. Psych. Punked. Punk back. Scratch and claw. Skater bitch. Mama Bear. Get between me and my baby, you die.

"Jasmine? Lost you for a second there!"

"Sorry. Like, they'd say I'll do anything. To bring home the bacon. 'Cause my baby's all I have. And if you don't take me on to code, that's on you. 'Cause I'll do anything. I'll walk out of here and I'll keep going. I'll hit up every software company in town."

Except I don't need to do that, she tells me. She spins her phone. Her daughter's eyes wink at me.

"What size shirt do you take?" she says at last. "We'll get you some printed. And a swipe card. What would you think about starting Monday?"

*

I code like someone drowning. Flapping, grasping. Ripping little scraps of lifesaving Java from message boards and Stack Overflow and Reddit and Codeshare and cramming it into my scripts and hoping it works. I'm part of this group in Slack called 'Code Acad Gradz' and I'll chuck some lines of code in a message and ask people why it's not passing, and they spit the answer back at me and I float—*barely*—in the coding world. *Barely* gets me out of my horrible apartment though.

I can ride my board across the lobby and straight into the elevator and bring home two grand a week for me and my daughter. I can skate to her daycare with zero guilts because I pay my bill in advance, these days.

I'm free, and Warwick may be trolling me, but it don't stop this badass bitch.

He fucks with my Facebook first. I can't prove that it's him—but no one else in the world hates me. And no one else can run a code cracker script like him, hammering trillions of word combinations into my account, brute force, using up server power. The cheek-boned man with the scratched-away arms wrapped in clingfilm, up all night in his black hoodie ordering digital assassinations on me.

I'm in a scrum meeting when my phone starts pinging. Shitloads of messages. My Facebook's been hacked. I'm some sort of Klan-loving racist fascist now, apparently. I haven't checked it in eight hours and in that time, there's been this series of memes posted on my timeline about Jews and so-called niggers and Proud Boys and extinction theory. Tagging my mum, my friends. Fine. Whatevs. People can think what they want. Delete, delete, delete.

I delete my whole account. Can't fuck via Facey if Jazmine doesn't have an account anymore, Douchebag.

He does it to my LinkedIn, too. That's annoying. Says all this anti-capitalist shit. He includes the CEO of Oracle in little blog post update things. It happens on an afternoon when I'm balls-deep in code trying to get a ticket completed by five. Again, I'm over it. A little scary; heaps embarrassing. But I tell my team leader I'm being trolled and she says she's got my back. I delete my LinkedIn account and carry on with life.

Chase me all you want, Warwick. I'll unplug from anything to get away from you. 'Cause I made you itch, and I blew up your ass and I poisoned your coffee and I took your status, motherfucker.

I'm not a bug in your terrarium anymore. It's been three years. You don't own me.

You don't own me, WARWICK MEGALOMANIAC YANG. You don't own me when I take Saffy over to Brisbane and we grin a week away at Warner Brothers Movie World and Wet & Wild and my baby turns five and I hold her over my head posing beside an animatronic Daffy Duck robot-puppet with a sensor that greets people as they walk past, and the robot says, "Cunt," and I put my daughter down and cover her ears.

"You heard me, cunt," it goes, and we back away up the path. It's got a video screen on its chest, Daffy has. Interactive; it's supposed to show a map of what events are going on around the park.

Except the screen goes black. Reappears with red letters.

SAFFIRE UR MOTHER IS A CUNT

CUNT CUNT CUNT CUN—

He gets me on the flight back, too. Through the tablet in the back of the seat of the passenger in front of me. The crossword clues on my interactive screen make fun of me, okay. I take it. I accept it. One question about IoT; one about algorithms. A question pops up on Saffy's screen and simply says, "HOW DUMB IS UR MUM 2 FUCK WITH TH CODING GOD?"

Hurl whatever, Warwick, I tell myself for months. 'Cause I've got a thick skin. I gave birth to a BABY, faggot. And I raised her up all by myself. That makes me tougher than you.

No matter how terrifying the stupid little messages that worm their way into my work email, or show up on the screen while I'm standing on the bus, or infiltrate TV adverts and digital menus and train timetables. No matter if he messes up every website I build, makes 'em all disappear. Even when he gets inside the digital billboard on the side of the Millennium Hotel over on Courtenay Place which, as I'm walking under it, displays a picture of a BMW running over a little girl with two pigtails in her hair, one pink, one—

I put my earbuds in and carry on. I like my new life with the terror and harassment. Great excuse to limit my screen time outside of work. Shit's been stripped down simple. I'm not really in touch with people on social anymore. I can login to my bank, my work intranet. He knows he has to keep his little revenge private; knows he'll get slapped if he fucks with Oracle. Oracle's got way more power than little old Jazmine Tauariki. Until then, I'll consider us even. And that's cool. He can feel like a big man, messing with websites. It's all just virtual. Barely affects me in the real world. Plus, that wannabe-monk-lonely-introverted-psycho-pathic-Unabomber-control-freak-COCKSUCKER can't touch my daughter in her final week of daycare. She's about to move on to school. She's practically an adult, I tell myself with a sniff.

It's Friday now and I feel this whole chapter of my life is ending. The score is 1:1 and I feel fantastic. I skate to work. I code and eat lunch and have sprint meetings and squirt eye drops and pull my hood over my head and get lost in white letters and black depths, emerging only to test my scripts on my browser, and I slurp coffee and chamomile and crunch nuts and blow bubblegum and nibble toothpicks and finally—FINALLY—it's 4.15 and I start gathering up my shit, clearing my Tupperware out of the dishwasher, stepping into the elevator hitting the Ground Floor button, ratcheting the straps on my backpack.

I put my skateboard on the tiles. Skate across the lobby. Slow for the plate glass doors.

My phone pings.

A PDF arrives in my inbox from Anonymail.com, that famous Deep Throaty website people use to send untraceable emails. It's got some auto-display code written into the header, evidently, because the PDF pops open before I can even hit the trash can button.

It's a form, filled in by hand.

Not my hand, though.

BrightSparkz

"Where sharing knowledge is caring knowledge."

AUTHORIZATION FOR PICK-UP AND DROP-OFF

I, __[insert signature]__*Jazmine T. Tauraiki*, _____ authorize the following

Name: *Warwick Yang*

Relationship: *Superior.*

To pick up _____[print child's name]__*Saffire Tauariki*_____.

Superior?! Ohhhhhh, you absolute arrogant asshole. The form's been filled in with my handwriting and my signature – well, a lookalike fake of my handwriting and my signature. A few frustrated heartbeats collide with a sudden sinking feeling. I sift through the heavy sledgehammer emotion. Tranquilo, girl. Take a breath. He's just trying to fuck with you. He's tried this shit before and you've overcome it every time. There is zero chance he'll go near your child. Delete it and forget about it.

My phone pings again.

More devastating this time.

It's a multimedia message with a video attached, 41 megabytes.

Quick check of some stupid video. 15 seconds, it looks like. Someone's hacked the security camera at BrightSparkz childcare center. We see a spindly skinny Grim Reaper with the hood of its coat pulled up unlatch the gate at Brightsparkz. Disappears for ten silent seconds. Returns with a girl whose hair looks familiar. Tied up in pigtails, two different colors. The hooded skeleton coaxes her out, holding a chocolate Santa Claus with one claw.

In its pocket, a wooden handle.

The handle of a meat cleaver.

But the video's fucked. It's warped and rippling. Underwater. Either that or I'm crying.

Tears dissolve the front of my face. I've collapsed on the ramp in front of work.

In the video—unannounced, unexplained, unlabeled—the hooded specter with the bone-thin arms leads my girl out of daycare. The way she stumbles into his legs, pulled, yanked, spirited away. The way she twists around to check with her teacher if it's okay to go with the man in the black hood.

You can call it a deepfake. Say it's a cleverly edited digital animation. Brilliant depth. Perfectly veristic shadows and postures. You can even see the bystanders, the people-who-don't-help, the fat old saggy-titted head teacher with her smile lines following Saffy to the gate and flapping goodbye.

I'm crying cause I know it isn't fake. I'm sprinting to the bus stop and pounding on the glass panels but there's no bus. I'm stomping my skateboard, c'mon, c'mon, weaving through fuckers down the Terrace WHO NEED TO SERIOUSLY GET OUT OF THE FUCKING WAY THIS INSTANT.

Kicking my board away. Tearing the door off a taxi and screaming directions. Bursting into BrightSparkz.

But I didn't need to do all that shit, cause the Authorization To Pick-up form is there on the counter at BrightSparkz, and the sign-in sheet is there, and the jolly fat woman who runs the place is there telling me I just missed my superior by ten minutes, and Saffy's already gone.

ABOUT THE AUTHOR

Michael Botur, born 1984, is the author of five acclaimed short story collections, four novels, page and pub poetry collection *Loudmouth* and the children's book *My Animal Family*. He has won awards for short fiction in the US, Australia and New Zealand. Botur has published journalism in most major newspapers and magazines in New Zealand and is working on screenplays in 2022. He lives in Whangarei with his two kids, who beg Daddy to tell them synopses of the scary stories he's writing.

In 2021 Botur was the first New Zealand winner of the Australasian Horror Writers Association Short Story Award for 'Test of Death.'

ABOUT THE PUBLISHER

The Sager Group was founded in 1984. In 2012 it was chartered as a multimedia content brand, with the intent of empowering those who create art—an umbrella beneath which makers can pursue, and profit from, their craft directly, without gatekeepers. TSG publishes books; ministers to artists and provides modest grants; and produces documentary, feature, and commercial films. By harnessing the means of production, The Sager Group helps artists help themselves. For more information, please see www.TheSagerGroup.net.

MORE BOOKS FROM THE SAGER GROUP

The Swamp: Deceit and Corruption in the CIA
An Elizabeth Petrov Thriller (Book 1)
by Jeff Grant

Chains of Nobility: Brotherhood of the Mamluks (Book 1-3)
by Brad Graft

Meeting Mozart: A Novel Drawn from the
Secret Diaries of Lorenzo Da Ponte
by Howard Jay Smith

Death Came Swiftly: Novel About the Tay Bridge Disaster of 1879
by Bill Abrams

A Boy and His Dog in Hell: And Other Stories
by Mike Sager

Miss Havilland: A Novel
by Gay Daly

The Orphan's Daughter: A Novel
by Jan Cherubin

Lifeboat No. 8: Surviving the Titanic
by Elizabeth Kaye

Hunting Marlon Brando: A True Story by Mike Sager

See our entire library at TheSagerGroup.net

THE SAGER GROUP
Artifex Te Adiuva